the
SUMMER
OF
Weddings

FIVE ISLAND Cove

JESSIE NEWTON

ISBN-13: 978-1-63876-444-1

Chapter One

R obin Grover stared at her phone as if it had personally betrayed her. As a wedding planner, she should expect problems—and she did.

At the same time, she'd planned and executed dozens of weddings where emergencies didn't happen, Mother Nature played nice, and everything went off without a hitch.

But apparently, Liam and Julia's wedding tomorrow—*tomorrow*—wasn't going to be one of them.

She let her eyes fall closed, and she held the position as she breathed in deeply. It was her job to find solutions to the emergencies.

Flowers, she thought even as the florist's panicked voice echoed through her head. There had to be thousands of flowers in Five Island Cove. Robin just needed to find them and get them to the white sand beach on the south side of Diamond Island.

No big deal.

She opened her eyes and started scrolling through her contacts. She had whole binders filled with vendors, and she landed on a name—Poison Ivy. Maybe not the best name for a wedding florist, but a florist all the same.

In fact, with seven weddings—yes, seven—on the calendar in the next six months, the desk in her office had disappeared beneath a sea of binders, sample books, and to-do lists. Her wedding planner's emergency kit—a massive file folder box filled with everything from safety pins to smelling salts—sat open on the counter lining the built-in bookshelves, ready for tomorrow's festivities.

Hey Jessa! she said, texting the owner of Poison Ivy. *Wondering if you have flowers for a wedding tomorrow? Colors are sage, pumpkin, and sky blue, but I'll take anything you can get close. There's been an emergency at my regular supplier.*

Robin didn't have to apologize for not booking Poison Ivy the first time around. She just needed to find center-pieces for tomorrow's beachside dinner.

Duke appeared in the doorway, his broad shoulders filling the frame. "What's going on? I've yelled for you three times. Lunch is here."

Robin looked up at the shortness in his tone, realizing she'd fallen into her work again. "Sorry," she said with a sigh.

"Bad news?" Duke came forward, and Robin eased herself into his arms. He hadn't gone to Alaska this summer for the first time in years, and she prayed every night that the catch here would be enough to pay their bills.

They had a wedding to pay for too, after all.

"The florist just called. Their refrigeration unit broke down overnight." Robin stepped back and ran her fingers through her honey-blonde hair, not caring that she was destroying the careful styling she'd done for today's final venue walkthrough.

It was supposed to rain anyway—just one more thing Robin needed to solve. But she couldn't reach up into the atmosphere, throttle Mother Nature, and make her blow the approaching storm away from Five Island Cove.

Robin looked at the scrawled note on the notepad on her desk. "Half the flowers for Julia's centerpieces are wilted beyond salvation."

"Well, that's not good." Duke huffed out a breath, and he was such an amazing man and perfect partner that he'd probably go anywhere to get Robin the flowers she needed for tomorrow's nuptials. "Can they get more?"

"They're trying, but it's *June*, baby. Every florist on the Eastern Seaboard is booked solid with weddings—and it's not like I can just run to another city and get some."

Robin picked up her planner and flipped through it with such force she nearly tore a page. "I've got seven weddings this summer, Duke. Seven."

One of which was their daughter's, and fine, Robin could admit having her twenty-year-old get married wasn't exactly the most comforting thing in the world for her.

"And the first one is falling apart before my eyes."

Duke placed his hands on her shoulders, his touch instantly grounding her. "Robin, love, if anyone can find a few flowers, it's you."

Robin leaned into his solid warmth for just a moment before pulling away. "I need to call Maddy, because she's meeting me for the walk-through tonight, and we need to make sure the impending rain isn't going to ruin the whole day."

"It's supposed to blow over overnight," Duke said.

Robin barely heard him. "I still need to meet Alice to go over the legal paperwork for our three family weddings."

"I thought you finished the paperwork last week?"

"That was just Julia and Liam's, and another client, McKenzie. Alice is helping with all the marriage licenses, prenups, and property agreements for the kids."

"Mm-hm, sure."

"Ginny just confirmed she's moving her wedding from October to August, and Mandie—" Robin's voice caught as her emotions surged. "Our daughter moved her wedding from next summer into Ginny's spot."

They'd so planned that too, which didn't surprise Robin. Ginny, Mandie, and Charlie all lived together, and Mandie was best friends with her fiancé's sister. Her gaze swept the desk, the bookshelves, even the couch covered in fabric samples.

"I'm drowning in details."

"Come eat lunch." He took her hand and gently guided her out of the office. Robin loved her new house, including that she could close the door on her wedding planning and leave it behind to deal with later.

Duke actually pulled the door closed with a final click, then took her into the kitchen, where the scent of coffee mingled with the vinegary one of her balsamic vinaigrette.

Duke poured her a fresh cup of coffee and slid it across the counter as she sat at the bar. "I'm glad I decided to skip Alaska this season."

Robin paused, the mug halfway to her lips. "I don't know what I'd do if you weren't here."

"You'd manage." Duke kissed her forehead and transferred her salad from the plastic clamshell container to a bigger bowl. He poured in the vinaigrette and handed her a fork. "But I wouldn't miss our daughter's wedding for anything, even if it did get moved up by nine months."

Duke had definitely been handling Mandie and Charlie's engagement better than Robin, though she thought she'd been hiding her worries fairly well.

Robin's phone buzzed just as she'd forked up her first bite of lettuce, avocado, and chicken. "Oh, it's Jessa."

She'd barely seen the first few words of the text—*Let me see what I can do and*—before her phone rang. Julia's name covered the text, and Robin very nearly dropped her phone in surprise.

"It's Julia," she said, abandoning her salad completely. "I'm going to put her on speaker."

"We've got this." Duke sat beside her and picked up his BLT.

Robin swiped on the call. "Julia, hey."

"Robin, I just checked the weather app again."

"I told you not to do that," Robin said. "It's June, and we live in the middle of the ocean." The weather changed minute by minute, and checking the weather now for an afternoon event tomorrow didn't help anyone.

"Sixty percent chance of rain tomorrow at four o'clock," Julia said. "That only goes up by five." She didn't speak in a supersonic voice, the way some of Robin's hysterical brides did. But her even, almost dejected tone was somehow worse.

"I just need you to be straight with me," Julia said. "Will we be able to have the ceremony on the beach?"

"I don't know." Robin sighed and looked over to her husband. "Maddy and I are going over there in a couple of hours. And Julia, the Winehouse knows what to do in the case of inclement weather. They'll have a plan, and the wedding will be absolutely beautiful."

She refrained from adding anything else. The wedding *would* be beautiful, period.

"I know," Julia said, but she didn't sound like she believed Robin.

"Did your boys make it to the cove?" Robin asked, deftly guiding the conversation somewhere else. For a few months, Julia wasn't sure all three of her sons would be able to attend her wedding, as her youngest worked for the FBI, and apparently had a lot of red tape to go through to get time off.

But Andrew had managed it, and Julia's three sons and

her one daughter-in-law should've arrived on the eleven-fifteen flight from New York.

Yes, Robin had too many details in her head.

"Yes," Julia said, her tone brightening then. "They've all arrived, and we just sat down for crab cakes."

"Then why are you on the phone with me?" Robin laughed lightly and shook her head. "I'm hanging up. I've got everything handled, Julia. You have nothing to worry about."

"I don't know what I'd do without you," Julia said, and Robin let her end the call.

Robin sighed, her shoulders pressing forward as if she carried something heavy there.

"You didn't tell her about the flowers," Duke said.

"It's policy to only tell the bride what she needs to know." Robin picked up her fork and stuck her bite of salad in her mouth.

Duke chuckled and shook his head. "All right, but I saw that note in your office that said Liam's mother is allergic to daisies, so..." He nodded to her phone. "You better check with Jessa to see what she's got."

Robin practically dove onto her phone. "I forgot about the daisies." That would've been a disaster. But things didn't get better when she saw Jessa's messages.

Let me see what I can do and I'll get back to you.

I can get you a bunch of lilies, roses, peonies, and garde-nias. Not sure on the colors, but I can see?

Just heard back from Greg, who's in the city today. I

spoke too soon. He can only get peonies and gardenias. He's sending pictures.

The next few texts showed white flowers, along with some nice, pink peonies. Too bad pink wasn't a color Julia had chosen for her ceremony.

How many centerpieces can you do with that? Robin sent her. *And what am I looking at in terms of cost? The wedding is tomorrow, Jessa...*

She started thinking about dying the white flowers the color she needed—which was totally insane. Robin didn't have time for that, did she?

"Hon, you need to eat." Duke plucked her phone from her hand and turned it over before setting it down on his other side. "What can I do?"

Robin thought for a moment while she took another bite of her salad. "Call your fishing buddy, Steven. Marianne has that cutting garden, right? See if she has any orange tiger lilies, or anything white that isn't a daisy that I could buy."

"On it." Duke pulled his phone out. "What else?"

"I'm going to pick up the table runners from the dry cleaner on my way to the Winehouse, but I'd love it if you could follow up with Mandie on the bridesmaids' gifts. She was supposed to be getting those from the jeweler next door to the drug store today, and I don't want her to forget."

"Your daughter? Forget something?" Duke scoffed, but his fingers continued to fly across the screen. He grinned at her and leaned over to give her a quick kiss. "I can see you're dying without your binders."

He picked up her phone and handed it to her. The way it vibrated as she took it told her someone else had messaged. Hopefully Jessa, saying the flowers were free and they'd be here by five o'clock tonight so Robin could inspect them.

"Go. Take your salad back to your office and save the world."

Robin took an extra moment to kiss him properly, savoring the way her love for him sparked and kindled way down in her stomach. She smiled as she ducked her head, the moment lengthening and reminding her what weddings were really about.

Love. True love, like the kind she shared with Duke.

She wished that for all of her brides that summer, especially her own daughter. As she gathered her salad and took it and her phone with her, something inside her calmed when she thought of Mandie and Charlie.

They'd been together for a long time, and Robin didn't need to doubt either of them. So she thought they were too young; it didn't mean getting married wasn't the right thing for them.

Heck, she and Duke had gotten married young too, and Robin refused to be like her mother in any way. She would not say anything to Mandie that might indicate that she didn't trust her, or believe in her, or that she might not —even slightly—support her.

When she needed to leave, Robin gathered her planner, phone, and an emergency notebook just as a crutch. She found Duke asleep on the couch, the neighbor's cat curled on his chest, and a bolt of gratitude struck her fully in the chest.

He got up at three in the morning to go fishing, and he'd given up his position on an Alaskan team that had earned them enough to pay for this beautiful new home, support Robin and the girls, and provide them with the amazing life she enjoyed.

And he'd been doing it for decades.

She smiled softly at him, grabbed her keys, and slipped out of the house. After taking a moment to text Jamie— *I'm doing the walkthrough on the beach tonight. Dad's asleep on the couch, and Mandie's closing the drug store. Tell me you're going to be responsible about coming home after work—no side trips to see anyone—and that you can help Dad get dinner on the table*—she took a deep, cleansing breath.

Thankfully, Jamie didn't have a boyfriend, and she did have a job at a cookie company that had come to the cove. She still seemed to be boy-crazy, and Robin didn't quite know how to deal with it. Mandie hadn't really been like that.

I'm finishing up now, and Paulo brought over a bunch of pizza that didn't get sold during lunch, so I'll have dinner for everyone.

Perfect, Robin said, and then she flipped her minivan into reverse and got herself down to the beach to make sure tomorrow's wedding went off without a hitch.

She noticed the crystal blue water, then the way the clouds rolled in and cut off the sunlight casting sparkles everywhere. Robin peered up through the windshield, actually glad to see the arrival of the storm. That meant it would bluster throughout the night and leave tomorrow alone.

As she pulled into the Winehouse, her phone buzzed with a text from Alice: *At the courthouse. Got all the paperwork for Julia and Liam.*

Thank you, Alice, Robin texted back. *You're a lifesaver.* She reached over to her bag and pulled out the clipboard. She checked off *marriage certificate* and looked at the long list of things still to do before the I-do was said.

A great sense of overwhelm hit her, but she reminded herself sternly, "You've done this before. It'll all come together."

Dead flowers, threatening rain, panicking and yet dejected bride...so about usual.

And Robin *would* handle it all, the way she always did.

She caught sight of Maddy as she stepped elegantly out of a RideShare, and Robin reached for her bag and heaved it across the console and into her lap.

"All right," she told herself, straightening her shoulders. "Time to go make some wedding magic happen."

Chapter Two

Julia Harper stood on the sidewalk, the beach expanding in front of her as her heart fluttered like the white ribbons adorning the ceremony chairs. The afternoon sun kissed her skin, warm and gentle—nothing like the torrential downpour that had rattled her nerves the night before.

"I can't believe it," she whispered, gazing at the perfectly blue sky. It seemed to shine with a glow all its own, and Julia's soul soaked it all up. "Robin promised the weather would clear, but I didn't believe her."

Maddy, her unexpected best friend, squeezed her arm. "Five Island Cove magic. It never fails."

From their vantage point, Julia could see the entire setup on Diamond Island's south beach. White chairs arranged in neat rows on the smooth, white sand. An elegant driftwood arch draped with flowing fabric and the most beautiful floral arrangements she'd ever seen—

peonies and roses in soft blush and cream, with lilies in her deeper, darker pumpkin orange.

Robin had added pink at the last minute, claiming the blue sky would compliment it all beautifully—and there'd been a floral emergency that Julia hadn't known about until this morning. Robin had solved it before telling her, and Julia's joy seeped through every cell in her body as she gazed at the perfect arrangement in front of her.

The ocean stretched beyond, a glittering backdrop of endless blue that seemed to cast the color over everything exactly the way Julia wanted it to—just as Robin had said.

"Mom?" Will's voice came from behind her. "Ian's ready for you."

Julia turned to find her oldest son standing there, handsome in his charcoal suit. At twenty-eight, he looked so much like his father she sometimes got caught off-guard. But the warm smile he offered belonged only to him.

"Thank you." She leaned into him, careful to pass her bouquet to Maddy first. "I'm so glad you came." She pulled back and smiled at him. "The next wedding we attend will be yours."

Will ducked his head, though he'd asked his long-time girlfriend, Rachel, to be his wife a couple of months ago. They'd set a date for next April, in Washington D.C., and Julia thanked God every day that her nightmarish divorce had not poisoned her sons against marriage.

She stepped away from Will and into the arms of her second son, Spencer. He'd been married for a couple of years now, and Julia kept hoping for a grandchild. He'd finished up his electrician's license and now worked in the city as a Journeyman, while Allison, his wife, worked in an accounting firm.

They'd been the most supportive and communicative with Julia since the divorce, what with her move to Nantucket, and then Five Island Cove.

"Mm, I love you," she whispered to her son, and he murmured the words back. She gave Ali a squeeze, and they positioned themselves behind Will and Rachel to walk down the aisle in Julia and Liam's wedding party.

She faced her youngest son—Spencer. He'd let his hair grow far too long, but Julia hadn't verbally commented on it. She'd simply swept her fingers through the long fringe when she'd picked him up from the airport, no words necessary.

He'd had a rough go of finding a girlfriend, and his job with the FBI didn't help. Julia herself didn't even know what he did, and he said everything was classified. She wasn't sure if that was true, or if he just used it as a way to avoid talking about his job. He too lived in New York City, where Julia had raised her sons, and as long as she heard from him a few times each month, she tried not to worry.

After hugging him, she sighed and smoothed her hands over her simple silk dress, its ivory color complementing her sun-kissed skin and dark hair. Her gaze fell on the mob of police officers heading her way, and a smile lit up her face.

She'd spent the last three years in Five Island Cove

rebuilding her life after her divorce, never expecting to find love again—certainly not with Liam Coldwater, the outgoing, outspoken second-in-command at the Five Island Cove Police Department.

But he made her so, *so* happy, and Julia blinked back tears, not wanting to ruin the careful makeup Maddy had applied.

"Ready to get married?" Aaron Sherman asked when he arrived. He was the Chief of Police, Liam's best friend and boss, and married to one of Julia's best friends.

Julia nodded, her smile growing enough to crowd out the tears. "So ready." She didn't see Eloise anywhere, and then she remembered that this wasn't a traditional wedding. There wouldn't be groomsmen and bridesmaids marching down the aisle in matching sets.

She'd wanted her sons and their significant others there, and Liam had said he'd bring "his boys." He was a single father to a teenager, and Julia had arranged to have Ian walk her down the aisle—about the only "traditional" thing happening that afternoon.

She did have a couple walking the aisle—Maddy and Ben, of course. They'd been so instrumental in Julia's life these past several years, and she couldn't imagine the event without them.

In fact, Maddy lifted her voice above those of the officers and said, "We're moving in two minutes, you guys. Get ready, and be quiet."

"Yes," Robin called as she arrived on-scene. She carried a clipboard and a very business-like expression. "Get in line like we practiced." Her eyes landed on Julia. "What are you doing here?"

She threw a panicked look down the beach. "Liam will see you." She hissed the last few words as she grabbed Julia's arm and pulled her into the tent that had been designated as the bridal room. Julia had gotten ready in there with the help of all of her friends, but now, only Ian stood there.

The seventeen-year-old looked like he'd break many hearts in his life as he stood near the doors on the other side of the tent in his black tuxedo. He lifted one hand in a wave but said nothing as Robin muttered something else and then ducked back out into the sunshine.

She moved toward him, realizing her hands were empty. "My bouquet." She turned back to the entrance she'd just come through just as Aaron ducked inside.

He held the flowers and practically threw them to her, as if they were a football. "Robin is not happy," he said before ducking right back out.

Julia took a moment to collect her breath and straighten an errant bloom. Then she turned back to Ian, hoping she hadn't made things too hard for Robin. But Robin was Robin, and she'd be stressed no matter what. Julia supposed she'd paid her to be that way today, so she wouldn't have to be.

"You look beautiful," Ian said as she met him. He offered her his arm.

"Thank you, Ian." Julia smiled and looped her hand through the crook of his arm. "Thank you for doing this."

"Yeah, of course." Ian had agreed readily when Julia had asked him to walk her down the aisle. Her emotions wavered at the first sounds of louder music, the gentle melody that had been playing on an acoustic guitar getting replaced with frillier, more wedding-appropriate fare.

She'd invited her parents, but both of them had questioned whether the other would be there. In the end, Julia didn't want to pick which one she'd "uninvite," so she'd told them yes, the other would be there.

They'd both opted to send congratulations virtually and stay home. Her father still lived in Long Island, where Julia had grown up, but her mother had moved to Toronto to be closer to her sister. Their divorce had been long and painful, and while Julia wouldn't mind having them both there, her father said it was best if he didn't put himself in the same room as her mother.

He didn't want to cause more problems, he said.

"They're moving," Ian said, edging closer to the tent flaps they'd exit through.

Julia went with him and pulled back one of the doors enough to see Maddy and Ben leading the wedding procession down the sandy aisle. The crowd had stood, and so much love lifted into the air, Julia swore she could see it shimmering in the sunlight.

Her sons went next, all of them stopping in front of Liam, who now stood at the arch. He wore his full Deputy uniform, with all the stripes and gold and the hat, and Julia couldn't wait to be his wife.

Her sons surrounded him and drew him into a four-way hug that made Julia's heart sing.

The police officers had not followed everyone else down the aisle, and as her sons moved to take their seats in the front row, her gaze moved to them. Aaron stood out in front of everyone else, and they'd partnered up in a line behind him.

"What is happening?" Julia asked just as Aaron lifted one white-gloved hand to his mouth.

Before Ian could speak—even if he knew—a whistle shrilled into the air. The music had cut off, and the noise went on for several long seconds.

Aaron then lowered his hand, and into the resulting stillness and silence that a whistle commanded, he yelled, "Let's go, boys!"

He then took one shuffling step down the aisle by himself, leaning low into a...dance move. He bounced forward over his right leg for a one-two count, then stepped forward into his left for the same one-two count.

Snickers and smiles filled the crowd, but Julia simply stared. Liam's police officer friends were going to dance down the aisle? In silence?

Then the music blared to life as the first pair behind Aaron shuffled forward onto their right legs and did the same two-beat bounce he'd done. This music had a beat, one that made Julia want to bounce and tap her toe too.

Pairing by pairing the officers bounce-step-danced down the aisle. When they reached Liam, they grabbed onto him and man-clapped him on the back in a hug, then gathered around him and step-clapped to the beat until every last officer had arrived at the altar.

Julia had never seen anything like it. Liam shone like the stars in heaven, all the new pennies in the world, and every ounce of sunshine that had ever come to earth. He laughed and hugged every man at the department, until the last one did a spin in the sand and pushed his officer's cap forward over his eyes in a total Michael Jackson move.

The music faded, and the crowd that had assembled in their wedding finest went wild. Cheers and whoops, whistles and catcalls, filled the beach, and Julia found she could not stop smiling.

"We have to follow that," she said to Ian just as Robin looked their way. Liam smoothed his dark hair back and reseated his hat, his eyes coming to the tent too. Suddenly nervous, Julia let the flap on the tent fall back into place, hiding everything beyond it.

Ian looked at her, and she looked at him. "Ready?" he asked.

She nodded, now saving her voice for when she told the sexy Deputy "I do."

Ian reached up and swept the tent flap to the side, and someone was there to secure it. Duke did it on the other side, and murmurs and sighs moved through the crowd down as they focused on Julia.

She felt like a butterfly emerging from the cocoon after a very long time curled inside. So much inside her had broken when her first marriage had fallen apart. She'd left behind everything she'd built and had ever known when she'd first gone to Nantucket to revitalize a run-down inn.

So much had happened there; many things that had blown her toward these five islands in the Atlantic Ocean, where a group of women had been waiting to further heal her.

And who would've ever predicted or guessed that she'd have someone as amazing and handsome as Liam living here too?

He seemed to only have eyes for her as she glided out of the tent, her bare feet relaying the heat from the sand. She could barely feel it, and she certainly only focused on Liam as the scene shifted before her.

Robin had clearly given some sort of signal, because the people who'd been sitting—or rather, standing—in the path from the tent to the driftwood arch-altar moved. They picked up their chairs and moved, creating a brand new aisle that only she and Ian would walk down.

Ian kept taking one more step, one more step, and Julia went with him. The faces of friends and neighbors blurred together—except for the front couple of rows, where Julia slowed.

Robin now stood on the end with Duke, both of them beaming with love and happiness. She hugged them both, hoping she wasn't taking too long.

You have the beach until ten p.m., she reminded herself. And this was her wedding. She could take a few seconds to hug those who had influenced her, changed her, helped her, and loved her.

Alice and Arthur embraced her as a unit, and Eloise and Aaron enveloped her straight into their chests. Kelli and Shad, AJ and Matt, Jean and Reuben, Clara and Scott, Laurel and Paul—who'd both shuffle-stepped down the aisle.

Then came Tessa, Kristen, Mandie, Ginny, and Aaron's girls, Billie and Grace.

Finally, only Maddy and Ben stood between her and Liam, and Julia took all the time she wanted to lean into their arms, accept their whispered congratulations, and let Maddy swipe her front curl back and wipe under her eye.

"Go on," she encouraged. "Go make that man yours."

Julia finally stepped back to Ian, feeling stronger and more loved than she ever had before. She let him lead her the last few steps to Liam, who engulfed them both in his broad wingspan, bringing them both against his chest with the words, "My two favorite people ever."

"Dad, you're breaking my back," Ian complained, and Liam released them. He hugged Ian separately, and he went to sit with her sons.

Then Liam looked at her, pure male desire shining in those deep, dark eyes. "You're breathtaking," he whispered for her ears alone. "I am so in love with you, I feel lost."

"You had the officers dance down the aisle," she whispered back, making him smile. "And I love you for it."

He pressed his lips to her temple for a moment, and then looked down at her bouquet. "Uh...I smashed that."

Julia looked at it too, a flash of regret lancing through her, quickly followed by panic. The pictures...

Then Robin plucked it from her hands, passed it to someone before Julia could even look up, and when she did manage to look at her wedding planner and friend again, Robin held a brand-new, second bouquet.

"What in the world?" Julia asked, but Liam filled the sky with his big belly-laugh.

"Thank you, Robin," he said, and Julia barely managed to rescue the new bouquet from Robin before Liam grabbed onto her and gave her a crushing hug too.

And Julia knew: Love multiplies, it doesn't divide.

Liam moved back to her side and took her hand. Together, they faced the pastor, and Liam practically yelled, "Okay, I think we're ready to get married now."

Julia giggled along with the many others who laughed, though she'd been ready to marry Liam for a long time now. As the pastor started his speech, she let the breeze drift through her hair and the sun soak into her soul.

She sighed in pure happiness that she got this second chance at life, love, and happiness, and then she looked at Liam and told herself to focus.

After all, not everyone got to have someone as amazing as him later in life, and not everyone got to live in such a beautiful place, and not everyone experienced joy the way she currently did.

She needed to be grateful for it—and she didn't want to miss a moment.

Chapter Three

Alice Rice checked her watch for the third time in as many minutes as the RideShare driver maneuvered the car along the curved road, the cliffs on her left. They'd gone past her parents' house a few minutes ago, and Alice had texted her father to set up a lunch date next week.

Just one more thing to press down on her, reminding her of all the things she currently had sitting on her plate. She hadn't had anything on her schedule this morning, though she got up early to see Charlie off to the docks— his summer job—and make sure she saw Ginny before her daughter left for her job working at a specialty doughnut shop.

She wouldn't have either of them home with her next summer, as they were both getting married this summer, if October could be considered summer. "In some states," Alice murmured, drawing the attention of the RideShare driver.

"Hmm?" she asked.

"Nothing." Alice settled back into the seat despite her screaming nerves. "Sorry, just talking to myself."

"Honey, I do it all day long," The RideShare driver giggled, and Alice flipped her phone over and slid it on.

She'd expected to catch up on paperwork in her home office, but her phone had buzzed with a text from Edna May Cavanaugh's granddaughter at precisely 7:03 AM.

Grammy's having a good day. If you still want to talk to her about the lighthouse, come at 10.

So here she rode to the remote beach cottage on Rocky Ridge at 9:52, and Alice's heartbeat thrashed with a mixture of anticipation and nervousness. After *months* of researching the lighthouse's murky ownership history, she might finally have a breakthrough.

The Cavanaugh home sat perched on one of Rocky Ridge's highest points—a weathered blue saltbox with white trim that had withstood decades of Atlantic storms. Alice knew Rocky Ridge better than most, as she'd grown up on this island and had once owned a vacation home here. Just this past Christmas, she and her friends had rented a place to spend the holidays together, and she let the comfort of this place she knew so well settle her slightly.

"Here you go," the RideShare driver said, twisting to look at Alice. "You think an hour?"

"Yes, please." Alice released her seatbelt and glanced at the well-maintained garden where peonies nodded in the morning breeze as she got out.

She gathered her leather portfolio containing all her lighthouse research and tugged down the hem of her blouse. Edna May liked things to be proper, Alice had learned. So she'd swept her dark hair back into a neat chignon, and she wore a cream blouse and navy blazer with her matching slacks.

Edna May might be ninety-three, but Alice knew better than to underestimate her. The woman had a reputation for being sharp as a tack and twice as pointed when the occasion called for it. And her granddaughter, Margie, had been most helpful in answering Alice's questions about the older woman.

The front door opened before Alice reached it. Edna May's granddaughter greeted her with a warm smile. "Morning, Alice," Margie said. "Grammy's in the sunroom. She's been talking about your visit all morning."

"Thank you for arranging this," Alice said, following Margie through the house. The interior smelled of lemon polish and freshly baked bread, and oh, yes, it looked like a ninety-three-year-old woman lived here alone. Tchotchkes lined every shelf and surface, as did crocheted doilies made with the smallest of needles and the deftest of hands.

Alice actually smiled at them, because they reminded her of visiting her grandmother's house as a teenager. Oh, how she'd hated going there, mostly because her father had made her wear knee socks and sweaters—and he'd escape to the bar.

She couldn't really blame him, as he'd lost his wife in a

terrible storm and at least he hadn't left Alice and her brother home alone.

"Honestly," Margie said. "She's thrilled, because she doesn't get many visitors who want to talk about the old days."

Alice wasn't sure that was exactly what she wanted to talk about, but she flashed Margie a tight smile.

The sunroom overlooked the harbor, with Sanctuary Island visible in the distance. Edna May Cavanaugh sat in a wicker chair, a crocheted blanket across her knees despite the June warmth. Her white hair flowed in neat waves, and she wore a blue dress with a cameo brooch at the collar.

"Mrs. Cavanaugh," Alice began.

"It's Edna May or nothing at all," the elderly woman interrupted, her voice stronger than Alice had expected. "And you're Alice Williams—no, it's Rice now, isn't it? Arthur's wife." Her keen eyes locked onto Alice's even as a friendly smile graced her weathered face.

"Yes, ma'am." Alice smiled, taking the seat Marjorie indicated. Then the younger woman slipped out of the sunroom, leaving Alice and Edna May to their business. "Thank you for seeing me."

"Margie says you're asking about the lighthouse."

"Yes." Alice carefully placed her portfolio on the small table between them. It bore lemons and leaves, reminding her of something from a by-gone era. "I've been researching the ownership situation for Kristen Shields. There's some confusion about whether the lighthouse was actually sold to the Fisherman's Coalition in the Fifties."

Edna May snorted. "Sold? Heavens, no. The lighthouse was never for sale."

Alice's pulse quickened, a million questions immediately crowding into her mind. "Tell me about it," she said instead, as she'd learned a lot of patience over the years—and that people would talk more if she simply invited them to tell her something.

"My Harold was treasurer of the Coalition for twelve years." Edna May's chest puffed up for a moment, and then her eyes grew distant with memory. "Rose Worthington was in a bind after her husband died. The lighthouse needed repairs, and she had no income to speak of. The Coalition offered to help."

"So they paid her something?" Alice asked carefully, reaching for her recorder. "Can I record this? Sorry, I just thought of it."

Edna May looked at her and then the recorder. "I suppose it's okay."

Alice pressed the button and set the recorder back over the lemons. "So the Coalition paid the Worthington's something for the lighthouse? Or...?"

"They gave her a loan, with the lighthouse as collateral. But it was always understood she'd get the title back when times improved." Edna May's gnarled fingers tapped against the arm of her chair. "Rose was proud—she wouldn't take charity. So they called it a sale in the papers, but everyone knew it wasn't permanent."

"Do you remember if there was any paperwork?" Alice asked, trying to keep her excitement from showing.

"Harold kept everything. Minutes of every meeting in those little notebooks of his." Edna May gestured vaguely. "Margie found boxes of them when cleaning out the attic. I don't know what she did with them." She harrumphed. "She wanted to donate or throw out almost everything. I'm lucky I have anything left in my house at all."

Alice would ask the young woman before she left, and she offered Edna May a kind smile. "My father is getting to the point where he's about to throw everything out, or donate it, too."

Edna May smiled too. "Your father's a good man, Alice."

Alice nodded, her emotions wavering slightly, especially with so many changes in her own core family happening this summer. "So the arrangement was temporary, not an actual sale?"

"Absolutely," Edna May said firmly. "I used to attend those meetings with Harold, because we had to travel to Diamond for them, and I didn't have anything keeping me at home."

Alice nodded, though Edna May didn't need the encouragement to keep talking.

"Rose's boy, Kenneth, came back from college eventually. He started working with the Coalition himself. By then, everyone had forgotten about the loan. The Shermans just kept running the lighthouse like they always had."

"Did the loan get repaid?"

"Of course," Edna May said like Alice had just asked the dumbest question anyone could ask.

Alice bent and pulled a sheet of paper out of her brief-case. "Mrs. Cavanaugh—Edna May—would you be willing to sign a statement about what you've told me? It would help establish the Shields' family claim to the lighthouse."

Edna May's eyes narrowed shrewdly. "A statement?"

"It's just something I can show the judge, since we have no records of this. I've been—" She cut off, because she wasn't sure she needed to get into the Destroyed Public Records Act with Edna May. "I'm trying to get a replace-ment title for Kristen Shields, but the judge needs more than what I've been able to find."

She held up the paper. "It's just everything you said." She nodded to the recorder. "I'll type it up exactly as you said it, and your signature goes on this, and I can present it to the judge in my case."

She inhaled slowly and held the air in her lungs while Edna May looked at the piece of paper like it might bite her and leave poison in her veins.

For the next hour, Alice constructed the affidavit with Edna May, carefully recording additional details about the arrangement between Rose Worthington and the Cove Fisherman's Coalition. By the time she called for Margie to witness the signature, Alice had more than she'd hoped for —a firsthand account that could finally resolve the light-house ownership question.

And if she could find Harold's notes from the meetings, as well as the repayment of the "loan," Alice didn't see how the judge could dismiss her again.

"Thank you," Alice said as she prepared to leave. "This means a great deal to Kristen and her family."

"I'm glad to help," Edna May called after her. "Come visit me again, Alice."

She nodded without promising anything, because Alice already had far too many balls up in the air. As Margie walked her through the house again, Alice asked, "She said something about Harold's old notebooks from the Coalition meetings?"

"Oh, sure," Margie said. "I donated those to the Historical Society. They'll have them at the office on Diamond."

Alice nodded, making a mental note to track them down. As a lawyer, she felt like tracking down details was all she did. Honestly, sometimes the work exhausted her.

The ferry ride back to Diamond Island gave Alice time to go over what she'd learned, call the Historical Society and ask about the records—they did have them—and send a quick text to Kristen: *Good news about the lighthouse. Can I call you later?*

Kristen's reply came almost immediately: *Yes, of course, dear. After dinner? Around seven?*

Alice confirmed and tucked her phone away, gazing out at the water. She didn't have to work on the ferry, and she needed a moment to breathe. The lighthouse stood tall on Diamond Island's eastern coast, its white tower gleaming in the midday sun. She could almost imagine

Rose Worthington standing at its base, making the difficult decision to entrust it to the Coalition during her time of need.

How many stories like that were hidden in Five Island Cove's history? How many arrangements and understandings had been lost to time, preserved only in the memories of people like Edna May?

By the time Alice pulled into her driveway, it was nearly one o'clock and her stomach growled. Arthur worked most of June, hardly ever in July, and was back in his counselor's office at the beginning of August to help all the high school students get the classes they needed.

The number of them who needed class changes was staggering, and Alice was glad someone enjoyed working with teenagers. She had barely survived hers, and she had great kids. Now, she wished she had *more* time with them before they got married and started their own core families, and she paused on the front porch before entering the house.

"You did a good job with them," she told herself in a whisper. "They'll be fine."

It was okay that Ginny had only known Bob for a year now. They got along really well, and Alice had seen them with one another. Bob adored her daughter, and he'd take good care of her. It was okay that Charlie and Mandie were getting married; they'd been together for years now, and despite the fact that they were only twenty years old, they'd figure things out.

Alice had to believe that, and she reached for the doorknob as laughter echoed from inside—young voices that made her smile despite her mental and emotional fatigue.

She found Mandie and Ginny in the kitchen, soda cans in hand. They sat at the island counter, wedding magazines spread between them. Ginny looked up first. "Hey, Mom. How did your mysterious meeting go?"

Ginny's dark hair—so like Alice's own—was pulled into a messy bun, and she wore one of Bob's old t-shirts over denim shorts. Her fiancé lived and worked in Boston, where he and Ginny would live once they got married, but he came to the Cove every weekend.

"It was great, actually." Alice set her portfolio on the counter and kissed Ginny's forehead. "Hey, Mandie." She hadn't expected to see her today, but it wasn't like Mandie needed to make arrangements to come over.

She was engaged to Alice's son, and she dropped by whenever she wanted. Alice wanted her to do that, even if a hint of squeamishness still squirreled through her whenever Charlie took her upstairs to his bedroom to spend the night.

They'd lived together for nine months in the city, but since they weren't married, and they didn't want to pay for an apartment in the cove, they'd moved back in with their parents for the summer.

Thus, Charlie and Ginny lived here, and Mandie lived with her parents. Alice's best friend. Charlie had spent the night at Mandie's too, and Alice and Robin had had one conversation about it and left it at, *They're adults, engaged, and have lived together before. What are we going to do?*

They both wanted their children to be able to come to them with anything, and Alice had never expressed her own awkwardness to anyone except Arthur.

Mandie gave her a bright smile. "I came to steal wedding ideas from Ginny. And to raid your fridge, obviously."

"Obviously," Alice echoed, amused. She opened the refrigerator and pulled out the pitcher of lemonade. "Have you two eaten lunch?"

"Not yet," Ginny said. "We were waiting for Charlie. He's supposed to be done at the docks soon."

As if summoned by his name, the back door swung open, and Charlie stepped inside. His dark hair was damp with sweat, his t-shirt clinging to his shoulders, as the scent of fish and saltwater came with him. At twenty, he looked so much like his father that sometimes Alice had to catch her breath.

"Hey, Mom," he said, crossing to the sink to wash his hands. "How was the old lady?"

"Charlie," Alice admonished, though she couldn't help smiling. "Edna May Cavanaugh is not just 'the old lady.' She's a living piece of Cove history."

"Sure, okay." Charlie grinned at her, but Alice frowned at him as he neared.

"You need to shower," she said.

"I will." Charlie moved behind Mandie, placing his hands on her shoulders. She tilted her head back to smile up at him, and he dropped a kiss right on her mouth. Alice looked away, feeling like an intruder in her own kitchen. It wasn't that she disapproved of their relationship—far from it.

Things were just...a lot sometimes.

"I'm going to make something for lunch," Alice said.

"I'm going to shower," Charlie said as he bent into the refrigerator. "Save me some lunch."

As he disappeared upstairs, Alice got out everything she needed to make sandwiches. As she assembled turkey and cheese, Mandie turned back to Ginny. "I've been looking for my grandmother's bracelet to wear for the wedding. You know, something old."

"I've never seen it," Ginny said, flipping through a magazine. "What does it look like?"

"It's silver with these little blue stones—maybe sapphires—and emeralds. My dad says Grandma Nancy wore it at her wedding to Grandpa Jason."

Alice only half-listened to their conversation as she assembled a platter of cold cuts, cheese, and bread. She turned back to the fridge to get the condiments.

"Is it at your mom's house?" Ginny asked.

"I'm assuming," Mandie said. "You can help me find it this weekend when you're there for your consultation."

"Two months to go," Ginny said, a note of anxiety creeping into her voice. "I still can't believe we moved it up. Bob's mom is freaking out."

"Robin Grover is on the case," Mandie said confidently, and the two of them dissolved into giggles immediately afterward.

Alice smiled at them, because while they could poke

fun at Robin, the fact was, Mandie had spoken true. With Robin as the wedding planner, anything and everything would be handled.

"Your wedding will be perfect," Mandie assured Ginny.

Alice set the bottles of mayo and mustard on the counter with the sandwich fixings. "Make yourself a sandwich, guys. And Ginny, don't worry about the timeline. If Robin says she can handle it, she can."

"I know," Ginny flipped closed her magazine and pushed it out of the way. Then she reached for a slice of bread. "It's just that everything's happening so fast. Bob got the job offer, and we decided to move up the wedding, and now we're scrambling to make it all work."

Alice understood her daughter's stress. When Ginny's fiancé, Bob, had received an unexpected job offer at a prestigious firm, they'd decided to move their October wedding to August. It made sense—they'd be married before moving—but it had thrown their careful planning into chaos.

"At least you have a venue," Mandie said, assembling a sandwich. "Charlie and I are still debating between the beach and the Cliffside Inn."

"The inn would be beautiful," Alice said. "And more predictable than the beach, weather-wise."

"That's what I keep telling him," Mandie said. "But he's obsessed with this sunset ceremony idea."

Alice smiled, remembering how beautiful Julia and Liam's beach wedding had been this past weekend. "It's

not a bad idea, and in October, the sun sets decently early."
She raised her lemonade to her lips. "You could have a
gorgeous dinner afterward, and the whole thing will be
beautiful."

"Yeah, it will," Ginny said, grinning.

Mandie nodded more slowly. "That does sound nice,
but I don't know if we can afford a full dinner."

Alice's heart squeezed, because she wanted Mandie,
Charlie, and Ginny to have everything they wanted. At the
same time, learning to compromise wasn't a bad thing.
And being disappointed taught amazing life lessons.

After a few moments of silence, where the girls made
sandwiches, Mandie said, "Anyway, I really want to find
that bracelet. My mom says it's the perfect 'something
blue' too." She took a bite of sandwich and shrugged one
shoulder. "I'll show it to you when you come on Saturday."

"What should I do for something blue?" Ginny asked.

"I thought you were going to go with that bra and
panty set."

"I don't know," Ginny said with a sigh, and Alice once
again felt like an intruder inside her own kitchen, with her
own daughter and a young woman she'd known for years.
"It doesn't *mean* anything."

She cut a glance over to Alice, who didn't know what
to say. Thankfully, her phone chimed with Arthur's notif-
ication sound.

*Lunch with the superintendent running long. Home by
3. Love you.*

She texted back quickly, then looked up to find both girls watching her with identical knowing smiles.

"What?" Alice asked.

"Nothing," Ginny said innocently. "It's just cute how you still get that look when Arthur texts you."

"What look?" Alice asked

"The 'my husband is the most amazing man in the world' look," Mandie said. "It's sweet."

Alice's cheeks warmed. "Well, you two should see yourselves when Charlie or Bob text either of you."

"I do not look like that when Charlie texts me," Ginny said, her smile only growing bigger as she half-stood and reached for the bag of potato chips further along the counter.

"Golden hour is going to be off the hook tonight," Charlie said as he thundered down the last of the steps. He grabbed a plate and started making two sandwiches at the same time. "I'm going to take my camera out on Houston's boat tonight."

He looked at Mandie, then Ginny, then Alice. "If anyone wants to come."

"Are you sleeping on it?" Alice asked, her maternal worry already starting to fire. She'd prefer he anchor the boat and sleep there until he could see to dock over trying to come back in the dark, but both scenarios weren't exactly ideal.

"Yeah," Charlie said. "I'll have to be back at the docks at dawn, and Houston needs the boat for a family thing."

He slathered mayo and mustard over all four slices of bread without looking up.

"I'd love you to turn on your pin," Alice said. Charlie's photography had evolved from a hobby to a serious passion over the past year. His Instagram account, featuring moody black-and-white images of New York City architecture, had gained a substantial following.

"I will, Mom."

"I'd go out on the boat tonight," Mandie said, and Alice turned away from the conversation with a reminder that her son had lived with Mandie in a really small NYC apartment.

"Great." Charlie grinned at her, something passing between them that Alice couldn't decipher as she passed her son.

"Oh, that reminds me," Mandie said. "Charlie, did you talk to your boss about having next Thursday off?" She lifted her phone and flipped it over. "The photographer can do our engagement photos then."

He looked up, something sheepish on his face. So that was a no, he hadn't talked to his boss.

"Charles," Mandie said.

"I'll text him right now." Charlie took a monster bite of his ham and cheese sandwich and picked up his phone.

"Where are you going to do the pictures?" Ginny asked. She and Bob had done theirs in Boston, as Ginny spent every spare moment of her time in that city. She'd transferred from NYU to BU for this upcoming fall, and

Alice simply prayed and hoped her daughter would be happy.

Bob makes her happy, she thought, and it rang true.

"I was thinking the lighthouse," Mandie said, her expression turning wistful. "It's so romantic up there."

Alice's thoughts returned to her meeting with Edna May and the affidavit now safely stored in her portfolio. "Speaking of the lighthouse," she said. "I have a phone call to make."

She reached for her phone, scrolling to Kristen's number. As she pressed dial, she caught Mandie's next words to Ginny.

"So you'll come Saturday? I'll show you the bracelet if we find it—it's really beautiful."

"Definitely," Ginny confirmed. "I need all the 'something old, something blue' inspiration I can get."

The line connected, and Alice stepped onto the porch for privacy.

"Hello, dear," Kristen said, and Alice sank into the comfortable sound of her voice. She released the tight air in her lungs and sat on the top step.

"Kristen," she said, smiling into the noon-day sunshine. "Good news."

Chapter Four

M andie Grover sat in her mother's office, surrounded by a hurricane of wedding planning materials. The once-immaculate space now resembled a fabric store after a tornado—swatches of material in every shade of autumn sprawled across the desk, sample invitations fanned out like playing cards, and at least three binders lay open to different pages.

"What do you think about these centerpieces?" Mom asked, sliding a photo across the desk toward Ginny, who leaned forward to examine it.

Mandie had seen her mother's office like this before, with other brides, and she curled into the corner of the couch and watched her best friend and future sister-in-law tilt her head thoughtfully. Ginny's dark hair fell across her shoulder as she considered the arrangement of crystal clear vases filled with deep red and orange blooms, with lighter peaches and cream flower printouts being held up by Mom beside them.

"I love them," Ginny said finally. "They're perfect for August."

"And they'll complement the bridesmaids' dresses," Mom said, flipping through her planner with practiced efficiency. "Now, let's talk about the cake tasting next week. I've scheduled it for Tuesday at three."

She looked up and raised her eyebrows. "Does Bob want to be there? I could potentially try to get a weekend date, but they're harder to schedule..."

"Tuesday is fine," Ginny said. "Bob doesn't care, and I'm done at the bakery by two."

"Yes, that's why I grabbed three," Mom said, making a mark in her binder. "And we need to do the last fitting on your dress in the next couple of weeks. I called, and they gave me dates for the week after the Fourth."

Ginny picked up her phone, and she and Mom went back and forth about a date to complete the final fitting before the August wedding.

Mandie shifted in her seat, fighting the urge to check her phone and check out. While she was genuinely happy for Ginny, her own wedding plans remained in limbo. She and Mom still couldn't agree on a venue, and October would be here before they knew it.

Something needed to get booked, and soon.

"Okay," Mom said. "I think that does it for you." She switched her hawk-like gaze to Mandie, who blinked with a bit of surprise. That had ended so suddenly, and she'd had no time to transition to her. "But you and I need to get something booked if you really want to get married in October."

"Sorry," Ginny stood and glanced at Mandie. "I know that must've been boring for you."

"No, it's fine," Mandie assured her. "I need all the ideas I can get. Charlie and I still haven't decided on anything except that we're definitely getting married." She switched her gaze back to her mother, giving her some of her steely-eyed glare back to her. "In October."

"Then get over here and let's get a venue decided on." Mom switched her binder for her planner, her honey-blonde hair catching the afternoon light streaming through the window. "October is not busy in the cove for weddings, but there will be other things going on. Proms, anniversary parties, etcetera."

"I know, Mom." Mandie sighed as she got to her feet. Ginny took her spot on the couch while Mandie sank into the seat in front of her mom's desk. "I just can't decide if it should be outside or not."

She'd loved growing up in the cove, and she actually hoped she and Charlie would end up back here one day. He'd decided he wanted to be a pharmacist, though, and that would be several more years of college. A Ph.D.

Her mother's expression softened as she flipped a page. "Outdoors, the second week of October...the Keystone has a beautiful beach with the ability to cover the whole thing in case of rain." She turned another page. "It's the wind we'll have to worry about."

"There's always wind in the cove," Mandie said.

"It's worse in the spring and fall," Mom said without missing a beat. "Sunset still?"

"Yes," Mandie said, leaning forward. "How much is the Keystone?"

Mom lifted only her eyes without moving her head. "We can afford it."

Mandie swallowed, because she knew her parents didn't make a whole lot of money. Certainly not as much as Charlie and Ginny's parents. "I've been thinking about a sunset dinner, Mama. How much would that be?"

Mom dropped her eyes and flipped a page. "Sit-down dinner? Or a buffet?"

"I don't know," Mandie said.

"The Gardenia has a stunning outdoor-indoor facility, with a ballroom that spills out onto a terrace that over-looks the ocean. They have on-site catering, where we can get a discount on both the venue and the food when we book them together."

She got up and plucked a new binder from the shelves built into the wall. She moved to Mandie's side and opened the binder as if she were a hostess at a high-end restaurant, handing Mandie a menu.

"Charlie and I can pay for the dinner," she blurted out.

Mom simply smiled at her. "It'll be thousands, honey." She shook the binder, indicating Mandie should take it.

Mandie swallowed and relieved her mother of the binder. "We want to contribute."

Mom nodded, respecting the boundary even if Mandie could see she didn't fully agree with it. Her mother rounded the desk again and sat down; Mandie focused on the binder, too many things streaming through her to look at her mother in that moment.

The glossy brochure in front of her seemed too good to be true, from the two-story ceilings, with stained glass in every window along the chalet-style front of the building, with marble in the floor, the pillars, everywhere.

"I don't think we can afford this." Mandie snapped the binder shut. "Mom, that's too nice."

"I get a discount," Mom said breezily.

"Then they won't give us a discount on the catering." Mandie's stomach clenched, and while she wanted a big, grand wedding, in the end, she didn't need it. She just needed her family there, and Charlie waiting at the altar.

"I wanted to ask about—"

"Mandie," Mom said firmly and kindly at the same time. "You can't change the subject. We need a venue. Today." She picked up her phone. "Should I text Naomi about this place?"

"It's on Bell?"

"Yes," Mom clipped out. "Up on that cliff above Kaleidoscope Beach." She held her phone at the ready, and Mandie's mind fractured.

"It feels too nice," she finally said.

"It's perfect for an autumn wedding," Mom said

matter-of-factly. "If it's bad weather, they can do the ceremony indoors. If it's beautiful, as October sometimes can be, they can arrange things outside."

Mandie nodded, that lump back in her throat. She waited until her mother had sent the text, exhaled heavily, and set down her phone. Then she asked, "Mom, I've been meaning to ask—do you know where Grandma Nancy's fisherman's bracelet is? The silver one with the blue stones?"

Mom looked away from the next item on her list, her brow furrowing slightly. "It should be with the rest of the family jewelry." She sat back in her chair, a glorious smile gracing her face. "I loved wearing that bracelet, though I didn't want to at first."

Mandie smiled back at her mother. "That's just because Grandma didn't like you marrying a fisherman."

Mom laughed lightly. "In the end, it became this physical symbol of my choice." She focused on Mandie. "And I know you're not marrying a fisherman, but it's not about that. Our family is from the cove. We're fishermen, even if that doesn't continue."

"There's still hope for that," Mandie said, grinning. "With Jamie."

Mom scoffed and folded her arms. "We both know Jamie is going to leave the cove, go off to somewhere like Montana or Texas, find a cowboy, and tip her hat to the rest of us here."

Mandie sobered, swallowing down the lump in her throat. "Charlie and I want to come back here eventually," she said. "Maybe he won't be a fisherman, but boats are in his blood, and we both love it here."

She got to her feet. "Ginny and I are going to go look for the bracelet. You think it's in the attic?"

"Yes, all the heirloom pieces are in the cedar chest in the attic. I packed them away when we moved here last summer."

Ginny stood up too. "Maybe I'll get some inspiration for my something old or something blue."

"Those aren't required for weddings now," Mom said, but Mandie just linked her arm through Ginny's, and they bent their heads together.

"It's tradition, though," Ginny said. She giggled. "And it drives Bob's mom nuts, so I'm so doing it."

Mandie laughed with her. "I thought you liked Bob's mom."

"I do," Ginny said. "She's great, but she's just...she has really strong opinions, and she gets so riled up over the simplest things."

Mandie pulled down the steps to the attic and climbed up them first, excitement bubbling in the bottom of her stomach. The bracelet wasn't just beautiful—it represented her family's deep connection to Five Island Cove and the fishing traditions that had sustained them for generations.

The attic held the summer heat and smelled of cedar and old paper. Sunlight streamed through the small dormer windows, illuminating dancing dust motes and the jumble of boxes that had been put here, never to be unpacked.

"Wow," Ginny said, looking around. "I forgot how much stuff your parents brought from the old house."

"Dad can't bear to throw anything away," Mandie said, picking her way through the maze of storage. "Mom says it's because he spends so much time at sea—he likes knowing his things are waiting for him when he gets back."

They made their way to the far corner where a large cedar chest sat beneath the sloped ceiling. Mandie knelt before it, running her hand over the smooth wood.

"My grandfather made this for my grandmother when they got married," she said, lifting the heavy lid. The familiar scent of cedar and lavender sachets wafted up, along with memories of childhood afternoons spent exploring its contents and dreaming of the day when she'd be the one walking down the aisle.

Inside lay neatly folded quilts, boxes of photographs, and several smaller containers. Mandie carefully lifted out a velvet-covered jewelry box.

"This should be it," she said, settling cross-legged on the floor. Ginny joined her, peering over her shoulder as Mandie opened the box.

Inside lay her mother's pearl necklace, her grandmother's cameo earrings from Torre del Greco in Italy, and several rings and earrings carefully wrapped in soft cloth.

But no bracelet.

Mandie frowned, digging deeper as she carefully

moved items aside. Finally, she started handing them one by one to Ginny, just to make sure she didn't miss anything.

"This is fantastic," Ginny said about an enormous, diamond-shaped ring with a tiny, thin band. "It's so vintage."

Mandie barely glanced at it. "I remember my grandmother wearing that. She loved it, and the top of that diamond went clear up to her second knuckle." She managed a smile. "She couldn't even bend her finger when she wore it."

Ginny fitted it onto her middle finger. "I love it."

When Mandie had gone through the whole box and still not found the bracelet, she finally gave up. "That's weird. It should be here."

"Maybe it's in another box?" Ginny suggested.

They spent the next twenty minutes methodically going through every container in the chest, but the bracelet was nowhere to be found.

"I don't understand," Mandie said, sitting back on her heels. "Mom always kept it in this box."

"Could it be somewhere else?" Ginny asked. "Maybe she took it out for cleaning or something?"

"Maybe." Mandie closed the jewelry box and replaced it in the chest. "Let me show you what it looks like, at least."

She moved to another box labeled *PHOTOS* and pulled out a thick photo album bound in faded blue fabric. Flipping through the pages, she stopped at a formal portrait of her grandparents on their wedding day.

"There," she said, pointing to her grandmother's wrist. "See?"

Ginny leaned closer, studying the black and white photograph. "Oh, it's gorgeous."

Even in the old photograph, the bracelet's beauty shone through. It circled Grandma Nancy's slender wrist like a silver ribbon, the intricate carvings of fish and waves catching the light. Tiny gemstones—sapphires and emeralds—were set into the fish scales, creating a shimmering effect.

"It's a fisherman's bracelet," Mandie said. "My great-grandfather made it for my great-grandmother over one hundred years ago. It's been worn by the Grover brides ever since."

She turned the page to show another photograph, this one of her parents on their wedding day. The bracelet gleamed on her mother's wrist, a perfect complement to her classic white gown.

"Mom wore it, Grandma Nancy wore it, and Great-Grandma Eliza before that." Mandie's voice softened. "I've always known I'd wear it too."

"It's beautiful," Ginny said. "We'll find it." She spoke the last words with conviction, but a sense of unease settled in Mandie's stomach.

Mandie nodded, letting the story she'd heard many times flow through her. "My great-grandfather carved each fish by hand," she told Ginny, tracing the image in the photograph. "He was at sea for months at a time, and he worked on it during the long nights. The sapphires and emeralds came from a treasure box he found in a shipwreck."

"Really?" Ginny's eyes widened.

"That's the family story, anyway," Mandie said with a small smile. "Dad says the truth is probably that he saved up and bought them in Boston, but I like the shipwreck version better."

They continued looking through the album, Mandie pointing out other family heirlooms and telling stories about her father's fishing ancestors.

"I can see why this bracelet means so much to you," Ginny said when they reached the end of the album. "It's not just beautiful—it's your heritage."

"Exactly." Mandie closed the album carefully. She loved history, and tradition, and all the old stories passed down from generation to generation.

She loved feeling that connection to her past, her ancestors, and she wanted to feel the weight of the bracelet on her wrist now that she was an adult—and actually engaged.

"I can't imagine getting married without it," Mandie said, then she took in a sharp breath through her nose and forced a smile to her face. "We'll find it."

"We'll find it," Ginny said again, her voice as strong as Mandie's had been.

Mandie nodded, trying to believe it. But as they left the attic, she couldn't shake the feeling that something was wrong. The bracelet wasn't just misplaced—it was missing. And without it, a crucial piece of her family's legacy would be absent on the most important day of her life.

The bracelet's disappearance felt like more than just a missing piece of jewelry—it was a break in the chain that connected Mandie to her family's past.

She simply had to find it.

Chapter Five

E loise Sherman stood at her kitchen counter, watching steam rise from the pot of boiling pasta while her mother and stepdaughters moved around her in a synchronized dance they'd perfected over years of family dinners. The familiar rhythm should have been comforting, but instead, a knot of tension tightened between her shoulder blades.

"The sauce needs more garlic," her mom said, peering into the simmering pot of marinara as if she could divine its future. Her silver-streaked hair caught the evening light streaming through the kitchen windows, making her look almost ethereal.

"I already added three cloves, Mom," Eloise said, reaching for the wooden spoon to give the sauce another stir. She gently moved in front of the pot, easing her mom away from it.

"You can never have enough garlic," her mom insisted,

opening cabinets in search of more. "Where do you keep it these days?"

"Left of the stove, Grandma," Billie answered before Eloise could, though her mother had been to the house plenty of times and should've known that.

At seventeen, Billie had grown into a confident young woman who seemed to navigate the world with an ease Eloise sometimes envied. "But Mom's right—it's perfect already."

Eloise shot her stepdaughter a grateful smile, her patience for this dinner almost waning completely away. Since she'd decided to sell Cliffside, she found she had hardly any patience for anything at all. Not the best thing, especially since the inn had been up for sale for a little over two months now, and while there had been some initial interest, Eloise hadn't heard from her real estate agent in a couple of weeks.

And life went on at the inn. Busy, chaotic, and steadily clomping forward now that the summer season had arrived.

Eloise dipped the tip of her pinky in the sauce and slid it in her mouth. It definitely had enough garlic. "Taste it, Mom," She held out the spoon so her mother could swipe up a taste too.

Mom waved it away. "I can tell just by the smell." She continued her search, opening the refrigerator next. Eloise watched her, completely baffled for a moment.

Grace, sitting at the kitchen island with her eReader in front of her, looked up and caught Eloise's eye. At fourteen, she was the observer of the family, taking everything in with those thoughtful eyes that reminded Eloise so much of Aaron.

"Grandma," Grace said quietly. "Why are you're looking in the freezer?"

Mom blinked, looked like Grace had flicked icy salt-water in her face, and then laughed. "I don't know." She closed the freezer door with a soft thud. "My mind wanders these days."

The casual comment sent a chill through Eloise. These little moments had been happening more frequently—Mom putting her reading glasses in the utensil drawer, forgetting appointments, calling Eloise by her aunt's name. Each incident alone could be dismissed as normal aging, but together they formed a pattern Eloise wasn't ready to acknowledge.

"The garlic's by the stove, like Billie said," Eloise reminded her, keeping her voice light.

"I have it." Billie looked up from the hot dog buns she'd been buttering to make an easy rendition of garlic bread. "But I really don't think we need more. There will be plenty of garlic on the buns, too, remember?"

Mom moved down to stand next to Billie. "Are you still going to go to culinary school?"

Eloise hid her smile as she flipped off the burner beneath the sauce. It had been bubbling and boiling away for long enough. They just took jarred sauce and zhuzhed it up with sautéed garlic and a bit of onion, oregano, and fresh parsley. Simmer for a half-hour while they put together the pasta and bread, and Eloise had a family dinner in under forty-five minutes.

"Yeah, maybe," Billie said without looking over to Eloise. "Ian says I'm bossy enough for the job." She grinned at Eloise's mother. "He means it in a good way. Chefs have to be in-charge in the kitchen."

"Is your boyfriend coming over tonight?" Mom asked.

Billie's cheeks flushed pink. "No, I don't think so."

Ian Coldwater didn't usually come to family dinners. He was polite and could carry on a conversation with Eloise and Aaron if he had to, but Billie didn't bring him around much. When Eloise had asked her where they went, she'd said, "The lighthouse. We just sit there and watch the sun go down and talk."

Eloise had nodded, though she knew teenagers had different versions of what "talking" meant these days. She was pretty sure some kissing went on in between the actual words, as she knew Billie had kissed Ian in the past.

But she and Aaron had talked to both girls so much about boys and sex, that Eloise had simply nodded.

The front door opened, and Aaron's voice called out, "Something smells amazing."

"Dad's home," Grace announced unnecessarily, closing her novel as she stood up to go greet him. She loved her father endlessly, as evidenced by the way she squealed as he embraced her.

Aaron wore his police chief's uniform as he followed Grace back into the kitchen, his dark hair slightly rumpled from whatever had happened at the police station today.

His eyes found Eloise's immediately, and the warmth in them loosened some of the tension in her shoulders.

"How are my girls?" He crossed to Eloise first and pressed a kiss to her temple, his hand finding the small of her back—a gesture so familiar it felt like breathing. "How was your day?"

"Busy," Eloise said, leaning into him briefly and wishing he could hold her indefinitely. "The inn's booked solid through Labor Day." She stepped out of the way as Billie slid the buttered and garlicked hot dog buns into the oven. "Billie's been working hard at the inn, and Grace did a sewing project with my mother this afternoon."

She smiled fondly at the girls as Billie moved into her father and hugged him lightly.

"What'd you do at the inn today, baby?" he asked.

"All the laundry," Billie said. "Then I played lifeguard at the pool in the afternoon."

"Oh, that's hardly working," Aaron teased, and Billie smiled good-naturedly too.

"Daddy, I wanted to ask you about this weekend," she said, and Eloise catalogued the way her throat moved as she swallowed.

"What's this weekend?" he asked, as Aaron sometimes only focused on this very moment to stay sane.

"It's the balloon festival on Pearl," Billie said. "Remember?"

"Oh, sure." Aaron plucked a crouton out of the stream as Grace poured them over the lettuce. He glanced at

Eloise for a moment, and she felt certain he knew where this was headed.

"There are a few people sleeping over on Friday night," Billie said, immediately clearing her throat. "Camping on Shipwreck Island—you know the beach that's not really an island? They allow public camping."

"I'm aware of what beaches allow public camping," Aaron said, a frown appearing between his eyes.

"I'd go after work on Friday," Billie said. "Grace can come too." She shot a look over to her younger sister as surprise flowed freely through Eloise. Billie had always been kind and inclusive with Grace, but they were a few years apart, didn't share the same friend group or interests, and rarely hung out together outside of family activities.

"The balloon festival starts at six a.m.," Billie said. "Pretty much if you want to be there to see the balloons lift off, you have to stay overnight on Pearl. Since I'm saving for school, I thought camping would be the cheapest. It's only eight dollars per tent."

"Do we own a tent?" Grace asked.

"I own a tent," Eloise's mother said, perfectly timed.

Eloise swung her stunned attention to her. "You own a tent? Why would you own a tent?"

The timer on the pasta went off, and Eloise moved robotically to silence it. She'd already set the colander in the sink, and she poured the pasta and water into it, the steam rising around her face like a veil.

But there was no escaping this conversation. She and Aaron had talked about Billie countless times since they'd gotten married. Eloise had tried to be the best mother she could be to the girl, while gently teaching Aaron to speak softer, listen more, and helping him understand how girls thought and lived—and loved.

Billie asking to sleep overnight on the beach two islands away only reinforced what Eloise wanted in her life. More time with the girls before they left home. More involvement in their lives, despite the fact that she took them to Sanctuary Island and the inn every day with her.

Time was so slippery, and Eloise hated feeling it cascade through her fingers like sand. She was tired of not having enough of it.

"How many people are going?" she asked as she set the pot aside and lifted the colander to pour the pasta into the sauce.

"Six or seven," Billie said. "If Grace comes, she can share a tent with me and Addie."

"So Addie's going," Aaron said. "Boys?"

"Yes, Daddy," Billie said. "There are some boys planning to go."

"Ian?"

"Yes." Billie nudged Eloise out of the way to crack the oven door. "These are done, El."

"Yep." She backed up to let Billie open the oven and get the toated garlic buns out. "Take them to the table. Mom, can you grab those hotpads on the corner of the counter and put them on the table for Billie?"

She exchanged a glance with Aaron. "Dinner's ready."

That was wife-code for, *Don't say anything. Give this thirty seconds to sit inside your head while we sit down for dinner.*

His mouth tightened, but he took a step over to Grace. "Salad is done?"

"I got it," Grace said, taking the bowl to the table too.

Eloise grabbed a towel to use to hold onto the handles of the sauce pot, and she nodded to her husband. "I need a trivet for this too, hon."

They bustled around, taking their seats and getting all the food placed. Once they'd sat, Eloise looked past her mother and Billie on one side of the table, and Grace on the other, to her husband. "I want to talk about the inn too."

Aaron reached for the tongs to pick up a piece of garlic bread. "Any word from that buyer? The one from Providence?"

"Daddy," Billie said, her voice sharp but not whiny. "I'm going to be seventeen this year and out of the house in two years. I should be able to camp on the beach for a single night with people we know and trust."

Aaron lasered his attention on Billie, and Eloise picked up the salad bowl. The whole house and everything in it held its breath.

"Yes," Aaron said quietly, powerfully. "You should be able to do that."

Billie blinked, clearly surprised. "Regina Thomas is going with Krista. Me and Addie. Grace if she wants to." She shot her sister another look. "Ian is planning to go—

he has to talk to his father too, but he just got back from his honeymoon this morning—with Noah and Henry."

Eloise and Aaron both knew who Ian's friends were. Noah's father owned the largest creamery on the island, and everyone knew the Turndales. They were a good family, with good kids.

"I just said you should be able to go," he said. "If El can get you to the south ferry station."

Billie looked down the table to her with wide, blue eyes. "Ian said he could drive us," she said. "It's fifteen dollars to park overnight at the ferry terminal, but he says he has enough money."

"What are you going to do for food?" Eloise asked. Living in a small micro-chasm of a place like Five Island Cove definitely provided some opportunities for the girls that others didn't have, but camping wasn't one of them. "Dinner and at least breakfast the next morning?"

Billie took some bread too, then passed a bun to Eloise's mother. She hadn't taken any food yet at all, and barely seemed to know she sat at a table with other people. Eloise catalogued that for now, but watched as Billie tonged pasta onto her plate next.

"Well, uh, Ian and I were planning to go out here before we catch the ferry to Pearl," she said. "And then—"

"As a date?" Aaron asked.

Billie nodded and served her grandmother some spaghetti too. "Addie, Regina, and Krista are going to meet us for the last ferry. I think Noah and Henry are going down earlier, to get the tents set up."

"And it'll just be you and Addie in a tent," Aaron said.

Billie looked at him again. "Yes." She drew in a breath. "We were planning to walk to Capitol Bagel on Saturday morning, after the balloon launch. Or see if they have food trucks in the park where the balloons lift off from. They did last year, remember?"

Eloise had not attended the balloon festival last year, but the girls and Aaron had gone down on the first ferry. The brightly colored orbs had already been in the sky, and Billie adored them.

She looked down the table and met her husband's eyes. "I want text updates for everything," he said. "When you're leaving the house, where you and Ian eat, when you're leaving there, when you're on the ferry, when you get to the beach."

Billie shone now, and her neck appeared to be rubber she nodded so much. "Yes, sir."

"Camping, parking, food," he mused. "I'll give you a hundred bucks to make sure no one starves or goes without."

Eloise grinned. "Did I ever tell you guys about when I went out to Friendship Island with my friends?"

"Only a thousand times," Grace said, finally contributing to the conversation.

"Did you want to go to the balloon festival with your sister?" Aaron asked, looking at his youngest.

Billie and Grace watched one another across the table for a long moment. Then Grace shook her head as her cheeks turned bright red. "No, I don't think so," she said.

"That's because—" Billie started.

"Don't you dare," Grace cut off Billie with a growl. "I'm going to tell them myself."

"If you say so," Billie said, though she seemed a bit surprised that Grace had stood up to her. Eloise certainly was.

She glanced over to her mother and reached out to touch her forearm. "Mom, you can eat."

Her mother startled and pulled her arm away as if Eloise had shocked her. She said nothing, but she did pick up her fork and start to twirl some pasta around it. Eloise frowned and looked back over to Grace.

The fourteen-year-old had turned a horrible shade of red, and it wasn't fading. "This, uh, boy—I mean, this friend of mine who happens to be a boy—this—" She coughed and reached up to wipe her right eye. Was she crying? "Maybe you should tell them," she said to Billie.

Everything about Billie softened, and she shook her head, her white-blonde hair swinging gently. "No, Gracie. You can tell them. They won't be mad. It's exciting." She gave her sister an encouraging smile, but Eloise's stomach rioted. She was pretty sure she and Aaron wouldn't think Grace's news would be "exciting."

Grace looked at her, and Eloise found herself giving the girl a calm smile. "I was hoping I could have the afternoon off at the inn, because I've been invited to a bowling party."

"A bowling party," Aaron stated. "With whom?"

"Fenn," Grace said, practically scraping the name out of her throat.

"Fenn?" Aaron asked. "Is that his whole name? First or last?"

"It's Fennrick Castleton," Billie said. "His grandfather owns the bowling alley, Daddy." She nodded back to Grace.

"He's having a summer party," Grace said, her skin softening back to its normal shade. "And he invited me, and I'd like to go."

"Sounds like a big party," Eloise said almost nonchalantly. She took her first bite of the spaghetti, and sure enough, the sauce had the perfect amount of garlic.

"Sort of," Grace said. "There will be about fifty people there—to fill all the lanes. Fenn asked if we could go together. You know, share a lane."

"Share a lane," Aaron repeated. He grinned down the table to Eloise. "Is that what young people are calling it these days?"

"Calling what?" Billie sniped at him. "Fenn's a nice boy, Daddy, and he likes Grace, so he asked her to go with him and bowl with him. It's not naked bowling, for heaven's sake." She rolled her eyes, then her whole head, and bit off the end of her garlic roll, clearly wishing it was her father's head.

"Fenn likes you?" Eloise asked.

Grace ducked her head and wiped her eyes again. "He says he does."

"How did he say that?" Aaron asked, his glare still on

Billie. He switched his gaze to Grace, and everything softened.

"He told me on the last day of school," Grace said.

"Look up at me, baby," Aaron said. "I promise I'm not mad. Remember how I just have to know all the information so I can make a good decision?"

Grace lifted her head and looked first at Billie, who nodded at her again. She breathed in and seemed to grow in confidence with the added oxygen. "He told me he thought I was the prettiest girl in school, and that he liked how smart I am at science, and that he hoped we'd be able to hang out this summer."

Aaron nodded and threw another look down to Eloise, who stuffed her mouth with more noodles. Then she wouldn't have to talk and everything would seem normal.

"Then he's been texting me. I text him back. It's…" She looked over to Billie again. "Exciting. He's cute, and I want to go to the bowling party with him."

"Okay," Aaron said. "I want to see the texts."

Grace leaned up onto one hip and pulled her phone out. She handed it to him. "It's nothing, Daddy."

"It might be something." Aaron set the phone facedown beside his plate and didn't look at it. "Remember, sometimes fathers get feelings for their girls." He looked solidly at Grace, then Eloise, then Billie. "Right?"

"Yes, sir," Grace and Billie said together, and Eloise simply smiled at him. He'd come so far in only a few years, and she reached over and patted Grace's arm.

"It's very exciting, Grace. You *are* the smartest and prettiest girl in the cove."

"Hey," Billie said, and that made everyone smile and laugh.

"Let's talk about the inn," Aaron said just before he finished his garlic roll.

Two potential buyers had already backed out after expressing initial interest—one citing the seasonal nature of the business, the other balking at the asking price.

"If this firm from Providence doesn't come through, maybe we should lower the asking price," Eloise said.

"The price is fair," Aaron said firmly. "The right buyer will see the value in that place. It's incredible, El."

She nodded, wanting to believe her husband.

"What's this about a buyer?" Mom asked out of the blue. "Are you selling the house?"

Eloise exchanged a glance with Aaron. "No, Mom, I'm selling the inn."

Mom's brow furrowed. "The inn? But you love that place."

"I do," Eloise said, frustrated by a great many things. "Mom, we've talked about this."

Her mother turned to her, genuine fear flashing in her eyes. "I'm losing my mind, aren't I?"

"No," Eloise said quickly, though her heart clenched. "You just forgot. We all do it."

"Not like this," Dawn said. "I can't remember anything, Eloise. Important things. Sometimes I wake up and for a moment, I don't know where I am."

Eloise shot a look down to Aaron and then took her mother's hands, noticing for the first time how fragile they felt. "Have you talked to Doctor Winters about this?"

Mom looked away, across the table and past Grace, as if she weren't even there. "He wants me to see a specialist in Boston."

"When were you going to tell me this?" Eloise asked, trying to keep the hurt from her voice.

"I didn't want to worry you," Mom said. "You have enough on your plate with the inn and the girls."

"You're my mother," Eloise said firmly. A keen sense of helplessness filled her immediately afterward. The inn, the balloon festival, the bowling party, all of her responsibilities—all of it seemed to fade in front of her eyes.

Her mother needed her. Not eventually, not when the inn sold, not when the girls were grown and gone, but now.

Everyone watched her, and oh, how Eloise hated that. She gave herself a mental shake and said, "I'll talk to Doctor Winters tomorrow."

Tomorrow, tomorrow, tomorrow.

LATER THAT EVENING, AFTER HER MOTHER HAD left to return to Sanctuary Island, after the girls had gone to bed, Eloise finished her skin care routine and sighed as she climbed into bed with Aaron.

She slid over and curled into his side as he made room

for her there. He'd been everything for her since she'd returned to the cove, and she loved him with her whole heart.

As his thumb traced a gentle circle on her arm, she allowed herself a moment of weakness and closed her eyes. "I'm worried about my mother," she whispered.

"I know. Me too."

"I need to sell the inn, Aaron. I can't do both anymore."

"I know." He shifted to face her, and Eloise looked into his handsome face. He touched his lips to hers gently, a seal of love and a promise of something more. "The right buyer will come."

"What if they don't?" she asked, voicing the fear that had been growing for months. "What if I'm stuck waiting while everything around me falls apart?"

Aaron pulled back to look at her, his gaze steady. "Then we adjust. The inn doesn't define you, Eloise. It never has."

The simple truth of his words washed over her. The inn had been her dream, her creation, her identity for so long. But perhaps it was time to let it go, regardless of whether the perfect buyer appeared or not.

Some sacrifices were worth making.

She nodded and pressed her lips to his. "Make me forget for a while," she whispered, and Aaron deepened the kiss and did just that.

Chapter Six

K risten Shields spread the quilt across the warm sand, glad when Parker stepped onto it to smooth the corners back. She couldn't get up and down off the ground as easily as she once had. Or at all these days.

The June sun bathed Diamond Island's west beach in golden light, glinting off the waves that rolled gently to shore on this perfect summer Wednesday. Pure happiness filled Kristen as she drew in a long breath through her nose.

She loved Five Island Cove, and though there had been some changes in the past couple of years, Kristen didn't mind them too much. She enjoyed the new seafood stands, and the additional housing, especially for seniors, and the increased opportunities for those she loved to have jobs and support themselves while being able to stay in the cove.

Stay with and near her.

She let the morning breeze stream across her face as she smiled into it, wondering how much longer she'd have here on Earth.

"Kristen," Parker said, and she blinked her way back to the present. She loved Kelli's son, and she was glad he hadn't gone to New Jersey to stay with his father this summer.

"Mm, yes," she said. "Did you want me to do your sunscreen?"

The teenager got to his feet and nodded. He followed her into the shade, where Kristen sat in one of the beach chairs that Duke had set up for her. She bent to retrieve the spray can of sunscreen from the oversized bag Kelli had brought to the beach that day. Once she had Parker completely covered, she clicked the lock into place on the can and said, "There you go, buddy. If you go swimming, be sure to tell someone, okay?"

"Okay." Parker jogged back toward the blanket out in the full sun and sank onto it with Grace and Jamie. Mandie and Ginny would come over during their lunch hours for the first Beach Day Luncheon of the summer. Eloise planned to come with Billie and spend the afternoon, while Mandie and Ginny had to go back to work. Charlie had taken a summer job at the fishing docks, and he finished up around noon, so he'd be here then too.

"Beach day," someone called, and Kristen turned to see Alice carrying a bag over each shoulder as she shuffled through the sand toward them.

Kristen loved the Wednesday luncheons, even if only a

few people could come. She lived for summer, when someone would text, *I'm thinking a Beach Day this week. Who can come?*

Things spiraled from there, and as Kristen accepted a cold bottle of strawberry lemonade from Robin and then sipped it slowly, the sand filled up with her beloved extended family.

Alice, Robin, and Kelli sat talking nearby, with another space reserved for AJ. In front of them, Reuben set up a couple of chairs while Jean worked on a breezy playpen for Heidi.

"I'll take her," Kristen said, reaching for the little girl—her granddaughter. Jean passed her over easily, and Heidi babbled happily to herself while Kristen settled her in her lap.

"Go see if he'll play with you," AJ said, and Kristen watched as her little boy, Asher, who'd be four years old in a couple of months, sprinted toward the teenagers on the blanket.

His cute little voice floated on the air, and Kristen smiled as Parker got to his feet, swept little Asher into his arms, and headed for the water.

"He needs sunscreen and water wings," AJ said in a tired voice. She took the empty seat next to Kelli, and the two of them started to blow up the water wings for Asher. "Where's Daphne?"

"I left her with Shad," Kelli said. "She was sleeping in her carseat, and he'll bring her when she wakes up."

AJ nodded, finished up with the water wings, and

looked over to Kristen. A soft smile filled her face. "Hey, Kristen," she said.

"Hello, dear."

Heidi started to flap her arms, and Kristen passed her to AJ, who rubbed sunscreen into the almost-three-year-old's chubby arms and hands and face. She giggled with the baby girl and cooed at her. Once she was covered up, she fixed Heidi's hat back on her head about the time Jean turned to collect her.

Kristen enjoyed watching her friends and loved ones care for each other, talk, laugh, and play together.

"You want something to eat, Mom?" Reuben's salt-and-pepper beard caught the sunlight as he grinned at her, so much like his father it made her heart catch. "I brought lobster rolls."

"You have lobster rolls?" no less than three women asked.

Reuben opened a huge white bag and started passing out the brunch-ish lobster rolls while Jean said, "I'm going to take her down to the water for a minute, and then maybe she'll nap."

"Sure thing," Reuben said. He kissed his wife and baby and watched them walk out of the shade and toward the glittering water.

Clara and Lena arrived, and Kristen lumbered to her feet to greet them. She grinned as she hugged her other granddaughter, who carried a giant, bright pink bag over her shoulder.

"I brought my yarns," she said in a loud voice.

"Oh, yeah?" Kristen stepped back. "What are you making?"

"Jean's taught her how to crochet," Clara said as she smiled and accepted a hug from Kristen too. Kristen marveled at the happiness pouring from her daughter. Only a couple of years ago, Clara had broadcasted unhappiness from every pore of her body.

She hadn't enjoyed growing up in the cove, and she and Scott had made their home in Vermont for decades. But life circumstances had forced them back to the cove, and after a failed attempt to revitalize an inn on a tiny island off the coast of Rocky Ridge, Clara had settled into this new version of herself. She currently worked as a manager at the Cliffside Inn, while Scott drove the ferry from Diamond to Sanctuary five days a week.

"I'm making this one blue," Lena said as she moved over to a chair her father had brought for her. "For Laurel's boy baby."

Kristen looked toward the parking lot, but she didn't see Paul or Laurel or their son, James. Laurel had said they'd be there that day, but she was due with her second baby in only another week.

Paul didn't go anywhere without Laurel, as last time she'd gone into labor, she'd passed out. She said he was being overprotective, but Kristen found him sweet and attentive—and what woman didn't want that?

"Aaron has a grill," Duke said. "I told you we should've brought ours." He got up and went to help Aaron pull the enormous silver bullet-like grill across the sand. It had big, all-terrain wheels, and it didn't take them long to get it on the edge of the shade created by the umbrellas and tents that had been set up.

"I'll come help with the coolers," Reuben said just as Aaron asked, "Who brought lobster rolls?"

"Don't worry," Alice said. "We'll be plenty hungry for burgers in a little bit."

Aaron harumphed, and Kristen smiled at his back as the men headed back across the sand. Robin got up and started to set up the folding table they'd brought, and coolers got arranged underneath it, creating a border on the left side of their group, along with the grill.

When Aaron, Reuben, and Duke returned, they had Paul with them. He carried James, and Kelli said, "I'll take him, Paul."

"Where's Laurel?" Alice asked.

"She's coming over with El," Paul said.

Jean came back up from the water with a dripping wet Heidi, and Kristen took her though the salty water seeped into her clothes. She didn't care one whit, because she'd much rather be here, surrounded by sunshine and friendship, love and laughter, than sitting in her condo alone.

"Jean," Lena said. "Look at this blanket."

Jean picked up her towel and wrapped it around herself as she sat down next to Lena and started examining her stitches. The friendship between them warmed Kristen's heart, especially seeing how it gave Lena so much confidence.

Kristen turned to her daughter. "How's she doing with getting ready to move out?"

Clara adjusted her sunhat and smiled over to Lena. "We've had a couple of meltdowns, mostly over what she wants to take with her. But in all, she's still set on it."

"She's all set for August first," Scott added. "We got the contract last week."

A momentary squeeze of worry filled Kristen, but she pushed it away before it could grow roots.

"Room for one more?" Laurel asked, walking slowly into the shade with Eloise at her side.

"Two," Eloise said. "And Ginny just got here with Billie and Mandie."

"Oh, really?" Robin checked over her shoulder. "They're early."

Kristen didn't manage everyone's schedules, and she shifted her chair back as more people arrived and wanted some space in the shade. No one would kick her out, she knew, and eventually, she ended up beside Alice.

"I filed the affidavit with the court yesterday," Alice said, her voice low enough that only Kristen could hear. "Edna May Cavanaugh's testimony was compelling. I have a hearing scheduled for next month."

"That's wonderful," Kristen said, hope blooming in her chest. The lighthouse had been part of her life with Joel for so many decades—their home, their livelihood, their legacy. The uncertainty of its ownership had been a shadow hanging around her neck for a while now.

"Don't celebrate yet," Alice said. "But I'm optimistic. I

found the records at the Historical Society too, and while they're not official city or state documents, they prove that the lighthouse wasn't actually sold."

"Thank you." Kristen reached over to squeeze Alice's hand. "For everything you're doing."

"Of course," Alice said simply, then brightened as she spotted someone. "Oh, the twins are here." She got to her feet to go welcome them and make sure they had somewhere to sit, see if they needed anything to eat.

Charlie stood at the table with Duke and Aaron, and their group swelled when Shad arrived with Daphne, and Arthur strolled onto the sand in his business casual clothes, obviously coming straight from his job as a high school counselor.

The scent of cooking meat filled the air as Duke and Reuben started to grill, and Kristen gave her order to Charlie when he came around.

Mandie pulled up a chair next to her, and Kristen reached over and squeezed her hand. "How are you, my friend?"

"Good," Mandie said, her voice a bit too high and the answer coming a bit too fast.

Kristen waited while Ginny lay out a towel right in front of them and sat on it. "We wanted to ask you about wedding traditions," Ginny said.

Kristen looked between the two engaged young women. "Oh? What could I possibly know about wedding traditions?"

"Bob's coming this weekend," Ginny said.

"He comes every weekend," Mandie threw in.

"And I don't care if he sees my dress, but my mom—"
She glanced around quickly. "She sort of threw this fit."

"I'm definitely more traditional than Ginny," Mandie
said. "I'm not going to let Charlie see my dress."

"My mom thinks Bob's mom sends him to do...recon
or something." Ginny huffed out her breath. "Like she's
going to take over the wedding. It's ridiculous. The whole
thing is practically planned already."

"Robin is very thorough," Kristen said, still a little
dumbfounded these women had settled here to talk to her
about this.

"Oh, the party can start!" someone called, and
Kristen looked up to find Julia and Liam making their
entrance.

"The newlyweds are back from their honeymoon!"

Maddy and Tessa arrived too, and the conversation
with the girls disintegrated while Kristen got up to greet
them all. Hamburgers got passed out, and Kristen loaded
her plate with her favorite cheesy chips, put ketchup and
mustard on her bun, and topped it all with lettuce,
tomato, and red onion.

Back at her seat, she found Mandie and Ginny had
moved on, and she hoped they'd come talk to her at any
time should they need to.

Kristen ate while Robin directed Charlie and Parker in
how to set up the volleyball net. Her honey-blonde hair
was pulled back in a practical ponytail, and she gestured
with the authority of a field general. Once everything was

set, and most people had eaten, the men and teens went out into the sunshine to play.

Alice, Eloise, and Robin circled up around her, and Kristen accepted another lemonade from Jean as more women joined them.

"I have some news," Eloise said.

"We could do a round of news," Robin said.

"Not everything has to be fancy," Alice said. "Not everyone has news all the time."

"I know that," Robin said. She glared at Alice for a moment, and then all eyes switched to Eloise again.

"My mother isn't doing very well," El said, her gaze distant and out on the horizon somewhere. "I'm going to go to Boston with her in a few weeks, to a specialist."

"What does the doctor here say?" AJ asked gently.

Eloise blew out her breath, her chest seeming to collapse in with the loss of air. "Early signs of dementia," she said, her voice almost getting swallowed by the sound of the sea, though it sat a dozen yards away. "The doctor wants more tests, but I couldn't get her in until the third week of July."

Kristen patted her arm. "I'm so sorry, El."

"We can all help with the inn," Robin said as she held a bottle of lemonade she hadn't opened yet.

"You have six more weddings in the next four months," Eloise said. "My real estate agent is meeting with someone out of Rhode Island next week." She shrugged and tipped back her iced tea. "That's it. I'm done. Someone else say something."

Kelli looked at AJ, who looked at Jean, who looked at Laurel. The group dissolved into giggles, and then Alice said, "I'm getting closer to a resolution on the title for the lighthouse."

"You're kidding," Jean said, her voice full of awe. "Reuben will be so happy."

Kristen nodded at her, and Clara pointed to Lena. "Go ahead. Say it. They'll listen."

Lena swallowed, her cheeks pinking up. "I—I want to do a fundraiser to help me move out," she said in the blunt, loud way she had. "My mom said we might do a yard sale where I could collect items from everyone and put them together, do the—the—"

She looked over to Clara.

To Clara's credit, she didn't jump in to save her daughter. Lena struggled to find the right word, and Kristen's heart only filled with love for her.

"I'll find a place, and a date, and do all the stuff to do it," Lena finally said. "I just need more items to sell."

"I've got plenty of stuff you can have," Alice said.

"Same," Robin said. "Mandie and Ginny were in the attic over the weekend, and they said I have boxes up there I never unpacked from when we moved."

"I have a whole bunch of stuff you can have," Jean said, and she met Kristen's eye. "And I think Grandma has some stuff still in the cottage where she used to live." Jean's worry flashed across her face as all eyes moved to Kristen.

She cleared her throat this time. "Yes," she managed to

say. "Whatever is there, you can have, Lena. It's time it found a new home."

A comfortable silence fell over the group, broken only by the sound of waves and laughter and calls from the volleyball game. Kristen looked around at these women—her girls, as she still thought of them—and marveled at the journey they'd traveled together.

Kristen took it all with quiet pride. This was her legacy —not the lighthouse itself, but the community it had helped foster. These connections, these relationships that had grown and strengthened over decades.

Laurel groaned, and Kristen's gaze flew to hers as Kelli said, "Laurel?"

"Oh, this is bad," Laurel said.

"Where's Paul?" Robin demanded, jumping to her feet. "Paul!" She marched out of the group and toward the volleyball game.

"Definitely a contraction." Laurel looked up, her eyes wide against the whiteness of her skin.

"Let's get you up," Alice said smoothly. "We'll start toward the car. Paul's coming right now." She glanced over to the game, where sure enough, Paul already jogged toward them.

Kristen simply stayed out of the way while Robin said she'd take James home with her, and Alice and Arthur assured Paul that they'd get all of their things and put them in their garage.

Paul shored up Laurel as they took painstaking step after painstaking step across the sand. As they left, and the energy returned to normal, Kristen turned toward the sea, its endless blue stretching to meet the horizon.

Behind her, the lighthouse stood in the distance, a white sentinel against the sky. The place she'd always looked when she felt lost or overlooked, when the world had become dark and she needed an anchor.

"Let this baby come into the world with joy," she whispered, a prayer carried on the salty breeze she'd loved her whole life.

Robin came to her side, and Kristen leaned into her hug. "They're going to be okay," Robin said.

"Are *you?*" Kristen asked. "You're so busy this summer."

Robin exhaled, the rushing of air joining the wind as it brushed by. "I guess we'll see." She tried on a smile, but it didn't fully fill her face, and it fell off quickly. "I can't wait to meet that baby."

She sniffled, and Kristen let her cover up her emotion and stress with that, and she simply put her arm around her so Robin would know she too never had to face a storm—or seven weddings in one summer, including her own daughter's—alone.

Chapter Seven

R obin's running shoes pounded the hard sand in a steady rhythm as she pushed herself to keep going. Sweat trickled down her back despite the early morning breeze coming off the harbor. Usually, this five-mile loop around Diamond Island cleared her head, but today her thoughts raced faster than her feet.

She glanced at her fitness tracker: 6:43 a.m. She'd need to be showered and at her desk for her first call of the day —a final meeting with the venue for McKenzie's wedding next week—by eight

That would make two down, five to go.

Once she tore herself away from the never-ending to-do list that came with wedding planning, Robin planned to be at the hospital this afternoon to see Laurel and her new baby girl. It had only been a couple of days since Beach Day, but Robin already needed the rallying support of her friends.

Her phone chimed from the armband, and Robin slowed to check it, hoping and praying with all she had it wasn't another crisis.

Eloise to the group: *I have another walk-through of the inn coming up! And my realtor said she's had two more people call about it this week!*

Congratulations started pouring in, at least from those awake this early. Robin quickly sent her own, *That's so exciting, El! That inn is going to be sold so soon!* before she tucked her phone away and picked up her pace, running until her lungs burned. By the time she reached her driveway, her legs felt like jelly, but her mind still buzzed with unchecked to-do lists.

Duke's truck sat in the driveway. He must have come home from his early morning fishing run. A wave of relief rushed through her—at least she wouldn't have to make breakfast too.

She found him in the kitchen, still in his work clothes, scrambling eggs.

"Morning, beautiful," he said, looking up with a smile that still made her heart skip after all these years. "Thought you might want some protein after your run."

"You're a mind reader." Robin grabbed a bottle of water from the fridge and drank half of it in one go. "Did Jamie get up yet?"

"Not a peep." Duke slid the eggs onto two plates alongside toast. "But it's summer, and I checked the calendar. She doesn't have to work until nine-thirty."

Robin checked the clock again. "I need to be at my desk by eight."

"Plenty of time." Duke set the plates on the table and pulled her in for a kiss. His arms encircled her waist, and for a moment, Robin let herself lean into his solid warmth, his steady touch, the absolutely masculinity of him.

"You're all sweaty," he murmured against her hair.

"You smell like fish," she whispered back. "Sorry I stink."

"Didn't say I minded." His hands slid lower, sending fire through Robin's bloodstream. But they really didn't have time to do this right now, so she pulled back reluctantly. "Later," she promised right before kissing him again. "Tonight. Right now, I need to shower."

Duke grinned and passed her a fork. "Eat first, shower next, and tonight is ours."

Robin ate quickly, grateful for the food and even more for Duke's steady presence. As she stood to clear her plate, Jamie shuffled into the kitchen, her hair a tangled mess and her eyes still half-closed.

"Morning, sunshine," Duke said, sliding the last of the eggs onto a plate for her.

Jamie grunted something unintelligible and headed straight for the fridge, where she pulled out a strawberry-banana protein shake.

"Sleep well?" Robin asked.

Jamie shrugged, peeling off the wrapper from her shake. "I guess." She took a sip and seemed to come alive slightly. "Mom, can I go to the balloon festival on Pearl tonight? Zoe and Tara are going, and they're staying at Zoe's grandma's house."

Robin exchanged a glance with Duke. "Honey..." She drew in a breath. "How will you get there?"

"RideShare and a ferry," Jamie said like Robin was the stupidest person alive. "Zoe's grandma said we can sleep out on her back deck."

"So you're going to take a sleeping bag with you on the ferry?" Duke asked.

Jamie's face darkened as she glared at him. "Why not? It's not like they're heavy."

"I know, but—" Robin started.

"You let Mandie go everywhere when she was my age," Jamie interrupted, her voice rising. "You guys never let me do anything fun."

"That's not true," Robin said, trying to keep her voice level. "And this isn't about Mandie."

Jamie rolled her eyes and peeled the plastic off the lid of her protein shake. "It's always about Mandie. Everything is."

Duke set down his coffee mug. "Jamie, that's enough. Your mother has a lot on her plate right now, and it's a big deal to go off-island overnight with people we don't know."

"You know Zoe," Jamie said. "And Mom's always busy doing something for someone else." She glared at Robin. "Never something for me."

Robin's heart stopped, though her mouth said,

"That's not true." Didn't Jamie know that *everything* Robin did was for her? How could she not know that?

The words stung from every angle, and Robin didn't know how to make it stop. She took a deep breath. "Eloise mentioned that Billie and her friends were going to the balloon festival tonight," Robin said. She looked over to Duke. "They make Billie text in every step of the way, and she has to activate her pin."

Her chest tightened, though she knew Duke would back her up. "If you agree to do those things—and send me Zoe's grandmother's address and phone number—then you can go."

With a shaky hand, she lifted her coffee to her lips and took the last sip. "I thought you were coming to the hospital with me this afternoon."

"I'm still planning on it," Jamie said coolly.

"Then, if you pack before you go, I can drop you off at the ferry station on my way home."

Jamie's eyes widened, all of her darkness gone. "Really?"

"Yes, really. But I need confirmation by..." She glanced at the clock, now dangerously close to having to do her meeting in a tank top that showed her sports bra straps and a sweaty ponytail. "Noon, or it's a no."

Jamie's mood transformed instantly. She grabbed her phone from her pajama pocket. "I'll text Zoe and get all the info right now." She looked over to Duke. "Will you help me turn on the pin?"

Duke sighed and rolled his neck. "Fine, but you owe

your mother an apology. She works as much as she does to make sure you have everything you want." He nodded over to Robin, whose chest tightened all over again, just for a different reason now.

Jamie rushed over to her. "I'm sorry, Mama." She hugged her tight, and Robin accepted her apology.

"Noon," she said as she stepped back. "In the time zone where we live. None of this, 'it's noon in California' crap you've tried to pull on me before."

"Noon," Jamie said, and she rushed back upstairs.

Duke raised an eyebrow at Robin. "You said yes."

"She's almost sixteen years old," Robin said. "Soon enough, she'll be able to storm out of the house, car keys in tow, and go whether we want her to or not." She put their plates in the sink. "I'd rather have her tell me where she is and who she's with."

She sighed as she faced her husband again. "I'm going to go shower."

"Want company?" Duke stepped closer and took her hand. Without waiting for her to answer, he led her into their master suite and helped get every inch of her skin scrubbed clean.

THE MATERNITY WARD AT FIVE ISLAND COVE Hospital was quiet when Robin arrived, a soft pink gift bag tucked under her arm. She found Paul dozing in the chair inside Laurel's room, his uniform wrinkled as if he'd slept in it. Laurel and the baby weren't anywhere to be found.

"Paul," she whispered, touching his shoulder gently.

He startled awake, blinking rapidly. "Robin, hey." He rubbed his face. "Sorry, I was just..."

"Getting some much-needed rest," Robin finished for him. "How are they?"

A smile broke across his tired face. "Perfect. Absolutely perfect. They just had to take Emily for some tests, and Laurel wanted to walk around, so she went with."

Robin smiled at the name, though Paul had sent it out to everyone on Wednesday night. Emily Isla Lehye, that subtle nod to the sea so beautiful in Robin's mind. "Emily is such a beautiful name."

"Laurel wanted to honor her grandmother," Paul said. "They should be back really soon."

Robin lifted the gift and looked over her shoulder as the door opened again. This time, Jamie held it for Laurel as she entered, pushing the wheeled bassinet holding her newborn in front of her.

"Wow, look at you," Robin said. "Up and about and doing great."

"I want to go home," Laurel said, shooting Paul a look. She hadn't had any complications with this birth, and she should be able to go home in the morning.

"And they want me to walk to do that, so walking I have done." She sighed as she sank onto the edge of the bed, and Robin stood out of the way in the narrow room while Paul helped Laurel back into bed, covering her all the way to her shoulders with the blanket.

"I'm going to go get coffee," Paul said, leaning over to kiss her. "Can I get you some pie from the cafeteria?"

"I want apple and chocolate," Laurel said with a smile. "Thank you, love."

"Can I hold her?" Jamie asked as Paul slipped out of the room.

"Yes, go sit," Robin said, taking charge in a way she knew how to do. She carefully lifted the precious bundle out of the clear bassinet and gazed down at the perfect little girl in her arms. "She is so beautiful, Laurel."

She looked at her friend. "Look at all this hair."

"She has it on her shoulders too," Laurel said fondly, her head falling back against the pillow. "She's like a kitten."

Robin giggled quietly, leaned down and pressed a gentle kiss to the newborn's head, and carefully settled her into Jamie's arms. She had texted by ten-thirty with the required address and phone number, and Duke had helped her get her pin activated, so he and Robin could see where Jamie—or at least her phone—was at all times.

Robin moved to set the gift bag on the bedside table before she faced Laurel. "How are you feeling?"

"Like I've been hit by a truck," Laurel said with a weak smile. "We didn't sleep much last night." Her gaze drifted to Jamie, gently patting the baby as she swayed slightly. "She's not as good of an eater as James was."

"Not yet." Robin perched on the edge of the bed and smiled at Laurel.

"I can't believe I have two children now," Laurel said, her voice filled with wonder. "Sometimes I still feel like I'm playing a game, and someone will show up and be like, 'just kidding! There's no way you know how to keep humans alive. We have to take them back now.'"

She gave a weary smile and let her eyes drift closed for a moment.

"That feeling never completely goes away," Robin said as she fiddled with the edge of the blanket. "Even when they're adults, and living their own lives, and getting married."

Laurel focused on Robin and squeezed her hand. "I can't even imagine. How are you holding up with Mandie's wedding?"

Robin sighed and dropped her chin. "Honestly? It's harder than I expected. Not the planning—that's the easy part. It's..." She trailed off, searching for words. She wasn't usually one who struggled to come up with something to say, and she never really let herself get too down.

"Letting go?" Laurel suggested.

Letting go.

Why was letting go so hard? Why couldn't she just open her hand and do it?

"Yes," Robin said as she lifted her head. She glanced over to Jamie, who gazed at the baby, and then lifted her eyes to meet Robin's. "One minute they're this size, these perfectly helpless beings, and the next they're asking to stay overnight on other islands, and sneaking out to meet boys, and then shopping for wedding dresses and apartment hunting in New York."

She smiled wistfully, because being a mother had been her greatest joy. The hardest thing she'd ever done, for certain, but also the most joyful.

"I just worry," she said. "I have an advanced degree in it." She smiled at Laurel, who'd always been so even, so classically beautiful, so steady.

"That's what mothers do," Laurel said. "I'm already worrying about college funds for this one, and she's only two days old."

Robin laughed softly. "It never stops." She carefully got to her feet so she wouldn't disturb Laurel. "Speaking of which, I should get going. I have a wedding in a few more days, and Jamie needs a ride to the ferry station."

"McKenzie and Trent?" Laurel asked.

Robin nodded, impressed. "You remember their names?"

"Paul mentioned it. He's on security detail."

"Right." Robin reached for the gift bag. "This is for Emily. Just some essentials and a little something I bought from Lena that she made for you."

Laurel peeked inside and pulled out a tiny blue blanket Lena had been working on at the beach only a couple of days ago. "I love that girl," she said with a smile. She dipped her hand back into the bag and pulled out the gift card. "Robin, thank you. I can't believe I have two babies under the age of two. This is going to help so much with diapers."

She leaned forward, and Robin bent down to hug her. "It's nothing," Robin said, because gift cards hardly took work. "Call if you need anything, okay? Meals, babysitting, someone to talk to at 3 a.m.—anything."

"Yeah, because my mom doesn't sleep," Jamie said as she stood and carefully laid baby Emily back in the bassinet. "She's amazing, Laurel. I'm happy to babysit anytime too."

Laurel reached for Robin's hand and squeezed it. "You guys are the best."

"Mama!" The door opened and Paul entered with James in his arms.

"See? She's right there. Remember, you have to be soft, buddy."

James would be two in August, and he grinned from ear to ear as Paul set him in bed with Laurel. "You guys are leaving?"

"Yes," Robin said. "We have a lot going on, but I had to see this baby." She gave him a quick hug. "You have a beautiful family, Paul."

He beamed as he pulled the chair closer to Laurel's bed and sank into it.

Robin dropped Jamie off at the ferry station and watched her meet up with two other girls before they entered. She pressed one hand to her heart and prayed, "Keep them safe tonight."

Before she could pull out, her phone chimed with a text from Mandie.

Found Grandma Nancy's wedding veil in Dad's fishing trunk! But still no bracelet. Ginny and I came over and went through your jewelry box, and nothing. Sorry to go through your stuff, but Dad said it would be okay.

Robin sighed and leaned her head back against the headrest. "Where is that bracelet?" There was no way she'd get rid of it. She'd worn it to marry Duke, and his mother and grandmother had worn it before her.

No problem. We'll find it. She sent the text and searched her memory as she drove home. She distinctly remembered putting the wedding bracelet back in its velvet pouch every time she got it out. She'd told its tale to both Mandie and Jamie as little girls, but they'd grown up, and she didn't have the opportunity to get the bracelet out and tell stories of true love much anymore.

She'd find it, because that bracelet had to be somewhere.

But once she got back to her office, she needed to finalize the numbers for the Peterson wedding next weekend, check on the custom invitations for the Hendersons, confirm the menu tasting for Ginny and Bob, and make sure she had her emergency kit ready for McKenzie's wedding in only a few days.

By the time Robin reached her office, her momentary peace from the hospital had evaporated. She sank into her chair and pulled up her wedding planner software, trying to focus on McKenzie's timeline.

Her phone rang—Mandie's ringtone.

"Hey, sweetie," Robin answered, tucking the phone between her ear and shoulder as she continued typing.

"Mom, I'm freaking out," Mandie said without preamble. "I went through Dad's fishing trunk, the attic boxes, your jewelry box—the bracelet is nowhere."

Robin closed her eyes briefly, the stinging that came with telling her she needed to get off the computer. "Honey, we'll find it. Maybe it's at Grandma's house."

"I already called her. She hasn't seen it in years." Mandie's voice cracked. "Mom, what if it's lost forever? It's been in our family for generations."

"It's not lost," Robin said firmly, though she had no idea if that was true. "We just can't find it right now."

"That's the same as lost."

"Mandie, I need to finish a timeline for a wedding on Wednesday. Can we talk about this later?"

A pause came through the line that set Robin's nerves rattling. "Sure, Mom. Sorry to bother you."

"You're never a bother," Robin said quickly. "I just—"

"It's fine. I understand. Love you."

The call ended before Robin could say more. She set her phone down, guilt washing over her. Robin rubbed her temples, where a headache was definitely brewing. Opening her desk drawer, she pulled out her emergency stash of chocolate and unwrapped a piece, letting it melt on her tongue as she returned to the wedding timeline.

Mandie wasn't getting married for four more months. They had time to find the bracelet.

One task at a time. That was the only way through this summer.

By the time Robin realized Duke had made dinner, the sun had started to set outside her big picture windows with the plantation blinds.

As if reading her mind, Duke appeared in the doorway, drying his hands on a dish towel. "Are you almost done?" He crossed to her and kissed her forehead, immediately pulling back. "Rough day?"

"Not a super smooth day," Robin said, leaning into him and letting him pull her to her feet. "You made dinner?"

He guided Robin to the kitchen. "Not just dinner, hon. I made your favorite."

Robin inhaled the familiar aroma of Duke's seafood pasta—and found it sitting in a pan on the counter, ready to eat. Her mouth watered, and she couldn't remember the last thing she'd eaten that day. Maybe that chocolate.

"You're a saint."

"Just a man who knows when his wife needs a break." He pulled out a chair for her. "Sit. Relax. I have red wine or white."

"Red, please," Robin said.

Duke poured two glasses of red wine and set one in front of her. "Mandie called a few minutes ago. She wanted to know if she could come over tomorrow to look through some old photo albums."

Robin nodded, taking a sip of wine. "She's obsessed

with finding that bracelet, and I kind of snapped at her earlier."

"I know." Duke served two plates of pasta and sat across from her. "I went through my old sea chest after she called. Thought maybe it got mixed in with my stuff during one of our moves."

"Any luck?"

He shook his head. "Nothing."

Robin sighed and twirled up a bite of creamy pasta and shrimp. "I feel terrible. That bracelet means so much to her."

"We'll find it," Duke said confidently.

"It's irreplaceable," Robin said, some of her daughter's panic starting to build inside her.

Duke reached across the table and squeezed her hand. "One problem at a time, love." They ate in comfortable silence for a few minutes before Duke spoke again. "So, Jamie's all set for the balloon festival?"

"Seems like it. I got the phone number and address."

"She texted me about twenty minutes ago that they got to Zoe's grandmother's house, and she'd made pizza. So she won't starve." He grinned at her, and Robin fell in love with him a little more.

"This is our future, you know," she said, waving her fork between the two of them. "Just me and you, alone in the house."

"Mm, I love that."

After dinner, Robin insisted on cleaning up while Duke checked the tide charts and current ocean conditions that would last through the night and into the morning, when he left to go fishing.

By the time she finished loading the dishwasher, exhaustion had settled deep in her bones. Duke edged up behind her, wrapping her in the safety and warmth of his arms. "About that rain check from this morning..."

He touched his lips to the back of her neck, and Robin leaned into the kiss. She felt herself melting into him, the day's stress dissolving as he took it from her.

His hand slid beneath the hem of her shirt, tracing patterns on her stomach that made her shiver. "I've been thinking about this all day," he murmured against her neck.

"Me too." Robin turned in his arms and met his eyes. "I'm so lucky I have you."

He grinned at her. "You're still and forever my favorite person."

He'd just led her into their bedroom when her phone shrilled out, filling their empty nest with noise.

They both froze.

"Ignore it," Duke said, his voice husky.

Robin was tempted—so tempted—but the ringtone was the one she'd assigned to her brides. "I can't," she sighed, reaching into her back pocket for the phone.

The caller ID showed McKenzie's name. Robin sucked in a breath and sank onto the bed as she swiped on the call. "McKenzie? Is everything okay?"

Duke stripped off his shirt and flopped back against

the pillows with a resigned sigh as Robin listened to the panicked bride on the other end of the line.

"Slow down," she said. "What do you mean the venue is flooded?"

As McKenzie explained through tears that a pipe had burst at the reception hall, flooding the entire main floor, Robin's heart sank through the floor.

This wedding was in four days. There was no time to find a new venue, rearrange all the vendors, notify the guests...

"McKenzie, listen to me," Robin said firmly. "I will fix this. I promise. Try to get some sleep, and I'll call you first thing in the morning with a solution." She ended the call and stared at the phone in disbelief.

"What happened?" Duke asked, sitting up beside her.

"The Harborview's main floor is under six inches of water," Robin said numbly. It never ended. And Robin wondered, not for the first time that day, how much longer she could keep all these plates spinning before everything came crashing down around her.

"There's nothing you can do tonight," Duke said, gently taking her phone from her. "Come on, sweetheart. Let me make love to you, and we'll deal with this tomorrow."

Tomorrow.

Robin let the word seep through her as she kissed her husband. Yes, tomorrow, she would tackle the to-do list and slay the wedding venue dragon.

Tomorrow.

Chapter Eight

G inny Kelton paced in front of the ferry terminal, checking her phone for the time for the fifth time in as many minutes. Bob's ferry from the mainland was due ten minutes ago, but the early morning fog had rolled in thick today, slowing everything on the water to a crawl.

It took him five hours to get here from Boston. He could fly in less time, but then he had to deal with parking, security, and wait times at the airport. In all, it still took about five hours.

The first ferry left Cape Cod at six a.m. on Saturdays, and that got him to Five Island Cove by ten-fifteen. But that meant he had to leave his apartment in Boston by four-thirty to make the hour-plus drive to the ferry station there.

He had to switch ferries in Nantucket, with the Steamer between there and the cove taking the last hour.

Ferries left Cape Cod every hour, and his return trip on

Sunday actually took him almost six hours, as the schedules didn't line up that great between the ferries on Nantucket.

Ginny loved him more and more with every weekend trip he took to come see her. She knew it was a sacrifice for him, as he'd stayed in Boston this summer to get ahead on his classes and do a clerking internship. He claimed he used the transit time to study, which then allowed their hours and brief days together to be all about them.

She tucked a wayward strand of hair behind her ear as the wind tried to rip it from her head and peered toward the glass exit doors again. The anticipation of seeing Bob after two weeks apart made her skin tingle. They'd been dating for a year, engaged for three months, and still, every reunion felt like this—electric, urgent, necessary.

Her phone buzzed, and she glanced down to see a text from her mother.

Don't forget dinner tonight. Seven p.m. Arthur's making the lobster mac and cheese and a Boston cream pie.

Ginny smiled and typed back: *Yum! We'll be there. Bob can't wait.*

That was true, at least. Bob genuinely enjoyed her parents' company, especially Arthur. Her stepfather had been nothing but supportive of their relationship from the beginning, while her mother—well, Mom meant well, but her cautious, lawyerly nature sometimes clashed with Ginny's more spontaneous approach to life.

To be honest, so did Bob's, as he was studying the law too. Science and technology even. He was the smartest person Ginny had ever met—and both of her parents were lawyers. Sometimes she wondered what Bob saw in her, a majorless sophomore who wasn't even sure she wanted to continue college.

She had transferred to Boston University, and she was enrolled in fourteen credits for the fall semester. She'd been taking business courses, simply because she liked them, and eventually, she'd have to declare a major—probably in busines or business management.

"Where is he?" she muttered as people started streaming out of the building. So the Steamer had finally let its passengers disembark. Ginny bounced on the balls of her feet, her anxiety and excitement combining together into one amazingly awful ball of nerves.

She couldn't wait to see him, couldn't wait to take him to the new taco truck for lunch, lay on the beach with him, and show him where they'd get married. Her mother had supported that, just as she'd taken the move-up of the wedding. Ginny still saw the set line of her mouth before Mom could erase it, though.

And she absolutely didn't want Ginny to show Bob her wedding dress.

"It's bad luck," her mother had said yesterday, her voice carrying that familiar note of concern. "The groom shouldn't see the bride's dress before the wedding day."

"Mom, that's an old tradition," Ginny had said, because she didn't care as much about decades-old traditions. "Besides, Bob's helping pay for the wedding. He should see what he's getting. I want him involved in every step."

"It's *your* dress," her mother had said. "He didn't pay for any of it, and grooms have no say over what the bride wears."

"Okay, Mom." The argument had ended there, as Ginny knew how to shut down her mother before she truly got started into a lecture. She hadn't agreed not to show Bob the dress, nor had she said she wouldn't. She'd just ended the conversation, though Ginny knew her mother still disapproved.

A horn blared, startling Ginny out of her thoughts. She resumed her search for Bob, but he still hadn't come out yet. Then, suddenly, he pushed through the glass doors, his tall frame moving with purpose as he started looking for her.

He wore a pair of khaki shorts, a bright blue polo, and a backpack. He carried a Duffle bag in one hand and glanced down at his phone in the other. Ginny lifted her hand and waved it. "Bob!"

His dark hair had grown long this summer, and the wind tried to get a piece of it as he looked up. When he spotted her, his face lit up with a smile that made every cell in her body rejoice.

He jogged toward her, laughing, as Bob was one of the happiest, most amenable people she'd ever met. "There's my girl." He dropped his Duffle and swept her into his arms.

She giggled as he enveloped her, the scent of his

cologne, his clothes, his skin, like coming home and sinking into a hot bath. "You're here," she said needlessly.

He steadied them and bent his head toward hers. "I'm here." His lips found hers, and Ginny melted against him, not caring who might be watching. She lost herself a little bit when with Bob, and he thankfully had enough wherewithal to keep things from going too far. When he pulled away, she kept her arms looped around his neck and her eyes closed.

Her smile felt etched on her face, and she finally opened her eyes to look at him. "Hi, Bobby," she said, suddenly shy despite her open feelings for him.

"Hi yourself, sweetheart." He brushed his thumb across her cheek and tucked her hair. "Mm, I missed you." He kissed her again, a quick, chaste union, and moved to pick up his bag. "I got early check-in, so we can go to the hotel first and drop off my bags."

He flashed her a smile while she dug in her purse for her keys. She'd been here less than thirty minutes, so she'd parked in the waiting lot, and she wouldn't have to pay.

"How was the trip?" she asked. "Is the seven o'clock ferry more crowded than the six?"

"A little," he said. "And it was fine. I got all my homework done for next week." He took her hand as they walked toward the parking area. "I'm at The Bungalow again."

Ginny squeezed his fingers, knowing the quaint hotel he liked to stay at. Every room was really a bungalow that faced the beach, and they only rented sixteen of them per night. Bob had booked there every time he'd come to the cove this summer, and Ginny suspected he had a standing reservation for Saturday night there all summer long—at least until August twenty-third, when they'd get married.

"I've got plans for us today."

"Do any of these plans involve us being alone?" Bob asked, his voice dropping to a suggestive murmur.

Heat rushed to Ginny's cheeks, though of course she wanted to be alone with Bob. "You said you got early check-in, right?" Her stomach growled, as Bob had arrived closer to lunchtime today, due to a late meeting at his internship firm last night. But she could wait to eat if her prize was Bob.

Bob's eyebrows shot up. "Yes," he said.

"And we're going there first," she said as she pressed the button to unlock the car she shared with Charlie while they were in the cove. She glanced over to him as they separated, her to move to the driver's door while he opened the passenger back door to put his bags in.

Once they had both climbed into the front seats, she looked over to him. "Does The Bungalow offer any sort of in-room dining?"

"They serve nachos and tacos on the beach," he said. "You know, in that little area meant only for hotel guests?"

Ginny gave him a smile and leaned toward him again. With her lips brushing against his, she whispered, "So maybe we just...relax in your room and then get tacos on the beach."

She kissed him, a thrill moving through her whole body.

"You wanted to take me to that new taco truck," he murmured as he slid his lips down the column of her neck.

"Plans can change," Ginny whispered, the feeling of being treasured and cherished running through her. "The tour at the venue isn't until two-thirty."

Bob lifted his head. "So you're still going to show me?"

"My mom isn't right about everything," Ginny said with a small shrug. "It's our wedding, and we're paying for almost all of it."

"Ah, so we're rebelling." Bob grinned and faced the front again. "Lead the way, my beautiful rebel." He laughed as Ginny shook her head and smiled. She started the car, got the AC pumping, and pulled out of the parking space.

"So how's the internship going?" Ginny asked as she navigated along Diamond Island's winding roads toward the south-west beach where The Bungalow waited. Bob had started an internship at a prestigious law firm in Boston just three weeks ago, and would have a paid position starting on September first, which was part of why they'd moved the wedding up.

"It's good. Intense. The partners are already throwing me into the deep end with case research." He rolled down the window, and the salt air rushed in. "But I love it. It's exactly what I wanted, and it'll be a great first job."

Plus, he still had two years of law school left, and Ginny heard her mother's words in her head yet again. *He has two years left, Ginny. So do you. There's no reason you can't graduate.*

No, there wasn't, other than Ginny didn't feel passionate about anything. Plus, just because she got married didn't mean she was going to drop out of college. One didn't influence the other.

"I'm so happy for you," Ginny said, meaning it. Bob worked incredibly hard, often studying until the early hours while holding down a part-time job. He'd worked for a few years before even starting college, which was why he was twenty-six and still had two years left. No matter what, his determination was one of the things she loved most about him.

"How about you? How are things here?" He watched her for a moment, and Ginny knew what he was really asking. Could she build a life she loved in Boston? Or did she still feel like Five Island Cove was—and always would be—home?

"It's good," she said lightly. "My job is great, and it's fun to be here with Charlie and Mandie."

Bob reached over and drew her fingers through his. "I know, sweetheart."

Ginny looked out her side window as she turned onto the coastal road that would take them along the beach. She'd miss her twin and her best friend this fall. She'd lived with Charlie and Mandie this past year, and she wasn't that excited about moving to a new city, with new every-thing, despite Bob being there. She'd have to learn where to buy groceries, how to get to a new campus, and how to be a wife all at the same time.

Honestly, Ginny carried a backpack that someone had packed bricks into almost all the time, and the pressure of it nearly choked her sometimes. She'd told Charlie about the weight of the expectations she carried, and he'd joked that she needed to mess up more.

"Then there are no expectations," he'd told her. And it was true that their mother didn't view her and Charlie the same. He'd definitely rebelled more as a teenager, and he'd hated high school so much that everyone was relieved when he actually graduated.

And now, it felt like the tables had turned. Charlie was literally going to be a doctor, and Ginny had no purpose past the date of her wedding.

That's not true, she told herself, though it certainly *felt* true.

"Did you talk to your landlord?"

"Yep," Bob said. "He only rents to single students. We're going to have to find somewhere else to live."

Ginny sighed and nodded. "Okay, I can start looking. I have a few places bookmarked."

"Hey." Bob reached over and squeezed her knee. "We'll figure it all out. I live there, and there are thousands of apartments in the city."

"Ones we can afford?"

"Of course," he said. "There are apartments for all budgets, baby." He gave her a grin, and that was so Bob—

always the steady one, the voice of reason. The perfect counterbalance to her sometimes negative energy.

She took the slight right onto the road that led along the back of the bungalows, and she let Bob run inside to check-in. He came out only a few minutes later with two water bottles, a brochure, and his key card.

"Number nine," he said. "It's just down a couple."

"You've stayed in three, seven, and now nine." She smiled over to him and continued down three more bungalows to a bright blue one with a giant nine on the back of it. It had one parking spot in front of it, and Ginny pulled into it.

She and Bob walked around to the front, the glorious, blue ocean stretching in front of them. The breeze kicked up too, as it was wont to do along the seaside, and Ginny took a deep breath of the salty air.

"I love the cove," she said wistfully as Bob moved to unlock the door. The single-story bungalow had a separate bedroom, a tiny kitchen, and a living room with two couches in it, a big TV mounted to the wall, and a bathroom. It was perfect for a couple who wanted to walk out their front door, take a few steps, and be on the sand.

The Bungalow had a small private beach back in front of the main building, with an infinity pool there too. As she entered behind him, Ginny suddenly didn't want to leave this bungalow again this weekend.

"Maybe we can just stay here." She leaned both palms into his chest after he'd dropped his bag onto the small dining table. "For the whole weekend." She pressed her eyes closed and settled her cheek against his chest.

He brought his arms around her and stroked one hand down the back of her head. "Feeling overwhelmed?"

"Yes," she murmured.

"Why?"

Ginny blew out her breath and stepped away. "Mandie can't find that bracelet, and I don't know. I feel like...I need to help her. The wedding is in less than two months, and there's all these little details that have to be done. My mother still doesn't really approve of us getting married, and it feels like every time we have to talk about something, all this tension comes roaring back."

Bob wore a look of sympathy. "I know, sweetheart. We don't have to get married if that will help."

"How would that help?" Ginny took the bottle of water he offered her and moved further into the bungalow. It boasted floor to ceiling windows along the front of it, but Ginny went by those and into the bedroom. This room also had windows taking up one whole wall, and she stood there and took her first sip of the ice-cold water.

Bob gave her a few seconds, and then he came into the room too. "I just mean—plenty of people live together without being married."

"I think that would be worse."

"Your own twin did it," he said.

"With the intent of getting married this summer." She shot him a fierce look. "I don't think that will help."

He stood beside her but didn't touch her. "So it's not really about getting married."

"I don't know."

"Is it about you going to BU?"

"How can it be? It's still school."

"So it's just us being together at all."

"I don't know," Ginny said again. "Charlie says I read too much into what my mom says and does."

Bob didn't agree or disagree; he just stood at the windows with her and watched the breeze fiddle with the leaves outside. After a long minute, he turned toward her. "I'm sorry I've caused problems with you and your mom."

"You haven't," she said. "She just thinks I'm too young."

"I wish I'd met you later in my life then." He grinned at her. "Or do I? I was lost without you, Ginny." He sobered and took her into his arms. "Meeting you was the very best thing that's ever happened to me, and I can't be sorry about it." He pressed a kiss to her hairline. "Forget I said that."

Ginny reveled in the warmth of his embrace, and she tipped her head back to receive his kiss. "Can we please just stay here all weekend?" she asked.

"Did you pack a bag?" His voice came out husky, his desire for her evident in his tone.

She nodded and leaned into him, enjoying the weight of his hands on her waist. "Make love to me, Bobby," she whispered just before she claimed his lips again.

He turned with her in his arms, his mouth so preoccupied at the moment that he couldn't answer verbally. But she didn't need him to.

"THIS IS IT," GINNY SAID A COUPLE OF HOURS later, unable to keep the excitement from her voice as they approached Driftwood Gardens, where they'd be married. "What do you think?"

Ginny loved the high hedges that lined the road and made everything feel exclusive and private. She'd always had a soft spot for driftwood, and she loved the way the event coordinator here took something discarded and forgotten and made it glorious and beautiful again.

"The ceremony is outside," Ginny said as the clubhouse came into view. She pulled into an available space and killed the engine.

She got out first, with Bob right behind her. He took her hand as they approached the elegant stone building, which sat perched on the edge of the cliff, its wide windows facing the Atlantic.

Taking him past it, down a sidewalk she hadn't seen the first time she'd come here with her mother and Robin, she led him to the viewpoint where the events coordinator took all prospective brides.

The lush, manicured gardens opened up, colorful blooms bursting through the shrubbery and shorter trees typical of Five Island Cove.

Bob let out a low whistle. "Gin, it's incredible." He

leaned forward against the railing, taking it all in. "This is where we're getting married?"

"The ceremony will be in that garden right there." She pointed to the one with the two-story driftwood arch, the arms of it angling and branching out at strange angles. Ginny smiled, because she loved that arch with her whole soul.

"We can decorate that arch with anything we want— flowers, ballons, other décor, or a mix-and-match." She pointed to the pavilion. "The luncheon will be served in the pavilion, which has panels that can be raised and lowered, depending on the wind and position of the sun."

"It's fantastic," he said, grinning from ear to ear. His joy made her happy too, and Ginny linked her arm through his.

"Do you really like it?"

"Ginny, I love it." He turned into her and took her face in both of his hands. He searched her face for a long moment. "It's perfect. It's going to be absolutely amazing, though I would marry you anywhere." He touched the tip of his nose to hers. "Anytime, sweetheart. Anywhere. I only need me and you there."

Relief washed over her. They'd discussed venues over video calls, but seeing his genuine approval in person meant everything. "But your parents are coming, right?"

"Yes, baby." He pulled back. "They're coming, and they're going to love it, and they already love you, and they'll love everything we do." He grinned at her. "Let's go; I want the whole the tour."

He probably didn't, but they spent the next hour exploring the grounds, Ginny pointing out where the altar would be set up, where guests would sit, the spot she'd chosen for photos with the ocean as backdrop. Bob listened attentively, occasionally offering suggestions or asking questions, but mostly just watching her with a look of pure adoration.

"What?" she finally asked, catching his gaze.

"Nothing." He smiled. "I just love seeing you this happy."

Ginny's young heart expanded. "I can't wait to marry you."

"Eight more weeks," he said, pulling her close. "And then you're stuck with me forever."

As they walked back to the car, Ginny's phone chimed with a text from Mandie.

Any chance you can help me look for the bracelet on Thursday? Mom's swamped with wedding stuff, and the house will be empty.

"Everything okay?" Bob asked, noticing her frown.

"It's Mandie. She still can't find her grandmother's bracelet—the one she wants to wear for her wedding." Ginny typed back a quick reply: *Of course. After work?*

"That's too bad. She still doesn't know where it is?" Bob asked.

Ginny slid her phone back into her pocket. "She's looked through a bunch of boxes and totes, but she likes to go when her mom isn't there. She says it worries her, and Robin has a million weddings this summer."

She drew in a deep breath and turned away from the view at Driftwood Gardens. "Okay, so we have to stop by the lighthouse to get some things for Kristen and Lena, and then...on to see my parents." She made it sound like it would be a grand party, and she even wiggled her hands like jazz hands.

Bob laughed and slung his arm around her. "I like your parents, Ginny. It kind of is a party there."

"Is it?"

"They have a pool," he said, as if that alone meant her house was party central.

The drive to the lighthouse took them along the coastal road to the north side of Diamond Island. Ginny loved this lighthouse, though she herself didn't have the deepest connection to it.

Her mother did, and Ginny had heard so many stories of the Seafaring Girls from both her mom and all of her friends, that the tall, towering structure somehow infused her with strength and light too.

It stood out on the very edge of the rocks, with nothing else around it. But the cottage where Kristen had once lived with her husband once they'd retired from taking care of the lighthouse sat back a bit, nestled among pine trees. Its weathered gray shingles and blue shutters gave it a quintessential New England charm.

"It's been empty since Kristen moved to the condo downtown," Ginny said as she used the key Jean had given her to unlock the front door. "But it's part of the lighthouse property, and Lena needs some things for her yard sale."

Inside, the cottage smelled of cedar and sea salt. Dust motes danced in the sunbeams that streamed through the gaps in the blinds, which had been pulled closed. The rooms had clearly been untouched for some time. A few pieces of furniture remained, draped in white sheets like silent ghosts.

"Wow," Bob said softly, taking in the vintage décor. "It's like stepping back in time."

Ginny ran her hand along a bookshelf she could take. She wasn't sure when Lena would have everything in place for the yard sale, but she could help her clean and restore some of these bigger items. "Jean said to focus on the spare bedroom. That's where most of the boxes are stored."

The cottage was a squat square, and it didn't take long to carry the boxes out to her car. "We can take the bookshelf, and the recliner," she said. "I think Duke is going to bring a truck to get the table and chairs."

"Where are we taking this stuff?" Bob bent to lift the recliner, and a puff of dust rose into the air. Ginny got the box from the dining room table, which contained old kitchenware, some used books, and a beautiful handmade runner for a table.

"These copper molds should sell well." She took the box out to the car and dug through a box or two while Bob returned to get the bookcase. Old fishing gear, a collection of seashells in a shadow box, an antique compass in a brass case.

A book of old photographs. "Mandie would love all of this," she mused, and she pulled out her phone to text her friend.

I'm picking up some things for Lena from Kristen's old cottage, and there is so much old stuff here! It'll be in my mom's garage, and you'd love it.

Oooh, I can't wait to look through it, Mandie said. *How's Bob?*

Ginny smiled at the question, said *He's great,* and went back to leafing through the photo album. She stalled mid-flip when an old picture caught her eye.

It was in color, so not terribly old, though it had definitely started to bleed along the edges. It showed a much younger Robin and Duke on what appeared to be their wedding day. Robin wore a simple white dress, her honey-blonde hair crowned with flowers, and on her wrist—

"The bracelet," Ginny whispered. She picked up the book and examined the picture closer. "Look, Bob. This is it."

The silver band circled Robin's wrist, its intricate design and blue stones catching the light even in the faded photograph.

"No wonder Mandie wants to wear this," she said as Bob peered over her shoulder.

"It's nice," he said. "Bookshelf is in."

"Okay." Ginny pulled out her phone, snapped a digital image of the picture, and texted Mandie again, this time attaching the evidence. *You won't believe what I just found at Kristen's cottage. A picture of your mom wearing THE bracelet on her wedding day.*

Mandie's response came almost immediately. *We have to find it.*

We're going to find it, Ginny promised her.

Bring that album. I've never seen that picture of my parents.

Ginny dropped the book back into the box she'd been casually going through and looked up. "Ready?" Bob asked, as if he'd just been standing there, waiting for her to be ready.

"Yes." She drove them from the lighthouse to the house she'd lived in for the last few years of her childhood and parked along the curb.

Inside the house, the scent of cheesy goodness filled the air, and she found Arthur bustling around the kitchen, stirring this and salting that.

"There you are," Arthur said warmly, wiping his hands on a dish towel before embracing Bob. "Good to see you, son."

He wrapped Ginny in a hug too as Bob said, "You too, sir."

"Where's my mom?"

"Right here," Mom said as she came out of the master bedroom. She wore a cream-colored blouse tucked into a pair of navy shorts. Of course. Ginny had never seen her mother look anything but like a sophisticated fashion model from the pages of an upscale boutique that only rich women knew about.

"Hey, you." She hugged Bob too, her smile genuine and wide. She switched her gaze to Ginny, whom she saw every day. "Where have you two been all day?"

"Just showing Bob around," Ginny said vaguely, and hoping she wouldn't have to go into more detail. "We walked around Driftwood Gardens, and then stopped by Kristen's cottage to pick up some things for Lena's yard sale."

"And?" Mom asked, turning back to Bob. "Did you like the gardens?"

Bob claimed Ginny by pulling her against his side. "They're the most incredible thing ever."

Mom's grin widened, thankfully, and Ginny ducked her head so she could hide her own smile. She knew her mother liked Bob, and that her worry over their marriage was perfectly normal.

"Are Charlie and Mandie coming tonight?" Bob asked.

Ginny shook her head. "Mandie's working late, I thought, and Charlie picked up an excursion."

"They're trying to save money for an apartment in the city," Mom said with a sigh. She moved into the kitchen and started to get down plates.

"Yeah, we've got to do the same," Bob said.

"Oh." Mom spoke in a bright voice and turned back to Ginny and Bob. She wore wide eyes now, and clutched four plates like she could barely hold them. "Eloise is going to Boston in a couple of weeks with her mother, and she's going to check with her tenants there. She thought they might be moving out this fall, and she'll need renters."

Ginny's eyes grew wide too. "Mom, you're kidding." She turned excitedly to Bob. "She has a brownstone in Boston, Bobby. A *brownstone.*"

Bob wore a sparkle in his eyes too. "That must cost a fortune," he said gently.

"She'd give it to you for a good price," Alice said. "I think she owns it. Eloise didn't get married until she moved back here."

"Wow, well, yeah, of course." Bob grinned around at everyone. "We want more information on that for sure."

Mom nodded and deftly moved past them to put the plates on the table. Ginny recognized this behavior, and she too went into the kitchen, this time to get utensils. Maybe then her mother would say what was on her mind.

"I picked up your wedding dress today," Mom said as Ginny laid down the first fork. "It's in my closet if you want to show Bob." She looked up then, plenty of fire burning in her dark eyes.

Ginny stared at her mom, completely shocked. "I thought I had to go in with Robin to do a final fitting."

"You do," Mom said airily. "I only got it for the weekend. They'll take it back for the fitting."

Ginny blinked, and then she tossed down the remaining forks and moved around the table and straight into her mother's arms. "Thank you, Mom," she whispered.

Her mother hugged her fiercely, and while Ginny didn't know what it felt like and meant to be a mother, she sure was glad she had a good one.

Chapter Nine

~~~

Alice stood in the kitchen, methodically slicing heirloom tomatoes for the Caprese salad. The sharp knife glided through the flesh, creating perfect rounds that she arranged in an alternating pattern with fresh mozzarella on a white serving platter. She'd then sprinkle the bright green basil over it all, creating a feast for the eyes before anyone took a single bite.

"Taste," Arthur said, appearing beside her with a wooden spoon extended. He'd spent the last hour perfecting his seafood risotto, a dish Charlie had specifically requested for tonight's dinner.

Alice obediently opened her mouth and sampled the creamy rice. "Mm, perfect. Maybe a touch more salt?"

Arthur's eyes crinkled at the corners as he smiled. "Already on it." He squeezed half a lemon into the pot, tossed a pinch of salt in, and stirred with practiced precision. "This is almost done, but it's fine to sit."

Alice checked the time—six-forty-five. Duke and Robin should be here with Mandie at seven, while Charlie was upstairs showering after his day on another excursion. He'd been picking up more of the afternoon groups, and Alice worried he might be working too much.

Even young people needed to sleep.

She'd just finished sprinkling the basil leaves across the tomatoes and mozzarella when the doorbell rang. A moment later, Robin's voice said, "...don't need to ring the doorbell and wait. We just walk in, Duke."

Alice still had to drizzle the balsamic glaze over her Caprese salad, but she wiped her hands and turned toward the mouth of the hallway that led to her front door. Robin led the way into the back of the house, with Duke in her wake.

"Hey," Alice said warmly. This dinner had been Alice's idea—a chance for both families to discuss wedding details for the October nuptials. But as the time arrived, a familiar tension crept up her spine.

She loved Robin with her whole heart, but she did have a controlling streak. They'd also made a pretty stringent rule that Alice wouldn't circumvent Charlie and Mandie and try to get information from Robin.

Alice didn't see how asking questions about her own son's wedding—to the wedding planner—was a problem, but apparently Mandie and Charlie did. In the end, Alice had been trying to accept that this wasn't really her son's wedding—it was Mandie's.

"Welcome," Arthur said as he bumped by Alice.

She blinked and stumbled after him. "Yes, come in." She didn't see Mandie, and she leaned in to hug Robin as she glanced down the hall. "Where's Mandie?"

"She's on the way," Robin said. "She was closing again tonight."

Footsteps thundered down the stairs, and Charlie appeared, his dark hair still damp, wearing a button-down shirt she'd never seen before.

"Is that new?" she asked, momentarily distracted.

Charlie glanced down at his blue shirt. "Mandie got it for me. She said I needed something that wasn't a t-shirt or fishing gear." He grinned at her and then moved to hug both Robin and Duke.

They smiled at him, seemingly totally at-ease with having him as a son-in-law. And why shouldn't they be? Charlie was an amazing person, and he loved Mandie.

Alice smiled, seeing the way Charlie ducked his head, slightly embarrassed, as Duke said something about the shirt too. "It looks good," she said. "Come help me set the table."

"Sorry, we're early," Duke said. "Trying to get Robin to stay home when she has somewhere to go is pretty hard."

"Hey," Robin said. "We were ready, and it's not like we need an appointment." She looked over to Alice. "I was a little restless."

"I took away her planner at five o'clock," Duke said good-naturedly. "She just finished a wedding, and she can take a Friday night off."

"Yes, she can," Alice said, though she understood the workaholic tendency. She had the same thing, and she'd set strict rules and alarms for herself to ensure she made time to relax, to take care of herself, to be Arthur's wife and the twins' mother. A good friend. An attentive daughter.

"Hon, can you scootch over?" Arthur touched her forearm, and Alice once again found herself startling back to attention. He threw down a crocheted hotpad and set the enormous pan of risotto on it.

The bright green peas shone against the creamy rice, which nestled the scrumptious shrimp.

"Wow," Duke said. "That looks amazing."

"Alice just needs to dress her salad," Arthur said, giving her a pointed look for a single breath, and then switched his vibrant gaze back to Duke. "And then we'll be ready."

"I'm here," Mandie said as she came bolting through the garage entrance. "I—Do I have time to change my clothes?"

"Hey, baby." Charlie abandoned his assignment to set the table, and he held the plates to the side as he drew Mandie into a hug. "You have plenty of time. It's not a formal affair."

Mandie hugged him and then pulled back. "You're wearing my shirt." She beamed up at him, and Alice saw in that moment how much Mandie loved her son. Her heart squeezed in her chest as she realized how...grown up the teenagers she'd known for the past several years had become.

For some reason, she still held Charlie in her mind at

certain ages. A baby, a five-year-old who skipped down the street to get on the school bus for the first time, a surly teenager who hated going to school.

Now, right before her eyes, she got a new snapshot of him—a handsome young man who had his whole life in front of him...with the woman he loved.

Then Mandie ducked into the bathroom, and Charlie stepped out of the kitchen to set the table, as asked.

"You don't need anything else?" Robin looked gorgeous as always, her honey-blonde hair pulled back in a low ponytail, wearing white capris and a coral blouse that complemented her summer tan. She lifted the bottle of wine Alice had missed a moment ago, her eyebrows going up too.

"It's that Pinot Grigio you loved at the Lighthouse Bistro."

Alice took the bottle. "Thank you, Robin."

"Of course." Robin set the wine on the table.

The simple statement eased something in Alice's chest. Yes, their children were getting married, complicating their relationship with new titles like "in-law," but at their core, they were still Robin and Alice, friends who had weathered far more than wedding planning together.

Alice drizzled olive oil and balsamic glaze over her salad and put it in the spot on the table Arthur had left for her. He'd engaged Duke in easy conversation, as Arthur always did. Mandie emerged from the bathroom, looking softer and more lovely in a simple sundress, her blonde hair now falling in loose waves around her shoulders.

She and Charlie seemed to lean toward each other, as if connected by an invisible thread, as she joined him at the end of the table and slipped her hand into his.

"Let's sit," Alice said. "Let me get the wine key." She hurried into the kitchen to get the corkscrew while chairs scraped the floor and people started to sit. Mandie and Charlie took the kitty-corner seats, and Robin and Duke filled the side facing the windows, leave another corner situation for Arthur and Alice.

She took the seat on the end after handing the corkscrew to Robin. "You open that for us, okay?"

Robin picked up the bottle of wine, and a moment later, the resounding *pop!* of the cork coming loose filled the room. Alice looked down the table to Mandie on the other end, keenly aware that neither she nor Charlie would be able to drink at their own wedding.

They really were young, but Alice set the thought on a shelf in her mind. People younger than Mandie and Charlie got married all the time.

Once everyone had their glass of wine, Alice raised her glass. "To our children." Charlie grinned at her.

"And to us," Robin added. "For raising such amazing kids." She laughed lightly, and Alice joined her.

They clinked glasses, and Alice took a sip, letting the crisp wine wash away some of her anxiety.

"So this is Charlie's favorite," Arthur said, reaching for the spoon to start dishing up the risotto. "Don't hold back, guys. It's just food." He grinned and put a big spoonful of risotto on his own plate. That seemed to break the ice, and Duke picked up one of the hard rolls while Mandie reached for the Caprese.

"How are the wedding plans coming?" Alice asked, deciding to just get the conversation going.

Robin set her glass down and took a roll from the basket Duke passed her. Alice handed her plate to her husband, and Arthur dished her some risotto too.

"Good," Robin said lightly. She glanced over to Mandie and smiled. "We booked at the Gardenia. Didn't Charlie tell you?"

"No," Alice said.

"I meant to," Charlie said from down the table.

"That's why I invited you to dinner," Alice said, sliding a couple of slices of tomato and cheese onto her plate. "Charlie...well, he's never been a fount of information." She smiled at him, and he had the decency to look ashamed.

"I've been working a lot the past couple of weeks," he said. He took a bite of risotto as Mandie stared at him. "And we wanted to talk to you guys about some stuff too."

Alice's eyebrows went up. "Oh, yeah?"

"We've been thinking," Mandie said, her voice steady though her fingers fidgeted with her fork. "And we want to keep things really simple."

"Simple is good." Robin took a bite of her roll and watched the couple. "The Gardenia will be a ton of sophistication. There's not much more you need to do if you want to keep things simple."

"Like, really simple," Charlie said now. "We're

thinking just immediate family, actually. Ceremony at sunset, dinner immediately afterward." He grinned at Mandie. "Just something small and nice and intimate."

Alice watched him too, and she knew why they'd been thinking like this. She truly didn't care if the whole town of Five Island Cove came to the wedding, or if there was a band, or about any of it, really.

She'd given up appearances when she'd left the Hamptons.

"Sometimes the wedding isn't about just the couple," Robin said in the most diplomatic voice Alice had ever heard her use.

"We want something that feels like us." Mandie looked at her mother with intensity in her eyes that spoke of how much she wanted something small and simple. But the Gardenia...the stone and archways of that place definitely spoke of class and elegance.

She exchanged a look with Robin. "We just want your day to be special."

"It will be," Mandie said. "Because we'll be marrying each other." She leaned into Charlie as he put his arm around her. "That's what matters to us."

Robin nodded slowly. "I understand that. But can I ask why the change? You seemed excited about a bigger celebration before."

Mandie and Charlie exchanged another look, and this time Alice caught something more—nervousness, perhaps. Or determination.

"We've been doing some math," Charlie said. "And

with rent in New York, my tuition, and trying to save for the future...we'd rather have the nice venue with less people than all the bells and whistles."

"I gave you a budget," Alice said, switching her gaze to Robin. "Did he give you my budget at least?"

Robin nodded. "Yes, I got your budget, and with ours, it's enough to have the ceremony where you want it, with the dinner." She frowned, still obviously confused. "I'm not sure what else you think we'll be doing."

"Flowers," Mandie said. "Bridesmaids dresses."

"Décor," Charlie said. "Centerpieces."

"You don't need more décor at the Gardenia," Alice said, hoping she was right.

"You can," Robin said. "But no, it's not necessary." She shot a look at Alice that gave her permission to say nothing. "You'll want flowers, Mandie, and I thought you were having two bridesmaids—Ginny and Jamie."

"Yes," Mandie said.

"I can buy my own daughter a dress to wear," Robin said.

"Same," Alice said, hoping the word would be taken for what she meant it to be—supportive.

"So that's a zero cost," Robin said. "The food and venue come together."

"It's thirty-three dollars per plate, Mom," Mandie said. "We can't—"

"Baby," Duke said. "How many people do you think we're going to invite?"

"You and Mom know everyone in the cove," Mandie said. "And Arthur and Alice do too."

"We just want to start our life together without debt or obligations," Charlie said.

"Do you trust us so little?" Alice asked. "I'm not going to approve tens of thousands of dollars. That's why I gave you a budget."

"Of course I trust you," Charlie said.

"Okay," Arthur said. "Let's not get all worked up."

"We're not children anymore," Charlie said, his eyes meeting Alice's directly. "We want it to be—" He looked at Mandie.

"Classic and small," they said together.

"So are we talking just parents and siblings?" Robin asked. "Because I can't imagine not inviting at least Kristen, Kelli, El, and AJ." She threw a panicked look at Alice. "And their families."

Alice had made guest lists before, and with their friend group, it didn't take long to get to fifty.

"We counted all of them." Mandie picked up her phone. "I think between us, we got to seventy-two."

That was much bigger than Alice had assumed from the word "small."

"Oh, that's not too bad," Robin said.

"We want to pay for the food," Charlie said. "If you guys can do the venue, the dress, and...the flowers."

"We don't need flowers," Mandie argued.

"Yes, baby," Charlie said. "We need flowers. They won't be that much." He looked down to Alice, who gave him a small smile. Yes, she would pay for the flowers. No problem.

"We've already got the venue," Robin said. "And we're going dress shopping this week."

"What about the bracelet?" Mandie asked. "None of it will matter if I can't find that bracelet."

Alice had heard about the bracelet, and Mandie, Ginny, and Charlie had shown her a wedding picture of Robin and Duke where Robin wore the beautiful piece of jewelry. "Any luck finding it?" she asked.

Mandie shook her head. "Not yet."

"We'll find it, I promise," Robin said. "We have to have it somewhere."

"Speaking of finding things," Duke said, turning to Alice. "How's the lighthouse case coming?"

Alice welcomed the change of topic, and she smiled gratefully at Duke. "I have a hearing scheduled for July fourteenth. With Edna May's affidavit and the records from the Historical Society, I'm cautiously optimistic."

"That's wonderful," Robin said. "Kristen must be thrilled."

"I don't want to jinx anything," Alice said. "But yes, I think we're close to resolving this once and for all."

"Mom's being modest," Charlie said. "She's been working on this case for months, digging through archives, interviewing old-timers. She's like a legal detective."

Alice scoffed and shook her head, though this case wasn't her usual fare. "It's important to Kristen, so it's important to me."

"That's what I love about the cove," Mandie said. "Everyone takes care of each other." She looked at Charlie, such hope on her face. "It's one of the reasons we want to come back here someday."

Alice's head snapped up. "You do?"

Charlie nodded. "Eventually, yeah. After I finish school and all that. But we both love it here."

Something tight in Alice's chest loosened. The thought of her children building their lives far away had been a constant ache. Knowing they might return someday felt like a gift she hadn't dared hope for.

"Well," Arthur said, raising his wine glass. "I think that calls for a toast. To Charlie and Mandie, and their future together—wherever it takes them."

Everyone raised their glasses, and Alice found herself smiling genuinely for the first time that evening. Perhaps she couldn't control how their wedding unfolded, but she could support their choices and trust that they knew what they were doing.

As the conversation flowed forward into other things, Alice reflected on a conversation she'd had with Arthur this week.

She'd been lamenting that she'd missed when her children had grown up, as she could so clearly remember when Charlie had first learned to ride a bike and Ginny hosted tea parties for her stuffed animals.

She'd said, "I miss them already, and they're not even gone yet," to which Arthur had held her close, touched his lips to her neck and murmured, "You're their mother; they'll always come back to you."

Now, sitting at the table with good friends and good food, Alice watched her son for a moment. Yes, he'd come back to her, and Alice felt it stronger than ever as her handsome son tipped his head back and laughed at something Duke and Mandie were talking about.

Chapter Ten

Mandie adjusted the vintage American flag scarf tied around her ponytail and smoothed her hands over the white sundress with its subtle red pinstripes. She turned to check her booty, noting that the fabric hugged her curves in a way that would have made her self-conscious last summer, but now?

She wasn't sure she cared.

"Mm, you look hot," Charlie said as he entered his bedroom on the second floor of his parents' house. Heat filled her face as she turned away from her reflection to ease herself into his arms. She suddenly felt beautiful in the dress, especially when Charlie looked at her the way he did right now.

"It's my new dress," she said. "But it looks old, like it's vintage." Mandie adored old things—and anything that looked old or spoke of bygone fashions.

"I like it on your body, and I'd be just as happy to see it

crumpled on the floor." He grinned at her, his hands warm on her hips. He leaned down and kissed her, and Mandie let herself get lost in his touch, the slight dampness in his hair from his shower.

She'd slept in this morning while Charlie had gone to his early-morning job on the docks. The fishermen had come back early today, as today was Independence Day, and the town of Five Island Cove had plenty planned to celebrate. Everything from food trucks on various beaches on every island, to the traditional boat parade here on the biggest beach in the cove—the western beach on Diamond Island—to fireworks being lit from the parking lot at the lighthouse, flying high enough for everyone on all five islands to see.

"Mm, you need to behave," she murmured to her fiancé as she stepped away. She peered back into the mirror, her bright red lipstick now smudged. "Look what you did."

He wrapped her up from behind. "Sorry, sweetheart." He grinned at her in the mirror, clearly not *that* sorry. "You're just so sexy. I can't control myself."

"Yes, you can." She turned sideways as Charlie stepped back. He'd gotten a gray T-shirt with the American flag at the drugstore late last week, and he'd paired that with a pair of beige khaki shorts. She found him incredibly attractive too, but she hid her blush by studying her profile.

"Seriously, Mandie. You're the most beautiful woman in Five Island Cove."

She smiled and turned toward him. "Okay, sweet talker. We need to get going or we'll miss the boat parade."

"Yeah, Ginny texted and said she's downstairs with Bob."

"Let's not keep them waiting then." Mandie grabbed Charlie's hand as she passed, and they laughed as they went downstairs, hung a left, and exited the house. Sure enough, the sedan Charlie and Ginny shared waited on the curb, as Ginny stayed with her fiancé Bob when he came to the cove.

A twinge of jealousy zinged through Mandie, because she'd love to have somewhere private and romantic to sleep over with Charlie. But getting a hotel would just cost money, and they were pinching ever penny in preparation for their upcoming wedding and life together afterward.

Charlie had borrowed his boss's boat once this summer, and Mandie had slept over with him then, but otherwise, she sometimes stayed over at his house, and he sometimes slept in her bedroom at her parents' house.

Neither situation was ideal, and Mandie couldn't wait to tie the knot.

The Diamond Island Marina buzzed with activity as they arrived. Red, white, and blue decorations adorned every lamppost and railing, and the scent of grilling hot dogs and hamburgers, as well as super-buttery popcorn, filled the air. Children ran around with sparklers despite the daylight, their excited shrieks blending with the music pouring from speakers set up along the boardwalk.

"Here we are," Ginny said after she'd found a parking space. She opened her door and stood, and Mandie did the same from the backseat. Ginny wore a blue sundress with white stars, and Bob came around the front of the sedan in khaki shorts and a red polo shirt. They were the picture of all-American sweethearts.

Mandie linked her arm through her best friend's. "You guys look so cute and coordinated."

"Like we planned it." Bob laughed from the sidewalk.

"We did plan it," Ginny said. "I texted you what to wear, remember?"

"Right, right." Bob reached for her, and Ginny stepped up onto the sidewalk. Mandie followed her and let Charlie take her hand so they wouldn't get separated in the growing crowd.

"My dad's boat is in the parade this year," she said as they followed everyone else streaming down onto the beach. "He and his fishing buddies decorated it yesterday."

"Where's the best spot to watch?" Bob asked.

"Everywhere," Ginny said as the golden sand spread before them. Plenty of families and people had already arrived, with lots more coming behind them.

"I love your bandana," a young woman said, smiling at Mandie.

"Thanks," she said, automatically reaching back to tighten it.

"Where'd you get it?"

"At the little store next to the prom shop," Mandie said

with a smile. "I was there last week, looking for a wedding dress, and I got so stressed, I just slipped in there. They have amazing vintage stuff."

"Oh, is it that new place? Old Beginnings?"

"Yeah," Mandie said, the name popping into her head. "That's it."

The other young woman nodded, and Mandie had no idea if she was still in high school or what. She'd only graduated a couple of years ago herself, but Mandie didn't recognize her. "Thanks."

A bearded man approached, and she took his hand, and the pair of them continued down the sidewalk. Happiness streamed through Mandie, and she went with Bob and Ginny as they started navigating the crowd to find somewhere to sit.

As they walked, Mandie spotted familiar faces everywhere—acquaintances from high school, then Eloise and Aaron with Billie and Grace near the judges' stand—and Billie's boyfriend—Mandie's boss from last summer, a man who'd dated Tessa Simmons for a while. Mandie had loved working with Tessa at the library too, but there hadn't been any openings this summer, and she didn't actually know if Tessa and Dave were still dating or not.

Until she saw him approach Tessa, hand her a bright red snow cone, and laugh. So apparently, they were still together. Mandie used to be able to keep up with everything in the cove, everything in New York City, everything with school, Ginny, Charlie, all of it.

But now, Mandie could barely focus on what she

needed to get done that day, and life felt heavier than it had last summer. Maybe it was the diamond on her finger, and the impending threat of having to pay for an apartment in New York City with only the money she and Charlie could make.

She exhaled, because she didn't need to carry those burdens today.

"I love this," Mandie said, breathing in the festive atmosphere.

Charlie squeezed her hand. "It's a great celebration."

"How about here?" Ginny asked about a spot with plenty of room for all of them.

"Sure," Charlie said, and he spread out the blanket he'd been carrying. Bob set down the small cooler and opened it to offer drinks. Mandie took a can of Sprite and a granola bar, though she wasn't that hungry. They'd get lunch after the parade, and Mandie really wanted clam chowder in a bread bowl, even if it was hot outside.

"So," Ginny said, settling cross-legged on the blanket as she popped the top on her can of ginger ale. "How did dinner go?"

Mandie exchanged a look with Charlie, knowing immediately he wasn't going to say anything. "It was fine," Mandie said. "Your mom was actually really supportive about us wanting to keep things simple."

"And your mom?" Ginny asked.

"She's—I don't know. She's frustrating," Mandie said. "She acts like we have a ton of money, when I know we don't."

"She does get discounts at places," Ginny said, her dark eyes wide and innocent. "And she can work miracles."

"Yeah," Mandie said, because she'd witnessed—and had even helped—her mom make miracle weddings happen. She'd seen her run a smooth event without any hiccups, and then been there when everything seemed to go wrong. Mom solved all the issues, and the I-do's still got said from a place of perfection. Usually, the bride didn't even know about all the problems.

"You promised to show me pictures of your final dress," Ginny said.

Mandie brightened instantly. "I totally forgot you had to leave early."

Ginny crowded closer as Mandie pulled up the pictures. "I know you're, like, this classic, satin type of bride, but I'm going with a ballgown."

"Ballgowns are classic," Ginny said. "Traditional, at least."

Mandie nudged her. "You hate traditional."

"I don't *hate* it."

"You kind of do," Bob said.

Ginny swung her attention to him. "I showed you my dress, you—you traitor." She grinned at him, and Bob tipped his head back and laughed.

Mandie passed the phone to Ginny. "Those last few are the final ensemble. They'll piece it all together. It should be done by the middle of September."

Ginny took the device and gasped after only one second. "Mandie, it's gorgeous!"

The dress was simple and elegant—a fitted bodice with delicate lace overlay that cinched at the waist with a sash, and then the big ballgown skirt flowed into a big bell. The dress wasn't overly formal, but it was undeniably bridal-ballgown.

"I'll wear a seven-layer crinoline," Mandie said.

"It's perfect for a sunset ceremony," Ginny said, still swiping on her phone.

Mandie's own excitement bubbled to the surface again. "And it was on sale, which made me feel better about spending the money."

"You're going to be the most beautiful bride," Ginny said, handing the phone back to Mandie. "And you're not showing Charlie, right?"

"No." Mandie quickly tucked her phone away, proud of Charlie for not even trying to look. She glanced over to him, and he reached for her. She scooted back into his chest just as a horn blasted across the harbor, signaling the start of the parade.

A cry rose through the air, mostly from excited younger children. Mandie focused toward the water as the first boat rounded the point, festooned with American flags and streamers.

Mandie grinned, because she absolutely loved the boat parade. The tradition in Five Island Cove dated back decades. Every year, locals decorated their vessels—everything from tiny rowboats to luxury yachts to fishing boats —and paraded around the harbor in a show of patriotic pride. The prizes were named fun things like "The Lady

Liberty Award," for the most elegant patriotic display, and "The Stars & Stripes Spectacular," for the best overall decoration.

"That one is going to win the quirky one," Charlie said as the second boat came into view.

"Red, White, and Quirky," Ginny said, and in fact, the crowd started to chant it as the fishing vessel drew closer.

Mandie suddenly jumped to her feet. "There's my dad's boat!" She started waving frantically as Dad's fishing boat passed directly in front of them. He'd strung big-bulb red, white, and blue lights across all the railings, up into the rigging, and wrapped right around the tower. He'd overlapped flags over the side so the whole thing looked draped in stars and stripes—but not in the classic, sophisticated way that would win some of the other awards.

Dad stood at the helm, wearing his captain's hat with an American flag bandana tied around it, and a cape—a legit cape—in red, white and blue fluttering behind him. His boat was crewed with his friends, all wearing capes, and as Mandie stared, wide-eyed, they started trying to crack open a giant hot-dog-shaped piñata.

"They went all out this year," Charlie said, chuckling.

"Dad's been planning it for weeks." Mandie laughed. "He's determined to win something, and it looks like he's going for the quirkiness."

A speed boat came next—a bright red luxury vessel that carried five or six young adults. All buff, all tan, wearing very little clothing. Short blue shorts for the men, and teeny tiny red bikinis for the women. They cheered and clapped together long red and blue tubes that then shot confetti into the air.

It came nowhere near the beach, but everyone on shore cheered nonetheless.

The parade continued, each boat more elaborately decorated than the last. The crowd cheered and clapped, with occasional bursts of laughter at the more outlandish displays. Mandie felt a surge of pride in her community, in this place that had shaped her into who she was.

When the last boat passed and the judges retreated to deliberate, Mandie's stomach growled, and she got up and started collecting their empty soda cans. Charlie folded up the blanket, and they packed everything back to the car.

The awards would be announced on the dock, and Mandie stayed close to Charlie, Ginny, and Bob as they joined the throng of people gathered around to hear who'd won. Food trucks had been parked down the other side of the lot, and Mandie tugged Charlie in that direction.

"Let's get something to eat while they dock and come ashore."

"All right." He went with her, and after surveying her choices, Mandie opted for the very patriotic hamburger and French friends—with her side of clam chowder—and they settled onto the seawall to eat.

Finally, the judges arrived, and Mandie stood with the last of her fries to hear the winners. The dock coordinator stepped up onto a podium, a mic in his hand, and beamed out at the crowd.

He wore a top hat in furry red, white, and blue, and he

started with the winners. "Most Patriotic goes to...Dylan Fredding and the Sea Maiden!"

The crowd whooped, with a section of it absolutely losing their minds. Mandie gave her fries to Ginny, though she and Bob had gotten fish tacos from a different truck.

The Lady Liberty award went to a summer resident who had a home on Rocky Ridge, and Charlie's one-time boss won the Yankee Doodle Dandy award.

The red speedboat won the Firecracker Spirit award, and only a couple remained.

Mandie's nerves twisted in her stomach as the coordinator said, "Up next is the Red, White, and Quirky award, and it goes to...Duke Grover and Friends, and their boat Northwind!"

Mandie screamed and started jumping up and down. She turned toward Charlie, who put his fingers in his mouth and whistled. She hugged him and couldn't wait to see her dad later. "He'll be so happy," she yelled above the applause.

"Your dad looks like he just won an Olympic gold medal." Charlie laughed and pointed up to where Dad was collecting his award.

"For him, this is bigger," Mandie said, clapping until her hands hurt and smiling until she thought her face would crack. Oh, how she loved small town celebrations like this, and she was so happy for her dad, who'd been there for her every single day of her life. Every hour, every moment.

He so deserved this, and she couldn't wait to hug him congratulations.

LATER THAT NIGHT, AFTER THE SUN HAD PAINED the sky in shades of pink and orange, Mandie and Charlie once again met up with Bob and Ginny, this time on the south side of Diamond Island.

More people would be clustered further north, closer to the lighthouse, but Mandie wanted darkness around her —and less people. So she spread out a blanket and pulled on a sweatshirt before settling down next to Charlie.

"I brought sparklers," Ginny announced, pulling a box from her bag.

"And I brought licorice." Bob handed her a bag of Red Vines, Mandie's favorite red licorice.

"Thank you," she said with a smile. She pulled out a piece and chewed on it while Charlie lit a sparkler for each hand.

Mandie watched the sparks dance and swirl, drawing patterns in the air. Charlie wrote her name in glowing letters that faded almost as quickly as they appeared.

"Make a wish," Ginny said, her face illuminated by her sparkler's glow.

Mandie closed her eyes briefly. *I wish I could always feel as happy and as free as I do right now.*

When the sparklers burned out and the fireworks hadn't started yet, Charlie lay back, pulling Mandie down beside him. She curled into his side, the darkness around them seemingly so vast and so deep.

Others had come to this beach, but not very many, and Mandie couldn't hear anyone nearby. Only the sound of Charlie's even, steady breathing.

"Look at all those stars," he murmured.

The night sky stretched above them, glittering with stars. Mandie felt small beneath it, but in a calm, comforting way. She expected the fireworks to start at any moment, and Charlie would pull up the website where Five Island Cove played patriotic songs timed to the fireworks for anyone outside the sound radius of the lighthouse.

"I've been thinking," Charlie said, his voice quiet enough that only she could hear.

"About what?" Mandie turned her head to look at him.

"Kids," he said simply. "I know we've talked about waiting until after I finish school, but…"

Mandie's heart skipped a beat. "But—what?"

"I wouldn't mind if it happened sooner." His eyes met hers in the darkness. "I mean, if it happened accidentally or something."

Mandie sat up, surprised. "Accidentally?" He knew how babies were made, right?

"Charlie, you have at least six more years of school, and I have two."

"I know how long we have left in school," he said evenly. "Lay down, sweetheart. I like holding you."

He was so nonchalant about things, while Mandie's heart now raced through the sky. She didn't want to shoot him down instantly, but they were already stressed about paying for an apartment, and he wanted to add a baby to it?

"We'd be trying to raise a baby in a tiny New York apartment while you're in pharmacy school and I'm working. How would we even afford childcare?"

"I know," he said. "I'm not saying let's try right now. I'm just saying I wouldn't be upset if it happened."

"I would," Mandie said, more sharply than she intended. "I mean, I want kids with you, Charlie. That's not the question. But not yet."

She couldn't even imagine *that* conversation with her parents.

The first firework exploded overhead, illuminating the crowd on this small beach on the south side of the island. Charlie wore a smile, and Mandie wondered what he'd see on her face if he looked.

"It makes more sense to wait," Charlie said. "I'm just saying—I'd be happy about it."

"Okay," Mandie said. "Are you going to put on the music?"

"Oh, sure." He lifted his phone and started swiping, the screen so bright as it glowed over them. He got that going as the second firework—a gold witch's hair explosion—landed in the sky.

Charlie kneaded her closer, tucking her flush against him. "I'll wait as long as you want, sweetheart. Okay?"

Mandie snuggled into him, relief washing over her. "Thank you for understanding."

"Always," he said, kissing the top of her head. He didn't seem to care about the fireworks very much, as he then said, "I love you, Mandie."

"I love you too," she whispered back.

"Let's find somewhere to stay tonight," he said. "I don't want to go back to my house or your house."

"Find somewhere? What does that mean?" Mandie pushed herself up again and looked down at him. "It'll cost money."

"I'm going to text a friend. He's in the city this week, and he's got a condo sitting empty." He sent a message quickly, and then pulled Mandie back to his side. "I can't wait until we're married."

Mandie watched the red and white sparks burst through the sky, the music still playing from Charlie's phone. "Do you ever worry that we're rushing things? Getting married so young?"

His body tensed. "Where is this coming from? Is it because I brought up kids?"

"No, not exactly." Mandie sighed into the night, glad it was dark and he wanted her glued to his side. Then she didn't have to look at him. "It's just...everyone keeps reminding us how young we are. My mom, your mom, even the wedding dress attendant mentioned it the other day."

"Do *you* feel like we're rushing?"

"No," she said immediately. "But sometimes I wonder if everyone else knows something we don't."

"Mandie, sweetheart." He shifted toward her and cupped her face in his palm. "I've wanted to marry you since we were sixteen years old. Who cares how old we are? What matters is that we love each other, and that we're committed to making it work."

"I know," she said. "And I do want to marry you. I'm ready." And she was.

"Then that's all that matters." He gave her a quiet smile and kissed her softly. "The rest we'll figure out as we go."

"You make it sound easy." She sighed back into his side as the finale started to ramp up. More and more fireworks exploded in the sky to the last strains of the *1812 Overture*.

His phone chimed among all the cannons and drums in the song, and Charlie looked at his phone. "I have the code to the lock on the front door."

"I don't have any other clothes," Mandie said.

"We don't need clothes, sweetheart." Charlie pressed a kiss to her forehead again and sighed as he gazed up at the sky, which lit up brightly as a whole arsenal of fireworks filled it.

Mandie grinned into the sky, because she loved the Fourth of July and all it stood for. The display ended, and Bob and Ginny started to get up on the other side of the blanket. Mandie didn't want this moment to end, but she reluctantly pushed away from Charlie and started gathering her phone and putting it in her bag.

As she and Charlie left the beach and bid good-night to Bob and Ginny, she drew in a deep breath of the cool night air. Maybe things were easier than she'd been viewing them. Maybe Charlie was right—all that mattered was that they loved each other and were committed to making their marriage work.

Sometimes things really were that simple—and Mandie craved simplicity.

Chapter Eleven

E loise sat at her mother's kitchen table, laptop open, nervously tapping her fingernails against her coffee mug. The Cliffside Inn's security cameras were pulled up on the screen, offering her a silent view of her realtor, Natalie, leading a well-dressed couple through the inn's grand foyer.

"Come on," she whispered. "Fall in love with it."

The couple—a man and woman who appeared to be in their fifties—paused to admire the original woodwork around the massive stone fireplace in the lobby. Eloise sat tensely, despite the fact that the chocolate chip cookies had been put out, along with the iced tea and lemonade—and the woman snagged a cookie. She took a bite, then moved to run her hand along the mantel, a gesture that made Eloise's heart flutter with hope.

She always left the inn during the showings, and it somehow felt like leaving behind her most trusted companion. She reminded herself that Cliffside was a building, not a person, and she *could* leave it in her past.

If only someone would buy it.

Natalie had been giving her notes on the interested buyers, though this was only the fourth time Eloise had scheduled a showing. She hadn't sat through watching the tour any of the other times, but today...she simply wanted to hear what they said straight from their own mouths.

She wouldn't be able to hear or see much once they got to the guest rooms, but Eloise had cameras in all the public areas of the inn—with microphones.

With her heart pounding, she tapped the volume icon in the bottom right corner, and the sound whooshed to life. "...lobby is inviting," the man said.

"There's a full kitchen, pantry, and storage area through this door," Natalie said in her crisp, professional real estate agent voice. "Right now, the owner offers cookies and drinks for check-in, and she employs a full-time chef, as they serve breakfast and dinner right here at the inn."

"But there's no restaurant, right?" the woman asked as she preceded everyone into the kitchen.

Eloise had poured her heart, soul, and plenty of money into the Cliffside Inn. She knew it was an amazing place; she also knew she was asking a lot for it, but she didn't want to compromise. She and Natalie had strategized a price that new owners could earn back in only three years, what with the bookings Eloise currently got—and that included being able to live on-site and pay themselves a good wage for Five Island Cove.

She just needed to find the right buyers.

"Oh, this is nicer than I thought it would be," the woman said. "How old did you say this building was?"

"It's one of the original structures in Five Island Cove," Natalie said, and Eloise had this speech memorized even if she hadn't heard it before. She knew the history of her own inn, after all.

As Natalie went through when it was built, who owned it, and when all the most recent renovations were done, the couple moved through the whole kitchen, actually turning on burners and walking into the big refrigeration unit in the corner.

"This door is actually non-functional right now," Natalie said, indicating the door in the corner. "It leads into the on-site apartment, which was originally built for the cook. But previous owners have lived here—anyone can live here. It's fully equipped with it's own bathroom, bedroom, and kitchen, and right now, the owner employs a night manager, and that's who lives in this apartment."

"Can we see it?" the man asked.

"Yes, of course," Natalie said, and she led them out another door that led into the back courtyard.

Eloise switched her gaze to that camera, but it too was muted. She sat back as they didn't pause to take in the gardens, shrubbery, or the pool just beyond that. Surely they would later, but for now, Natalie led them into

Rhonda's apartment. Her shift started at eight, but Eloise did see her during the day sometimes.

She'd been sure to tell her about this showing, and she didn't expect—or experience—any problems with the attached apartment.

The couple came back out, and Natalie led them through the courtyard, the back patio, pointing out the outdoor furniture, the chaise lounges around the pool, and the stunning views from atop the cliffs on Sanctuary Island.

Eloise's stomach tightened. She'd loved the Cliffside Inn for the past several years. It had brought her purpose and fulfillment in a way she hadn't known she'd needed. Yes, it was busy, but as she watched Natalie take the couple through the laundry facilities, and then finally upstairs to the guest rooms, Eloise's heart squeezed with love for the inn.

Her phone buzzed on the counter beside her laptop, and Eloise quickly swiped it up to read the text from Natalie. *They love the architecture. Asking about occupancy rates, and I can't find the latest report from the end of June.*

Eloise quickly typed back. *I'll resend it.* She tapped quickly out of the security camera feed to her financial documents. She found the occupancy rate, which showed Cliffside being completely booked for the months of June, July, and August—and December, April, and sometimes May—and sent it to Natalie again.

I can send the other averages for the off-season and the financials again, if they need them.

This should work for now, Natalie said. *Thank you!*

The camera feed showed Natalie gesturing animatedly as they entered the last room Eloise would be able to observe them in—the sunroom. Eloise switched to that camera view, watching as the couple's expressions brightened at the wall of windows overlooking the vast Atlantic Ocean on the east side of the inn.

It got morning sun, and Eloise sometimes called the room a library, and sometimes a game room. She rented it for a nominal fee to people who wanted to have meetings or conferences and were staying at the inn. When that didn't happen, the sunroom was open for any guest to simply come enjoy the sunshine, read, nap, or otherwise relax.

She'd only had four showings in the past couple of months, as the inn hadn't gone on the market until the middle of April. Two had amounted to nothing, with the other two resulting in lowball offers she'd rejected.

But this couple seemed different, though Eloise couldn't pinpoint why. Her phone rang, a shrill noise she used so she couldn't ignore it while working, startling her so badly she nearly knocked over her coffee.

Well, that ringtone would need to be changed when she sold the inn.

She quickly tapped on the call from her husband. "Hey," she said.

"Hey," Aaron said, his voice warm and carrying a hint of amusement. "How's the stalking going?"

"I'm not stalking. I'm...remotely observing." Eloise

smiled despite herself. "They seem interested. They've been there almost an hour."

"That's good, right?"

"I think so." She switched camera views again, watching as the couple exited the inn through the front door and paused at the bottom of the steps with Natalie. "The woman keeps touching things—the woodwork, opening the drawers, picking up towels by the pool." Eloise had no idea if that was a good sign or not.

"I'm just wondering if you want me to bring home dinner."

"What did the boys bring in?" she asked.

Aaron chuckled. "Terrance roasted a pig in his back-yard last night."

"Then yes," Eloise said instantly. She glanced over to her mother as she wandered into the kitchen. "I can make macaroni salad to go with it."

She angled her body slightly. "My mother is having a weird day. I'm going to try to get her to come stay with us until the appointment next week." Eloise had already made the suggestion to her mother—not that day, but a few days ago. It had not been received well, and Eloise didn't know what would happen if she had to insist her mother couldn't live on her own anymore.

"Oh, boy." Aaron sighed. Eloise bristled, though she knew his sigh hadn't come because he didn't want her mother in the house. It was because he knew how stub-born Mom could be.

Eloise supposed she'd inherited some of that trait, and

she frowned as her mother dropped a couple of ice cubes in her thermos mug and then poured hot coffee over them. Strange. She'd never seen her mother drink iced coffee before this very moment.

"Chief," someone said on his end of the line, and Eloise wasn't surprised to hear him say, "I have to run, El. Love you."

"Love you too," she said quickly, the call ending only a moment later. She sighed this time, and when she focused on the security camera feeds again, she saw that Natalie and the couple had left.

She dove onto her phone again, expecting some sort of report from her real estate agent. She had nothing.

Eloise got up and rounded the island countertop where she'd been sitting. "Aaron is bringing home pulled pork for dinner," she said casually. "One of his cops did a pig roast last night, so it should be excellent. Should I stop by and grab you on my way home from the inn?"

Her mother looked at her with clear, interested eyes. Eloise could *see* her there when she hadn't been able to earlier, and she didn't know if she should be happy about that or not.

"Sure, that sounds great," Mom said.

"If you want, you can bring a bag and stay the night," Eloise said as she opened the fridge. "Billie has that Morning Movie, and I know she's asked you to come."

"All right," Mom said, and Eloise watched her out of the corner of her eye. She didn't seem put out or argumentative, and she closed the fridge a moment later and returned to her devices.

Her phone vibrated in her hand as she lifted it, which meant she'd gotten a message. With a pounding heart, she slid it open and tapped to read Natalie's texts.

Quick report: No offer yet, but don't worry. They're asking a lot of questions, and they spoke about moving money right in front of me.

Eloise's heart leapt into her throat. *That's great! Work your real estate magic.*

Natalie obviously got paid based on the sale price, and she wouldn't want a low offer either. *I'll keep you updated. They're in the cove through the weekend, and they said they might have their son come look at it with them. I told them anytime—except your check-in and check-out window. They said they'd let me know by tonight.*

Thank you, Natalie. Just let me know. We can pop out anytime.

She closed her laptop and let out a long, shaky breath. This could be it—the moment she'd been both longing for and dreading. Freedom from the inn's constant demands, but also the end of a chapter in her life that had defined her for so long.

"I HATE DOCTORS' OFFICES," MOM SAID, fidgeting in her chair. "They always keep you waiting."

Eloise reached over and patted her mother's hand. "It's

a specialist, Mom. They're always running behind." And they were lucky to get in as quickly as they had, but Eloise kept that remark to herself.

They sat in a sleek waiting room on the fourteenth floor of a medical tower in downtown Boston, surrounded by tasteful abstract art and the quiet murmur of hushed conversations. They'd arrived in the city yesterday, flying from Five Island Cove and staying in a boutique hotel that Eloise had really enjoyed.

Traveling with her mother, though? It had been easier than Eloise had anticipated, especially because her mother hadn't left the cove in years, and she had fears about flying and travel that couldn't be eased through reason.

"What time is it now?" Mom asked, squinting at the wall clock.

"Eleven fifteen," Eloise said patiently. Yes, she knew they'd been there for forty-five minutes, but what were they going to do? Stomp out in a huff and fly home?

Mom nodded, then looked around the room as if seeing it for the first time. "This is a fancy place," she said. "Must be expensive to rent a space like this."

"Mm." Eloise had found that humming usually satisfied her mother, and she honestly didn't have a reply to everything she said.

A nurse in navy scrubs appeared at the doorway, clipboard in hand, and Eloise watched her while she read something on it. "Dawn Hall?"

"That's us," Eloise said, standing and waiting while her mother gathered her purse and sweater.

They followed the semi-smiling nurse down a corridor lined with examination rooms until they reached a larger office at the end. Inside, a middle-aged woman with silver-streaked dark hair sat behind a desk, reviewing something on her computer screen. She looked up as they entered, her expression warm and professional.

She stood, revealing tailored clothes and pinpoint heels. How she worked in those all day, Eloise would never know. "Mrs. Hall? I'm Doctor Valencia. Please, have a seat." She gestured to two chairs facing her desk. "And you must be Eloise, her daughter."

"Yes," Eloise said, settling into one of the chairs. "Thank you for seeing us."

Dr. Valencia nodded, her attention focused on Mom. "Mrs. Hall, I've reviewed your records from Doctor Winters, and I understand you've been experiencing some memory issues and confusion. Is that right?"

Mom straightened in her chair, her chin lifting in a show of defiance. Eloise wanted to pull her aside and tell her to one—*be honest*, and two—*just listen*. Doctors trained for a long time, and *could she please just listen?*

"Some," Mom finally admitted. "I forget things. Names, where I put things. Sometimes I get confused about where I am—but only for a moment."

Dr. Valencia nodded, and to her credit, she didn't look over to Eloise to check the validity of her mother's answers. "How long has this been happening?"

Mom looked at Eloise, uncertainty in her eyes. "Um."

"It's been gradual," Eloise said, giving her mother a

small, kind smile. "I think I first noticed it a few months ago, actually. But I wasn't alarmed." She looked at the doctor, hoping to drive that home. "She's getting older, and even as I've gotten older, I have a hard time remembering everything."

"Naturally," Dr. Valencia said.

"But there have definitely been isolated incidents that stick out," Eloise said. "We eat dinner together as a family semi-often, but she lives on a different island than we do. She's made the trip hundreds of times, but one day only, oh, what? Mom? Five or six weeks ago, maybe."

"Yes," Mom said quietly, her hands wringing together. "Beginning of June."

"She remembers that—but only sometimes," Eloise said. "Like, she asked me if she'd need a hat and gloves for the boat parade on the Fourth of July. Like she didn't know if it would be cold or hot."

"Go back to the dinner," Dr. Valencia said kindly.

"Oh, right." Eloise took a centering breath, wishing she were anywhere but in this doctor's office, having this conversation. "She called me and told me she didn't know how to get to my house. When I asked her where she was, she said she hadn't left yet, because she didn't know how to get to the ferry station, or what ferry to get on, or what to do. It's a route and steps she's taken many, many times."

"Mm, yes," Dr. Valencia said, moving her attention to Mom again. "And you're seventy-nine?"

"Yes," Mom said. "My granddaughter told me I was looking for garlic in the freezer."

"After we'd already put in all the garlic we needed," Eloise said. "I don't think she remembered we'd done it."

Dr. Valencia nodded and made a few notes on the chart in front of her. "Mrs. Hall, with your permission, I'd like to perform a cognitive assessment today. It's a series of questions and tasks that help us understand what's happening with your memory and thinking."

"Will it hurt?" Mom asked, sounding suddenly much older and more vulnerable.

"Not at all," Dr. Valencia assured her with that wide smile that certainly put Eloise at ease. "It's just questions and some simple activities like drawing or remembering words."

Mom nodded slowly. "All right."

The assessment took over an hour. Eloise watched as her mother struggled with some tasks that should have been simple—naming animals when shown pictures, remembering three words after five minutes, drawing a clock face with the hands set to a specific time.

With each difficulty, Eloise's chest tightened further and further.

When the assessment was complete, Dr. Valencia asked a nurse to take Mom to another room for a brain scan, leaving Eloise alone with the doctor.

"What do you think?" Eloise asked, her voice barely above a whisper.

Dr. Valencia's expression was gentle but direct. "Based on the cognitive assessment and the symptoms you've described, I believe your mother is showing signs of early-stage Alzheimer's disease."

The words landed like physical blows, and Eloise sat back in her chair. "Wow, uh, okay. Are you sure?"

"The brain scan will help confirm, but the pattern of cognitive deficits is quite characteristic. Her short-term memory is significantly impaired, while her long-term memory remains largely intact. She's showing spatial disorientation and word-finding difficulties."

Eloise nodded, trying to process this information logically despite the emotion threatening to overwhelm her. Did Alzheimer's patients live alone? Could they if they couldn't navigate their world?

Billie had two years of high school left, and Grace was just beginning it. Eloise had a spare bedroom in the small house on the beach she shared with Aaron and the girls, but would her mother even consent to moving in?

You go to Sanctuary Island every day.

The words rang in her ears, but they weren't exactly true. If she sold the inn...

It had been eight days since the older couple had walked through Cliffside. They had brought their son for a second showing that weekend, but Eloise had not yet heard from Natalie on an offer or their intent.

Her last message had been on Monday—two days ago now—and she'd said, *They're trying to put something together.*

So hopeful. Good news. But Eloise would like more *doing* and less *trying to do.*

She took a deep breath and focused. "What happens now?"

"There are medications that can help manage symptoms, though they won't stop the progression. We'll set up a treatment plan, and I'd like to see her again in three months." Dr. Valencia leaned forward slightly. "But there's something else we need to discuss. Is your mother still living alone?"

"Yes, on Sanctuary Island out in Five Island Cove. I live on Diamond with my husband and stepdaughters."

"That arrangement may need to change sooner rather than later," Dr. Valencia said gently. "People with early Alzheimer's can often manage alone for a while, but there are safety concerns—forgetting to turn off the stove, not taking their medication, getting lost, wandering, falling."

Eloise closed her eyes briefly as the list of bad things that could happen ran through her mind again. She could only imagine her mother wandering around Sanctuary Island—a place she'd lived for decades—and not knowing how to get home.

No way would Eloise allow her mother to go through that.

"I currently work about ten minutes from her," Eloise said. "But I'm actually in the process of selling my business so I can be more available."

"Having family support makes a tremendous difference." Dr. Valencia handed Eloise several brochures. "These resources will help you understand what to expect and how to prepare. There are also support groups for caregivers that many find helpful."

Eloise stared at the brochures like they might grow scales and become venomous snakes. She looked up and blinked. "Tell me the first step."

"I'd help her set reminder alarms on a device or clock for her medications," Dr. Valencia said. "And the conversation about her either moving closer to you or in with you should start now as well. Some patients are definitely opposed to that."

Eloise scoffed, the sound quickly morphing into a strange sort of unhappy laugh. "Yeah, my mother would fall into that category."

Dr. Valencia smiled. "She's a beautiful person."

Tears filled Eloise's eyes, and she nodded in quick bursts. "Yes, she is."

"She'll change with this, but that doesn't mean she's not your mother," Dr. Valencia said. "Help her get on a schedule for the meds, and start the conversation about her living conditions."

"Do I need to do anything to make her home safer?"

"Eventually, depending on what she chooses to do. I've had some families put security cameras in a loved one's home, so they know when entrance and exit doors are open. They can see when their loved one leaves, and where they go. That kind of thing." She drew a breath. "As far as steps or anything like that, no. It's the short-term memory issues that you'll deal with the most. Her medications, feeding herself, personal hygiene. Those become issues, because she doesn't remember if she's done them or not."

"Sure," Eloise murmured. "Okay." She sucked in a breath through her nose and stood. "Thank you so much."

Dr. Valencia stood too. "I know it's a lot." She nodded to the brochures. "My number is on the back of those. I have a care line that's open twenty-four hours, seven days a week. Any questions. Any concerns. Someone will be able to help you, guide you, give you answers."

Eloise nodded again and carefully tucked the brochures into her purse. She waited out in the main lobby for her mother to return from her scan, and when she finally did, Eloise had composed herself enough to smile reassuringly. They scheduled a follow-up appointment, collected prescriptions, and headed back to the parking garage in silence.

In the car, Mom finally spoke. "It's bad, isn't it?"

Eloise reached across the console and took her mother's hand. "It's Alzheimer's, Mom. Early stage."

Mom nodded slowly, staring straight ahead. "I understand. I've been...losing pieces of myself. It's terrifying."

"You're not alone," Eloise promised. "I'm going to be right here with you."

"I don't want to be a burden."

"You're my mother."

They drove in silence for several minutes before Mom spoke again. "I don't want to leave my house. I have three cats, and they'll be so scared somewhere else."

Eloise worked hard not to sigh and roll her eyes, as cats

could certainly adjust to a new living environment. "Let's not make any decisions today. We have time to figure things out."

But even as she said it, Eloise knew time was the one thing they didn't have in abundance. The disease would progress, decisions would need to be made, and life as they knew it would change irrevocably.

"We're staying in Boston tonight, right?" Mom asked, her tone suddenly lighter, as if the previous conversation hadn't happened.

"Yes," Eloise said. "And we're meeting my old college roommate Melissa for dinner."

"The one with the red hair?"

"That's right." Eloise was surprised her mother remembered that detail, though it spoke to her long-term memory being preserved while her short-term memory failed.

"I also need to swing by the brownstone." Eloise navigated through Boston's busy streets, heading toward the historic neighborhood where she'd purchased a brownstone years ago, when she'd lived in Boston and worked as a professor at BU.

The brownstone was a three-story brick building on a tree-lined street in Back Bay, and Eloise's heart softened as she arrived. Oh, how she'd loved this place. Everything about it.

Now, it reminded her of a life gone by, something she'd lived long before returning to the cove and falling in love with Aaron. Today, it served as an investment property, rented to a series of graduate students or young couples as Eloise's attempt to try to make that difficult time of life easier in some small way.

She parked on the street and helped her mother out of the car. The current tenants, a young couple finishing up their master's degrees, had agreed to meet them briefly during their lunch hour.

"It's so charming," Mom said, looking up at the building with its bay windows and ornate cornice. "I always forget how lovely it is."

"It is pretty," Eloise said, leading the way up the steps to the front door. She rang the bell at her own house, and moments later, a young woman with glasses and a messy bun opened the door.

"Eloise, come in," she said, stepping back to allow them entry.

"Thank you, Teresa. This is my mother, Dawn."

"Nice to meet you," Teresa said, ushering them into the living room where her husband, a lanky young man named Marcus, was hastily clearing books from the coffee table.

"Sorry about the mess," he said. "End of summer session means papers and more papers."

"No need to apologize," Eloise said, remembering her own graduate school days. "How have you been?" She looked around the narrow living area of the brownstone, snatches of her own life caught in the walls. It looked well-maintained, despite the clutter, and Eloise sank into a smile.

"Good, busy," Teresa said. "Actually, that's what we wanted to talk to you about." She exchanged a nervous look with Marcus as he came to her side.

He put his arm around her and smiled at Eloise. "I got a doctorate spot in Chicago."

"Oh, congratulations," Eloise said, though her mind immediately jumped to what this meant for the brownstone.

"Yeah, thanks," Marcus said. "But that means we'll be moving out." He too wore a worried look. "I know we just re-signed the lease, but I got in last-minute, and..."

"It's fine," Eloise said, her smile seemingly stuck in place. "I'm not going to hold you to a lease when you won't be living here."

"Really?" Teresa asked.

Eloise shook her head and laughed. "Really. Do other landlords do that?"

"Well, yeah," Teresa said. "Or they make the tenants sell the lease to someone else."

"There are a million students in Boston," Eloise said with a wave of her hand, her mind buzzing and rotating as an idea emerged.

"We've got friends who'd kill to have this place for this rent," Marcus said. "Unless you're going to raise it."

Eloise shook her head. "I don't need you to find me new tenants. I think I already have someone in mind who might want it."

"Oh," Marcus said, and he truly looked surprised. "Well, if you do, we have friends staying in the city, and like I said, they'd kill if they knew how little we paid for this place."

"But it's a good place?" Eloise asked.

"The best," Teresa said. "We've absolutely loved living here, Eloise, and we won't move out until August fifteenth."

She nodded, properly reassured, before her phone rang. Natalie's name sat there. "Excuse me," she said. "I have to take this."

She swiped on the call and ducked back out onto the porch before saying, "Natalie? What's going on?"

"Are you sitting down?"

"No, I'm standing on the porch of my brownstone in Boston."

"Oh, well, that will do," Natalie said. "You'll be able to scream when I say—we got an offer on the inn!"

The air left Eloise's lungs. She didn't even have enough air to ask, *Wh-what?* or *Really?* or anywhere near anything like a scream.

Nothing.

She sank onto the top step, her legs a little numb and definitely too weak to hold her up.

"Rich and Sarah Eagan have come in only fifty thousand below the list price," Natalie said, her words almost rushing over one another. "Okay, fine, fifty-one thousand. They're offering seven-ninety-nine, no contingencies, and they do want the radon test and inspection."

Seven-hundred-ninety-nine. Thousand. Dollars.

Her mind spun. She looked up, and the summer trees blurred together as the sky started to whirl too.

"Eloise?"

"Yes," Eloise finally managed to say. "Yes, I'm here, and yes, they can have the inn for seven-ninety-nine."

"They pay for the inspection and radon testing," she said. "They'd like to close by the end of August, but that'll be a tight squeeze for commercial property like this. There's so much to transfer, and..."

Natalie kept talking, but Eloise looked over her shoulder as her mother came out onto the porch too.

"...send it over, okay?"

"Okay," Eloise said as her mom settled on the steps beside her. "I'll watch for it and get everything signed." She'd sold property before, and she'd have twenty-four hours to get her signature on the offer to accept it.

The call ended, and she beamed at her mother. "That was an offer on the inn. A *good* offer."

Her mom patted her leg, and Eloise leaned her head against her shoulder. "That's wonderful, dear."

Eloise had no idea what the future held for her, despite her attempts to make plans. Every day felt like standing at a crossroads, trying to decide the best path to take—the *right* path to take—with something valuable being left behind on the road she chose not to walk.

"I just need to send one more text," she said. "And then we can go back to the hotel for a nap." She certainly needed one after this morning's news, this lunchtime tenant development, and that phone call.

My brownstone tenants are moving out on August 15. I currently rent it for $4000/month. It can have up to 3 bedrooms, 2.5 baths, washer and dryer, with an office on the garden level (basement). It's four levels, 2653 square feet. You're responsible for all utilities on top of rent.

Eloise took a breath, not sure Ginny and Bob could afford even that. Eloise had actually paid off the brownstone a couple of years ago, using the extra money from the inn. She could give it to them for cheaper and be fine.

But for Back Bay, a fully intact brownstone... It was about three thousand dollars cheaper than any other comparable rental in the area.

Price is actually negotiable, Eloise added. *If you and Bob are interested, let me know.*

She read over the text, deemed it good, and sent it. Then she sighed as she got to her feet and stowed her phone in her back pocket.

"Come on, Mom." She helped her mother stand. "Let's get back to the hotel for that nap."

She probably wouldn't take one. She needed to call Aaron, and she fully expected Alice to call and semi-berate her about the brownstone offer.

But the inn had sold.

And if Eloise could convince her mother to move out of the house she'd lived in for decades, move to a new island, or move in with her, Aaron, and the girls, she'd be accomplishing a miracle.

Simple, right?

Chapter Twelve

Kristen adjusted her grip on the large plastic storage bin as she climbed the stairs to Lena's new apartment. At nearly eighty, her knees protested each step, but she refused to let anyone else carry this particular load. It contained Lena's stuffed animals, her emotional support items, and truthfully, Kristen couldn't carry anything much heavier.

"Grandma, thank you," Lena called from the landing above, her round face flushed with excitement.

"Of course, dear." Kristen paused to catch her breath. Once she made it to Lena's new apartment, she'd definitely just stay to help unpack. Lena didn't have that much, as the Harborview Assisted Living Center provided furnished apartments.

Sparsely furnished, but furnished nonetheless. A couch, a dining table and chairs, and a bed. Scott and

Clara had purchased kitchenware for Lena, and she had her favorite sheets already on the bed when Kristen finally arrived in her bedroom.

"It's nice, right?" Lena asked as Kristen lifted the lid on the bin.

Kristen gave her granddaughter a smile. "Yes, Lena, it's going to be very nice for you."

"You have to help *keep* it nice," Lena said. "Like, things have to be cleaned to stay nice, so my mom helped me make a cleaning schedule."

"That's great," Kristen said. "Where is it?"

Lena took out a stuffed tiger and clutched it as she moved over to a whiteboard that had been hung on the wall near the door. "Mom put it here. I'm supposed to check it every day. So today is Monday, and on Monday, I wash and dry my laundry."

Kristen smiled, because though Clara hadn't loved growing up in the cove—or the lighthouse—the things she'd experienced had obviously rubbed off on her. Kristen had always done laundry on Mondays. In fact, it was one of the biggest things she and Clara had argued about when her daughter was a teenager.

"If it's not in your hamper by Sunday night, it doesn't get washed," Kristen used to say when Clara would complain about something that hadn't been run through the washing machine.

Oh, how that had made her so mad. Kristen giggled to herself as she arranged the stuffed animals on Lena's bed and then slid the empty bin underneath it. It had been raised, the way college dorm room beds were, to make more room for storage.

The one-bedroom, one-bath apartment was only six hundred and fifty square feet of living space, but Lena turned back to Kristen with such a beaming, happy expression, that it didn't matter.

Lena had just turned twenty-three, and she'd never lived anywhere but down the hall from her parents. Kristen knew that Clara worried about Lena here, on the south side of Diamond Island, in this relatively new facility that boasted twelve apartments specifically designed for adults with developmental disabilities who could manage semi-independent living.

Kristen worried too, but she felt like this was the very best place for Lena. Each resident had their own unit, with shared common areas like a clubhouse, pool, and recreation areas, and best of all—Harborview had staff available around the clock.

"You don't need to do the laundry today," Kristen said. "Come on. Let's go get your kitchen set up." She stepped out into the hallway just as Scott and Duke came through the front door, the two of them carrying a large boxed item.

"Oh, in here, Lena." She grabbed onto her granddaughter's arm and tugged her into the bathroom, which sat at the end of the hall, right next to the bedroom. "I think they're coming this way."

"It's my desk," Lena said, crowding into the tiny bathroom with Kristen. "They're going to put it together with tools. Did you bring the tools, Dad?"

"I've got them, bug," he said, puffing out his breath as he navigated the tight turn into Lena's bedroom. Duke stutter-stepped after him, and a big thud sounded as they dropped the desk. Signs and groans followed, and then the sound of hands slapping.

Scott chuckled and said, "Okay, let's get this desk put together."

Kristen wanted no part of that either, as she wasn't exactly mechanically inclined. She'd always relied on Joel to handle the building and putting together of items. She could read recipes and put that type of ingredients together, but desks, tables, and anything that required a special tool? Not for her.

"Mom," Lena said, moving out of the bathroom. "Look at my home."

Home. The word settled in Kristen's chest with a bittersweet ache. She followed Lena down the hallway, noting the cheerful bright gray walls and the large windows in the living room that let in plenty of natural light. The building overlooked a small, rocky beach on Diamond Island, close enough to downtown that Lena could walk to her job at the grocery store.

"Where do you want this?" Robin asked, entering the apartment with a laundry bag bulging with clothes.

"Look how many people came to help." Lena moved

over to hug Robin, who grinned as she patted the young woman on the shoulder.

"Arthur is bringing up the bookcase," Alice said as she ducked into the small space too.

"We can't all stay here," Clara said in her usual take-charge way. "Almost everything goes in Lena's bedroom, but if it's for the yard sale, we can put it in the corner of the dining room."

"I'll be in and out," Robin promised, and she hurried down the hall. Alice carried a box that said *ATTIC* on it, and she went into the dining room to start the stack for the yard sale.

"How much yard sale stuff did you bring?" Kristen asked as she went into the U-shaped kitchen. Lena had enough room to work at a counter that had a bar long enough for two people on the other side.

"Just a few boxes," Lena said as Kristen started looking for something to cut through the tape on the boxes sitting on the stovetop and counters.

"I can help you go through it and organize it," Kristen said.

"Okay," Lena said. She stood at Kristen's side until she finally pulled out the keys to her condo and used the jagged teeth to get through the tape. Then Kristen pulled out the top item—a full utensil tray.

"Find a drawer to put that in, sweetheart." Kristen handed her the white tray holding knives, forks, and spoons, and Lena turned to look for a drawer.

The modest space buzzed with activity, with Arthur

and Matt now assembling a waist-high bookshelf for Lena's living room. The couch faced an empty wall, and they positioned the bookcase there, while Alice and Robin unwrapped a new flat-screen TV.

Jean entered with Kelli, and the two of them worked on getting homemade curtains in pink, with white fluffy rabbits on them, hung over the front windows. Lena didn't like it when people could see into her space at night, and that had been a pretty big sticking point for her in the past few weeks leading up to this move.

Clara had told Kristen and Jean on their small, three-person group text, and Jean had immediately volunteered to make some curtains. She'd met with Lena to pick out fabric, while Kristen had called Harborview to get the dimensions of the windows in both the living room and the bedroom.

Kristen kept Lena busy putting away dishes, bowls, and cups, then she opened another box and helped her make a cupboard under the sink for her trash bags, dish-washer pods, and dish soap.

"Look, Grandma." Lena held up a scrubbing wand with a smiley face cut into the bright neon yellow sponge. "He's as happy as I am to be living here." She giggled and stood the wand next to the sink.

"You have to put soap in that, dear." Kristen handed her the bottle full of blue liquid. Lena started that job while Kristen broke down the boxes they'd unpacked in the kitchen.

In the living room, Jean arranged colorful throw

pillows on the sofa, and Kelli, Alice, and Robin had a box on the couch they were pulling things out of. They looked like Lena's coloring books and puzzle books that kept Lena entertained.

They put them in the bookshelf, along with a few of her favorite CDs and DVDs.

"Desk is done, honey," Scott said. "Want to come look and make sure it's where you want it?"

Lena abandoned the dishwashing wand and went with her father, talking about where she'd put the dishes and forks. Kristen smiled to herself as she finished the task she'd given Lena.

She had thick fingers, and she hadn't even gotten the end of the wand off yet. Kristen did it quickly, added the dish soap, and set it all up for her granddaughter. She did wonder how Lena would manage here alone, but she pushed away the thought. The point was, Lena would manage. She'd learn. She'd figure it out, the same way Kristen and everyone around the world had to figure out how to get by.

"Hey, Mom." Clara joined Kristen in the kitchen, her eyes a bit watery. "Thank you for coming."

"As if you could keep me away." Kristen gave her daughter a loving smile. "She's very excited."

"Yes, well, we're all here right now." Clara looked down the hall, where voices could be heard. Lena didn't come out of the bedroom though. "I'm worried about when we have to leave."

"She's been alone before."

"Yeah, I know." Clara sighed. "It's not that, Mom. She's at home when she's alone. This is a new place, and I think we both know how Lena really does with new things."

Kristen nodded and turned to find a few bags of groceries had been abandoned in the corner of the kitchen. She took the two steps to them and started pulling out the food. "Are you planning to stay with her?"

"And sleep on that couch? Have you sat on it?"

Kristen laughed lightly. "No, I haven't."

"It's not great." Clara took the package of key lime yogurt and put it in the fridge. "But yes, I have an overnight bag in the car. I'm hoping I won't have to use it, but..."

They got all of Lena's groceries put away, as more were brought in by AJ and Laurel as soon as Kristen finished with the fridge goods.

Kristen pushed her hair off her forehead and looked at the women who'd joined her in the small dining room and kitchen. So much love filled her as she watched AJ and Kelli laugh about something, and Clara and Jean chitchat about this, that, and the other.

"Lunch?" Robin asked loudly.

Alice shook her head. "No, it would be brunch."

"Fine," Robin said with a smile. "Brunch. Who's in?"

Choruses of acceptance went around the room, but Kristen stayed out of it. She noted that Clara did too, and she moved over to Lena and said something to her quietly.

Lena nodded and then walked over to the front door.

"Thank you," she yelled into the fray of voices. "Thank you all for coming to help me move into my new home." She bounced on her toes slightly and clapped her hands.

"Of course, my dear." Robin hugged her first, and that just started a hugging line. Everyone smiled and congratulated Lena before the stepped out of the apartment, until finally, it was just Lena, Kristen, and Clara.

"You go," Kristen told Clara. "I'll stay and help Lena organize some of her yard sale items." She smiled at her granddaughter and held her breath slightly as Clara hesitated.

Finally, her daughter nodded, and she stepped right in front of Lena. "Have Grandma help you put out your photos too, okay?"

Lena nodded and hugged her mother. "Thank you, Mama. I am so happy, I promise."

"I'm glad, honey." Clara sniffled, ducked away from Lena, and turned to follow everyone else out of the apartment. Kristen caught her daughter's eye from the kitchen. They shared a silent moment of understanding—the grief they'd both carried, the ways they'd learned to move forward without forgetting.

The moment broke, and Clara left, finally pulling the door closed behind her, which sealed out the summer heat and gave Kristen relief from the busyness of the morning move-in.

Lena exhaled heavily and faced Kristen. "I want to do the yard sale stuff first."

"Okay," Kristen said, as she at least knew where that

was. Who knew where the pictures had been stashed, and by whom?

Thankfully, Lena didn't seem to want to talk as she put the first box of yard sale items on the dining room table. She knew exactly why Clara was worried; the first child leaving home was always the hardest, even when it meant a huge amount of growth had happened. She'd felt the same bittersweet pride when Clara had first moved away, and again when Reuben left for college. The letting go never got easier.

Because, yes, Lena had reached the point where she could—and wanted to—live on her own. But that only meant she had a whole bunch more growing to do, and growth and change was hard for all involved.

Lena pulled out an unopened set of dinnerware and walked it down to the end of the table. "I have a couple of bins in my bedroom," she said. "But not anything for the kitchen yet."

"What do you have in there?" Kristen asked.

"One bin for books," Lena said. "And one for jewelry. And one for clothes."

"Are you letting others know to organize their items in the same way?"

Lena blinked, her expression blank. "I will write that down." She pivoted on her heel and left the kitchen.

"Lena," Kristen said after her, then decided not to argue. She'd be back soon enough. She pulled out items she could categorize herself, but she wanted Lena to have the opportunity to do it.

No, she hadn't been able to get the yard sale organized and accomplished before her move-in date, but she still had a couple of good months left in the cove for such a thing.

Her goal was to do it before school started, which gave her another month, and Kristen was determined to help her.

"I wrote it down," Lena said. "I will text everyone when I have a few more categories."

Kristen nodded to the things she'd pulled out of the box. "Who did you get this stuff from?"

"Alice," Lena said, and Kristen shouldn't have been surprised to see so many new items. Many of them looked suspiciously like wedding presents, and they probably were things Alice didn't personally like but hadn't done anything with.

"Kitchen," Lena said. "This is a picture frame." She looked over to Kristen. "It's not clothes or kitchen or books."

"Housewares, maybe," Kristen suggested, almost making it sound like a question.

"Housewares," Lena said. "Let's use that box for housewares." She put the empty picture frame back in the box Kristen had taken it out of.

Kristen let her categorize the other items, her thoughts now on Alice. The hearing about the lighthouse title had gone well, and the judge had submitted the application to the state of Massachusetts to get a new title, this time with Reuben's name on it.

Kristen had almost started crying when Alice had told her, but she didn't want to celebrate until the title arrived at the lighthouse, and Reuben and Jean had it in their possession.

Then, she planned to throw a huge party.

The doorbell chimed, and Lena nearly jumped out of her skin. Then she yelled, "It's my apartment, so I get to answer my door!"

She lumbered over to the door and pulled it open without checking through the peephole. This facility had gates and security guards, so Kristen wasn't too worried, but she still might mention it to Clara.

You will not, she told herself sternly as Eloise leaned in to hug Lena.

"I'm so sorry I'm late," Eloise said. "There's so much going on with the inn, and I had to be there for the radon testing guy this morning."

"It's okay," Lena said. "Grandma and I are just going through some yard sale stuff."

"Good morning, El," Kristen said. "The others went to brunch. They just left about ten or fifteen minutes ago, and I bet you could catch them."

"Oh, it's fine," Eloise said, waving away Kristen's suggestion. "I had pumpkin chocolate chip muffins on the way here."

"Pumpkin already, huh?" Kristen grinned at her. "You love bringing out the autumnal flavors early."

"The *guests* love it," Eloise said as she joined Kristen and Lena at the table. "Wow, Lena. Look at all of this stuff." She smiled at the young woman. "I have things in my garage."

"I'm making categories," Lena said.

Eloise blinked and said, "Okay."

"Let's keep going," Kristen said, and she let Lena get the next box. She pulled out a jewelry box and marveled at its age. It also looked slightly familiar. The small, wooden box contained intricate carving on the lid—fish and waves, which wasn't that unusual for the cove.

She opened it, expecting to find costume jewelry inside, but the box sat empty save for the deep burgundy velvet lining. "This is nice," she said. "Lena, who gave you this stuff?"

"I don't know," Lena said.

Kristen looked back at the box, where the words *ROBIN—STORAGE* had been scrawled on the side in black marker.

"I wonder if Robin meant to donate this," Kristen said. "It looks old and maybe like an heirloom." She looked over to Eloise, who gently took the box from her.

"And Mandie still hasn't found the wedding bracelet." Eloise met Kristen's eyes, and then lifted the lid on the box, as if the missing bracelet would be stashed inside and Kristen had just missed it.

Of course they both knew about the missing bracelet. Mandie had been looking for it for six weeks now, and Robin had texted everyone to commiserate and get support.

"Jewelry," Lena said, taking the box and putting in her

jewelry pile. Both Kristen and Eloise kept their eyes on it for a moment, and then Lena snapped her fingers.

"Grandma, get me something else."

Kristen flinched and looked into the box. She pulled out a napkin holder that looked like it was made from sterling silver. She handed it to Lena as Eloise removed a set of salt and pepper shakers.

Kristen pulled out an ancient shoebox and lifted the lid. Fake gems glittered back at her, and she passed the costume jewelry to Lena. She loved sparkly things, so Kristen wasn't surprised to see her move down the table to the other jewelry items and start to rifle through the bangles, rings, and hoops.

"This is going to take forever to price," Lena said, looking up.

"You could put different items—like bracelets or rings —in a basket for a single price," Eloise suggested.

Lena frowned without answering as she reached into the box and lifted out a deep, dark blue, velvet pouch. "This has something inside it."

"Let's see." Kristen took it from Lena and gently loosened the drawstring before handing it back to Lena.

She tipped the contents of the pouch into her palm, and a flash of silver crossed Kristen's vision.

Lena sucked in a breath at the same time Kristen's pulse picked up speed. "It's so pretty," Lena said.

The silver bracelet bore immaculate carvings of waves and fish, with glimpse of blue and green from the embedded gemstones along the scales and crests.

"Oh, wow," Kristen said.

Eloise cried out and said, "Let me see it, Lena." She very nearly grabbed the bracelet from Lena and held it out in front of her. "Is this what I think it is?"

Kristen didn't have to hold the bracelet to know. "Yes," she said. "That's Robin's wedding bracelet."

Chapter Thirteen

R obin's phone buzzed against her hip as she arranged the last of the centerpiece samples on her dining room table. She'd been up since five, organizing everything for her afternoon meeting with the Hendersons, who were getting married in September.

The text from Kristen made her pause.

We found something I think belongs to you. Can you come to Lena's apartment this morning?

Robin's brow furrowed. What could Kristen possibly have found that belonged to her? She'd helped with Lena's move yesterday, but she hadn't left anything behind that she could remember.

Sure. Need to finish setting up for a client meeting at 1:00, but I can be there by 10:30?

Perfect. See you then. Kristen added a smiley face emoji, which was unusual enough to make Robin wonder what this was about.

She returned to arranging silk flowers, linen samples, and photos of table settings. The Hendersons wanted a rustic autumn theme for their wedding, and Robin had spent hours putting together options that would work with their venue and budget.

Duke came in from the back porch, coffee mug in hand. "You've been at this since before the sun came up."

"I know." Robin straightened a photo that had slipped out of alignment. "But the Hendersons are my most indecisive couple yet, and I want to make this easy for them."

Duke came behind her and placed his hands on her shoulders, kneading the tense muscles. "You always do." He pressed a kiss to the top of her head. "I'm heading out for the lazier fish. Need anything while I'm out?"

"No, I'm good." She leaned back against him for a moment, drawing strength from his solid presence. "Oh, Kristen texted. She found something of mine at Lena's, apparently. I'm going to run over there before my meeting."

"Ooh, mysterious." Duke gave her shoulders one final squeeze before stepping away. "Maybe it's those earrings you thought you lost last summer."

Robin laughed, though she'd for-sure lost a lot of things in the move. She usually took great care to know where she put things, but the move had been stressful, and they'd had so much help, that by the end, Robin was just letting people put boxes anywhere.

"Those turned up in Jamie's jewelry box, remember?"

She glanced at her phone to check the time. "I should wrap this up and get going."

"Same." Duke grabbed a protein shake and headed out while Robin finished her set-up on the table. Then she took a quick shower and dressed in a light blue blouse and white capris. Professional enough for her meeting, but comfortable for the August heat already building outside.

The drive to Lena's new apartment took less than fifteen minutes. Robin parked and headed up to the second floor, curious about what Kristen had found. She knocked lightly on the door, hearing voices inside.

"My apartment!" Lena pulled open the door a moment later, joy bursting on her face. "Robin, you are going to die."

"Let her in, dear," Kristen said. "Show her what you found."

"Come in," Lena said, sweeping her arm into her tiny apartment. Robin grinned at her and eased into the room.

"Wow, look at this place." With everything unpacked and put away, the apartment looked lived-in and comfortable. Lena had put out family photos on the top of her bookcase, pushing the TV she and Alice had set up to the very end.

The curtains had been thrown open, and Lena had all the lights on too. The younger woman moved over to the dining room table and picked up something. "This was in one of the boxes you gave me for the yard sale."

When Lena turned, a dark blue velvet pouch dangled from her fingers and a wide smile graced her face.

Robin sucked in a breath and pressed her hand to her throat. The weight of everything in the known universe rode on her shoulders, and at the sight of that velvet pouch —which she knew held the family wedding bracelet—it all lifted.

She hadn't even realized how heavy her guilt had been that she couldn't produce the heirloom for Mandie as she planned for her wedding.

She knew now, and she stumbled a step over to Lena's couch and leaned into it. "The bracelet." She finally tore her eyes from the pouch to look at Kristen. "Is the bracelet inside?"

Kristen nodded, her smile infectious. Robin found one forming on her face, and she quickly approached Lena and gently took the pouch from her, though she wanted to rip it out of her fingers.

She opened the pouch and removed the bracelet, the silver catching the light as Robin studied the intricate wave patterns and tiny blue-green gemstones. They glinted in the happiest way, and she instantly got transported twenty-five years into the past, when she herself wore this bracelet.

She'd stood in front of the mirror in her wedding gown and admired the fish scales and ocean crests, carved with exquisite detail, wrapped around the band, just as she did now.

"Oh, my," Robin whispered, her voice breaking. Her legs suddenly felt weak, and she sank onto the nearest chair. "It's the bracelet. Mandie's bracelet."

"*Your* bracelet," Kristen corrected gently, sitting beside

her. "Duke's grandmother's bracelet. The one all you Grover women wear on your wedding day."

Robin's vision blurred with tears as she cradled the precious heirloom against her bosom. "Mandie will be so relieved." Her fingers traced the familiar patterns, memories flooding through her.

"I'm sure she will be," Kristen said as she set a cup of tea on the table in front of Robin. "Breathe, dear. This is happy news."

Robin looked up and wiped her eyes. "I feel like I've been running five different marathons, each of them pulling me in a different direction."

"I bet." Kristen reached out and smoothed Robin's hair back off her face. "Take a moment, dear. The world isn't going to end in the next moment."

Robin did exactly what Kristen said—she sat there and breathed in and out, feeling the air enter her lungs in a calm, easy way for the first time this summer. She'd completed three more weddings in July, bringing her summer count to four. She only had three more to get through; two this month, and then Mandie's in October.

"Where was it?" she asked. "How did it end up in a yard sale box?"

Kristen patted her hand. "It was in a box labeled 'Robin—Storage.' I can make all kinds of assumptions, but..."

Robin's brow furrowed. "A storage box." She looked across the table, but it didn't hold anything else. "What else was in there?"

"Uh, Lena, do you remember what else was in Robin's box?"

"A napkin holder, housewares," Lena said. "Salt and pepper shakers, kitchen stuff. A big box of costume jewelry —except that. Grandma says that's a family...token, and I can't sell it at the yard sale."

Robin managed a small smile in Lena's direction.

"There was a pretty nice jewelry box," Kristen said. "Lena has agreed to let you have that back too, should you want it."

Robin knew the box instantly, and she nodded. "Yes, please, Lena. Duke's grandfather carved that, and Duke himself relined it for me several years ago."

"I'll get it." Lena left the room in favor of her bedroom, and Robin lifted the teacup to take a sip.

The warm liquid tasted like herbs and honey, and it soothed her even further.

"I told Jamie to get all the boxes up in the attic for Lena's yard sale," Robin said, her crushing guilt suddenly landing on her shoulders again. "I thought Mandie had looked through everything up there, and I didn't even check them."

She closed her eyes, regretting her busy life this summer. And her own daughter had been paying the price, while Robin was off planning everyone else's dream wedding.

"Hey, we found it," Kristen said in the soft, soothing voice she had. "Stop beating yourself up."

"I'm—not."

Kristen titled her head and gave Robin a *Really?* look as she sat down at the end of the table. "I know you better than that, dear."

Lena returned with the jewelry box, and Robin got up to hug the girl. "Thank you so much, Lena. You've saved the whole summer of weddings."

"Did you see me answer the door at my own apartment?" Lena asked as she stepped back from Robin.

Robin burst out laughing, because sometimes life was as simple as answering the door at her own apartment. "Yes," she said. "You sure did, sweetie."

She held out the bracelet, admiring it once more. "This has been in my family for four generations. My husband's great-grandmother received it as a wedding gift from her husband. He was a silversmith who specialized in jewelry inspired by the sea."

She turned it to see all seven fish, with their blue and green scales. "Seven fish for the seven seas. And if you look closely, each wave also has a tiny blue or green stone embedded right in the top of it. See, the Grovers are fishermen, and they feel a great connection to the sea and Five Island Cove."

"It's beautiful," Lena said. "I really liked it, but Mom says it's way too nice to sell at a yard sale."

Robin smiled and slipped the bracelet onto her wrist, feeling its familiar weight. It fit perfectly, just as it always had. "I wore it when I got married." She touched the silver fish with her fingertip, remembering. "Duke's mother told me that as long as I wore this bracelet, I'd always find my way home—just like the salmon returning to their birth-place." She smiled softly. "I told Mandie the same thing when she was little."

"She's going to be overjoyed," Kristen said.

"I need to call her right now." Robin reached for her phone and quickly snapped a picture of the bracelet encircling her own wrist. Then she dialed her daughter. The line rang and rang, but Mandie didn't pick up.

She frowned at the phone as her daughter's voice started to instruct the caller to leave a message. "She should be at work, but she can almost always take a call." Robin took a deep breath. "Let me text her to see when she's free." Robin quickly typed a message to her daughter: *I have great news! Can you stop by the house after work? I have something important to show you.*

While they waited for a response, Lena offered them lemonade, proudly serving it in her new glasses. Robin sipped the too-sweet drink, her mind swirling with relief and memories.

She loaded the picture of the bracelet to her friends' group chat and sent it. *Lena found my missing bracelet! I had errantly put it in one of the boxes that got put in my attic, and we accidentally donated it to her yard sale.*

YOU'RE KIDDING, came in from Alice almost immediately.

This calls for a celebration, Eloise said. *I'm taking the afternoon off and will be at your house with champagne later!*

I'm in on that, AJ said. *I'm so happy for you, Robin!*

Oh, Mandie will be thrilled, Kristen said, though she stood five feet from Robin.

She smiled over to her as Kelli said she'd be on Diamond Island that afternoon, and she'd leave Parker and Daphne with Shad and join everyone at Robin's for a toast.

"I guess I'm hosting happy hour tonight," she said as she got to her feet. "Thank you so much, Lena. I have to get back for a meeting." She hugged her one more time, then gripped Kristen in an embrace that said so much more than words could.

She wiped her eyes again as she left the apartment and then the assisted living facility. She returned home, ate a quick lunch, and welcomed the Hendersons to her home before she realized Mandie hadn't answered her text yet.

MANDIE HADN'T ANSWERED BY THE TIME ELOISE showed up on the front porch with Alice's arm linked through one of hers and holding a bottle of bubbly in the other. She lifted it and said, "It's pi-ink," in a sing-song voice.

Robin laughed and stepped back to welcome her friends into her house. "AJ just texted to say she's walking over, and Jean said she can't make it."

"We've had a lot of wind on the east side," Eloise said, her mood a bit darker now. "They've been losing shingles on the lighthouse."

"That's what she said." Robin left the front door ajar, so the others could just come in when they arrived. "So it's just AJ and Kelli?"

"Maddy's at the restaurant tonight," Alice said. "Clara's still at Cliffside with Julia. Tessa went to the mainland with Dave, and—"

"Can we talk about Tessa and Dave?" Eloise asked. "Because they have been getting *chummier* and chum-mi-er."

"Chummier?" Robin gaped at Eloise. "Have you already opened that champagne?" She took the bottle from her friend, but it weighed plenty, and the cork was still intact.

Eloise waltzed out onto Robin's back patio, and Alice watched her too. "I didn't smell anything on her," she said.

"Maybe she's just overjoyed with this being her last month at Cliffside," Robin said. She popped the top on the champagne and started pouring it into flutes.

"We're here," AJ called.

"In the kitchen," Robin called back, and a few moments later, she picked up two glasses and went to meet AJ and Kelli. "I think it's just us."

"Laurel is on the way," AJ said. "Paul just got home."

"Oh, perfect," she said. "I haven't looked at my phone in a half-hour. It's been glorious." She laughed and went to get her own glass of champagne. Alice had taken hers and one out to El, and Robin joined them.

She sighed as she sat down around the table, the umbrella and the trees in her yard providing shade at this time of early evening. "I can't believe we found that bracelet," she said.

No, Mandie still hadn't responded to her text, and Robin did pull out her phone to check it. A moment later, Alice plucked the device out of her hand.

"Hey," Robin said.

"No phones at happy hour," Alice said. "Even you can do sixty minutes without your device."

"Of course I can," Robin said. "I was just checking—"

"There's nothing to check tonight." Alice set the phone on the table out of Robin's reach and lifted her glass. "To finding the bracelet."

"To finding the bracelet," everyone chorused, and Robin lifted her glass and said it too.

"To young love," AJ said, lifting her glass a smidge higher.

Robin glanced at Alice as she said, "To young love!" along with the others. She lowered her glass then, took a sip, and sighed as she leaned back in her chair.

Then she swung forward again and lifted her glass, "To El selling the inn."

"To El selling the inn!"

She grinned at her friend as a hint of redness crept into Eloise's cheeks. "You know what we haven't done this summer?"

"We're not doing it tonight either," Alice said dryly. She lifted her champagne to her lips and took the tiniest of sips. She'd let her hair grow a bit this summer, but Robin suspected she'd cut it before Ginny's wedding.

"No Tell-Alls. No nothing," AJ said. "It's just happy hour."

Kelli nodded. "It's been a pretty drama-free summer, and I want to keep it that way."

Robin saw no reason to push them into doing or saying anything they didn't want to do or say. It was happy hour, and she had plenty to celebrate.

Soon enough, AJ groaned and said, "I have to get home."

"Same." Kelli covered her mouth and made a tiny hiccup. "Oh, wow, I don't drink very often." She giggled and got to her feet.

"I'll make sure you get in a RideShare and text Shad," AJ said.

Robin stood along with Eloise and Alice, and she led the way back into the house. Everyone put their glasses in the sink, and Robin hugged Eloise just as her phone rang.

"Oh, it's my mother." Eloise bustled down the hall and out of the house.

Robin watched her and turned back to her friends. "Has El said anything about getting her mother to move to Diamond?"

Alice shook her head. "Dawn is really fighting it."

"She's doing okay in her place," AJ said. "El told me she takes her meds and hasn't wandered off once. She still comes to dinner every week or so, and she hasn't gotten lost again."

Robin nodded, her own brain a little fuzzy from the sparkling wine. "Dealing with aging parents isn't all that fun." Being part of the sandwich generation herself, Robin knew from first-hand experience how difficult it could be to navigate new ground with her mother while trying to provide everything her daughters needed as they became adults themselves.

"You're not kidding," Alice said. "My dad and Della got old very suddenly this summer." She sighed and tapped on her phone. "I just called a RideShare, and it'll be a few minutes."

"Stay as long as you want," Robin said.

"Our ride is here," AJ said just as Robin's phone chimed and buzzed simultaneously. She opened the message and froze, her stomach dropping.

Mom, don't freak out, but Charlie and I are in New York City. We needed to get out of the cove for a few days.

As she tried to wrap her head around those words, another text came in.

I'm sorry I didn't tell you. I'll explain everything when I'm back.

Robin stared at the phone, a chill running through her despite the warm evening air. Why would Mandie and Charlie suddenly leave for New York without telling anyone?

"'Bye, Robin," AJ called, and Robin set her phone on the counter so she could go say good-bye to her friends. After hugging AJ and Kelli and waving them down the driveway to their ride, Robin returned to her kitchen.

With just her and Alice—and the lead in her stomach —Robin picked up her phone and handed it to Alice.

"What's going on?" she asked, confusion riding her brow.

"Do you know where your son is?" Robin asked.

"He's—" Alice blinked and looked at the phone, tapping and sliding.

"Spoiler alert," Robin said, needing another glass of sparkling wine. "They're in New York City."

Chapter Fourteen

Mandie stood at the window of their hotel room, fifteen stories above the bustling streets of Manhattan. The city sprawled before her—a concrete jungle so different from the quaint seaside charm of Five Island Cove that it might as well have been another planet. She pressed her palm against the cool glass, watching yellow taxis dart between buildings like schools of tropical fish.

"I still can't believe we did this," she said, not turning around.

Charlie's reflection appeared behind her in the window. "Having second thoughts?" His voice carried that note of concern she'd grown to recognize over the years— the one that meant he was trying to sound casual but was actually worried.

"No," she said quickly. "Not about coming. Not about us. Just...processing." She leaned back against him as his arms encircled her waist. "My phone's been blowing up all day."

So much so that she'd silenced it before lunch, ignored her mother's calls, and then finally texted her that she'd come to the city. Then, she'd promptly turned off her phone and plugged it in.

Her mother would be *losing her mind* about now, and Mandie wasn't sure how long she could put her off.

"Mine too." Charlie rested his chin on top of her head. "Ginny's sent about fifteen texts."

"Your mom will be next." Mandie sighed, guilt gnawing at her insides. "Because my mother knows now, and if she can't get in touch with me, she'll call your mom."

"We can call them now if you want."

Mandie shook her head. "Not yet. I just wanted a day away." And she wasn't even sure why. Or from what she needed to "get away" from.

She suspected the answer was...herself, and she didn't know how to stop being her.

She turned in his arms to face him. "Maybe we should consider Brooklyn more seriously. I know it's further away, but we're never going to live right next door to campus, and if we have to get on the subway for twenty minutes, what's forty?"

"It would be cheaper," Charlie said, his eyes searching hers. "We'd get a bedroom instead of a studio with our budget."

She nodded, knowing she was the one holding them

back from living further from campus. In fact, Charlie had said several times that he didn't care where they lived; he just wanted to get a lease signed.

School started in a month. A single month. Four weeks. Thirty days, and they still didn't have anywhere to live.

Charlie smiled down at her, and that familiar flutter stroked through her chest. No matter how many times he kissed her, no matter how often they made love, he still stoked something inside her.

"Can we eat first, and then go to Brooklyn and look at that place you found?"

"Do we need to schedule something?"

"It's open season," Mandie said, knowing that wasn't quite right. "Or open applications, or something. They have an apartment to show at any time. It's like a walk-through."

"An open house," Charlie said with a smile. "And I'll only go if we can eat in Chinatown."

Mandie grinned up at him and touched her smile to his. "I love you."

"Yeah," he said over a chuckle. "You just like the egg rolls from Dim Sum Choo more than me."

She laughed and turned to face the room, face her phone. Her mind switched, and she crossed to where she'd plugged in her phone. "I'm going to call my mom right now. Then it won't be hanging over me while I'm eating the most delicious egg rolls on the planet."

She sank onto the bed, grateful when Charlie joined

her. She leaned into him as her device powered up, and it didn't take long for the messages and missed call notifications to hit her screen. "It's New York," she grumbled. "We've lived here for two years."

"She probably just wonders what you mean by 'needed to get away for a few days.'"

Yeah, Mandie wondered that herself. She took a steeling breath and tapped to return her mother's latest call. The line only rang once before Mom said, "There you are." She sounded pleasant, but Mandie had grown up with the woman, and Robin Grover had a Ph.D in Worrying-And-Trying-To-Cover-It-Up.

"Hey, Mom." Mandie got to her feet, suddenly unable to sit. She hated showing Charlie this anxious, messy side of herself, but he should probably know now that she cried sometimes for no reason, and that she couldn't have a hard conversation without pacing the room.

"I just—we need an apartment, and we weren't finding one in the cove," Mandie said, jumping on that angle though she knew her need to come to the city with just Charlie had more teeth than that. What those were, though, still eluded her.

"So you're apartment hunting."

"We're within a month, and yes, there are a lot of things open right now as things shift."

"Well, good," Mom said airily. "I hope you find one."

"We're considering Brooklyn." Mandie paused in front of the windows again, her thumbnail migrating to her mouth. "We're headed out there to look right now."

"Okay," Mom said. "When are you coming home?"

"Friday," Mandie said. Then they wouldn't have to pay weekend rates at the downtown hotel. "I'm working at the drugstore all weekend, and Charlie has excursions."

"Mandie," Mom said, and that sounded like the ramp-up to a lecture. But then she just sat there, silent. Mandie couldn't hear anything else on the her end of the line, and she released her breath, the tension in her muscles going with it.

"I don't know, Mom," Mandie said, her voice pitching up. "I don't know why I'm feeling how I am—I don't even know what it is. I just—we needed an apartment anyway, and I just felt like everything in the cove was suffocating me."

"Me?" Mom asked.

"No." Mandie shook her head and sighed. "I mean, not really, Mom. It's not a you-problem. This is a me-problem, but I don't know what it really is or how to solve it."

"Maybe you'll feel better when you find an apartment."

"I'm sure I will," Mandie said, though she wasn't sure of anything at the moment. "You said you had great news?"

Mom pulled in a sharp breath. "We found the bracelet."

The words sat there, spoken from one hundred miles away, ringing in Mandie's whole body. "What?" she asked.

Mom giggled—actually giggled. "Lena and Kristen

were going through some donated items for the yard sale, and they found the bracelet. I have it on my wrist right this moment."

Mandie spun from the window, her eyes wide and her heart pounding in her chest. "You're kidding. Charlie, they found the bracelet!"

He looked up from his phone and rose to his feet too, his smile coming easily. "That's great, sweetheart."

She hippity-hop-stepped over to him and looked up at him, pure joy and wonder streaming through her. "Okay, Mom, we have to go look at that place in Brooklyn now. I just didn't want you to worry."

"I'd appreciate it if you could turn on your pin," she said. "Up to you, but it is a big city, and things happen."

"I will," Mandie said, though she was with Charlie and didn't think for a moment something would happen to them. They'd lived in this city for two years now, and the vibrancy and culture of it suddenly thrummed through the floorboards at her feet.

"I love you, Mom."

"I love you too, Mandie. Be safe, okay?"

"Okay." The call ended, and Mandie sighed out the last of her tension. "I can't believe they found the bracelet. Now we can for-sure get married."

Charlie's eyebrows went up. "Would you have called off the wedding if you couldn't find it?"

A bit startled by his question, Mandie took a moment to consider it. "You know what? It's definitely been plaguing me. It felt like this...this bad omen. Like, I know it's stupid, but without the bracelet, maybe we weren't supposed to get married."

Charlie frowned and turned away from her. "Nice to know a bracelet was deciding that for you and not how you feel about me." He grabbed his wallet from the top of the dresser and stalked toward the door. "Not that you *want* to be with me and *want* to be my wife."

"Charlie, wait. It's not that."

"I don't want to talk about this right now." He left, the door slamming closed behind him, as they were all on such wound-tight springs.

Tears pressed into Mandie's eyes, and she grabbed her purse and followed him into the hall. She sincerely hoped he had a key to the room, but she wouldn't allow herself to ask as she jogged after him.

He stood, tall and broody, in front of the elevator, his hands stuck deep in his pockets. He'd already pressed the button, and he didn't look at her as she stood next to him.

"Of course I wouldn't have called off the wedding if the bracelet had never been found."

Charlie turned his attention toward her in slow-motion. His glare didn't comfort her, and Mandie didn't quite know what to do with it.

"I love you," she said next. "I want to marry you, bracelet or no bracelet."

"What did you mean by bad omen?"

"I don't know." Mandie threw her hands up as her first tears fell. "Everyone in my family going back three generations has worn that bracelet on their wedding day, and I want to wear it while I marry *you*. That's all."

Charlie softened and pulled her into his arms. She wrapped her arms around him and pressed her face into his chest as she cried. "I know I'm a mess," she said. "I know it makes no sense to you that we needed to come to the city this week, and that we couldn't tell our parents, and all the stuff about the bracelet."

"It's fine," Charlie said softly. "I just don't like seeing you stressed and upset."

"I know."

"I want every day to be us going to Chinatown for eggrolls, and spending time together, and holding hands as we wander the city."

"I want that too."

The elevator dinged, and Mandie turned her back on the car as the doors opened. She wiped her face, and then let Charlie take her hand and lead her onto the elevator. Thankfully, no one else stood on the car, and she managed to stifle her sniffles before they reached the lobby.

Outside, the August heat hit them like a wall, but Mandie welcomed it. The noise, the crowds, the endless motion of the city—it all felt like possibility. She'd fallen in love with New York during a rare family vacation her parents had brought her and Jamie on for Christmas. She'd been thirteen, and she hadn't met Charlie yet.

Everything had been new, charming, exciting, full of energy. She loved the city almost as much as the slower, softer, filled-with-sunshine pace of summertime in Five Island Cove.

Now, as she walked hand-in-hand with Charlie down Amsterdam Avenue, she felt that same sense of adventure returning. "I love this city," she said. "I've missed the energy, the diversity, the feeling that anything can happen." She gestured around them, to the tall buildings, the greenery among all the glass and steel.

"I love the cove, but sometimes it feels so...contained. Like I already know exactly how my life will unfold there."

Charlie nodded, understanding in his eyes. "I love both places too."

"Do we eventually want to be back in Five Island Cove?"

"I don't know, sweetheart. It's hard for me to predict where the enormity of my life will take me."

"But, like, we don't see ourselves in say, Vancouver." She looked up at him, and Charlie grinned and shook his head.

"I think you'll wither and die if you're more than two hundred miles from your mom."

"Hey, no, I won't." Mandie steered him over to the subway entrance, thinking about her relationship with her mom as she went down the steps. Yes, they were close. Mandie loved to call her mother and talk about everything that happened that day, but she didn't do it every day.

"Fine, I like talking to my mom."

Charlie laughed down on the subway platform. "I don't mind it, Mandie, but no, I don't see why we'd go to

Vancouver. You're studying history and design, and I'm going to be a pharmacist in like, a decade. There will be plenty of jobs for me close to the cove."

"We're just going to take it one day at a time," she said. Her phone rang, and Mandie tugged it from her purse to check it. "It's Ginny."

Charlie swore and took Mandie's phone. "I forgot to text her."

Mandie let him handle it, and he gave her the phone back when they got on the train. "Is she mad?"

"Yep." Charlie lifted his arm over her shoulder while Mandie checked the phone. Ginny did sound a bit peeved, but Charlie had talked her down, the way he always did.

Truth be told, Charlie calmed Mandie down on a pretty regular basis. She stuck her phone in her purse and leaned back into him. She closed her eyes, and said, "I'm sorry I'm so wired."

"It's fine, sweetheart." He ducked his head closer. "I know who you are, Mandie, and I love you."

She smiled, the genuine way he spoke warming her from the inside out. She loved Charlie too, and she decided it didn't matter where they lived, what they could afford to eat, none of it, as long as she could be his, and he could be hers.

A couple of hours later, filled with delicious Chinese food, and now across the Brooklyn Bridge, Mandie pulled open the door to the apartment building Charlie had found.

"Doesn't smell like curry," Charlie murmured as he followed her.

The lobby itself seemed nice enough too. The floors boasted a speckled terrazzo, clean and slightly shiny in the summer evening light. A potted plant—fake, but trying its best—stood cheerfully beside the elevator.

The mailboxes were all chrome with black numbers that had seen better years, and a cork board held all kinds of handwritten notes and fliers, including one for a "free couch in unit 6F."

Mandie took a breath, trying to picture herself here... and she could do it. She could see herself coming into this building with bags of groceries, crashing after a long day of classes, kicking off her shoes, making love to Charlie, making a life with him here.

"I like it," she said.

"I think we have to buzz up to 3A for the tour," Charlie said, leading her over to the intercom next to the elevator. He studied it like it was a puzzle to solve for a moment, then pressed a button.

"Hey, there," a woman chirped. "Did you want to walk-through our one-bedroom or two-bedroom apartment?"

"One-bedroom," Charlie said.

"Great, I'll buzz you up. Floor three," the woman said. "My name is Jo, and I'll meet you when you get off."

Charlie reached out and pressed the elevator button. The ring around up arrow lit up and then immediately went off.

"I think you have to wait a second," Mandie said.

He gave it four or five, and then pressed the button again. This time, the light stayed on, and the elevator lumbered to the lobby after several long moments.

It rattled and hummed on the short ride up, then delivered them to the third floor, where a narrow hallway holding a tall, leggy blonde greeted them.

"Hey," Charlie said, shaking Jo's hand. "I'm Charlie, and this is my fiancé, Mandie."

"Great to meet you," Jo said. "Have you guys lived in the city before?"

"Yes," Mandie said amidst the faint smell of takeout and laundry detergent. "We're both going to be juniors at NYU this fall." She looked over to Charlie. "Next month." Her breath sort of burst from her body in a laugh. "We're getting married in October, and we need somewhere to live."

"Sure." Jo led them to the corner unit—3A, and used an electronic keycard to open the door. "All of our units come with keycards like this," she said. "It gets you on the elevator too, as well as up to the rooftop, where we have a garden area where people can sunbathe, eat, hang out. It also gets you into the courtyard."

She pushed open the door and gestured for Mandie and Charlie to enter first. "This building is rent-controlled for students and young couples without kids. It forms one side of a square with four other buildings, and we share a courtyard that has a pool, a picnic area, and a small park with a fountain and benches, that kind of thing."

"Wow," Mandie said, stepping inside first.

"This is technically a studio," Jo said behind her. "The bedroom only has a sliding barn door, but it's surprisingly bright for a Brooklyn shoebox."

The apartment was small, yes, but not suffocating. A trio of tall windows directly across from the door let in warm light, overlooked the strip of kitchen in front of them, and shone light onto the scuffed hardwood floors that spanned the whole space.

The cabinets had been painted white and the kitchen also housed a refrigerator, a gas stove, and a deep sink—no dishwasher.

"Enough room for a small table here," Jo said. "Every three floors has a laundry room the units share."

"How many units on each floor?" Charlie asked.

"Eight," Jo answered. "Four on each side of the elevator, with a mix of one- and two-bedroom on each floor. The laundry room for this floor is down off the lobby, and right now, we have only two of these studio-one's left."

"Really?" Mandie asked, a slip of panic making a pit form in her stomach. "I thought you guys had a lot right now."

"Our open house today has gone really well," Jo said. "But our incentives are all still intact. First month's rent is half-off, and we've worked a deal with the utility companies to waive their set-up fees for new tenants."

She smiled and gestured toward the fridge. "Bathroom is on the other side of the fridge there, and you can see the bedroom straight ahead."

So that was the whole apartment.

Mandie checked out the bathroom, which contained white tile on the floor, a medicine cabinet with a mirrored door, and water pressure that Jo promised was "excellent if you like showers that wake you up."

No tub, because there wasn't room for one. Mandie didn't particularly mind that, and there was a high window in the shower.

She joined Charlie in the faux bedroom, which had three full walls, with corners on the fourth that faced the living room-slash-kitchen area and held the barn door.

There was a long, deep closet on the left wall, with a window on the right, and Mandie realized that if she let herself, she could start imagining where things would go. Her books. Charlie's jackets. The thrift store rug they'd bought last fall for their previous place.

Charlie stood beside her, hand brushing hers. "It's no penthouse," he said

"No," Mandie said, smiling. "But it'll hold our bed, and there are windows."

"This is a corner unit," Jo said. "So our inward units just have the windows on the right."

"Sure," Mandie said. But every room had a window, and Mandie actually thought this apartment was pretty great. "But all the windows overlook the courtyard?"

"Yes, ma'am," Jo said. "You come in off the street, but all the apartments extend toward the back." She walked over to the window. "And...I don't know if you noticed, but this is actually a hatch window. It opens."

She gave it a good shimmy, then lifted it. "There's a tiny terrace out here."

Mandie watched in wonder as the taller woman folded herself through the window and waved to them from the other side of it.

"That's amazing," Charlie said. "Talk to me about your rent-to-own deal that comes with signing a lease."

"Oh, sure." Jo climbed back into the apartment. "Before that, you've got central air and heat, and we help you get the applications out to the utility companies. Internet is on your own, and yes, we have two partnerships with rent-to-own centers that can help you get the furnishings you need."

"What are you thinking?" Mandie asked. They'd left their bed, couch and love seat, and a dresser in a storage unit in the city.

"I don't know," Charlie said. "Just asking."

"I can give you the packet when—or if—you sign the lease." Jo led them toward the door. "I can show you the rooftop and the courtyard if you want?"

Mandie nodded, though she wanted to simply sign the lease. They'd looked at three other apartments already today, and this one was comparable and cheaper.

The rooftop was amazing, and the courtyard made her smile. Especially when Jo said, "We have unique partnerships with specific food and drink vendors. They're not allowed to bring their full-sized trucks back here, but they can bring their carts."

She indicated a coffee cart that had Mandie's mouth watering. "And they give residents a discount."

Charlie bought her an iced coffee and an Americano for himself, and they settled on a bench with the promise that they'd come check-out with Jo when they were ready.

Mandie fell silent as she sipped her coffee, her thoughts running wild. In the courtyard—and Brooklyn—the rushle-bustle of the city seemed far away, though Mandie still felt the vibrant energy, and the ever-present hum of the city remained.

"I'll just say it," she said. "I want it."

Charlie finished his coffee and let out a long sigh. Mandie couldn't read his expression, and her pulse shrank in her veins.

Then he grinned and said, "So do I."

"Will you take me to that bookshop in the Village tomorrow?"

"Sure, baby."

"And can we get a footlong from one of the carts around Central Park?"

"Whatever you want." Charlie lifted his arm and tucked it around her.

A perfect sense of peace settled over her as she watched a man jog by in front of them. Yes, they'd run away. Yes, they had problems to solve and decisions to make. But right now, in this moment, sitting in this gorgeous court-yard, everything felt possible.

This city had been her first taste of independence, her first step away from the sheltered life of Five Island Cove.

She'd grown here, discovered parts of herself she never knew existed. And yet, the cove was home—the place where her roots ran deep, where her family and friends formed a network of love and support that couldn't be replicated.

Mandie suddenly understood something important: it wasn't about choosing one place over the other. It was about embracing this chapter of her life—the city, the education, the growth—while knowing that the cove would always be there, a constant in a changing world.

She and Charlie could build a life here for now, knowing it wasn't forever. They could experience everything the city had to offer, then return to the cove when they were ready, bringing back all they'd learned and become.

Exhaling, she stood up and faced the man she loved. "Come on. Let's go sign the lease on that studio-one-bedroom. They only have two left, and it's the best thing we've seen."

Charlie stood too, took her in his arms, and leaned down to kiss her. "You're the best thing I've seen."

She grinned up at him, and while she didn't normally hesitate once she'd made up her mind, she took a few second to kiss Charlie so he'd know he was the best thing in her life too.

Chapter Fifteen

Eloise served Sarah and Richard Eagan their third cup of coffee as they pored over the booking software on her laptop. The soon-to-be owners of the Cliffside Inn had arrived promptly at eleven that morning—right after check-out—eager to learn everything about the business they'd be taking over in just twenty days.

"So this is where you can see all the upcoming reservations," Eloise said, pointing to the calendar view on the screen. "Green means fully paid, yellow means deposit only, and red means they've reserved but haven't paid anything yet."

Sarah tucked a strand of silver-streaked auburn hair behind her ear and leaned closer. "And this September is completely booked already?"

"Yes," Eloise said, pride warming her chest despite the bittersweet feeling that had been her constant companion since accepting their offer. "Fall foliage season is huge for us. People come from all over to see the colors change across New England, and I had a marketing manager a few years ago that helped me set up a campaign to get spillover from that."

Eloise had agreed to turn over everything having to do with the inn, and that campaign and all the contacts her marketing manager had put together existed in a digital folder on her laptop. She'd give it to the Eagans to do with what they wanted.

Richard nodded appreciatively, his salt-and-pepper beard catching the morning light streaming through the office windows. At fifty-seven, he'd recently retired from a career in corporate hospitality, and the Cliffside Inn represented his and Sarah's dream of running a small, upscale bed and breakfast.

"The vendor network you've built is impressive," he said, flipping through the physical binder Eloise had prepared. "Local fishermen, farmers, bakers—I can see why your guests rave about the food."

"Duke Grover brings us the freshest catch every Thursday, Friday, and Saturday," Eloise said. "Your busiest days, of course. And Mabel's Bakery delivers those cinnamon rolls Sarah loved at breakfast. They're our most requested item. Everything else is made right here on-site by Marge. You'll love her."

Sarah smiled. "I'm sure we will. I've gained five pounds just by sampling the food here this week."

"Worth every ounce," Richard said, patting his own substantial middle.

They'd agreed to keep the staff for at least a term of six months, at their current wages, and that had pleased Eloise greatly. The inn's rooms had been booked this week, so Sarah and Rich were staying somewhere on Diamond Island and coming out to meet with Eloise during the quietest times at the inn—between check-out and check-in.

Eloise couldn't help but like them. They were kind, enthusiastic, and clearly committed to maintaining the inn's character and quality. If she had to sell the Cliffside, she couldn't imagine better buyers.

And yet.

Every explanation felt like giving away a piece of herself. Every detail shared was another step toward the reality that soon, none of this would belong to her.

"The housekeeping staff all plan to stay on," Eloise said now that she'd mentioned Marge, pushing through the tightness in her throat. "Rhonda, our night manager, is thinking about moving closer to her daughter in Providence, but she's agreed to stay through October to help with the transition."

"That's more than generous," Sarah said. "We'd love to keep her longer if she's willing."

"So you don't want to live on-site?" Eloise asked. After all, she lived here in Five Island Cove, and she'd more than likely see Sarah and Rich around the islands.

"I don't think so," Rich said. "We're looking at places here on Sanctuary, so we can have a separation between work and home."

Eloise nodded, though she knew how very difficult that separation could be.

A knock at the office door interrupted them, and Eloise looked up to see Natalie, her realtor, standing in the doorway with a thick folder.

"Sorry to interrupt," Natalie said, her professional smile firmly in place. "I have the inspection to go over with the Eagans, and I was out here on Sanctuary to do a walk-through."

Eloise nodded, grateful for the momentary reprieve. "Why don't we take a break? The dining room should be cleaned by now. You can go over things there while I check on a few things."

As the Eagans followed Natalie to the dining room, Eloise escaped to the kitchen, pressing her palms against the cool stainless steel and taking a deep breath.

"Are you okay, El?" Marge asked as she came out of the walk-in fridge with an enormous lamb shank in her hands.

Eloise gave her a smile. "Yes. I just needed a break from things."

Marge smiled at her, as Eloise had often escaped to the kitchen to get away from the "things" beyond it that stressed her.

"I need to put in the pantry order. Thank you for sending me the menu for the rest of the month."

"Of course," Marge said. She normally sent the menu in two-week increments, but Eloise only wanted to do one more order for the month, as she'd only own the inn for another twenty days.

Less than three weeks.

She wasn't sure why this thing she'd wanted, worked for, prayed for, made tears burn in her eyes.

She busied herself by checking the pantry inventory, a task she'd done hundreds of times over the years. The familiar routine calmed her, the soft ticking of pencil against paper so soothing, and by the time she rejoined the Eagans in the dining room with the order form, she felt steadier.

"Everything looks in order," Richard said, sliding the paperwork back toward Natalie. "Just a few questions about the property taxes."

As Natalie explained the tax structure, Eloise's phone buzzed with a text from AJ.

Still on for our walk at 4:00? Jean's coming too.

Absolutely, Eloise said. *Meet at the lighthouse trail?*

Perfect. I finished a batch of iced tea this morning, and I'll bring some for everyone. AJ included a picnic basket emoji, complete with a red checkered cloth spilling out the top, something Eloise would've never predicted for the strong, stubborn sports journalist.

AJ still wrote on select projects, but she did everything from the comfort of her home office here in Five Island Cove.

The prospect of an afternoon walk with her friends

lifted Eloise's spirits. She returned her attention to the meeting, answering questions about the inn's seasonal events and local partnerships, and then walking the Eagans through how she did pantry orders.

"One last thing," Sarah said as the time for check-in approached. "We'd love to keep the Starry Night package you offer. The guests' reviews of the private cliffside deck dining are incredible."

"Of course," Eloise said, pleased they wanted to continue one of her favorite offerings. "I'll introduce you to Marcus, our astronomy enthusiast who helps set up the telescopes."

She kept her smile hitched in place until she could escape to her office alone. Then, she locked the door behind her, sat down at her desk, cradled her head in her hands, and wept.

THE LIGHTHOUSE TRAIL WOUND ALONG THE western edge of Diamond Island, offering spectacular views of the Atlantic. Eloise spotted AJ and Jean already waiting at the trailhead, each holding a glass of amber liquid like they were doing a whiskey tasting.

"There she is," AJ waved and picked up a third glass. She smiled as Eloise arrived, handed her the glass, and gave her a quick hug. "How does it feel to almost be done with the inn?"

Eloise couldn't help smiling. She took a sip of the ice-cold iced tea. "Mm, AJ, this is amazing."

"Matt's mother finally taught me how to make it," AJ said. "I don't think she hates me quite so much anymore."

"Of course she doesn't hate you," Jean said. "You always say that, and she shows up weekly with something new for Asher."

"Well, she loves Asher," AJ said. "Who wouldn't?" She grinned and set her glass down on the bench at the trail-head. "I'm just going to leave this here and get it on the way back."

Eloise took another swallow of tea, thrilled she'd left the inn right as check-in was beginning. Then she put her glass with AJ's, and Jean made it a trio. AJ turned and started down the path that would widen once they got past the initial bottle neck between the cliffs and the trees.

Eloise went last, which was where she wanted to be on any type of group activity. Jean twisted and asked, "How did today with the Eagans go?"

"They're lovely people," Eloise said, keeping her eyes on the path at her feet. The last thing she needed was to fall and hurt herself. "They really care about preserving what makes the inn special."

They went single-file by the trees, and then Eloise picked up her pace for a couple of steps to fall into step beside them. She took a big breath, enjoying the August heat tempered by the cool ocean breeze as it entered her lungs. "I love the cove."

"You didn't say how today actually went," AJ pointed out, peering past Jean, who walked between them..

Eloise sighed. "What do you want me to say?"

"The truth," AJ said.

"It feels like I'm giving away my child." Eloise frowned at the blue sky to the north. "Which is weird, because I don't even have kids, and I have no idea what that would even be like."

"You have kids," AJ said promptly. "Billie and Grace are absolutely yours."

"I agree," Jean said quietly, the perfect complement to AJ's stronger personality.

Eloise nodded, because she loved her girls with her whole heart. They walked in comfortable silence for a moment, the rhythmic sound of waves crashing against the rocks below filling the air.

"How's your mom doing?" Jean asked gently.

"Some days are better than others." Eloise stepped carefully around a jutting rock on the path. "The medication seems to be helping with her confusion, but she's still adamant about staying in her house."

"Have you talked to her about moving to Diamond Island?" AJ asked.

Eloise nodded. "Multiple times. She always has a reason why she can't—her garden, her neighbors, her cats, her car." She sighed. "She acts like she has the only car on Sanctuary, and there's no way to get it to Diamond."

"Cats can become like children," Jean said with a small smile.

"I know," Eloise said. "I've told her they can come too —Prince is very good with cats—but she just changes the subject." They reached a wooden bench overlooking a particularly stunning vista and sat down by unspoken agreement.

"I've given her a brochure for where Kristen lives—and they allow cats. But she won't even consider moving right now." The words tumbled out now, and a burden lifted from Eloise's shoulders as she spoke. "I'm trying to help her, to make things easier before they get worse, but it's like she doesn't see anything beyond the moment she's living."

"Maybe she doesn't," Jean said.

Eloise turned to look at her. "Yeah." She sighed. "Maybe she doesn't."

"My dad's said all the same things you say your mom is saying," Jean said. "He doesn't want to give up his dog, who will take the bicycle back to little Jerry down the road who keeps leaving it on the wrong lawn?" She smiled. "And all I or my mom could talk to him about was the safety concerns we had, how he couldn't even divvy out his own pills, how he couldn't keep up with the outdoor chores."

Eloise could've said all of those things about her mother, though she hadn't gotten so bad that she couldn't put her pills in a daily pill box. Eloise had helped her set up alarms to make sure she took them, and Eloise had taken to simply texting her every once in a while to make sure she was eating, bathing, and generally doing okay.

She stopped by a few times per week, and her mother came to dinner slightly more often. Eloise had brought up leaving Sanctuary, and she'd given her mother as many options as she and Aaron could come up with.

Nothing had worked.

"So what changed his mind?" AJ asked. "Because they just moved into a new place, didn't they?"

Jean nodded. "Yeah, my mom got him to agree to a fifty-five-plus community, and they're like this pseudo assisted living facility; they have two full-time nurses who live on-site."

She reached into her pocket and pulled out a tube of Chapstick. "My mom and I decided to stop talking to him about dangers and all the things he couldn't do. That only made him dig his heels in and try to prove us wrong. Instead, we started talking about all the positive things a different housing situation would provide."

As Jean spoke, something shifted in Eloise's understanding. She'd been so focused on the practical aspects—the safety concerns, the logistics of care—that she hadn't fully considered that everything she said caused fear.

"We stopped telling him he needed to move 'because he needed help' and started talking about how much better his life would be." Jean smiled. "My mom is a saint, and she made it about what he could get from the facility, not what he *wasn't* able to do in their current situation."

Eloise nodded slowly, turning the idea over in her mind. She considered herself a positive person, but she'd been focused on helping her mother her way, and perhaps she needed to change her tactics.

Mom hadn't had anything too scary happen yet anyway, and Eloise reminded herself that they'd *just* gotten the diagnosis.

She reached over and curled her fingers around Jean's, a sudden rush of gratitude for these women, for the way they could see through her frustration to the heart of what mattered, for the way they cared about her in silent—and loud—ways.

AJ exhaled heavily as she got to her feet. "I have to get going. Asher will be up from his nap by now, and Matt has to stage for night golf this weekend."

They continued their walk, making the loop that brought them back to the bench where they'd left their iced tea glasses.

"Anyway," AJ said. "That's the latest on Kelli and Shad."

Eloise had hardly seen Kelli this summer, as Parker had stayed home from his dad's in New Jersey, and Kelli had a toddler and a busy yoga studio on another island.

"Well, I hope everything turns out okay with his job," Jean said.

Eloise nodded, not much more to add, because she hadn't even know Shad wasn't happy with his city government job.

"Same time next week?" AJ asked as they reached their cars.

"Definitely." Eloise drove home with the windows

down, letting the salt-tinged breeze rush through the car. For the first time in weeks, the thought of selling the inn didn't feel like an ending, but more of a...transition—a door closing so that another could open.

The scent of roasting chicken greeted Eloise as she entered the house, followed by the unmistakable rich aroma of chocolate.

"Aaron?" she called, setting her purse on the entryway table.

"In the kitchen," he called back.

She found him standing at the counter, carefully spreading Eloise's favorite food in the whole world— German chocolate cake frosting. She could eat the creamy, coconutty, walnutty treat by the spoonful, no cake needed.

"What's all this?" She approached and leaned into his side, swiping her pinky through just a titch of the frosting. She put it in her mouth as he grinned at her.

He swiped his finger through the frosting too and held it out for her to taste. She sucked it off his finger, their eyes locked. Aaron then took her into his arms and kissed her, a growl emanating from way down deep in his body.

"I thought we'd celebrate," he said. "I took the afternoon off, sent the girls to my parents' house, and made this cake."

"A celebration," Eloise repeated. "Of what?"

"Of you." He kissed her softly this time. "Of this new chapter you're starting, where you're home more, and doing more of what you love, and I'm able to come home in the middle of the day and make love to you."

She smiled up at him as her heart swelled with love. "I suppose that does call for a German chocolate cake."

"It sure does." Aaron touched his mouth to hers again. 'The real question is if you want to eat it now or after."

"Mm, after what, Chief?"

Without answering, Aaron stepped away and wiped his hands on a dish towel. "The chicken needs another twenty minutes." He took both of her hands in his. "Come to bed for a few minutes."

Eloise giggled like a teenager as she went with him down the hall, where he locked the door behind them and showed her how very much he loved her. She lay in his arms, her eyes closed, when his alarm went off.

"Chicken's done." He groaned as he rolled away from her. "Do you want a minute to shower?"

"Mm, yes," Eloise said, and she watched as Aaron pulled on a pair of gym shorts. As he left her in their darkening bedroom, she had the overwhelming thought that this was where she needed to be. *This* was the life she wanted to pour herself into now.

She showered, redressed in a soft pair of summer sweats—capris and a short-sleeved hooded sweatshirt—in violet, and headed back out to the kitchen.

Aaron had the table set, with candles burning, that chocolate cake standing tall and proud right in the middle of it all.

"Wow," she said. She pulled him into her arms. "You're my favorite person in the whole world."

He beamed down at her. "I just want you to know

how much I appreciate you," he whispered. "You took on my girls—and me—and you're flawless at taking care of us and loving us, and I know I don't tell you enough how much I appreciate it."

Eloise nodded, letting his words fill her mind and then her heart. How she felt in the bedroom echoed through her, and she said, "This is the life I've always wanted, Aaron—and *you* gave it to me."

"Let's eat," he said, and Eloise took her place at the table while he went to fill their plates with food. Her phone buzzed, and Eloise twisted to retrieve it from the corner of the counter where she'd left it when she'd walked in.

"I hope this isn't anything from Cliffside," she said with a frown. Instead, she saw a name she recognized as her mother's next-door neighbor, Janice, on Sanctuary Island.

Eloise, your mother just showed up on my doorstep. She asked me for her spare key, but I've never held a spare key for her. I've brought her inside, but I'm not sure what to do.

Eloise sat up straight, alarm coursing through her. "No."

Aaron put a steaming plate of golden brown chicken, mashed potatoes, perfect asparagus spears, and the glossiest gravy ever in front of her. "What is it?"

"It's my mom," Eloise said, her reality splintering. "She's wandered over to the neighbor's house and doesn't seem to know what's going on."

Aaron turned and swiped his keys from the countertop. "I'll drive."

Eloise tapped and lifted her phone to her ear as she looked around for a pair of shoes. "Janice, hi, it's Eloise," she said when the woman answered. "Aaron and I are on our way to Sanctuary, but can you stay with my mom until we get there?"

All Eloise could think as Janice agreed to stay with Mom was, *An hour. An hour. An hour. It'll take us at least an hour to get there.*

Chapter Sixteen

A lice tapped her fingernails against the polished wood of the post office counter, trying to keep her impatience in check. "I'm sorry to keep stopping by, but are you absolutely certain there's nothing for me? The courthouse said the title generation was completed four days ago, and it should be here."

Whatever that meant.

Mabel Pierce, who'd been Five Island Cove's postmistress for nearly three decades, gave Alice a sympathetic look over her wire-rimmed glasses. "I've checked twice, Alice. Nothing from the Massachusetts Land Court has come through for you or Kristen."

"Could it be misrouted? Or stuck somewhere in processing?"

"It's possible," Mabel said. "But unlikely. Mail doesn't just disappear these days, especially official government documents. They're barcoded and tracked."

Alice exhaled slowly, mentally counting to five to find a hidden well of patience. "Is there a way to check the tracking?"

"If you have the tracking number, sure."

"Which I don't," Alice said, more to herself than to Mabel. "Because the courthouse clerk said she'd 'look into it' and call me back." She didn't bother to hide her frustration, though an unarrived document wasn't Mabel's fault.

"I'll keep an eye out," Mabel promised, just as she had yesterday. "And I'll call you the minute anything arrives."

"Thank you." Alice forced a smile to her face. "I appreciate it."

Outside the post office, she groaned as she sank into her sleek sedan. She'd promised to meet Ginny at the florist at eleven to finalize the bridesmaid's bouquets, which gave her just enough time to make one more call to the courthouse.

She sat facing the water, the air conditioning blowing, and pulled out her phone. She and dialed the now-familiar number for the Land Court Clerk's Office in Boston. She'd been down to the Five Island Cove Registry of Deeds to find out why the title for the lighthouse hadn't come yet, though she already knew all certified land documents came from the central office in Boston.

She'd been told as much, and she'd requested the number for them and called several times now. There'd been a backlog in generating the duplicate title in the first place, but they claimed to have mailed it on Monday.

It didn't take that long for mail to come from Boston;

it usually arrived overnight, in fact, and Alice's frustration felt too familiar as she navigated through the automated system and got put on hold. The tinny muzak only added to her irritation, and she decided she'd rather drive than sit.

She put her phone on speaker and tucked it into against her collarbone, using the contraption Ginny had put on the back of it to snap her collar between the pieces to hold it in place.

She left the tiny parking lot at the post office and pulled out onto the main road that circled Diamond Island.

"Massachusetts Land Court, how may I direct your call?" a bored voice finally answered.

"This is Alice Rice again," she said, trying to sound pleasant rather than desperate. "I'm calling about the Five Island Cove lighthouse title. I spoke with someone named Denise earlier this week?"

"One moment, please."

More waiting. Alice drove past fishing boats rocking gently in the harbor, remembering how her father had taught her to sail in these waters. The lighthouse had been a constant in her life, a beacon guiding her home. Now, after all the work she'd done to legally secure it for Kristen and her family, the final piece was frustratingly out of reach.

"This is Denise."

"Denise, hi," Alice said as she came to a stop at an intersection. "I still haven't received that duplicate title for the lighthouse here in Five Island Cove."

Silence. Maybe some faint clicking in the background, which made Alice roll her eyes. "I'm showing that the title was processed on August third and mailed out on August seventh."

"Yes, you told me that on Wednesday," Alice said. "And Tuesday, and I've been checking at the post office every day, and we haven't received it."

"Sometimes these things take time," Denise said as if Alice didn't understand how US mail worked.

"Denise, my friend," Alice said. "Since I've spoken to you three times in a week, I think we can be friends. I've lived in Five Island Cove for a great many years, and nothing takes five days to be mailed from Boston."

She drew in a breath that did little to calm her and reached way, way, way down deep for another shred of patience. By some miracle, she found one. "The post-mistress said if I had the tracking number, I could see if it has been snarled up somewhere. Is there any way I can get that tracking information from you?"

"A tracking number..." Denise practically slapped her keyboard. "I can email you those details. Let's see..."

Alice remained as silent as possible, not even daring to breathe lest it come out aggressive and scared Denise away from giving her the tracking number.

"Okay, the email on record for this title is Alice Rice at Family Firms dot com. Is that right?"

"Yes, please," Alice said. "Will there be instructions for where I can check the number?"

"It's the USPS," Denice said.

"Oh, sure," Alice said, a measure of foolishness filling her. "Thank you so much, Denise."

"I've just sent that email. Did you want to confirm you got it before I let you go?"

"Yes, please. Give me one second." Alice practically swerved into oncoming traffic to make a left turn into a parking lot at a row of shops. "I'm really sorry to bother you again. It's just been a long process to get this title, and this is important to a lot of people here."

She brought the car to a stop and quickly tapped away from the call and into her email. The top email, in all bold typeface, was from the Land Court office. "I have it," she said. "Thank you again. I *really* appreciate your help."

She ended the call and sat for a moment, trying to make sense of what she'd just heard. She quickly long tapped and dragged over the tracking number, then copied it before switching to her Internet browser and searching for "how to track mail—USPS."

She put the tracking number in the slim entry box there and tapped the blue arrow. For some reason, her heartbeat throbbed in her throat as her phone WiFi struggled to complete her request.

Her phone buzzed with a text, and the message rolled down from the top. *Ginny: At the florist. Where are you?*

Alice sighed and dropped her phone into the cup holder again. Her daughter was getting married in three days, and right now, that took precedence over everything else.

After all, Bob would be arriving in the cove that

evening, and Alice would be lucky if she saw Ginny much between then and Tuesday morning's ceremony.

ALICE STARED AT THE BRIDAL BOUQUET, something motherly and lawyerly combining into a terrible funnel inside her. She told herself to hold her tongue, that Ginny could be the adult here.

"That's not what I ordered at all," her daughter finally said.

The florist looked from the purple, blue, and white arrangement, her smile faltering when she met Ginny's eyes. Alice had already seen the horrified widening of her daughter's eyes, and she shook her head slightly as Felicia met her eye too.

"No?" she asked. "Are you sure?"

"Am I sure?"

Alice covered Ginny's hand with hers. "Felicia, her colors are peach, pink, and mint. There's no way she ordered this. Are you sure you have the right bouquet to show us?"

There were a lot of weddings in the cove in the summer. Some people came here for destination weddings, for crying out loud.

Felicia's mouth straightened into a thin line, and her expression told Alice she didn't like being questioned. "Let me—"

"I'm pretty sure the name of the bouquet was 'pastel summer,'" Ginny said.

"Pastel summer is very popular," Felicia said diplomatically. "Let me go check on this." Thankfully, she took the incorrect bouquet with her.

Ginny scoffed once Felicia had disappeared into the back room. "I don't think she even believed me."

"They'll fix it," Alice wondered how many more fires she'd have to put out before Ginny and Bob said I-do. "When is Bob arriving? He's flying this time, right?"

Ginny brightened, though she sighed. "Yes, he's flying, and he's not leaving Boston until four-thirty."

"So not until later tonight."

"Ten-thirteen, I think." But Ginny knew, and Alice knew she knew. Her daughter had an amazing memory, so all the things that required that—spelling, math—Ginny had been very, very good at.

"You're right," Felicia said as she returned. "That was for another wedding. I'm so sorry." She held out a bouquet that was exactly what Ginny wanted for her bridesmaids. "This is the Pastel Summer, and I have you down for four of these."

Ginny got to her feet. "Yes, this is it." She held it in front of her the way a bride would and gazed at it. She looked up at Alice, her eyes bright and filled with joy. "It's great, right, Mom?"

A pang moved through Alice's chest, pressing out against her ribs. Watching Ginny's joy... When had her little girl grown up enough to be choosing wedding flowers? It seemed like just yesterday Ginny was collecting seashells on the beach, her chubby hands filled with treasures she'd toddled back and shown to Alice with the same bright-eyed look on her face.

"And I have you down for our White Ranunculus boutonnieres," Felicia said, now checking a clipboard. "Just two of those. Is that right?"

"Yes," Ginny said.

Just Charlie and Bob's brother.

Alice's heart jumped again, because Bob's parents would be arriving tomorrow. Alice would be in full entertainment mode then, and she hadn't done that long-term since leaving the Hamptons.

"Now, you're at Driftwood, yes?" Felicia asked, and Ginny nodded.

"They're doing all the on-site set up," Ginny said. "I believe Jazzy coordinated the centerpieces through you." She whipped her gaze to Alice and then looked back at Felicia.

"Yes," Felicia said. "We have them as the Pale Boho. Is that right?"

When Ginny looked like she'd been asked a question in another language, Felicia reached for an overstuffed binder and started flipping pages. She finally found the one she wanted and pointed to a beautiful, mostly cream-colored arrangement with a splash of peach and the beige pampas grasses that Ginny loved.

"That's it," Ginny said. "I believe there are fifteen tables."

"That's what I have in my notes too," Felicia said. "Now, the ceremony is at eleven?"

"Yes," Ginny said. "We're expecting guests as early as ten-fifteen."

"We'll have everything done before nine," Felica assured her. "Including your bouquet and the bridal bouquets. Everything will be at Driftwood by nine a.m. They have a fridge there we've used in the past."

"Okay." Ginny sat back down, and Alice recognized this look too. Overwhelm. Thankfully, Felicia wrapped things up quickly, and all Alice had to do was sign the invoice and pay the last half of what she owed for the flowers.

"I can't believe it's only three days away," Ginny said as they left the shop. "It feels like we just got engaged."

"Time has a way of speeding up when you're planning a wedding." Alice linked her arm through her daughter's. "Are you nervous?"

Ginny considered the question. "Not about marrying Bob. I'm sure about that. But the ceremony itself? Standing in front of everyone? A little."

"That's normal," Alice said with a grin. "I think we have everything set and ready." Now, they just needed the day to arrive.

"There's Mandie," Ginny nodded up ahead of them, to a café where they'd planned to meet Mandie and Robin. Then she came to a complete stop and darted in front of Alice.

"I still can't believe they just took off like that," Ginny said. "It's so unlike Mandie."

Alice searched her face, trying to find an answer that would satisfy her daughter. "You know how Mandie is; she's...she gets a little intense is all."

Ginny looked at the ground, her gaze rebounding to Alice's. "She told me she was jealous of me, just a little."

Alice's eyebrows went up, because she thought Ginny and Mandie were best friends. "Did she say why?"

"Because we have this amazing brownstone to live in, and it just fell into our laps." Ginny sighed. "I couldn't really argue with her. But Dad's helping them with their apartment, so it's not like she can really complain."

Alice blinked, because she hadn't heard any of this, from anyone. "Your dad is helping them with the apartment in Brooklyn?"

Ginny sighed and looked away. "It's not a big deal, Mom. All Dad knows how to do is transfer money. It doesn't make him a good dad."

A lump formed in Alice's throat, and she couldn't swallow past it. "I—Arthur and I have money."

"Charlie won't even take it," Ginny said. "He's not even talking to Dad right now, because he and Mandie want to do things for themselves. But I didn't know they'd had this big fight about it—I mean, an argument."

Ginny smiled at her. "Put your eyebrows down, Mom. It wasn't a fight."

"You said the word fight." Alice had to work to get her

eyebrows to go down. "Charlie argued with your dad about taking his money?"

"Yes," Ginny said. "But I didn't know that, and when Dad offered to help me and Bob in Boston, I said yes." She rolled her neck and wiped her hand across her forehead. "That made Charlie mad too, and now, I don't know. Things are a little weird with them right now."

"But you'll work it out," Alice said. "Right? I mean, I haven't noticed anything." She glanced over Ginny's shoulder to the café, but Robin and Mandie had gone inside, probably to escape the heat.

"We'll be fine," Ginny said. "Mandie's intense, like you said. And Charlie usually calms her down, but he's been really intense about the whole money thing with Dad." She blew out her breath. "I'm just—I told you, because— do you think me and Bob are mooching off others? That we're not 'real adults' because we're letting El give us a good deal on the brownstone, and I'm willing to take Dad's money to help with bills and groceries?"

Alice fell back a step. "Of course not."

"I know I'm young, but I can take care of myself. I do adult things, and I just don't think there's anything wrong with getting a little bit of help."

"There's not," Alice said quickly. "Everyone needs help sometimes." She took her daughter by the shoulders. "You don't have anything to prove to anyone, my darling girl. You are not Mandie, and you are not Charlie, and you don't need to do anything the same as them."

Ginny smiled and leaned her forehead against hers.

"You and Bob are amazing together. That man loves you with everything he has, and he looks at you like you single-handedly cause the sun to rise every morning."

Alice gave her a soft smile, though Ginny's shoulders shook as she started to cry. "You get to be Ginny and no one else, and you get to be Ginny-With-Bob, and you two get to decide what you should and shouldn't do."

She grinned and stepped back. "If it were me, I'd take as much of your dad's money as I could."

Ginny exploded into laughter, and she wiped her tears as she did. She looked everywhere but at Alice, and when she finally could meet her eyes, she dove into her arms.

"I'm going to miss you so much when we move to Boston." Her chest shook. "What am I doing? I can't get married and move away and be someone's *wife*? Who am I kidding?"

Alice held her tightly, her own heart breaking, and then healing, shattering again, and then reforming bigger and better able to love than before. "Sweetheart, you're getting married in three days, and it's going to be amazing."

Alice stepped back and peered into her daughter's eyes. "Boston isn't that far. I am always right here." She tapped Ginny's breastbone. "And a phone call away." She smiled so she wouldn't break down into tears too.

"I know," Ginny said, wiping her eyes. "I'm just— sometimes things are a lot."

"I know they are. Change is hard, even good change." Alice smoothed a strand of hair from Ginny's face. "But you're going to build the *most fantastic* life with Bob. I'm so proud of you, and everything you've done, and who you are. Okay?"

Ginny sniffled and nodded. "Okay, Mom." She took an extra moment to wipe her face and pull her hair back, breathe, and then face the café. "Okay."

They resumed walking, and an awful ache settled in Alice's chest—the bittersweet pain of watching her child stand at the edge of the nest, wanting to fly but terrified she might fall instead.

Alice told herself both of her children were ready to fly. She'd equipped them with everything they needed to be successful, and they just needed to take the leap.

Ginny will be fine, she thought, not sure where it had come from. But she felt the thought was true—and she hoped she'd be okay come Tuesday evening, when Ginny was Mrs. Robert Olsen and off on her honeymoon.

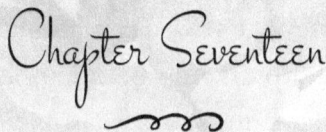

Chapter Seventeen

G inny woke with the rustling of sheets, her eyes flying open as awareness crashed through her. Morning had arrived. The morning of her wedding day.

"Time to get up," Mandie said, and Ginny rolled over. Her best friend in the whole world looked at her with soft eyes and an even quieter smile. "You're getting married today."

"Yeah." She lay perfectly still for a moment, cataloging the flutter in her stomach and the rapid beat of her heart. Was this normal? Was every bride supposed to feel like she might simultaneously burst into tears, throw up, or break into a song and dance?

"It's going to be amazing," Mandie said. She groaned as she rolled and then sat up, and Ginny did the same, sans the groan.

She picked up her phone on the nightstand, noting the time as the latest she'd slept all summer. Having a job at a bakery would do that. A smile filled her face when she saw Bob had texted.

Can't wait to see you at the end of the aisle. I love you more than all the stars in the sky.

The simple message settled something inside her. She'd had a couple of boyfriends before Bob, and from the moment she'd met him, she'd felt something different in his presence.

I love you too, she texted back. *See you soon.*

She stood and padded to the window in her bedroom, drawing back the curtain. The sun shone brightly, just as it had every day this August. Soon, rain and fiercer winds would come to the cove, but today looked glorious and perfect.

A soft knock at the door preceded her mother's entrance. Mom carried a tray with a steaming mug, a small plate of fruit, and a croissant—the way she'd done on Ginny's birthday.

Charlie got a box of his favorite cereal, but Ginny didn't like milk all that much. Her mother had gotten her chocolate croissants for the past couple of years, and Ginny loved them.

"I thought you might want something light before we head to Driftwood," Mom said, setting the tray on the dresser. "I know they'll have breakfast there, but."

She wore a wide smile with her casual day suit in black —a pair of flowing pants with a matching, wide-sleeved shirt. She'd pulled her hair back, had on minimal makeup, and so much joy oozing out of her.

"Come give me a hug." Mom opened her arms, and Ginny flew into them. "Mm, I love you." She stroked Ginny's hair. "Are you ready for today?"

"I think so." Ginny stepped back and moved over to the mug of tea. The warm ceramic seeped into her fingers, and she took a small sip of the chamomile and honey. "Thanks, Mom."

Mom perched on the edge of the bed. "How are you feeling? Really?"

Ginny considered the question, searching for the right words. "Like I'm standing on the edge of a cliff. Not in a bad way, just...I know everything changes after today. And I *want* it to change. I *want* to be Bob's wife. I *want* that life in Boston that's waiting for me." She picked up the chocolate croissant and sank next to her mother. "But it's still a little terrifying."

"That's how all the best adventures begin," Mom said. "A little terrifying, a lot exciting."

Ginny nodded, grateful that her mother understood. "Are you going to be okay with Dad here?"

A flicker of something—tension, resignation, acceptance—crossed Mom's face before she smoothed it away. "It'll be fine," she said. She sighed as she rose to her feet. "Today isn't about me, sweetheart, and I'm not going to make it anything but you and Bob starting your life together. That's all that matters."

"All right, Ginny, we—" Mandie cut off when she saw Mom standing there. "Oh, hey, Alice."

"I'll leave you girls to get your things together." She

ran her hand down the back of Ginny's head. "We have to leave in fifty minutes to get over to Driftwood for Shauna."

Ginny jumped to her feet and hugged her mother tightly. "I love you, Mom."

"Mandie will make sure you get everywhere you need to be on time." Mom smiled at her, and with only one awkward stutter-step, she moved into Mandie and hugged her too.

"My mother won't allow her to even be one second late," Mandie said.

"And we love her for that." Mom laughed lightly and glided out of the room like nothing was changing today.

Ginny met Mandie's eye, and they smiled simultaneously. "Do I have time to eat a little bit?" She took a bite of her chocolate croissant before Mandie told her that no, they'd set their alarm for as late as possible, and they needed to get all of Ginny's "somethings" in the tote, drop in the shoes, and grab her makeup kit.

Mandie would be doing that for Ginny, while a stylist through Driftwood, Shauna, would be doing her wedding up-do. Robin would have the dress and veil in the bridal room, and the wedding package that Mom had agreed to included a continental breakfast for the wedding party, two bridal rooms, a groom's room, and a family room.

Ginny had decided to dedicate the extra bridal room to her father, who was bringing his girlfriend-for-now. Ginny had met several over the years since her parents' divorce, and as she dusted the flakes of croissant from her hands and got to work packing up what she needed, she prayed her father would be on his best behavior today.

She was pretty much the only person who'd accepted his attendance at her wedding, and while Ginny wasn't playing by many traditional rules, she did want her dad to walk her down the aisle.

While Charlie wasn't super jazzed that Dad would be there, he'd agreed to help Ginny manage the situation. *I just hope there isn't one*, she thought as she left behind the rest of her tea and picked up her makeup tote.

In the kitchen, she found Arthur finishing up a plate of scrambled eggs and toast, already fully dressed for the wedding in a handsome, dark brown suit, complete with a pale pink tie with barely-there paisleys in a slightly darker thread.

"We're heading out," Ginny said. "We'll see you over at Driftwood."

Arthur grinned at her. "We'll be right behind you; your mother just went to answer a call."

Ginny hesitated, but in the end, she decided she didn't need to know who Mom was talking to. She'd handle it, set it on the virtual shelf in her mind, and be present for the wedding. At the same time, she'd been waiting for the title to the lighthouse for over a week now, and it still had not shown up at the post office in the cove.

The bridal suite at Driftwood held a waiting vanity table, where Ginny deposited her makeup kit before turning to Robin, who had been in the room already. Of course.

"Where do I need to be?" she asked.

"Right here," Robin said. "I'll go get Shauna. Mandie will get your makeup done. And we'll get you dressed when it's time." She smiled, the edges a bit pinched. She carried a clipboard and wore a flattering, professional dress in one of Ginny's wedding colors—peach.

"Have you eaten?"

"A little," Ginny said, pressing one hand to her belly. "I don't have a big appetite."

"I can send the leftover food home with your parents," Robin said, consulting her clipboard and making a check. "I think we'll have plenty between the breakfast and luncheon."

Mandie entered the room with Billie, Grace, and Jamie, and Ginny turned to greet them all. She'd never really gotten close to a roommate, and she'd spent so much of her summers with her mother's friends' kids. So she'd asked them all to be bridesmaids, and they each seemed excited to be there.

"Come sit," Mandie said. "Let's get your makeup started."

"The dress is right here." Robin indicated it hanging on the stand in the corner. "The photographer will be in to do details in twenty minutes, and we'll have her return when you get dressed."

"Okay, thank you, Robin." Ginny hugged her and went with Mandie while Robin moved over to Billie, Grace, and Jamie and started giving them instructions.

Ginny sat down, ready to be pampered as she got

prepared for her wedding. Women came and went, including the photographer, and then Mom arrived with the bouquets.

"I have flowers, girls."

That got everyone's attention, and Mom smiled as she passed out the bridesmaids' bouquets and the girls ooh'ed and ahh'ed over them.

"We'll want you guys to be ready for photos in a half-hour," Robin said. "Ginny, Shauna is here."

"I have to get my own makeup done," Mandie said. "A half-hour, Mom."

"Thirty minutes," Robin confirmed. "Set a timer, ladies. This is a morning wedding." With that, she left the bridal suite, and Ginny sat in front of the mirror again as Shauna plugged in her curling iron.

"Good morning," the older woman said with a smile. "Don't worry, you still have an hour to be ready." She combed her fingers through Ginny's hair. "Are you looking for something classic?"

"My hair is really thin," Ginny said, reaching to touch it herself. "So anything you can make look nice, I'll be happy with."

Shauna smiled at her in the mirror. "I'm sure we can do that." She got started, and Ginny made a conscious effort to close her eyes and bask in the activity and energy going on around her.

She didn't need to participate in it. She wasn't personally responsible for making sure every person got their hair done, and their shoe straps exactly right, and their makeup applied.

She just had to worry about herself, and Ginny smiled into the warm atmosphere in the bridal suite.

Soon enough, Mom returned, and Shauna stepped back. "Beautiful," Mom said. "Ginny, dear, let's get you in your dress."

She stood and took a moment to look at herself in the mirror. She had no idea who the woman was looking back at her, but she looked older and sophisticated. She looked confident, and when Ginny smiled, she did too.

All at once, Ginny realized who she looked like—her mother.

And her mother had taken on the hardest of things and come out the victor, and that meant Ginny could too.

"She wants all the buttons down the back," Robin said, and Ginny blinked away from her reflection to listen to Robin direct the photographer.

Her dress would become a second skin, and she wasn't surprised to be alone in the room with Mandie and her mother—with the photographer taking detail shots of items over on the vanity—while she quickly stepped out of her clothes and into her wedding underwear.

Her mom handed her the shapewear, though Ginny didn't have a lot of curves to deal with. With that in place, Mom held the dress, and Ginny took Mandie's hand and stepped into it. They shimmied the stretchy, tight fabric up over her hips and chest, and Ginny looked at herself in the mirror again.

"I love a mermaid dress," she said, her smile suddenly huge. The pearly satin was almost the color of white wine instead of the traditional blinding white of Mandie's dress. She stood very still while her mom and Mandie started doing up the fabric-covered buttons on the back of the dress, and Ginny adjusted the sleeves that hugged the sides of her biceps.

The camera clicked and clicked as the photographer got her photos, and then Mom finally smoothed her hand down Ginny's back.

"Now, we just need your somethings," Mandie said, pivoting toward the bin they'd brought that morning. She lifted the first one out. "Something borrowed."

She handed Mom a gold hair clip, and Mom sucked in a breath. "This is mine, from when I married Arthur." She smiled fondly, then tucked the pearled clip into part of Ginny's crown braid.

"Something old." Mandie moved to stand in front of Ginny, and she carefully lifted a necklace out of a black velvet box. The string of pearls—wine-colored, like the dress—emerged, and Ginny grinned as Mandie secured them around her neck. "Gorgeous."

"Where did you get those?" Mom asked.

"They're Arthur's mother's," Ginny said, lifting her hand to gingerly touch the largest pearl positioned perfectly against the center of her collarbone.

"Wow," Mom said. "He told me you'd talked to him about using something of hers, but I haven't seen these."

She too lightly touched the pearls, as if they might turn to dust if they got too much weight applied to them.

"Something new," Mandie said, handing Ginny the bottle of brand-new perfume they'd found just yesterday at an antique shop down on Pearl Island. Ginny took it from her, uncapped it, and spritzed the air in front of her. Then she stepped into the mist, the scent of tangerine, something fizzy and sparkling, and a tang Ginny couldn't quite identify dancing through her nose.

"Mm, I love this," she said, as she'd always preferred a fruity perfume.

"It's not bad," Mom said, though she liked a floral scent.

"Something blue," Mandie said, and Ginny's heartbeat skipped for some reason. Probably because this was the final step in her preparations. The photographer waited, because Ginny needed to slip on her shoes, and she wanted a picture with her Mom and Mandie in the bridal suite.

But Robin entered the bridal suite and said, "Ginny, eight minutes."

Mandie shook the something blue, which happened to be a pair of insoles in bright blue. They were made specifically for heels—wedding heels—to help a bride be more comfortable in what could be uncomfortable shoes, and Mandie stooped to slide them into Ginny's matching shoes.

The bright blue insoles seemed to smile up at her as she held Mom's hands for balance and stepped into the shoes.

They were more padded now, and Ginny rose three inches in the air, suddenly feeling like she could take on the world.

Or at least get married without throwing up.

Tears filled her eyes, but she blinked them back. She would not cry before she even left the bridal suite. She turned away from her reflection and gestured for her mother and Mandie to crowd in close around her.

"We need a picture," she said, and posing for the photographer gave her the space she needed from the moment to compose herself.

Then Mandie took her into a hug and said, "You're the most beautiful bride in the world," before she left with her mother.

Ginny caught a flash of black fabric when Robin paused to speak to someone, but she turned to her mother. "Well?"

"Stunning," Mom said, her voice catching on itself. "Your dad is right out there in the hallway. Bob will be at the altar, and I'll be in the front row." She cupped Ginny's face in her palm. "I'll see you out there."

Ginny nodded, her throat suddenly dry. She watched as her mother left, and she couldn't believe how alone she felt. Then the door opened again, and her father filled the entrance.

Ginny moved toward him as he scanned her from head to toe and back. "Wow," Dad said. "You look amazing, Ginny."

"Thank you, Dad." She stepped in to hug him lightly, then threaded her arm through his. "Are you ready for this?"

"Are you?" he asked.

"Yes," Ginny said decisively. "I'm so ready."

She moved with her father to the small anteroom off the garden where she'd be married, where they paused to wait for the music that would signal her entrance. She wanted to step to the corner and peek around it, just to make sure everything was in place.

At the same time, she wanted to experience the entirety of the gardens at once. The huge driftwood arch, which should bear flowers, ribbons, and pearls in her preferred colors. The drifting bows on the backs of the wooden chairs.

And all the driftwood, flowers, and shrubbery that came with the elegance of Driftwood Gardens.

"Your bouquet," Robin whispered, and Ginny twisted toward the sound of her voice.

"I didn't even realize I didn't have it." Ginny took the blooms from Robin, smiling softly at the peach and pink beauty of them. Robin nodded curtly and disappeared behind the closed door.

In the next moment, the music shifted, and Ginny recognized the cue. Her bridesmaids had already processed, and now it was her turn. She took a deep breath, her heart hammering against her ribs.

"Dad," she said.

He looked at her. "Yep, it's time." He tucked her arm tighter against his side, and she nodded, unable to speak past the lump in her throat. He stepped to the archway leading out of their hiding spot, and Ginny had no choice but to go with him.

She *wanted* to go with him.

He emerged first, and she went after him, quickly stepping to his side when he paused. In front of her, that towering arch beckoned to her, its magnificence rendering her still and mute.

Her eyes trailed down the dozens and dozens of blooms caught in the gorgeous driftwood—to the man standing in front of it.

Bob.

The assembled guests rose to their feet, but Ginny's gaze never left Bob's. He stood tall and proud, directly in front of her, his smile bright and infectious.

Time seemed to slow as she moved forward. She was vaguely aware of the guests—Kristen, Jean, and Clara whispering their congratulations as she passed, then Kelli, AJ, and Laurel whooping as she went by them.

Bob's parents and brother stood in the front row on the left, with Mandie, Charlie, Mom, and Arthur on the right.

But mostly, she saw Bob, his eyes never leaving hers, the sense of wonder etched in his eyes growing with each step she took toward him.

When she finally reached the arch, her father kissed her cheek and placed her hand in Bob's. The warmth of Bob's fingers entwining with hers grounded her, and the nervousness that had plagued her all morning evaporated.

"How gorgeous are you?" Bob murmured, quickly sweeping his lips along her temple. "Simply beautiful."

Ginny smiled as the officiant began speaking, but she heard only fragments through the rush of blood in her ears. Something about love and commitment, about the journey they were beginning together. She and Bob had written their own vows, and when the time came, Bob spoke first, his voice steady and sure.

"Ginny, I knew you were special from the very moment I laid eyes on you. You were the brightest person in the room—not just because of your intelligence, but because of how you light up every space you enter. You make me laugh, you challenge me to be better, and you remind me every day what it means to love completely."

He squeezed her hands, his eyes never leaving hers. "I promise to stand beside you through everything life brings us. I promise to listen, to grow with you, to choose you every single day. I promise that no matter where we live or what we do, home will always be wherever you are."

Tears threatened to spill down Ginny's cheeks as she began her own vows. "Bob, you came into my life when I wasn't looking for love, but somehow, you became everything I never knew I needed. You're my best friend, my favorite person to talk to, the one who makes even the ordinary days extraordinary."

She took a shaky breath, steadied by the warmth in his eyes. "I promise to be your partner in all things. I promise to face challenges with you, to celebrate triumphs with you, to build a life with you that's filled with laughter and love and adventure. I promise that no matter what the future holds, my heart is yours, completely and forever."

"And with that, I now pronounce you husband and wife."

Bob whooped, pumped one fist straight up into the air, and swept Ginny into his arms. "Bobby," she warned, but there was no stopping him as he dipped her low and pressed his mouth to hers in a sloppy, laughing kiss.

Ginny squealed, because she could barely walk in this tight mermaid dress. And being horizontal in Bob's arms? She had zero control and felt certain she'd fall flat on her back in front of everyone.

Then Bob lifted her up, turned toward the crowd, and raised their joined hands. Ginny held her bouquet out to the side as the crowd applauded and cheered.

She expected the first person to congratulate her to be Mom, but instead, Charlie swept into her space and grabbed onto her. "Wow," he yelled over the noise of the still-congratulating crowd. "Wow, wow, wow."

Ginny gripped him tightly, this person she'd spent every part of her life with. Her twin. They'd done so much together, and in so many ways, Ginny knew Charlie better than herself.

They hadn't always agreed, and Ginny found him to be the most stubborn man on the planet. But she loved him like she loved no one else, and dang it, one tear finally squeezed out of the corner of her eye as she hugged her twin brother.

Charlie didn't have to say anything else either. Ginny could hear his heart, just as he knew how to listen to hers, and they simply held one another in this quiet, profound space while everyone celebrated around them.

Chapter Eighteen

Kristen smoothed her hands over her lavender silk dress as she entered the pavilion at Driftwood Gardens, where the luncheon would be served at Ginny and Bob's wedding. The ceremony had been perfect—intimate and joyful, with Bob and Ginny radiating happiness that reached straight into Kristen's heart and reminded her that goodness still existed in the world.

Now, white-clothed tables dotted the garden terrace, each adorned with beautiful arrangements of cream, peach, and pink flowers, with an abundance of pampas grasses that reminded Kristen of the tufts of beach grass that grew through the sand.

Waitstaff circulated with flutes of champagne and trays of hors d'oeuvres, but in lieu of a string quartet playing, Bob and Ginny had opted for their own modern playlist. Kristen paused while she waited for someone to lead her to her assigned table, and she feasted on the scene before her.

Kristen had witnessed so many beginnings and endings in Five Island Cove. She'd been present for first steps, first heartbreaks, first homes, and now, watching the children of her beloved girls begin their own journeys felt surreal... and also perfectly right.

"There you are." Clara appeared at her side with a champagne flute. "I think we've earned one drink."

Kristen accepted the glass of pink, bubbly liquid with a smile, enjoying how even the alcohol matched Ginny's colors. "Thank you, dear."

She didn't have to ask Clara about Lena, because her granddaughter texted her all the time. She really seemed to be thriving in her new apartment, and she'd even set a date for the yard sale—this Saturday.

Clara took a sip of her bubbly, her eyes bright as she looked around the pavilion. "I have to admit, I love weddings."

"And Robin and Ginny put together something spectacular," Kristen said. She'd never been to Driftwood Gardens, because why would she? But the fragrant gardens, the hint of salty breeze from the nearby ocean, the gorgeous blue sky everywhere, it all entered her heart and made a memory there.

"I think Alice put you at our table." Clara glanced toward her husband, who was deep in conversation with Reuben while Jean bounced Heidi on her hip a pace away. "Come on, Mother."

Kristen stepped out of the line of people still waiting to be shown to their seats, and she navigated the huge rock slab carefully in her heels. She so didn't want to fall and break a hip, not here. Not ever, but especially not here.

Clara stepped over to Scott and looped her arm around his waist. He looked at her, his eyes bright as he leaned in and stole a kiss. "Hey, you found her." He turned his beaming expression on Kristen, and the maternal part of her that only wanted the best for her children sang.

For a while there, Kristen had thought Clara and Scott would separate and get divorced. Clara especially had come so far from the frightened, defensive woman who'd unwillingly returned to Five Island Cove, determined to rebuild an inn alongside her life.

The inn had failed, but Clara had rebuilt her life, her marriage, her relationship with her daughter, her brother, and Kristen. One day at a time. One meal like this one. One memory etched in the heart.

Now she stood tall, confident in her choices and her place in the community of islands which relied so much on each other to survive.

"Are you worried about the transition at Cliffside?" Kristen asked.

Clara took the last swig of her champagne and set the glass on a tray of a passing waiter. "A little," she said. "Eloise has assured us that part of the agreement is that we all get to keep our jobs at our current rate for six months. After that, the Eagans can change anything they want."

"It's going to be great," Scott said. "They've already told Clara how much they love her." He squeezed his wife closer to him and leaned his head down to say something else to her that Kristen didn't catch.

"Grandma," Lena said, squeezing into the circle with them. "Did you see that fountain over there? It's made of chocolate!"

"I haven't seen it," Kristen said with a smile. "Show me, okay?" She eased away from her children and their loved ones to go with her granddaughter. Sure enough, at the back of the pavilion where the buffet was set up stood a three-tiered chocolate fountain.

"Wow," Kristen said as the rich, deep, dark chocolate flowed from level to level. "And look, Lena." She pointed a bit down the table, on the other side of a platter of pound cake and biscotti, strawberries and bananas, and marshmallows and pretzels. "That one is a white chocolate fountain."

"Oh, my heck, I didn't even *see* that one!" Lena took a few steps toward it, then stopped. "They have popcorn, Grandma." She turned back to Kristen. "Can I have white chocolate popcorn?"

Kristen gestured her back to her side and squeezed her hand. "I'm sure you can, Lena, but we'll have lunch first."

She turned to lead Lena back through the crowd, most of whom stood near their tables but weren't actually sitting at them. She'd only taken two steps when she spotted Kelli and Shad standing with AJ, Matt, and Asher.

"Where's Daphne?" she asked as she joined their group. Lena kept going, and Kristen let her, because she certainly couldn't get into too much trouble here.

"She was fussing," Kelli said with a sigh. "Eloise took her to give me a reprieve."

"She's cutting teeth," Shad added, glancing left and then right, as if he might be able to find someone more interesting than Kristen to talk to. That irritated her slightly, but she also knew Shad had been looking for another job, and perhaps one of his contacts would be here.

"I can't wait for school to start," AJ said. "Then this little man will have a couple of days out of my hair every week." She grinned at her son, who had just turned four this month and would be starting kindergarten in another year.

"I'd love to go walking after you drop him off." Kristen had sometimes joined the moms who walked in the morning, but they went earlier than she liked in the summer months.

"Of course." AJ gave Kristen a side-squeeze. "We've been missing you."

"Who goes?" Kelli asked. She accepted another glass of champagne from Shad and lifted it to her lips.

"Me and Jean most days," AJ said. "Kate joins us sometimes, but it depends on how the morning goes for her—or really, the night before."

Kristen nodded, glad that AJ and Jean had befriended someone outside their core group. There'd been so many splinter cells of friends in the past couple of years, but the past six or eight months had seen very little drama.

"Julia sometimes comes," AJ said. "And Tessa almost always does."

"Tessa does what?" the woman herself asked as she joined their group. She'd brought Dave, her boyfriend, with her, and Kristen backed up a step and shifted to make room for the two of them.

"Walking group," AJ said. "Wow, Dave, look at that jacket."

He wore a burnt orange jacket in crushed corduroy, and he beamed down at it. "Isn't it great? I found it at the new vintage pop-up shop that travels around the islands."

"Great is...a word for it," AJ said, and she grinned as Dave looked up at her and grinned.

"You don't like it?"

"I think it's great," AJ said, clearly teasing him.

Tessa took his hand and leaned into his shoulder. "Are you going to tell them, or should I?"

Dave looked at her, then scanned the circle. "You go ahead."

Kristen leaned in as the group behind them erupted in laughter. She didn't want to miss the news, after all.

Tessa smiled, and Kristen was sure a hint of a blush crept into her face as she ducked her chin. "Dave and I... well, Dave's going to move in with me next month."

"I knew it," AJ said in a triumphant voice. She reached out and shook Tessa's shoulders. "Congrats, you two."

Kelli hugged Tessa, and Kristen took her turn too. No sooner had she stepped back than someone touched her elbow. She looked down and then over her shoulder to find El standing there with a very tired-looking little girl in her arms.

Kristen turned to face her. "Hello, dear." She reached out and traced one finger down Daphne's face, and the little girl reached for her. Kristen squashed her groan as she took the toddler from Eloise.

"She wanted to say hi."

Kristen smiled at her, and tugged down the hem on Daphne's pink dress. "You look lovely, El." She too wore a pale pink dress, with a gather and pleats on her left hip that hid all the parts of El she probably didn't like.

"Thanks," she said.

"Where's your family?" Kristen asked. "Did your mother end up coming?"

"Yes." Eloise pointed to a table a couple over. "They're right over there. Grace is entertaining her with stories about Ninth Grade Day."

Kristen went with her, unsurprised to find Paul and Laurel, along with Liam and Julia, chit-chatting with Aaron next to where Dawn already sat at her place. Eloise had had quite the scare with her mother a couple of weeks ago, and she'd been quite stressed on the group chat.

Kristen had taken her a big pot of clam chowder, as she'd managed to get her mother to come stay with her and Aaron temporarily, though Kristen hadn't heard of a long-term solution yet.

"Hey, there, Kristen," Aaron said. "Have you had any trouble at your condo lately?"

Kristen blinked at him. "At my condo?"

"We've had some calls about thefts specifically targeting seniors," Paul said.

Kristen wouldn't be able to hold Daphne for long, and Eloise seemed to know it. She took the little girl back as Kristen said, "No, I haven't heard of any of that where I am."

"She's on the north side of the island," Paul said. "It's a much nicer community than Rockford."

"We'll keep an eye on it," Aaron said.

"Where are your kids?" Kristen asked Laurel.

"Paul's sister is babysitting." She smiled and lifted a glass of much darker amber liquid to her mouth, and Kristen suspected it was sparkling cider. After all, Ginny herself wasn't old enough to drink champagne.

"I found our table," Maddy said as she maneuvered next to Julia. "I left Ben over there, because he's already peopled out."

Julia grinned at her. "Already? We've only had the ceremony."

"He's not exactly an extrovert," Maddy said with a smile. Kristen had always liked Maddy's husband, Ben, but he worked a lot and didn't seem to come to a lot of the bigger group events, that was true.

"You're not going to duck out early, are you?" Julia asked.

"I doubt it," Maddy said. "But I might cut him loose if he starts growling everything he says." She giggled and looked around the circle. "What's going on with Tessa?"

"Oh, you weren't here." Julia grinned over to Tessa

and Dave, who had fallen back a couple of steps and were engrossed in their own conversations. "They're moving in together."

"What?" Maddy turned and set her glass on the table and went behind Aaron and Liam to Tessa and Dave.

"If everyone could find and take their seats, please," a woman said over a public address system that didn't even squeak when she started. "We'd like to make sure everyone has a spot and is comfortable before we begin in about five minutes."

The group Kristen had been standing with broke up and moved around the table to take their seats, but Kristen wasn't sitting with the cops and their wives.

Maddy and Tessa and Dave started toward a nearby table, and a thrill moved through Kristen when she found Ben sitting at the table with Reuben, Jean, and Clara— who stood looking around for Lena.

AJ, Matt, Asher, Kelli, Shad, and Parker sat at the table right behind them, with Duke, Jamie, a spot for Robin, and an older woman Kristen didn't know. Kelli seemed to, though, and Matt seemingly knew everyone in the cove, due to him owning the golf course, and they both chatted with her easily.

The head table held Ginny and Bob, both sitting right in the middle, with Alice and Arthur beside Ginny, and Charlie and Mandie on the end. On the other side of Bob sat his parents, as well as his brother and a woman Kristen hadn't met yet. She assumed she belonged to Bob's family, though.

Kristen wanted to tell Alice how beautiful the ceremony had been, how gorgeous her daughter was. She wanted to hold Ginny close to her heart and advise her to make as many memories as she could while she was young, as they'd be what sustained her when she reached Kristen's age.

Her heart filled so full, she felt it might choke her from the inside out, and she swallowed against her emotion.

"Mom," Clara said, and Kristen turned from gazing at the head table.

"Yes, sorry," she said quickly, and then she practically fell into her seat. And while Kristen hardly ever spoke of her late husband, especially after everything that had come out following his death, she missed him more powerfully in that moment than any other over the past six years since he'd passed.

The crowd thinned as people took their seats, and Kristen's gaze once again migrated to Alice. She'd been trying to track down the title to the lighthouse for over a week now, and it still hadn't arrived in the cove.

She'd gotten a tracking number that hadn't come up in the USPS tracking system. Alice had called yesterday, but the contact she had at the Land Court office hadn't been in, and no one had been able to help her.

She'd promised Kristen via text that she'd figure this out, and Kristen didn't doubt her for a moment. Yes, a twist existed in her stomach that only that reissued title would fix, but she knew Alice had done—and was doing—everything she could.

"Welcome," a woman said, and the last few people took their seats and the chatter died into silence. "We're so glad to have you at Driftwood Gardens, and we aim to have every moment you're here be one of your happiest."

Kristen smiled and added her own gentle applause to that which filled the pavilion. "We're going to turn the mic over to Mr. and Mrs. Olsen, and then lunch will be served."

Without Joel, Kristen's girls and the families they'd built had become the heartbeat of Five Island Cove for her. She'd seen them heal each other, challenge each other, support each other through marriages and divorces, births and losses, triumphs and failures.

Her role had shifted over the years, from mentor to friend to something like the roots of a great tree—less visible perhaps, but no less vital. She provided stability, history, connection to the past as they all moved into the future.

Kristen looked west, toward the lighthouse, though she couldn't see it through the roof over the pavilion. But everything always drew her back to the lighthouse, the tallest, most steadfast structure in the cove, just as it always had. Just as she hoped it always would.

She'd had a good life there, with who she'd thought was a good man, and though some hard truths had been learned in recent years, the memories in her heart and mind couldn't be tarnished.

"Thank you so much for being here to celebrate with us," Bob said into the mic. "Ginny and I are just going to look at you for a moment, so we can remember your smiles at our wedding."

He paused, and he seemed to look straight at Kristen, if only for a moment. She sure liked him, and she did the same thing—she looked around and memorized as many smiles as she could.

After all, she didn't know how many more days, months, or years she had on this earth, and she wanted as many tender, amazing moments in her mind as she could get.

Chapter Nineteen

R obin arrived at the lighthouse an hour before the official start time of Lena's yard sale, her SUV packed with folding tables and a cash box. Lena had struggled to find a place to host the yard sale, as her assisted living facility didn't allow such things.

Until two days ago, Clara and Scott were going to host it on their front lawn, but then they'd had a pipe burst, and that yard had now been dug up.

It had been Robin who'd suggested the lighthouse, as it had a flat, open, rocked area where they could set up tables. Not only that, but parking in the cove was always an issue, and the lighthouse had a decently sized lot.

She'd been posting on social media like crazy to make sure everyone knew where the location of the sale had been moved to, and Jean and Alice had taken around new signs with the correct address.

The morning air held a hint of autumn's approach—

crisp and invigorating despite the August date on the calendar. As Robin wrestled the first folding table out of the back of her car, Lena called to her from the direction of the lighthouse. The wind whipped her words away, though, and Robin chose to focus on the table so she didn't smash a toe.

When she could finally look at Lena, she found the young woman wearing a bright yellow t-shirt with a colorful rainbow on the front, the swirling letters of her assisted living facility name going through the stripes.

"My parents are bringing doughnuts, and we decided to sell hot chocolate and coffee to go with them."

"That's a great idea, Lena." Robin nodded to the end of the table. "Help me get this set up, okay? Where do you want the tables?"

"I drew a map." Lena pulled a folded piece of paper out of her pocket. "I want to put the furniture along the sidewalk up here, with the table for the check-out."

"Great, let's put this one on the sidewalk then." They moved the table there, and Lena helped Robin pull out and secure the legs before they stood it up. By then, Scott and Clara had arrived, and Scott opened the back of their car.

It seemed everyone knew to come early to help set up, because Alice and Arthur arrived a moment later, with AJ following them, and Eloise and Aaron with a big truck Robin had never seen before.

When she greeted El and hugged her, she asked, "Whose truck is that?"

"It's the only one the police department owns," Eloise said. "Aaron put out a call for donations this week, and things have been piling up at the station." She beamed at Reuben and Aaron as they pulled a loveseat out of the bed of the truck. "There's a few loads of furniture—maybe something Mandie and Charlie will like."

"Oh, I'll text her to come as soon as she can. She's working this morning." And moving to New York City tomorrow. Robin and Duke had offered to go with her and Charlie, to help them get moved in and settled, but she hadn't heard yet if they were needed.

Robin hadn't seen her daughter's apartment yet, and she'd really like to, but it didn't have to be on the first day.

Barstools joined the loveseat, and Arthur carried a table up to the rocks. Lena moved up there to start setting out the items she'd sorted, while others brought her more and more and more boxes.

A familiar calm settled over Robin amidst all the activity. This was what she did best—organize, delegate, create order from chaos. But today, she reminded herself, she wasn't just here to manage. She was here to enjoy, to be present.

She emptied her car and moved it out onto the road, so others could have her parking space. When she returned, she found Jean setting up the cash box with Lena, patiently explaining how she'd gotten smaller bills for change. She also had a card reader, and she looked up as Robin joined them.

"There she is," she said to Lena. "Ask her."

"Will you run the cash box, Robin?" Lena asked. "Everything is marked with stickers." Lena picked up a sheet that had various colors of roun stickers on it, with handwritten dollar amounts beside them.

"If there's a blue sticker, that's one dollar," Lena said. "Red is two dollars." She went on to explain the entire chart, though Robin understood it after only the first couple.

She glanced over to the nearest item to the check-out table—a bookcase. It didn't have a sticker. "The furniture doesn't have stickers?" she asked.

Lena shook her head, almost a perplexed look on her face. "I made tags for them. They still need to be put out." She looked around. "But...I don't know..."

Jean opened the folder that had been under the sticker price sheet. "Right here, Lena."

"We've got the refreshments down at the end here," Clara said as she approached. "We're going to have people pay for them there, not here."

"Okay," Robin said.

"Mom, I need to tag the furniture."

"Okay, darling. Let's do it." She took Lena to do that, and Robin looked up the few steps to the grounds of the lighthouse. At least ten tables stood in a horseshoe shape, the lighthouse standing proudly behind them, as well as a metal clothing rack, where Alice stood arranging things on hangers, moving them here and there according to some system she understood.

"Wow," Robin said. "Look at all this stuff."

"It's incredible," Jean said. "She's been so excited to get things set up in her categories—housewares, books, clothing, toys, and kitchen items, cookbooks, jewelry, tools, and sports equipment." Jean ticked each one off on her fingers as she spoke. She trilled out a laugh. "*I* have them memorized, for goodness sake."

Kristen arrived, and she paused next to Robin and Jean. "This is so great," she said. She gave Robin a quick hug and then moved down the sidewalk to get a cup of coffee and a doughnut.

Customers started to arrive, and it warmed Robin's heart to see locals browsing tables and buying dog crates, shovels, and recliners.

Robin manned the cash box, keeping a meticulous tally of sales while Lena enthusiastically spoke with anyone who got close. Robin knew a lot of people in the cove, as she'd lived here her whole life, and she thanked every single person who came through.

"How's she doing in her new place?" one of Robin's contacts in the wedding industry, Anita, asked.

"Really well," Robin said. "All the proceeds from this sale will help her pay her rent and utilities." She handed the woman a couple of dollars in change. "She's worked all summer on it."

"You need a tip jar," Anita said. "Because I'd put this in it."

Robin held out her hand, and Anita dropped the bills into her palm. "Great idea," she said, looking around the table for something she could use.

She couldn't see anything, and Anita said, "I have just the thing. Wait here."

Robin certainly wouldn't abandon the cash box, and she watched as Anita bustled over to her car and opened the back passenger door. When she emerged from rifling through the backseat, she had a plastic container in her hands, the kind that had once chocolate-covered caramels.

She lifted it and shook it, and Robin picked up the permanent marker Lena had used to make her furniture tags. She took the plastic container from Anita with a grateful smile and wrote TIPS on it in all caps.

After setting it proudly in front of the cash box, she waved good-bye to Anita and looked at the next customer waiting to check out. "Oh, hello, Marisol." She picked up the stack of books, which went for a dollar each. "How's your sister?"

"Still in the boot," Marisol said, and Robin chatted with her while she tallied up the woman's purchases.

"Mandie and Charlie want that tall cabinet," Duke said as he pulled his wallet out of his back pocket. "I took pictures of all the furniture and sent it to them, because Charlie won't be in off the boat until noon, and Mandie's working until four."

"She can't get away for a few minutes?"

"Even if she could." Duke laid down a twenty-dollar bill. "Some of this furniture is going fast."

Robin had been so busy, she hadn't noticed. Familiar and unwanted worry bled through her, because she wanted

Mandie to have the things she needed for the apartment in the city.

Robin took the money and put it in the cash box. She handed Duke a piece of paper and the marker and said, "Go mark it as sold."

"I was just going to put it in the back of the car." He looked at the marker like it might grow teeth and bite him.

"Oh, sure," Robin said, glancing over as another customer approached the table to check out. They carried a whole box of housewares, and it took Robin several minutes to go through them all and add up the cost.

By then, a line had formed, but she didn't mind the pressure. She talked and added, took money, and noted that the tip jar was collecting a fair bit of change.

Then Alice appeared at the end of the table, a full box in her hands too. "Things for Mandie and Charlie," she said. "I did a video for him, and I guess I'm a personal shopper now."

She smiled as brightly as the sun, and Robin reached for the first item—a pot that would boil water in under a minute. A pang of something—not quite jealousy, maybe being left out?—ran through her.

"Did you talk to Mandie?" Robin asked as she pulled out a set of salt and pepper shakers for a dollar.

"No, apparently, they're swamped at the drug store this morning getting their new autumn windows done." Alice peered at Robin. "I guess she told Charlie to figure it out, that he knew what they needed."

"I'm sure he does," Robin said, adding a five-dollar set of mixing bowls to the tally.

Alice laughed, the sound rich and reaching right up toward the heavens. "I'm sure he doesn't," she said. "He did his best, though, and I suppose that's all anyone can ask for."

"You're absolutely right," Robin said, the last of her pinching feelings leaving. Jean came through the line after Alice had taken her box of kitchen and housewares, and she offered Robin a cup of coffee.

"Mm, yes," Robin said. "It's been busy."

"Do you want a break?" Jean pointed up to the table. "Lena needs some help with the clothing table, and you looked like you could use a break."

Robin smiled gratefully at Jean and sipped her coffee. "I'll go see what I can do." As Robin moved to the clothing table, she noticed Eloise and her mother, Dawn, examining a collection of vintage teacups. Dawn looked better than she had at the wedding—more present, her eyes clearer. Robin made a mental note to check in with Eloise later about how things were going.

"Robin!" AJ called, approaching with Matt and Asher in tow. "Please tell me you have something to entertain a four-year-old who's already bored with every toy he owns."

Robin laughed and nodded over to another table in the horseshoe. "Check the toy table. Lena has amassed quite a collection of toys, puzzles, and games."

Asher darted off toward the toys while AJ sighed

dramatically. "We've been here for three minutes, baby. Wait for your dad."

"There's a truck," Matt said as he leaned in to kiss AJ's cheek. "You just don't know what it's like to be a four-year-old-truck-obsessed-boy."

"No, I do not," AJ said as Asher turned with the bright yellow truck in his hand and yelled, "Momma! Look!"

"I see it, buddy," Matt said, and he growled like a dump truck as he scooped Asher and the truck into his arms. The boy dissolved into giggles, and Robin's heart squeezed with love. She could so clearly remember when her girls giggled like that when Duke came home from fishing. They'd always been so excited to see him, ask him about the sea that day, and listen to his stories while they ate dinner.

It was amazing to her how much of a thief time could be.

"You look happy," Duke said, interrupting her thoughts.

"I am," Robin said, surprised to realize how true it was. "This is nice." She folded a t-shirt and placed it back in the sliding stack she'd made.

"What? Not running around making sure everything's perfect?" Duke teased, bumping her shoulder with his.

"I'm evolving," she said with a laugh. She nodded over to the tools. "Those look a little picked over. Will you go straighten them up? We still have an hour left."

The sun rose higher and higher through the sky, until it was very nearly overhead, and Robin never did return to the cash box. She let Jean and Clara run it, and at the end there, Lena joined them too.

"Thank you," she said loudly to everyone. "Thank you for coming."

Once the yard sale ended, Robin looked around. There were still quite a few items, but Lena had managed to lighten the load by at least half.

"Thank you everyone," Lena said, turning in a full cirlce and waving both of her hands.

Everyone cheered, and a surge of pride ran through Robin as she added her applause to the noise rising from the lighthouse. This day wasn't just about selling old items —it was about helping Lena establish her independence, about community coming together, about the connections that made Five Island Cove special.

"We'd love anyone to stay and help re-box everything up," Scott yelled. "We'll be hauling it all to Good Will, and some to the Veteran Helping Hands as well. They said they can use any clothing we have."

Robin and Duke stayed to help, and once they had everything boxed up, in Scott and Clara's SUV, and their tables in the back, Robin started making her good-byes. Kristen, AJ, and Alice had already left, so she went around and hugged Clara, Jean, and El, and then she joined Duke in the car.

"Lunch?" he asked.

Robin nodded, glad to be off her feet and out of the heat.

"Cravings?" Duke asked.

"Anything," Robin said with a smile.

"Heard from Mandie yet?" Duke asked. "If I'm not going out on the boat tomorrow, I should probably let Derrick know."

"Nothing yet," Robin said. "Honestly, hon, I don't think we'll go."

"No?"

Robin shook her head. "I know Alice and Arthur are going, and how much help could they possibly need?"

Duke looked over to her. "So we'll plan a trip to the city in a few weeks. Mid-week, when the hotels aren't crazy expensive and everyone's in school. We'll go to the outdoor markets, see their apartment, eat all the pizza we can, and come home."

He grinned as he eased onto the highway and started taking them away from the edge of the island and back toward downtown Diamond, where some of their favorite cafés and bistros waited.

Robin's phone chirped from her pocket, and she pulled it out, expecting a message from Jamie or perhaps an update on how much money Lena had raised to help with her expenses from Clara.

Instead, Mandie's name sat on the screen.

Alice and Arthur are going to help us move tomorrow, and I don't think you and Dad need to come. Charlie's dad offered to pay for movers for the bigger items we have in storage, so we're all set. I hope that's okay. Love you, Mom!

Robin stared at the message, a lump forming in her throat. It wasn't that she wanted to spend her Sunday helping move furniture up narrow stairs to an eighth-floor apartment in Brooklyn. But being excluded stung more than she expected.

"What is it?" Duke asked, glancing over to her.

"Mandie," Robin said, handing him the phone after he pulled into a parking space. "She doesn't need us to help with the move tomorrow."

Duke read the message, then handed the phone back. "That's probably for the best. Those stairs in their building looked like a nightmare."

"I know," Robin sighed. "It's just—I don't know. I thought I'd be there."

"For every step she takes?" Duke asked gently.

"No, of course not. That's ridiculous." Robin shook her head. "I just didn't expect to feel so...replaceable."

"You're not replaceable," Duke said firmly. "You're her mother. That will never change."

Robin nodded, knowing he was right but still feeling the ache of transition. Mandie was building her own life now—one that included Charlie's family as much as her own. It was natural, expected even. But that didn't make it easy.

"Come on, hon." Duke got out and rounded the car to open her door for her. "Look at it this way." He led her toward the Seafood Shack, his arm snaking around her and holding on tightly. "We have the whole day to ourselves tomorrow. Maybe I'll skip fishing and we can stay in bed until lunchtime, and then start planning that trip."

Robin managed a small smile, and then a laugh when Duke grinned at her. "Maybe we can."

She knew he wouldn't skip fishing. They wouldn't stay in bed until noon, and they still had a daughter at home. Perhaps they would plan a trip, but that just meant Robin had to find someone to stay with Jamie while they went to the city.

Not only that, but Robin still had one more wedding this year—Mandie and Charlie's in October.

That's six weeks from now, she told herself as Duke opened the door to the Seafood Shack and waited for Robin to enter first.

She wanted to live this moment, not plan for a future one. So she tucked her phone away, as well as the message from her daughter, determined not to let her worry about tomorrow—or October—define lunch with her husband.

Change was inevitable—children grew up, made their own choices, created their own families. That was how it was *supposed* to be. That was what she'd raised her girls to do.

Likewise, Robin had her own life to live, her own choices to make. Perhaps it was time to focus a little more on herself and Duke, on the relationship that had sustained her through raising those girls and building a career.

As they waited in line to order, Robin leaned into her husband's embrace, allowing herself to imagine possibilities beyond wedding planning, raising children, and being the best girl mom she could be—possibilities that belonged just to her and Duke.

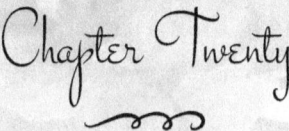

Chapter Twenty

A lice gripped the doorhandle in the backseat as the cab driver navigated through the chaotic Brooklyn traffic, horns blaring around them and pedestrians darting between cars with reckless abandon. The GPS had rerouted them three times already, and it seemed like they might never arrive at the right building.

We should be turning left here, she thought, but the driver made no effort to put on his blinker. She glanced down at her phone, where she'd put in the address and asked her app to map her to Charlie and Mandie's new apartment.

They definitely needed to turn left...right there.

She glanced over to Arthur as the cab flew past the street where she would've turned left. He looked at her and smiled, then reached over and took her phone from her. "He's driving; not you."

Small island life had definitely infected Alice's bloodstream, because she couldn't imagine living in the city like this. Once, it had been what revved her up, brought her joy. Now, she craved the slower, quieter streets of Five Island Cove, especially now that summer tourist season would officially end in only another week.

She and Arthur had spent the morning at a home goods store with Mandie and Charlie, getting all of the last-minute things they needed to turn their new apartment into a functional space to live.

They'd also brought over the boxes of items they'd wanted from the yard sale, and Robin said she'd ship them the cabinet they'd bought as well.

"Here you are," the cab driver said, and Alice blinked as she whipped her attention out the window.

"This isn't—"

"The front of the building is only accessible via the sidewalk," the driver said. "See? This street is pedestrian-only." He pointed straight in front of him, and Arthur opened his door.

"Thanks, brother," he said easily, and Alice hastened to follow him. The city air hit her—a mixture of exhaust, food from nearby restaurants, and that indefinable energy that was uniquely New York.

"We have a lot to carry," she said. "No one said we couldn't get dropped off in front of the building."

"This is a great place," Arthur said as the trunk lifted on hydraulics. He pulled out an enormous suitcase, and then the wheeled crate they'd bought at the home goods store. "We'll be able to get everything with this, remember?"

Alice felt like her head wasn't attached to her body, because no, she hadn't remembered they'd bought a wheeled crate to help them get everything up to the eighth floor—and Mandie and Charlie could take it to the grocery store and get their items home more easily too.

And bonus, it folded up flat, so they could store it in their place, which Charlie called, "a great deal," and Mandie called, "microscopic."

In the city, Alice believed both of their descriptions, and her anticipation of seeing the apartment for herself doubled.

She filled the crate with the few bags they had with them while Arthur hefted out the second suitcase.

Mandie and Charlie had brought three more suitcases between them, and their cab arrived just as Arthur closed the trunk. He banged on it, and their driver lifted his hand out of the open driver's window and called, "Thanks."

She helped Mandie and Charlie gather their first load of bags while trying to ignore how different this all felt from Five Island Cove. She looped the straps of an overnight bag over the handle of the crate, then adding another bag on top of it. Mandie and Charlie had packed up everything they owned and moved it over a hundred miles across the sea. This wasn't their first time doing it, though, and Alice marveled that two people's lives could be reduced to five suitcases, a few bags of purchased goods, and a wheeled crate, even as full as it was.

Oh, and their sofa set, their bed, and a nightstand they'd kept here in a storage unit in the city. Frank had paid a couple of guys to get those out of storage and deliver them to the apartment, and Alice looked up at the skyscraper in front of her as Charlie slammed the trunk on the second cab.

"All right," he said, reaching for the handle of one of the larger suitcases. "Can we get everything?"

"Yep," Mandie chirped, and they started down the street together, with Alice and Arthur bringing up the rear.

Alice had heard all about the apartment, the quad of buildings, and the courtyard between them. She'd looked at the website, which made the rooftop look positively enormous, and the pool like a tropical oasis only a stone's throw from a white sand beach.

Photos could so easily warp reality, and Alice's stomach thrummed with every step she took. In the lobby, Charlie and Mandie piled onto one elevator, and Alice put on as many suitcases as she could fit before the doors closed.

She and Arthur waited for the next car, with Mandie's keycard gripped in Alice's fingers. "This is a nice lobby, at least," Arthur said. "Look, you can see that courtyard through the door back there."

He nodded toward the back of the building, but Alice could barely see that far. Her anxiety over this move ran through her, but she wasn't sure why. "I just want to see the apartment," she said. "Then tour the courtyard."

"All right," Arhtur said easily, and he led the way onto the second elevator, then pulled on her suitcase too. They rode up to the eighth floor in an elevator that had definitely been faster in previous years.

Alice got spit out on the eighth floor, which was one long hall that went to the right and left, with the elevator right in the middle. Windows stood sentinel on both ends, but there was no salt breeze. No sound of gulls. No neighbors waving as they passed.

"Down there," Arthur said, nodding past her. Alice looked right to find Charlie waving to them from the end of the hall.

Alice steered her suitcase in that direction, soaking in the smile on her son's face. So maybe they didn't know another soul in this building, but strangers could become friends. And with a pedestrian-only street in front of the build, there wouldn't be the constant rumble of traffic.

In fact, as Alice approached, an actual tree stood outside the window, almost reminding her that beauty could be found in many places—even big cities with tall buildings and homes stacked on top of each other.

"Home sweet home." Charlie gestured for Alice to enter, and she left the suitcase for him to wrangle as she stepped over the threshold and into the apartment.

"The windows," she said, being hit with the sight of them immediately. They started about halfway up the wall and went all the way to the ceiling. Cabinets in the strip kitchen against the back wall broke up the windows, but one stood tall above the sink and let in plenty of light.

Frank had worked his magic, because the furniture had arrived, and the table had even been unwrapped and the plastic wrapping removed.

"The couch isn't where we want it," Charlie said. "But Arthur and I can move it."

"Sure thing, bud," Arthur said as he bumped the wheels of the suitcase into the apartment. "The AC works great too."

"Can you believe it has central AC?" Charlie let the door close behind him, and he reached to twist the deadbolt. Alice's mama-heart twisted too, because at least she could sleep at night knowing Charlie took security seriously.

The flooring throughout the apartment said many others had lived here, with every line and scratch having its own unique story to tell.

"Where's that rug?" Mandie asked as she came out of the bathroom.

"Dad said he'd left it on the bed."

She detoured into the bedroom, which only had a large sliding barn door to separate it from the main living space. "We have to put that down first, and anchor the couches on it."

With the bathroom, the whole place had two and a half rooms and couldn't be much bigger than a hotel suite.

"This is great, Charles." She wrapped her arm around his waist and leaned into his height.

"It's a little small," Charlie said. "But it's just me and Mandie, and we're going to use the table for a desk."

"You've got a little nook here," Arthur said, peering into the corner behind the wall of the bedroom. "I'm sure we could get something there, and it's right in front of the window."

"We got the end unit, too," Mandie said as she smiled around at the apartment and then laid out the rug. "So we have extra windows—and our balcony overlooks the courtyard."

"Yes," Alice said, moving forward to look out the windows. "This is very nice, you two."

"Suitcases in the bedroom," Charlie said, and he dragged two of them in that direction. Alice stayed in the kitchen while Arthur, Mandie, and Charlie each put a suitcase on the bed—which still needed to be made—and started unpacking clothes, linens, and towels.

Something beautiful touched Alice's heart as she watched them claim this space as their own, chatting about plans to put a couple of potted plants out on their tiny terrace, seeing possibilities rather than limitations.

Alice towed another suitcase toward the room and positioned it just outside. When Charlie finished with his, she took it and moved it over into the little nook. She and Arthur would nest the suitcases and take them home with them, only to bring them back if Charlie and Mandie needed to move again.

But now that they were getting married, Alice suspected they'd simply stay in the city during the summertime, where they'd been returning to the cove to work for the past couple of years.

Bit by bit, every article of clothing got hung in the closet, and Arthur assembled the over-the-toilet shelving, where Mandie then put their towels, wash cloths, and a stack of toilet paper.

Arthur and Charlie moved the couches where they wanted them, and Alice made up the bed while Mandie pulled out the kitchen items and situated them in the cupboards where she wanted them. She didn't mind cooking, and Alice took a moment to watch the younger woman as she bent to put the yard sale items with the things she and Charlie already owned.

Love filled her and filled her and filled her, and all of her doubts about Mandie and Charlie evaporated. They'd come to the city by themselves. They'd found this apartment. They'd both continue their educations, learn how to make a marriage work, and build a life together.

"And that cabinet will go here," Charlie said. "We can put our books in it, and anything else that doesn't have a home."

"No, we're not using that cabinet as a junk cabinet," Mandie said, giving him a pointed look. "You have drawers in the kitchen for that."

"Drawers aren't big enough for some junk," Charlie said, grinning at her.

She cocked one hip at him, her high ponytail swinging as she did. "You've used our credenza for that in the past. That's where your 'big junk' items go, Mister."

He tipped his head back and laughed, stumbling over

to Mandie and wrapping her in his arms. It took her a moment or two to soften, and then she giggled with him.

They did have a dark brown, wood credenza opposite of the couch, with a TV standing black and blank on top of it.

"Jean made us some pillows." Mandie stepped out of Charlie's arms. "But she's shipping them this week, so we don't have them yet."

Alice looked around at the apartment, which practically shone with homeyness. Her husband tucked one of the two chairs further under the table pushed against the wall, and said, "This is a great place, you guys. You're going to love it here."

"Do you want a tour of the rooftop space and the courtyard?" Charlie asked.

"And we can probably get lunch out in the courtyard," Mandie said, moving a few steps and plucking a paper that had been magneted to the fridge. "We get a list of what will be available every week. Let's see...today is Sunday..."

Charlie joined her and peered over her shoulder. "They have macaroons, a coffee cart, and oooh, paninis."

"In the courtyard?" Alice asked, her eyebrows going up at the same time she spoke.

Charlie looked up, and he shone as brightly as the sunshine coming in the windows. "I told you, Mama. They have agreements with carts and street vendors to come in and sell in the courtyard."

"And there's a great bodega right across the street,"

Mandie said. "Around the corner, maybe only a hundred yards away."

"The rolling crate will still be useful," Charlie said. "Mandie loves ice cream, and that stuff is heavy." He grinned at her, took the paper from her, and stuck it back to the fridge. "We can grab lunch down there, or walk down the street and see what else is nearby."

"And get groceries on the way back," Alice said, as she'd volunteered to fill Mandie and Charlie's fridge with food as they started the first semester of their junior year.

She'd done the same for Ginny, but she'd just sent her daughter with money, as Bob's parents had helped get them settled into the brownstone where they'd be living. Alice had plans to get to Boston in a few weeks, where she'd see her daughter, check out her living conditions, and go from there.

Ginny had sent her a complete video walk-through, complete with gushing about the "garden level office, Mom! That's what they call it—a garden!"

Alice had grinned and grinned along with Ginny as she showed Bob's office in the basement level of Eloise's four-story brownstone in a coveted neighborhood in Boston's Back Bay.

"Let's go," Charlie said. "I'm starving."

Alice watched as Mandie grabbed her purse without hesitation, clearly already comfortable navigating their new neighborhood. It struck her then—these weren't children playing house. They were young adults creating a life together, figuring things out as they went, just as she'd been so eager to do at their age.

A marriage at twenty to his high school girlfriend wasn't what she'd planned for her son, but maybe that was the point. He wasn't following her blueprint—he was creating his own.

TUESDAY MORNING FOUND ALICE ENTERING THE post office on Five Island Cove, a familiar sense of anticipation and dread mingling in her stomach. The lighthouse title still hadn't arrived, and she was going to get to the bottom of it today.

To-day.

She fitted her key into her legal box, her heart doing a complete bellyflop when she found an envelope inside. Her fingers shook for a moment as she fished it out, but she took one look at the top left corner and knew it wasn't from the Massachusetts Land Court. With a sigh, she tucked the envelope into her purse and stepped into the room where Mabel processed packages and solved problems.

"Morning, Mabel," she said.

Mabel abandoned her work station a few feet from the counter, her expression earnest as she came closer. "I'm so sorry there's nothing yet."

"It's okay," Alice said, a genuine smile touching her

face. "I'm going to call them again, because something isn't right."

"I even called," Mabel said. "Yesterday, because I knew you were still in the city. I told them the tracking number wasn't right, because we couldn't see anything on it."

Alice reached over and covered Mabel's hand with her. "How sweet. Thank you. What did they say?"

"They'd look—"

"—Into it," Alice said with her, already nodding. "Yes, I've been told that too." She suppressed the sigh threatening to steal her breath. "Thank you, Mabel. I'll call them."

She smiled herself out of the post office, and since she ran a law office of one, she had time to sit in her car right there in the parking lot and make the call. She had promised Robin they'd go to lunch today, and Alice would tell her all about the move over the weekend, though she knew Mandie had already called her mother and filled her in.

She dialed the now-familiar number for the Land Court Clerk's Office, mentally rehearsing what she would say. No more polite acceptance of excuses. She needed answers.

"Massachusetts Land Court, how may I direct your call?"

"Denise Johnson, please," Alice said firmly. "This is Alice Rice calling about the Five Island Cove lighthouse title."

"One moment."

The hold music played for what felt like an eternity before Denise's voice came on the line. "This is Denise." How she chirped her name like that *every* time she picked up the phone, Alice didn't know. Maybe an unending supply of candy.

"Denise, it's Alice Rice again," she began, keeping her tone professional but insistent. "I still haven't received the lighthouse title, and the tracking number you provided doesn't appear in the USPS system. There's a problem, and I need to know what it is, so I can get it resolved."

"Alice," Denise said. "You're saving me a call today. I know where your title is."

Alice pulled in a breath. "You do?" she asked when she wanted to snap, *And?*

"Yes, it's sitting right here on my desk."

The air in Alice's lungs leaked out, and she couldn't control it, keep it in. Confusion rode her brows down into a V. "Your desk? What—I'm so confused."

"I thought we'd mailed it out," she said. "But it got stuck to another piece of mail, got knocked loose in the machine at the post office, and returned to us."

"You're joking."

"I'm mailing it today," Denise said. "And I was going to call you with a new tracking number. Can you take that down now? A real one."

"Yes," Alice said, diving into her purse to find a pen. "I can take that number down now."

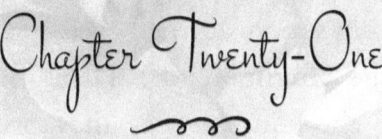

Chapter Twenty-One

T he door clicked closed behind Eloise with a finality that settled into her bones. The Cliffside Inn stood quiet in the noonday hush, the kind of silence that came only after the last guest had departed and no new ones would arrive. Not today, not tomorrow. Not ever again— at least under her care.

Rich and Sarah Eagan would own Cliffside in an hour, and they'd handle check-in on this solemn Wednesday afternoon.

She stood in the foyer for a long moment, her hand still on the golden handle behind her, her eyes traveling slowly across the wide-planked floors she'd refinished herself before re-opening the inn here in Five Island Cove.

The front desk sat pristine and vacant, her grandmother's crystal vase no longer holding their fresh flowers, the computer powered down now that check-out had finished.

They operated on a robust staff during the day, with

the personnel managers, Marge in the kitchen, and maids turning over rooms and prepping for check in and dinnertime.

But Eloise, Sarah, and Rich had agreed that Eloise would get the inn's rooms turned over, and then everyone would have the afternoon off. Then, Julia and Clara would handle check-in the way they usually did, and Marge would have dinner on the table for tonight's guests.

Eloise would be back on Diamond Island by then, getting dinner ready for her family.

"It's okay to cry," she whispered to herself, her throat tightening as she finally stepped away from the door. She walked past the breakfast nook where the smell of cinnamon rolls had once greeted her on select mornings, where Billie had written her first middle school essay on the corner table while waiting for Grace to finish swimming lessons in the inn's pool.

Every square inch of this place held a memory. A version of herself. A version of her friends, the employees who had become family.

She moved into the kitchen, the stainless steel gleaming under the overhead lights. Marge had left a note on the fridge—*Love you, El. Don't be a stranger*—held in place with a magnet shaped like a crab wearing sunglasses. Eloise touched the paper gently, then pulled it down and tucked the note in her pocket. A goodbye didn't have to mean a severing.

She paused at the French doors that led to the back

patio and pool, pressed her palm against the glass, and looked out at the ocean.

The cliffs dropped off just beyond the lawn, and the water stretched out beyond them, a shifting slate of blue and green with streaks of foam. The breeze fluttered the gauzy curtains at the edges of the doors.

She pulled out her phone, because she didn't need to wander the inn like a ghost, weeping over something she'd worked for, that she wanted. *Where are we meeting for lunch today?* she asked. *Am I too late to come?*

She hit send to the group thread and waited only a beat before the replies came in.

Robin: *You're never too late for a Wednesday luncheon. We just sat down at The Blue Buoy.*

Kelli: *Everyone's not even here yet. AJ missed the ferry.*

AJ: *Yeah, I won't be there for another twenty minutes. Clara is with me.*

Alice: *Kristen and I are waiting for a RideShare. The ferry was insane this morning.*

I was already on Sanctuary, Robin said. *I didn't realize.*

Eloise turned to leave the inn, tapping to call a ride as she went. The Blue Buoy served amazing seafood baskets down on the western beach of Sanctuary, and it would only take her ten minutes to get there once she got a RideShare.

I was at the library with Tessa, Jean said. *We finished up plans for the Seafaring Girl end-of-summer shindig this weekend on time, but the ferry system is a mess.*

We'll get there as fast as we can, Tessa said. *They're supposedly bringing another ferry from the Pearl-Bell route to replace the one that went down a couple of hours ago.*

The ferries are off, because they lost one on the route from Diamond to Sanctuary, Laurel said almost on top of that. *Oh, Tessa just said that.* She included a smiley emoji with it.

So I'm fortunate I live on Sanctuary, Julia said.

I'm on the way too, Maddy said. *Sorry if that mixes up the seating.*

It won't, Robin said. *There are enough seats for everyone.*

Eloise's phone chimed as she stepped outside, a signal that her ride was only a mile away. Eloise walked to the end of the sidewalk, arriving in the circle drive of the inn, the scent of late summer blooms still perfuming the air.

The breeze tangled in her hair as she took in the eastern view of the Atlantic Ocean. That hadn't changed; the water still danced, the sky still stretched endlessly above it, the smell of salt perpetually hung in the air.

Only *she* had changed.

Her RideShare arrived, and Eloise slid into the back seat with the words, "The Blue Buoy, please."

"You got it." The driver tapped on his phone for a moment, then looked out the windshield and eased away from the Cliffside Inn as easy as breathing. Eloise looked at it—that golden-pink stone she loved with her whole heart —and pressed her palm against the glass separating her from the inn.

The car moved around the corner and started down the hill, and just like that, the inn disappeared behind Eloise, both physically and in every other way.

She sat back in her seat and sighed, catching the attention of the driver. "You okay?" he asked.

Eloise nodded. "Yes."

"You own that place, don't you?" he asked.

"I just sold it," Eloise said, the words growing teeth in her mouth. "That was my last morning there." She gave him a smile and looked out the window, because by showing up at this luncheon, she'd have to tell ten more people she was okay.

Are you okay?

The question rang through her head in her own voice.

As she watched the familiar landscape of Sanctuary Island flow by, from cliffs to beach, Eloise smiled to herself.

Because she was absolutely okay.

She found Robin, Kelli, Alice, Julia, Maddy, and Kristen holding down a table for twelve out on the patio behind The Blue Buoy. She sank into a chair beside Kelli and sighed. "Hey, everyone."

"Oh, you're here." Robin reached across the table and squeezed her hand. "How was this morning?"

"Good," Eloise said. "Normal." She looked at her and then Alice. "I don't want to explain it to everyone. It was a good morning, and I wanted to sell the inn."

"Doesn't mean it's not emotional," Alice said while Kristen simply patted Eloise's hand.

"Right," Eloise said. "But I wasn't forced out. I actually made a lot of money on the sale of the inn. I'm not unhappy. It's just..."

Thankfully, Laurel, AJ, and Clara arrived, which stole the attention from her as everyone greeted them.

"Jean and Tessa are still about twenty minutes away," Clara said as she sat down next to Kristen. "But Jean texted me their orders, so we don't have to wait."

A pair of waitresses appeared, and drink orders got put in. Eloise caught one's attention and asked, "Can we get a basket of calamari and those seafood fritters for the table? Put them on my bill."

"Sure thing," the young woman said. "Anyone else want any appetizers?"

"I want the chips and street corn," Alice said, which drew a lot of raised eyebrows. Alice ate, but Eloise couldn't think of a time she'd ordered or eaten chips.

"What?" Alice asked. "I thought today was a celebration luncheon."

"Is it?" Robin asked.

"Yes," Kristen said with a smile. "So everyone get ready with one thing you're celebrating from this amazing summer."

Eloise volleyed her gaze from Kristen to Alice, but neither of them jumped right into their celebrations. The drinks came out quickly, and individual conversations broke out. Eloise sat between Kelli and AJ, and they spoke past her about their kids.

Eloise wasn't bothered that she wasn't involved in the

conversation. Her work at the inn had prevented her from attending so many of these luncheons, and she simply enjoyed that she could be here today, guilt-free.

She had nothing else pulling at her, demanding her attention—and it felt so, so good. Every woman at this table had shown up for her, for Aaron, or for one of the girls so many times.

Love seemed to reverberate through her in waves, and when she looked across the table, Robin's eyebrows went up. "What?" Eloise asked.

"You're quiet."

"Yeah," she said, lifting her Shirley Temple to her lips. "I'm the quiet one of the group."

"That's so not true," AJ said. "Kelli was the quiet one of our group."

Eloise grinned over to Kelli. "Never in terms of personality, though. She just knows that not everything has to be said out loud."

"Tell my son that, would you?" Kelli asked with a roll of her eyes. "He told me this week that I can't—and I quote—nag him to death this year."

"Over school?" Eloise asked.

Kelli nodded and sipped her pomegranate tea. "He doesn't get the best of grades. I told him he has to try in math this year, now that he'll be in high school, and that if he at least tries, he can go to the lighthouse the way he likes. If not..."

"Wow," AJ said. "You threatened to take the lighthouse from him?"

The lighthouse had always been the one place Eloise had felt safe, and she knew it still felt like that for some of the women at this table.

"He skipped a lot of classes last year," Kelli said. "And I was too busy and distracted to keep up. Plus, I thought—it's eighth grade. I get why he didn't care. But this is high school."

Robin nodded. "The high school grades matter, and it's hard to drive that point home to a teenager."

Eloise followed the conversation, because she had two teenagers now. Billie would be a junior this year, while Grace was still at the junior high...in eighth grade. Apparently, it had been Parker's hardest year, as well as Jamie's, and Eloise was so glad she'd be around more to help her girls.

The appetizers came out, and Eloise took some of everything as it went around. Jean and Tessa arrived, and the waitresses reappeared to take their drink orders and then get everyone's food order.

Eloise ordered the coconut shrimp basket and switched from her nonalcoholic Shirley Temple to an apple martini.

"I love calamari," she said, to which Alice and Robin agreed. With everyone there, it was way too hard to try to keep up with every conversation, so Eloise didn't even try.

"Okay," Alice called, lifting one hand into the air to get everyone's attention. When that didn't work with Maddy, Jean, and Tessa down on the end, Kristen whistled through her teeth.

"Ladies," Robin said into the resulting silence. "Alice and I would like to do a celebration announcement, kind of like how we do with our Tell-Alls or New Truths."

"So it can be a New Truth," Alice said.

"Or a Tell-All," Robin said. "We just want to get caught up. See, some of us have a Summer Sand Pact, where we unite like this every summer here in Five Island Cove, and now that you're all part of us, we want to extend that to you."

Eloise smiled, because she knew plenty of people who didn't maintain relationships with the people they grew up with. Heck, just seven years ago, Eloise had lived alone in her Boston brownstone, hardly speaking to anyone at this very table.

That thought reminded her that she'd made huge changes in her life in the past, and they'd blessed her life so richly.

"I'll go first," Robin said. "I'm celebrating my summer of weddings, having done six weddings in only three months, and though I have one more to go, this was one of my biggest, most successful summers yet."

"To the summer of weddings," Alice called, lifting her drink.

"To the summer of weddings!" Eloise joined her voice with the others and clinked her glass against Kelli's, AJ's, and Kristen's before taking a fruity sip.

"And as part of that celebration," Robin said. "I'm going to open a wedding planning firm and bring on at least one full-time person to help me with details."

"Wow," Alice said, her eyes wide. A tickle of surprise moved through Eloise too, but she applauded for Robin all the same.

"I'm celebrating the fact that both of my children are moved back to school," Alice said, continuing the chain. "And my New Truth is that I'm going to find some parenting classes specifically for how to deal with adult children."

"That's your celebration?" Eloise asked, shooting a look at Kristen.

"Yep." Alice looked at Tessa, who blinked at her.

"Dave moved in, and things are going well." She leaned past Alice and looked at Robin. "We might need to get on your schedule for a wedding...at some point."

"I'll have you call my new assistant," Robin said without missing a beat.

Eloise smiled as Jean said, "I had a great summer with the Seafaring Girls," she said. "That's what I'm going to celebrate."

"To the Seafaring Girls," Kristen said, and everyone lifted their glasses again.

Maddy grinned around at everyone as glasses got reset. "Ben and I are going on a cruise."

"For Christmas," Julia said from the other end of the table. "You'd think a man who spends most of his time on a boat would like to take a land vacation." She grinned from one corner of the table to the other, her eyes locked on Maddy.

"We like the rocking of the boat," she said.

A beat of silence covered the table, and then AJ giggled and said, "All right then," before Eloise burst out laughing. She loved her girlfriends, and they definitely had their problems, with some splinter groups that made others feel left out, and so many of them in different stages of life. They sometimes gossiped about one another, but they rarely brought their husbands into anything.

"I'm celebrating that Asher loves his pre-school," AJ said. "And my New Truth is that I'm going to start my own sports journalism YouTube Channel."

"What?" Eloise asked, her shock more palpable now. "Your own channel?"

"I thought you wrote columns," Alice said.

"I'm a sports reporter," AJ said. "And so many people do things from home on YouTube. I think we should do a channel on how to survive on islands." She looked around at everyone on the table. "People are fascinated by things like that—just search for channels on Alaska. You'll see."

Eloise would probably not do that search, but she believed AJ, and she reached around and gave her a quick side-hug. "That's awesome AJ. I hope it goes really well for you."

AJ wore bright eyes as she nodded. "Thanks, El. Your turn."

"I'm obviously celebrating the sale of the inn," she said, a true, genuine smile coming to her face. "Today was my last day, and I left the keys at the front desk for the Eagans."

She'd removed the security camera app from her

phone, and she didn't have to do any paperwork tonight to prep next week's menu, handle time-off requests, or work on her fall social media campaign.

"To the Cliffside Inn," Kelli said, grinning at El.

She ducked her head, shook it, and smiled as everyone else at the table called, "To the Cliffside Inn!"

Kelli took a breath. "I'm going to do a New Truth." She fiddled with her silverware for a moment. "Shad's going to quit at City Hall...and come work for me at Whole Soul."

She beamed then, clearly having been holding onto this news for just such an occasion.

"You didn't tell me that," AJ practically yelled, and Eloise had only known Shad wasn't very happy at work. Nothing more.

"We've been talking about it all summer," she said. "He's going to put in his notice next week and finish out the year. Then, we'll probably move to Bell to be closer to the studio." She shrugged one shoulder. "I'm very excited about it."

"Working together," Robin said. "As husband and wife. That'll be interesting."

"You hope she doesn't kill him, you mean," Alice said good-naturedly.

"I'm not sure I could do it," Robin said. "That's all."

"I think you'll do great," Eloise reassured Kelli, who seemed to thrive under the words.

They looked at Clara, who smiled around at everyone. "I think I'm celebrating that I finally feel like I belong here in Five Island Cove." Her eyes turned glassy, and she quickly reached for her mojito. She took a sip and looked at Laurel. "That's it for me."

Laurel waited, watching Clara for a moment before switching her gaze to Robin. "No one's going to force her to say more?"

"We don't *force*," Robin said.

"I've felt forced sometimes." AJ raised her hand and grinned at Robin.

"I only *insist gently* when I think it'll be good for you," Robin said, shaking her shoulders and drawing herself up tall. "And no, I'm not going to gently insist that Clara tell us more. I'm so glad she feels like she belongs here in the cove, with us, because she does."

"You really do," Laurel said. "My Tell-All is that I'm completely overwhelmed with two little kids. I'm outnumbered all day, and when Paul gets home, they act like he's the better parent." She sighed, and Eloise wanted to reach out and hug her.

Alice started to twitter, and so did Maddy.

"That's motherhood," Julia said. "It's the most wonderful thing in the world—and the most thankless."

"I see you, though," Eloise said. "And now that I'm not at the inn, I can come get one or both of the kids almost any day."

"I see you too," Robin said. "I've had those two little kids and a busy husband, and sometimes the days feel twenty-four years long."

"I see you," Alice said, and tears pricked Eloise's eyes.

Laurel wiped at hers as Kristen said, "I see you, Laurel," and so did Clara and Jean, AJ, Kelli, and Tessa.

Laurel sniffled and nodded, then took a long pull on her virgin peach cooler.

"I guess I'm going to celebrate being married again," Julia said.

"So things are great with Liam?" Robin asked.

"Really amazing, yes." Julia looked at Kristen, the last of them to say something.

She took a moment, then bent down and lifted something from her purse. "The title for the lighthouse arrived this morning."

Eloise sucked in a breath, a shriek building in her throat. But Robin beat her to it, emitting a little scream and grabbing the official piece of paper from Kristen.

"You're kidding."

"She's not kidding," Alice said, pure pride riding on her face. "Mabel brought it to my house. She rang the bell at seven-thirty."

Eloise lifted her martini. "To the lighthouse!"

Glasses got lifted again, and Kristen seemed to radiate the same light the lighthouse did on foggy nights.

"To the lighthouse!"

HER MOTHER'S HOUSE STOOD JUST AS IT ALWAYS had—white clapboard siding, green shutters, a riotous garden still clinging to its greenery for the year.

"Thanks," she said to the RideShare driver, and she stepped out of the car. She'd driven the girls to school for the first day of school, and then Eloise's whole day sat open before her.

Except for this one conversation she needed to have with her mom.

The door opened before she could knock. Her mother stood there, a cat twining around her ankles, her steel-gray hair pinned up in loose curls. "El, I wasn't expecting you today, was I?"

Eloise gave her mom the best smile she could muster. "Yes, Mom." She lifted the bag that held the bagel breakfast sandwiches her mother loved. "We planned to have breakfast in your backyard before fall really gets here."

She refrained from adding on, "Remember?" because Mom obviously didn't remember. Eloise stepped up into the house and moved past her mother. Her other two cats lounged on the armchair, and a kettle whistled softly on the stove. The scent of herbs and dryer sheets hung in the air as Eloise went into the kitchen.

"Your kettle is boiling," she said.

"Yes," Mom said. "I was just making us tea."

Only a single cup and bag sat ready on the countertop, but Eloise said nothing as her mother bustled around and made two cups of tea. She pulled out their sandwiches, and they sat at the kitchen table, the same one Eloise had done her homework on, the same one that had once been covered in bills, or a simple family meal, or a half-finished puzzle.

Her mother took a bite of her sausage, egg, and cheese bagel, her eyes somewhere out the window behind Eloise.

"I know you want to stay here," Eloise said as she unwrapped her sandwich. But she didn't think she could eat before getting all the words out of her mouth. "I know it's hard to think about leaving this house where you've lived for so long."

Her mother set down her sandwich and picked up her teacup. She usually fired back at Eloise, but today, she simply sipped silently.

"I'm not trying to take your independence," Eloise said, her voice cracking as her emotions overcame her. "I found a place on Diamond Island I think you would love. It's close to me, Aaron, and the girls. You'd have your own apartment. Your own space. And they allow cats."

Her mother blinked. "Three cats?"

"All three," Eloise said with a smile. "Yes, it's in a senior community, but Mom, you'd be so happy there. They play dominoes every Saturday and have tons of other games and activities."

And best of all, she'd only be ten minutes away from Eloise, instead of an hour.

Silence stretched between them.

Then, softly, her mother said, "It's probably for the best."

Eloise blinked. "You—what?" Hope ballooned inside her, but Eloise pushed against it, because the most dangerous thing in the world was hope.

"What do I have to do?" Mom asked. "Fill out an application?"

Eloise scrambled for her phone. "We can do it online."

Her mother looked at Eloise's phone like it had transformed into a scorpion. Then she took a sip of tea, picked up her sandwich and took a bite, and met Eloise's eye. She nodded, and while Eloise would like a verbal agreement that she'd move to Diamond Island, she'd take a nod if that was all she could get.

Chapter Twenty-Two

K risten breathed in the crisp September air as she made her way along the lighthouse trail, savoring the gentle resistance in her knees—a familiar companion these days, but not an unwelcome one. The path on this part of the trail wound through low scrub and sea grass, still damp with morning dew despite the sun having risen hours ago. The lighthouse stood tall against the cloudless sky ahead, its whitewashed walls gleaming.

"You're awfully quiet this morning," Jean said from beside her. Her dark hair was pulled back into a practical ponytail, and she wore a light jacket against the autumn chill that had begun creeping into Five Island Cove.

"Just enjoying the walk," Kristen said. And she was. After the whirlwind of this summer—the weddings, the yard sale, the lighthouse title finally coming through— there was something precious about an ordinary day with no particular agenda.

"I can't believe how perfect the weather is," Clara said from behind them. "The forecast said rain this whole week."

"The cove has its own weather system," AJ said. "Matt says the golf course gets sun when it's raining at the south beach."

Laurel, who had been trailing slightly behind with baby Emily strapped to her chest, caught up with them at the bend in the path. "Paul thinks the islands create some kind of microclimate."

Kristen smiled to herself as the women debated the peculiarities of Five Island Cove weather. These walks had become a cherished time for her, and she'd miss them when the colder weather forced her indoors.

Her knees would really act up then, and Kristen also strongly disliked being up and out of her condo before the sun rose. She usually spent winters baking, then taking her wares around to anyone she thought might need them during the sunniest parts of the day.

"Anyone heard from Eloise today?" Jean went first up the final incline to the flatter land where the lighthouse stood.

"It's barely nine o'clock," AJ said, matching Jean's pace.

Kristen let them all go ahead of her, because she'd be slow going up this final hill. Honestly, she felt slower and slower with each passing season, though walking with her girls helped her feel younger and more vibrant than she would've otherwise.

She listened to the others talk about Dawn and Eloise, speculating on whether the move would really happen or not. Eloise had been jubilant when she'd texted a couple of weeks ago to say she'd finally convinced her mother that a move to Diamond Island wasn't a loss of independence, but a way to maintain it.

Kristen had helped her by giving her the folder of research she'd done on the fifty-five-plus communities on the island, and Eloise had found a spot at one of the older ones, on the northeast side of town, before the wilds and cliffs took over and dropped off into the ocean.

She'd congratulated Eloise along with everyone else, but now, it was time to start packing and moving some of Dawn's items, with the goal of having her fully out of the house on Sanctuary and into the apartment here on Diamond before Mandie's wedding.

Then, Eloise wouldn't have to worry about storms preventing her from getting to Sanctuary, her mother wandering off in the dead of winter, or Dawn's symptoms worsening when Eloise couldn't be near enough to help.

She finally gained the top of the hill, where the other ladies had stopped to wait for her. Jean pretended she needed to stretch, but she just didn't like leaving Kristen behind.

"I'm heading over to help her pack some of her kitchen things after this," Kristen said. "Eloise said they're moving things slowly over the next couple of weeks."

"Moving from island to island is a huge pain," AJ said. "I can't believe Kelli's going to do it in the winter."

"Yeah, I'm going to try to be really sick that week." Clara grinned at everyone as she took the first step toward the lighthouse parking lot.

The title now rested safely in the lighthouse, where Reuben took care of it and everyone who needed a light in the darkness. She couldn't remember the last time she'd been as thrilled as she'd been when Alice had showed her the official documentation of what she'd always known in her heart—this beacon belonged to her family, as well as to this community.

They paused in the parking lot, where Jean moved to hug AJ. "I'm going to bundle Heidi up tomorrow, so I'm going to walk in your neighborhood."

"Perfect," AJ said. "Asher goes to pre-school at nine."

"So I'll come about then," Jean said.

"I'm helping Lena with a couch cover tomorrow," Clara said. "So I'm won't be there."

"I'll be brave and bring both kids," Laurel said. "My new double-stroller got here, and the wheels on this one actually work."

All eyes came to Kristen, and she smiled at them. "I can be at AJ's around nine-fifteen."

The group broke up with calls of "'Bye," and "See you tomorrow."

Kristen looked up at the structure that had been the backdrop to her entire life. Reuben took immaculate care of it, the same way his father had before him. Thankfully, it would continue to be what it always had been—a light to guide people home.

Kristen found herself missing Joel, and she quickly ducked her head and headed for the sidewalk so she could call a RideShare.

"Mom? I can drive you," Clara called out her open window. "You're going to the ferry, right?"

Kristen nodded and went to get in the car with her daughter. Sometimes she felt so stifled, as she couldn't talk about her late husband with her friends—and certainly not with her daughter. He and Clara had never gotten along, and she'd left the cove the moment she could to get as far from him as possible.

In fact, Kristen had barely gotten Clara to come to his funeral. She'd thought their problems were normal for a dad and daughter, but then other things had come out about her husband. Kristen still mourned him in a lot of ways, and she'd had no one to work through her complicated feelings with.

"Mom," Clara said, glancing over to her. "Do you think I held Lena back?"

"Of course not," Kristen said instantly.

"She's just doing so well in her new place, and I don't think I'd have ever investigated it if she hadn't seen the fliers at the grocery store."

"You did what you thought was best with the information you had," Kristen said. "That's all any of us can do as parents."

"I know. But seeing her thrive now...it makes me wonder what else she might be capable of that I've never considered."

"I can see why you feel like that," Kristen said. "What would be one of those things? School?" Lena had graduated from high school just fine, but she'd never gone to college. Scott and Clara had taught her everything she knew how to do, including cleaning around the house, simple cooking skills, and how to make and keep a budget.

She didn't drive, but she didn't have to, and lots of people didn't drive here or even own cars.

"Yeah," Clara said. "Perhaps she can take some online classes."

"Lena doesn't like the computer much," Kristen said gently.

"I'm going to ask her about it anyway." Clara put on her blinker and pulled into the ferry station. "Good luck with Dawn."

"Thanks for the ride, dear." Kristen took a moment and looked at her daughter, cataloguing the dark hair and eyes, so characteristic of her own reflection. "I love you."

"Love you too, Mom." Clara smiled, and Kristen headed in to catch the next ferry to Sanctuary Island.

As she waited, she found herself reflecting on how different her life looked now than it had a handful of years ago. The grief over Joel's death had softened into something more complex—an appreciation for what had been real and good in their marriage, an acceptance of the painful truths that had emerged after his passing, and gratitude for the life she'd built since.

The ferry arrived, and Kristen boarded, choosing a seat near the railing where she could watch the water. The journey to Sanctuary Island took about twenty-five minutes, but she treasured these moments of transition, suspended between destinations.

She climbed from the car at Dawn's house, her heartbeat suddenly trembling in her chest. She knew Dawn, of course, but they weren't close. She knocked and stepped back, expecting Eloise to open the door and welcome her inside the house.

But Dawn stood on the other side of the door as it opened, and her face brightened. "Kristen, hello." She looked past her, her gaze returning quickly. "What are you doing here?"

"I came to help you go through a few things in your kitchen," she said warmly. "Can I come in?"

"Sure." Dawn stepped back without asking any more questions, which alarmed Kristen a little bit. "El left a bunch of boxes for me."

"Yes," Kristen said as Dawn closed the door. "I thought she was going to be here."

"She texted a little bit ago and said something had come up at the station, and she'd be here later."

"Okay," Kristen said, and she entered the kitchen to find the countertops covered with everything from little bottles of spices to small appliances like a toaster, a hand mixer, and a Belgian waffle iron.

"It looks like you've started," Kristen said lightly, though not a single item had been put in a box.

"I don't know what to keep and what to get rid of,"

Dawn said. "It seems that everything I see holds a memory I don't want to lose."

"I understand," Kristen said, because she had gone through the same thing. "After Joel died, I had to go through everything we owned and decide what was worth keeping."

She picked up a whisk attachment and then set it back down. "You know what I learned by doing that?"

Dawn watched her with wide open eyes, but she remained silent.

Kristen looked down at the cat rubbing up against her leg. She smiled, as a stray feline hung around the condos who she put food out for from time to time.

"I learned that every object, every thing, every item you've accumulated had a purpose in that time. It meant something to the person you were when you got it and used it."

She took in the enormity of cooking and baking utensils, wondering how many Dawn actually used. "But you're a different person now, and not every item you own needs to go with you. Only the most important ones, for *this* time of your life."

Kristen picked up a bottle of nutmeg. "So. Do you make many things with nutmeg these days?"

"I don't even know when I bought that," Dawn said, her eyes bright and keen. "And no, I don't bake much these days."

"When I had people come help me," Kristen said. "We

made three piles: Keep, throw away, and donate. I think something like this, we can toss out."

Dawn nodded and turned toward the garbage can in the corner. "I agree."

Kristen smiled at her as Dawn herself put the nearly full bottle of nutmeg in the trashcan.

"I've never thought about things as serving their purpose for a time," Dawn said. "That makes so much sense."

Kristen nodded, her smile as kind as she could make it. As she worked and Dawn sorted, a slip of appreciation moved through her for her ordinary life filled with extraordinary moments of connection.

And in that moment, Kristen realized something that made her pause with a set of measuring cups in her hand. Perhaps the greatest gift of aging wasn't wisdom or perspective, though those were precious too. Perhaps it was the ability to find wonder in the quiet spaces between the big events—to recognize that a simple day helping a friend pack dishes could be just as meaningful as securing a historic lighthouse title or celebrating a wedding.

The real treasures were hidden in plain sight, in the rhythm of ordinary days strung together like pearls on a necklace—each one unique, each one perfect in its imperfection.

Chapter Twenty-Three

M andie stood at the window of the bridal suite at the Gardenia, watching the ferry cut through the water as it brought her wedding guests to Bell Island. She smiled at the merrily waving, bright pink flag that signaled the ferry as one designated for *her* wedding guests.

Her mother really did have a lot of connections in Five Island Cove, as Mandie had never seen a special ferry just for wedding guests—but she had one.

The October afternoon light cast everything in a honeyed glow, transforming the water into a shimmering tapestry of gold and amber. The warmth spread through her, and she leaned her head against the window, which sent a chill through her forehead due to the air conditioning in the suite.

"You're going to ruin your makeup," Ginny said, appearing beside her with a bottle of sparkling water. She held it up. "I put lemon in it."

Mandie straightened away from the window and took the bottle. "Did I leave all my foundation on the glass?"

Ginny grinned at her. "No, it's fine." She hooked her arm around Mandie's waist, making her feel loved and beautiful. She leaned her head against Mandie's shoulder as she took a long drink of the lemon-infused sparkling water.

"I think there's only one more ferry dedicated to wedding guests," Mandie said. "How are things going out there?"

"It's amazing," Ginny said. "Having the hors d'oeuvres was so smart. People are mingling, drinking, talking. It's a real vibe."

Mandie nodded, and she and Mom had planned the pre-ceremony mingle when they realized guests wouldn't all be able to arrive at the venue off the main island in Five Island Cove at the same time.

Mom had then arranged for a dedicated ferry to simply run back and forth, marked with a flag, and a dozen Ride-Share drivers to be ready at the ferry station to bring people up to the Gardenia overlooking Kaleidoscope Beach.

Mandie felt like the luckiest girl in the world. First, to be marrying her best friend today. Second, that she got to say the I-do's in such a beautiful place. Third, surrounded by so many people who loved her and her family.

The bridal suite at the Gardenia was nothing like the one at Driftwood where Ginny had gotten ready in August. This space was all creams and golds, with floor-to-ceiling windows that overlooked the beach below. The room held just a hint of autumn—burnt orange roses, tiger lilies, and deep burgundy dahlias arranged in copper vases, with apple-pie-scented candles flickering on marble countertops.

In truth, Mandie felt like a bit of a fraud standing there in a brand-new pair of sweats her parents had bought specifically for this day. "You'll want them for after everything too," Mom had told her. "Your flight is at almost midnight, and they'll make a great travel outfit too."

Mom loved things that served a dual purpose, and Mandie loved the sweats, so she was glad they ticked both boxes.

Her hair and makeup had been done for about twenty minutes now, and Mandie's stomach vibrated with nerves she didn't understand. Surely all brides felt like this on their wedding day, though.

"My mother is wondering if she can come up and help you get dressed." Ginny looked up from her phone, a certain measure of anxiety in her eyes. "It's okay if she can't."

Mandie glanced over to where Jamie loitered at a vanity, already completely ready for the ceremony, though it wouldn't begin for another hour. Besides her, Mandie's grandmother had popped in to congratulate Mandie and present her with the pale blue handkerchief that would serve as Mandie's Something Blue.

Mom had been in and out of the room all afternoon, staying to help Mandie with one thing, then leaving to check on something else happening elsewhere at the Gardenia. Mandie expected her back at any moment to help Mandie get into her dress, and she didn't care all that much to have photographic evidence of every moment of today.

She'd write it all out in her journal and remember it that way instead. The photographer had gotten a gorgeous photo of the dress on a padded hanger studded with pearls, hanging from the outdoor arbor, which was made up of three dark pieces of wood, affixed at ninety-degree angles, with an abundance of flowers in the top left corner and creeping down the right side.

Mandie had gasped when she'd seen that photo, and she couldn't wait to see what edits the photographer would do to make it even more beautiful.

"It's fine," Ginny said. "I'll tell her she can't—"

"She can," Mandie said, coming back to herself. She worried about her own mother feeling left out or over-shadowed, but Mandie was marrying Mom's best friend's son, so it made sense to Mandie that Alice would be present to help with the dress too.

Besides, she could use the help. The big, puffy ball-gown had a corset back that Mom had struggled to lace up very quickly, and Mandie prepared herself to stand still and be patient while they dressed her.

"Are you sure?"

Mandie nodded and finished her sparkling water. "Yeah, I'm sure." She smiled at her best friend and soon-to-be sister-in-law.

"Okay." Ginny focused on her phone and sent the text just as Mom re-entered the room...with Alice.

Their eyes met, and Mandie got the question even from across the room. *Can Alice come in?*

Mandie nodded and moved to throw away her bottle.

"I hope it's okay if I come help," Alice said, glancing over to Mom. "If it's not, I completely—"

"I already texted you, Mom," Ginny said. "She said it was fine."

"See?" Mom said, tugging Alice closer. "It's fine." She offered a kind smile, and Mandie's own worries about hurting her mother's feelings dissipated.

She approached Mandie and reached up to touch the spot where Mandie had leaned against the window. Of course. Mom-the-Wedding-Planner didn't miss a single detail. "Lindsey is bringing up the dress now. Just double-checking: Y0u don't want the photographer in here?"

Mandie shook her head. "No."

Mom nodded, her clipboard nowhere in sight. "The ferry just dropped off more people." She smiled and maintained her focus right on Mandie. "They're going back for one last ride, and then, everyone will be here."

Mandie nodded and stepped into her mother, because getting a hug from her had always calmed her. "Dad's here?"

"Yes," Mom said, though Mandie had arrived with both of her parents hours ago. "Grandma's here. All the ladies. Charlie."

Mandie sniffled and stepped back. "Okay." She

nodded and glanced out the window again. Sunset was definitely getting closer, and Charlie's dream of making her his wife as the sun settled into the ocean came with it.

"Well, you look amazing in these sweats," Mom said gently. "But it's time to get into your dress."

She wore a deep burgundy dress that complimented her honey-blonde hair, black high heels, and her mother's corsage. It matched Alice's, who wore the dark orange color in the most sophisticated way possible.

Her dress had wide straps that went over her narrow shoulders, with streams of silk falling toward the floor. Both Alice and Mom had pulled their hair back into elegant up-dos to mimic the classical, traditional vibe of Mandie's wedding.

The door opened, and everyone turned toward it. Lindsay, the wedding coordinator here at the Gardenia entered, Mandie's dress draped lovingly over her arm. She glowed as she smiled at everyone. "Look what I have," she said, and Mom went to get the gown from her.

"Thank you, Lindsay."

"We have twenty more minutes of hors d'oeuvres, and then we'll clear the terrace and make sure everything is set for the ceremony."

"Perfect," Mom said. "Thank you, Lindsay." She handed the dress to Alice and turned her back on Mandie. She leaned in and asked Lindsay something in a voice Mandie couldn't hear, and Mandie's natural instinct was to find out what was going on.

Then she reminded herself that her mother was in

charge, and this was what wedding planners did—they made sure nothing bothered the bride on her wedding day.

Lindsay left a moment later, and Mom wore nothing on her face to indicate there was any problem at all when she turned to face Mandie. "Let's get started. We'll want time to touch up your hair and makeup, and we need to add the jewelry too."

Mandie stepped behind the changing screen and shimmied out of her sweats. She wrestled with the tight, stretchy shapewear, finally getting it up and over her hips. "I feel like I just worked out," she said, to which at least Ginny giggled.

She pulled on her crinoline and velcroed it around her waist. After wiping her hand across her forehead—and smearing her makeup there—Mandie growled, dropped her hand, and reached for her slip.

"Okay?" Mom asked, peering around the side of the screen.

"I just have makeup everywhere," Mandie said as she pulled her slip over her head. She turned and stepped out from behind the screen, and took Ginny's hand to balance herself as she stepped into the gown Mom had prepped for her.

She and Alice pulled it up and over Mandie's shoulders, and then they started working on the corset back.

Mandie closed her eyes and let them pull and tug everything into place while Ginny moved to get the foundation and powder. "It'll take two seconds to cover that."

She listened to the sound of her own heartbeat in her

ears, until finally, Mom and Alice stopped and Mom said, "You're done. Let's get the shoes."

"I have all the somethings," Ginny said.

Mom pulled in a breath. "Did your grandmother bring the handkerchief?"

"Yes, it's here," Ginny said as Alice placed Mandie's deep red heels on the floor in front of her. She stepped into them and smiled as Mom presented the fisherman's bracelet.

"Something old," she said, sliding the delicate jewelry that meant so much to Mandie onto her wrist.

Mandie admired it for a moment, her emotions pinching through her. "I love this bracelet." She'd dreamt of wearing it when she got married, and that moment had arrived.

"Something borrowed," Alice said, and she took a black velvet box from Ginny and cracked open the lid. A gorgeous pair of earrings shone up at Mandie, all gold, with tiny pearls embedded in the teardrop shape."

"Wow," Mandie said. When she finally tore her eyes from the earrings, she smiled at Alice. "Were these yours?"

"My grandmother's," Alice said with a fond smile.

"Something blue." Ginny passed her the handkerchief, and Mandie tucked it under her dress, under her bra strap, hoping and praying she wouldn't need it. The goal was to smile for the rest of the day, not cry.

"Something new." Mom held up a gorgeous chain of pearls, their ivory opulence screaming through the room.

"Your father bought these for you, from a fisherman's wife he knows in Alaska."

Mandie turned and let her mother clasp her into the pearls, and then she moved over to the mirror to take in her reflection. With her hair up, her neck looked long and slender, with all the right pieces of jewelry in place.

She was ready.

Mom moved to stand just behind her, and Mandie met her eye, understanding passing freely between them. They'd had their moments of disconnection this summer —when Mandie had run off to New York without telling anyone, when she'd chosen Alice and Arthur to help with the move instead of her parents, when they'd argued about what her parents could and couldn't afford for this event.

But here they stood, together on her wedding day, the invisible thread between them stronger than ever.

She smoothed her hands over the lace, which reminded her of the patterns sea foam made when it retreated from the shore, on the top half of the dress. This ballgown style of wedding dress wasn't trendy or edgy, but it was timeless —like the cove itself.

Mandie didn't truly recognize herself, though she'd loved dressing up from the time she could pull on princess dresses. The woman staring back at her looked serene, confident, rooted in a way Mandie hadn't felt since getting engaged.

"You look like you belong in a fairy tale," Jamie said. Mandie put her arm around her younger sister and squeezed her.

"It's almost time," Mom said. "The last ferry should be here, and I've just sent for your father."

Mandie nodded, taking a deep breath. "I'm ready." She looked down at the silver waves of the bracelet, thinking of all the women who had worn this bracelet on their wedding days—her great-grandmother as a gift from her husband-to-be, her grandmother—the one Mandie had barely gotten to know before she'd been taken by illness— then her own mother, who'd married Mandie's father when she wasn't much older than Mandie.

And now her, stepping into marriage at the beginning of a new decade, in a world that seemed to change more and more every day.

Yet some things remained constant: the rhythm of the tides, the steadfast presence of the lighthouse, the bonds of family and friendship that had weathered countless storms.

Someone knocked, and then Lindsay poked her head in. "Can I get the moms out here? The father of the bride is here, and we need everyone else out on the terrace."

Mandie suddenly didn't want her mother to go. She rushed toward her and grabbed onto her. "Mom."

"Mm, you're beautiful." Mom gripped her tightly, pressing her cheek to Mandie's. "I love you, and you're ready for this." She stepped back and cupped Mandie's face in both hands. "Best of all, Charlie loves you." She nodded, her smile so huge.

Mandie nodded too, and then Mom turned and crisply

clicked her way out of the bridal suite, taking Jamie with her.

"This is it," Ginny said, and she too enveloped Mandie into a hug. "I so wish Bob and I were going to be in the city with you and Charlie this year."

"One day," Mandie said, hoping that wish and promise would come true. Ginny retreated to Alice's side, and Mandie went to hug her too. "Thank you, Alice."

"You are the best thing to ever happen to Charlie," Alice whispered. "Thank you for loving him." She pulled back, wiped her right eye, and left the room as well.

Lindsay remained in the doorway, and she bent to get the full bouquet of autumn blooms—dahlias and roses in rich burgundy and deep orange, with sprigs of eucalyptus and golden ferns.

Mandie moved forward and took the bouquet from her, took a big breath, and stepped out into the hallway with Lindsay. Dad stood there, looking smart and handsome in a dark black suit that seemed to swallow all color and light into it.

His face burst into a massive smile, and his big fisherman's laugh filled the hallway. He opened his arms, and Mandie flew into them, feeling safe, loved, and cherished in her father's embrace.

"You are so beautiful," he said. "I hope Charlie knows how lucky he is."

Mandie simply hugged him tightly, hoping he knew how grateful she was for everything he'd done for her over the years, for everything he was, for him being the best dad in the world.

"Let's go," he said. "Your mother will never forgive me if I can't get you to the altar on time." He grinned, but Mandie didn't want to draw her mother's ire either.

She linked her arm through her father's, and they followed Lindsay down hallways and steps until they reached the exit that would lead them out into the ballroom.

From there, the ballroom became the terrace, and because God had smiled upon them today, the weather had permitted them to get married right on the edge of the terrace, with the sunset the most perfect backdrop for a wedding.

Rows of white chairs faced the ocean, where the late afternoon sun hung low in the sky, casting long shadows toward Mandie's feet. Hurricane lanterns lined the aisle, their flames dancing in the gentle October breeze, and lighting the way to the tall arch with those gorgeous flowers.

Mandie stood at the back with her father, watching as Jamie proceeded down the aisle, followed by Ginny. Soft music played through the speakers overhead, a hauntingly beautiful rendition of "Somewhere Over the Rainbow"—Charlie's choice, a nod to the movie nights they'd shared on slow, easy summer nights.

"Ready, hon?" Dad asked, his arm tightening against hers.

She looked up at him, this man who had taught her to

fish and sail, who had checked under her bed for monsters and waited up when she missed curfew, who had let her go to New York with tears in his eyes but pride in his voice.

"I'm ready, Dad."

The music shifted to the bridal march, and the guests rose to their feet. Mandie took her father's arm, and together they stepped onto the sparkling stones that led to Charlie.

He stood tall at the altar, his dark hair tousled by the breeze, his eyes finding hers immediately. The smile that broke across his face was pure sunshine, and Mandie's heart expanded in her chest, making more room for all the love she felt in this moment.

Love from—and for—her parents. Love for their friends, who had so faithfully supported both her and Charlie over the years. Love for Ginny, Alice, and Arthur.

And so much love for Charlie. That seemed to grow and grow and grow, and Mandie wondered when it would stop.

As she walked, she was aware of the eyes watching her —Alice and Arthur beaming from the front row, Kristen dabbing at her eyes, AJ giving her a thumbs-up, Kelli bouncing baby Daphne on her hip. Eloise and Aaron stood with Billie and Grace, who waved excitedly. Julia and Liam held hands, while Laurel balanced Emily on her hip and Paul kept a watchful eye on James.

Tessa wiped her eyes as Mandie passed, and she sure did miss her days with the woman in the library here in the cove. Jean reached out and brushed her shoulder, her smile as large as Clara's. Maddy sighed, and Mandie nodded to her, a silent *thank you for coming.*

The whole tapestry of Five Island Cove was here, threads of lives interwoven with her own.

When she reached the altar, her father kissed her cheek and placed her hand in Charlie's. His fingers burned and stayed steady against hers, and the look in his eyes told her everything she needed to know. This man loved her, and Mandie had never been so sure of anything.

"Hi," he whispered.

"Hi," she whispered back.

The officiant—a family friend who had known Mandie since she was a little girl—began the ceremony with a warm smile.

"Friends and family, we gather here today, with the ocean as our witness and the setting sun as our backdrop, to celebrate the union of Mandie Karla Grover and Charles Frank Kelton."

The words washed over Mandie like the tide, familiar and soothing, because her wedding day had finally, *finally* arrived.

Chapter Twenty-Four

Robin's breath caught in her throat as Mandie and Charlie stood beneath the flower-adorned arch on the gorgeous outdoor terrace, the bottom rim of the sun just now kissing the water in the distance.

Just what they wanted—their sunset ceremony. A dream come true.

Her daughter stood radiant in the ballgown she'd chosen, the evening sunlight casting a golden glow over the ceremony that made everything seem like a golden, haloed dream.

Charlie's voice carried across the gathering, steady and sincere. "Mandie, we've shared a lot of things, but I feel like I'm still discovering new things to love about you every day."

Robin squeezed Duke's hand as Charlie continued with, "I promise to support your dreams, to listen when you need to talk, and to give you space when you need to breathe."

The words resonated deeply with Robin, reminding her of promises Duke had made to her all those years ago—promises he'd kept through fishing seasons and wedding seasons, through raising their girls and building their life in Five Island Cove.

"I promise to be patient when you're stressed, to make you laugh when you're sad, and to always, always come home to you, no matter where that home might be."

Robin couldn't help sighing, because who didn't want to have their safest, most-loved person to be the one they got to come home to every single day?

She certainly did, and she wanted that for both of her girls too.

Robin watched her daughter take a deep breath, those familiar blue eyes—so like her own—shining with certainty as she began to speak. "Charlie, loving you has been the easiest thing I've ever done. It happened so naturally that I didn't even notice until it was as much a part of me as breathing. But choosing to build a life with you—that's a decision I make with my whole heart, my whole mind, and my whole soul."

"She's so beautiful," Duke whispered, and Robin could only nod. She'd worried over Mandie so much, about plenty of things. This wedding at age twenty had not been on her plan, but now that it had come, Robin basked in the energy and love between her daughter and Charlie.

"I promise to stand beside you through celebrations and challenges. I promise to be honest, even when it's difficult. I promise to remember that we're a team, that your victories are mine to celebrate, and your burdens are mine to share. And I promise that no matter where life takes us, my heart will always find its way back to you—just like the tides always return to the shore."

Pride and love swelled in Robin's chest, nearly overwhelming her. This confident young woman speaking of love and commitment with such clarity had once been her tiny baby, her stubborn toddler, her headstrong teenager. Now Mandie spoke of making decisions with her whole heart, her whole mind, her whole soul—and Robin knew, with absolute certainty, that she'd raised a daughter who understood what commitment truly meant.

George, one of Robin's long-time friends who'd officiated several of her weddings, said, "Wow, what a couple amazing declarations of love." He clapped his hands together and grinned at Mandie and Charlie.

"Charlie Frank Kelton, do you take unto yourself Mandie Karla Grover, to be your legal and lawful wife, to love, cherish, and support?"

"I do," he said.

George switched his gaze to Mandie. "And do you, Mandie Karla Grover, take Charles Frank Kelton to be your legal and lawful husband, to love, cherish, and support?"

"Yes, I do," Mandie said.

With a chuckle, George practically bellowed, "Then,

by the power vested in me from the State of Massachusetts, I pronounce you, Charles Frank, and you Mandie Karla, husband and wife, legally and lawfully wedded for the rest of time."

He looked from Charlie to Mandie. "You may kiss your bride, Charlie."

He drew Mandie into his arms, and as Duke's arm slipped around her waist, Charlie leaned Mandie back and kissed her, the two of them smiling and giggling.

Applause erupted around them, and a sense of relief like Robin had never known cascaded through her. This was her last wedding of the year, and it felt fitting that it was her own daughter, marrying the man she loved so strongly.

Duke ran his lips along her hair, a silent question of how she was doing.

"Perfect." Robin dabbed at her eyes with the handkerchief Alice had pressed into her hand moments before the ceremony. "Absolutely perfect."

Mandie turned toward her then, and Robin took the few steps into her daughter and hugged her tightly. "That was so wonderful," she whispered.

She released Mandie to her dad and sister, and for a moment, Robin felt utterly lost at her own family's celebration.

Then Alice stepped to her side and linked her arm through Robin's, and the world righted. She felt like she'd just broken the surface of the ocean after being tossed overboard.

She looked over to Alice, who smiled at her with such love and kindness. "Well, they did it," she said.

"They sure did." Alice squeezed Robin's side, and she laid her head against her friend's shoulder, so much happiness and peace filling her from the soles of her feet to the back of her throat, where the emotion caught.

Eloise finished congratulating the couple, and she joined Alice and Robin, lacing her fingers through Robin's. "That was the most beautiful ceremony," she said.

Kelli arrived with Daphne, and she stood at El's side, silent and solid in her friendship. AJ spoke with Charlie and then Mandie, and she too joined the rest of them back by the arch, out of the way, where they could watch, observe, and bask in the good feelings streaming across the terrace.

"Robin, that was amazing," AJ said. "She's an amazing young woman."

"She sure is," Kelli said.

"Look how happy they are," Kristen said as she approached. She drew Robin into a hug, and Robin sank into the maternal embrace as tears pricked her eyes. Her own mother had lacked so much for Robin, but Kristen had filled that role flawlessly for decades now.

"Thank you for everything," Robin said to her mentor, one of her best friends, the woman who'd never judged her openly, but who had been there in Robin's head, guiding her silently, for so long.

"I love you," Kristen said. "And I love those kids." She

fell back and then moved to Robin's side. They edged back together as Mandie and Charlie finally made it past all those who knew them best.

Mandie lifted her bouquet in one hand, and Charlie lifted their joined hands, and they went down the aisle toward the ballroom to another raucous round of applause.

So much work went into preparing a ceremony, person, and party like this one, and Robin always felt a let-down after every wedding she worked on.

"Ladies and gentlemen," a cool female voice said. "Please make your way to the ballroom, where the bride and groom are delighted to share dinner with you before the sun disappears completely."

It only took about twenty minutes for the sun to dip into the ocean, and several of those minutes had already passed. So they definitely wouldn't have natural light all the way through this buffet dinner.

But the fairly lights and torches had already been switched on, lighting the space with happy, twinkling yellow-orange light.

"Let's go eat," Robin said.

"Wait," Alice said.

She'd already taken one step, but Robin paused and turned back to her friends. Looking at them, she could suddenly see each of them so clearly. Alice, with her quiet, constant sophistication. Her intelligence, and her passion for protecting her children.

Kelli, with her steady friendship, and her undying

commitment to those she loved. She and Shad were making even more moves to focus on their family, and Robin's own sense of loyalty always got strengthened when she spent time with Kelli.

She looked at AJ, who represented a strong woman to a T for Robin. She'd known her dreams and chased them, then returned to the cove and chased a new dream—one with true love, a husband, and the cutest little boy in the world in it.

She constantly reinvented herself, and her YouTube channel had been launched, and AJ worked every day to build it. To build herself.

Eloise blinked, and Robin admired everything about her. Her unwavering consistency, her ability to make big changes, her deep well of patience, love, and loyalty. Robin felt like she had so much more to learn from El, and she hoped she'd always feel like that.

That took her to Kristen, who had meant so much to all of them over the years. Robin had looked to the light-house time and time again, using it as the one thing in the cove—inside herself—that wouldn't change. That would always show her the way.

Kristen herself embodied the lighthouse, and Robin looked to her as the guiding light in her life when she felt overwhelmed, lost, or alone.

Tears splashed her cheeks as she opened her arms to her friends, and they crowded around, each of them wrapping their arms around one another as they made one big group hug.

"Oh, here's where we are," Jean said. She piled in, and Robin shifted to make room for her in the circle. Jean giggled, and the group shifted again when Clara arrived, and then Laurel.

Maddy, Tessa, and Julia piled around them too, and Robin found herself right at the core of the huddle, surrounded by those who loved her despite her flaws, her bossiness, and everything else about her that could be off-putting.

Perhaps they loved her *because* of those things. No matter what, Robin felt their love as it moved from them into her, and she never wanted to leave this circle of friendship.

ROBIN LACED UP HER WALKING SHOES AND MET Duke on the front porch. He'd come back from his morning fish already, his catch sold to the various restaurants and shops for the day.

She took his hand, and he smiled at her as they went down the front steps together. The crisp, morning air stung her skin and lungs, but the sun shone overhead, lending warmth to her clothes as it heated them.

"Jamie get off to school okay?" Duke asked as they set out, their pace leisurely.

"Yes, though I had to practically drag her out of bed." Robin hated being That Mom, but Jamie would take whatever she could get. "We never should've let her put her foods class first. She's acing it, so she thinks she never has to go."

"She is great in the kitchen," Duke said.

"That doesn't help me get her to school on time."

"I can talk to her."

"No," Robin said with a sigh. "I'd rather save you for the boys."

"Ugh." Duke groaned. "We just got one away from the boys; I can't deal with more boys."

Robin trilled out a laugh. "We didn't get Mandie away from boys. If anything, now she's even more anchored to one."

"You know what I mean."

"Do I?"

Duke looked over to her. "Are you still worried about them?"

Robin looked down the curved road where they walked, seriously considering his question. "I think I'll always worry about the girls, even when they're doing well. It's just..."

"What you do," Duke said. "Who you are." He squeezed her hand. "And what I love about you."

She scoffed and bumped him with her hip. "You're just glad I worry about the girls, so you don't have to."

"Hey, I worry about the fish," he said. "The bills. You." He looked at her with all seriousness in his gaze. "You're incredible, you know."

"I could never catch a fish," she said. "So I think you're pretty incredible."

He grinned at her as they rounded the bend that led to the eastern shore. "So, how does it feel to have completed your summer of weddings?"

Robin watched a pair of gulls wheel overhead. "Satisfying," she said.

"They were all amazing."

"Which was your favorite?"

Duke chuckled. "Our daughter's, of course."

"Mine too." Robin beamed up at him as they continued to walk, her shorter legs working harder to keep up with his longer ones. "That sunset happened right on time."

They walked along the boardwalk at the harbor, where fishing boats bobbed in the morning light. Duke's boat wasn't among them—he'd committed to only do the early morning fishing trip, and then his partner was doing the rest of the day's work.

He'd wanted to help Robin recover from the wedding madness and to simply enjoy being together. When he'd told her on Sunday evening, after the wedding, Robin had wept into his chest before falling asleep.

She'd spent a lot of time on her own in the past few years, and having Duke at her side meant so much more now. Soon, Jamie would be gone, and they'd be back to how they'd started their family—just the two of them.

She paused at the crest of the hill, looking out over the water. From this vantage point, she could turn in a full circle and see all five islands of the cove—Diamond beneath their feet, Sanctuary to the north and Rocky

Ridge a smudge on the horizon beyond that, with Bell and Pearl to the south.

"I still want to expand the wedding planning business," she said. "But the goal is to be more present in the daily moments of our life, like I was at the wedding. Not always planning the next thing or trying to solve everyone's problems."

"And you're telling me so I'll remind you?"

"Yes, silly. That's what you do." Robin bumped his shoulder with hers and then stepped in front of him and wrapped him in a hug. He automatically put his arms around her too and held her against his chest.

"I'd die without you," Robin whispered.

"That's ridiculous."

"I'm serious," she said. "You keep me sane, and while I love being the fixer, the planner, the one everyone counts on to make things happen, it means I miss the slow moments."

"I'll help you get to them," he said, leaning down to touch his lips to hers. Duke pulled away and tucked a strand of hair behind her ear, his eyes crinkling at the corners. "I've always seen you and loved you, Robin. Even when you're running around saving the world, I know your heart."

Something loosened in Robin's chest at his words. All summer, she'd been helping others navigate their big moments—Julia's new marriage, Ginny's whirlwind romance, Mandie's journey to the altar. She'd supported Alice through the lighthouse title saga, cheered Eloise through selling the inn, celebrated Kelli's business expansion, stepped in to help—and love—Lena and Clara no matter what else she had going on, and been the first to subscribe to AJ's new YouTube channel. She stood ready to babysit for Jean or Laurel, and she loved going to lunch with Julia, Maddy, and Tessa.

She'd been there for everyone, as she always wanted to be.

But *Duke* had been there for *her*. Steady, patient, loving her through her moments of stress and triumph alike.

The morning stretched before them as they continued their walk, unhurried and full of possibility, just like the future she'd been contemplating. As they rounded the final bend toward home, Robin thought about the summer that had just ended—the challenges and celebrations, the moments of doubt and the major wins. She thought about her daughters, one newly married and building a life in the city, one still finding her way through the complexities of adolescence. She thought about her friends, each navigating their own paths with courage and grace.

And she thought about herself—Robin Grover, wedding planner extraordinaire, devoted mother, loyal friend, beloved wife. A woman who had spent a lifetime holding things together for everyone else and was now learning, step by step, to sometimes simply let things be.

The lighthouse beacon flashed in the distance, visible even in the morning light—a reminder that some things remained constant while others changed. Five Island Cove would remain, its rhythm of tides and seasons marking time. Her friends would always be here, supporting each other through whatever came next. And Duke would always be at her side, his hand steady in hers as they walked together toward whatever the future held.

Robin breathed in the crisp autumn air, feeling more at peace than she had in months. The summer of weddings had ended, but something new was just beginning.

And she couldn't wait to see what it would be.

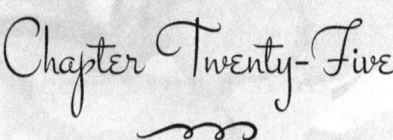

Chapter Twenty-Five

E loise maneuvered the last cardboard box through her mother's new front door, her shoulders and back aching from a full day of lifting and carrying. The afternoon light filtered through the windows of the condo, illuminating the hope that danced in the air.

"That's the last one," she called, setting the box labeled *KITCHEN—TEACUPS* on the counter in her mother's new kitchen.

Mom emerged from the bedroom hallway, a frown creasing her forehead. "I can't find Milo."

"Aaron has him at my house." Eloise gave her a smile and noted that nothing had been unpacked while she'd been bringing boxes in. "He's bringing all three cats over after we get things more put together. You didn't want to worry Genie."

One of her mom's cats really didn't like change, and she'd been yowling at Eloise's for almost a week now.

Relief softened her mother's features. "Oh, yes. I remember now."

These moments of confusion had been happening more frequently, which was precisely why Eloise had pushed so hard for this move. Having her mother twelve minutes away instead of a ferry ride apart meant Eloise could check on her daily if needed, at any time of day or night.

Billie rose to her feet in the living room, her silver-blonde hair pulled into a tight ponytail, arms laden with a potted fern. "Grandma, where do you want this?"

Mom's face brightened. "By the window there, dear. It needs morning light."

The condo was modest but perfect for Mom's needs—two bedrooms, an open-concept living and dining area, and a small kitchen with an island that doubled as a breakfast bar. The complex itself offered everything Eloise had hoped for: a community room where residents gathered for activities, a small garden area where Mom could tend to her beloved herbs, and most importantly, round-the-clock staff who could check on residents if family members couldn't reach them.

"El," Grace called from the spare bedroom. "Should I put Grandma's sewing machine in here or in the living room?"

"Ask your grandmother," Eloise said, beginning to unpack the teacups. Each one emerged from its newspaper wrapping like a small treasure—delicate bone china with hand-painted roses, sturdy stoneware collected from various island shops, a commemorative mug from the lighthouse's centennial celebration.

"In there, Gracie, please," Mom answered, moving to help Eloise. "These cups have stories."

Eloise handed her mother a blue-patterned teacup. "This one was from Aunt Meredith's collection, wasn't it?"

Mom nodded, turning the cup in her hands. "She left me her entire set when she passed. Said I was the only one who appreciated a proper afternoon tea." A shadow crossed her face. "I didn't bring the entire set, did I?"

"Just your favorites," Eloise said gently, once again holding back on the rest of the sentence. No, her mother hadn't been able to move her entire house full of items to a much smaller condo.

Eloise had been at her mother's house every day for over a month, painstakingly going through everything and deciding what to do with it all.

The process had been emotionally exhausting for both of them—each item a memory, each decision a small surrender to this new chapter, each day one closer to this one, where her mother was fully moved out of the house on Sanctuary.

Once Eloise got going, the unpacking actually went quickly, and Billie had the living room set up before she and her mother got the kitchen put together. She started helping break down the boxes, and then went to help Grace in the spare bedroom.

Eloise's heart filled with love that the girls were here on

probably one of the last Saturdays where they'd have good weather before winter, helping her mother—someone with whom they shared no blood.

Sometimes a found family was far better than one with DNA.

"All right," Eloise said as the first rays of twilight started to shine through the front window. "Should we check on the girls and see what's going on in the bedroom?"

Mom smiled and reached to hug Eloise instead. "Thank you, El," she whispered, her grip surprisingly strong for her petite stature and age.

"Of course, Mom." Eloise hugged her back, too many emotions to name mixing and tangling through her.

"Special delivery," Aaron said, and Eloise stepped out of her mom's embrace. He entered carrying a large pet carrier, from which emanated disgruntled yowls and pitiful meows. "The gang's all here."

Mom grinned and moved into the living room, where Aaron set the carrier on the couch. She opened the door, and a large orange tabby emerged, looking thoroughly offended by the entire experience.

"Oh, don't be like that, Milo," Mom said. "We're going to like it here." She glanced over to Eloise as she spoke, and Eloise felt the acceptance in the words settle in her heart.

Her mother *was* going to like it here.

The other two cats—the sleek black female named Genie and a gray-and-white Maine Coon called Pepper—

also came out of the carrier and immediately began investigating their new territory.

"Look, guys," Grace said. "We brought over your tree."

"And your condo," Billie said, trying to get Genie and Pepper to take their positions on the tall cat toys in the corner. But the felines seemed more canine in that moment, wanting to sniff and explore everywhere before settling in to glare down at everyone.

Eloise watched her mother with Milo, noting how her hands trembled slightly as she petted him. Mom had always been so capable, so independent. The woman who had raised Eloise and her brother alone after a divorce, who had worked two jobs to put food on the table, who had never complained even when things were at their hardest—that woman still existed, still shone through in the best of ways.

"This place looks incredible," Aaron said, coming to stand beside Eloise. He slipped an arm around her waist and pressed a kiss to her temple. "What do you think about ordering pizza for dinner?"

"That sounds perfect," Eloise said, leaning into him gratefully.

Mom's face shone with hope. "I live on Diamond Island now, and I can have pizza delivered to my house."

Eloise giggled as Aaron said, "You sure can, Dawn. So what do you want?"

"Sausage and olives," Mom said, bustling past them and into the kitchen. "I've got a salad I can mix up."

"I'll call it in," Aaron said. "Girls, come tell me what you want from the Pizza Parlour."

"Pepperoni, Dad," Billie said, to which Grace groaned and said, "We always get pepperoni."

"That's because it's delicious," Billie said.

"I want ham and pineapple with Alfredo sauce," Grace said, turning a hopeful face to Aaron.

Watching them, a wave of contentment washed over Eloise. For so long, she'd defined herself by her work—first as a professor in Boston, then as the owner of the Cliffside Inn. She'd poured everything into those roles, measuring her worth by her professional accomplishments.

But here, standing in her mother's new-to-her condo with the people she loved most, Eloise realized the roles that mattered most couldn't be listed on a résumé: wife, mother, daughter, friend.

And she wanted to embrace those things now, and see how good she could become at them.

As Aaron wrangled the different complaints of his daughters, Eloise's phone chimed with a text from Robin.

Just reminding everyone of brunch tomorrow at The Harbor Café, 10:30. Please let me know if you can't make it. El – did you ask your mom to come? Just let me know, so I can adjust the reservation if I need to!

Eloise looked up and eased into the kitchen, responses already coming in on the small group text that didn't include everyone. Robin and Alice had been doing things with the other empty nesters in their larger group—Tessa,

Julia, and Maddy—while the moms of younger children went walking in the morning.

Kristen sometimes went with the moms, and even Eloise had gone on a walk or ten after getting the girls off to school.

"Mom," she said. "My friends and I are going to brunch tomorrow morning." She carefully took the tongs from her mom and added, "We don't need the salad right this second. Aaron's still ordering the pizza."

Her mom blinked at her, eyes wide for a moment. "Brunch?"

Eloise smiled at her. "Would you like to come? I can stop by and pick you up about ten-fifteen."

Mom looked over to Aaron, who said, "Fine! I'll get a different pizza for everyone," and rolled his eyes.

Eloise laughed lightly, because they couldn't order pizza without having a fairly significant disagreement about what to get. She didn't mind, because they'd have pizza for lunches and leftovers for dinners for a couple of days now.

"I'd love to come to brunch," Mom said. "Just a perk of living so close, right?"

Eloise grinned at her. "That's right, Mom. You'll find there are a lot of perks to living on Diamond Island. It's totally different than Sanctuary."

Eloise loved both islands and always had, but no one could deny that Diamond had more restaurants, better beaches, and the most improvements out of all the islands. Yes, her mother would be very happy here, and Eloise felt a sense of peace and contentment completely different than when she'd sold the inn. Combined with that, she felt like a brand new person, rediscovering Diamond Island—and all her relationships—all over again.

And she was excited to keep doing so.

———

THE HARBOR CAFÉ BUZZED WITH SUNDAY morning activity, the clinking of coffee cups and murmur of conversation creating a comfortable backdrop as Eloise and her mother entered.

"Robin said she was here already," Eloise said, glancing left and right. The restaurant occupied the ground floor of a restored captain's house on Diamond Island, its wide windows in the back offering expansive views of the harbor, where fishing boats doted the sea.

"There they are," Eloise said, spotting Robin, Alice, Julia, and Tessa at a large round table near the window.

Robin waved them over, a huge smile on her face. She rose as Eloise approached. "Oh, you made it."

Eloise wasn't sure if they'd done Sunday brunches in the past she just hadn't been invited to. As she leaned in and hugged Robin, it didn't matter. She'd been so tired on the weekends, and she'd wanted to spend every spare moment she had with Aaron and the girls, so she wouldn't have come to brunch even if she'd been invited.

"This place smells amazing," she said as she hugged Alice next. She wore an elegant cream-colored sweater, and

Eloise stepped behind her to take the seat between her and Julia, who finished up what she was saying to Maddy across the table.

"Hey, you." Julia gave her a side squeeze after Eloise had sat down.

"Hey." Eloise smiled at her, then across the table to Maddy, then Tessa, who sat directly across from her.

"Good morning, Dawn," Robin said, and Eloise knew her being down on the end would kill her. And yet, she'd chosen that seat. "How did the move go yesterday?"

"Good," Mom said as she laced her purse strap over the top of the chair and twisted back toward everyone. She sat next to Maddy, which was another great place for her, as Maddy was an extrovert and very good at talking to and including strangers.

"I'm so glad," she said now. "El sent us some pictures, and it looked like you had everything done already."

"Just about," Mom said, her smile seemingly stuck in place. "It helped that I didn't have to move everything at once."

Yes, Eloise had been going back and forth between Sanctuary and Diamond for weeks now. They'd just moved the big things yesterday.

"What about cleaning your other house?" Alice asked as she spread a napkin over her lap. "Do you need help with that?"

"Nope," Julia said. "I'm sending the housekeeping team from Cliffside down to do it tomorrow." She beamed down the table at everyone, and Eloise had never felt such gratitude. Not only for Julia, who'd suggested a cleaning service for Mom's house, but to the Eagans for agreeing to pay their maids to come do it.

That had been Julia's idea too, and Eloise reached over and squeezed her hand under the table. "Thank you," she murmured.

"It'll go up for sale this weekend," Mom said. "The realtor has someone coming to take pictures this week." She let out a long breath. "So that's that."

"It's amazing," Robin said. She grinned down the table and lifted her mimosa. "Welcome, everyone, to the Sunday brunch club."

Eloise didn't have a drink yet, and she wasn't one for alcohol in the morning anyway. But she spotted a carafe on the table and reached for it. A sense of rightness settled over her as she poured herself a cup of coffee and had Julia push the sugar closer to her and Maddy call for the cream to be passed down.

"So I need some help," Julia said.

"Oh, here we go," Alice said with a grin. Eloise wasn't sure of the format of these brunches, so she settled back in her chair and looked at Julia.

"Liam's house is full of plants."

"Plants?" Robin asked.

"Houseplants," Tessa said. "Loads of them."

"*Loads*," Julia said. "I've killed two already, and it's only been four months. I fear he'll file for divorce if I don't figure out how to keep a plant alive."

Eloise giggled, as did everyone else. "He hasn't noticed the two you murdered?"

Julia gave her a severe look. "I replaced them while he was at the station, but he knows something is off."

Alice burst out laughing then, harder than before.

"This is serious," Julia said, though her smile widened and then widened again.

In that moment, the waitress arrived to take their orders, and the conversation about saving houseplants got put on hold while Eloise put in an order of eggs Benedict, and Alice asked about blueberry pancakes.

Once all the orders had been put in, Mom looked seriously at Julia. "Houseplants just need a little TLC," she said. "I could come show you what I do with mine to keep them alive."

"I'd love that," Julia said. "What are we talking? Plant food and sunshine?"

"I play music for mine," Mom said, and Eloise blinked at her.

"What?" she asked.

"They like it."

Eloise stifled another giggle, noting that everyone at the table wore a smile. "If you say so, Mom."

"It's a scientific fact," Mom said. "Mine like classical music the best." She nodded over to Julia. "You'll see."

Eloise—a scientist, for crying out loud—seriously doubted it. But she didn't feel like arguing with her mother about this. If she wanted to play Mozart to her houseplants, she could totally do that.

"At this point, I'll do anything," Julia said.

"He's not going to file for divorce over a few house-plants," Maddy said.

"Dawn, you must join our book club," Tessa said, effectively changing the subject. "We meet once a month, and there's always refreshments."

"And very little actual book discussion," Alice added with a laugh.

"That sounds lovely," Mom said, looking genuinely pleased. "I like reading almost as much as sewing. Oh! You know what I love best?" She wore diamonds in her eyes as she looked around at everyone at the table.

"Reading *and* sewing at the same time. Audiobooks have changed my life."

"Mm, I like a good audiobook too," Alice said. "Sometimes I just drive around and listen to one, to get out of the office."

The talk flowed around her, but Eloise found herself observing and listening, savoring the moment, the way she liked to do. These women had supported each other through lighthouse disputes and inn sales, through parenting challenges and health scares.

Now, they were folding her mother into their circle with the same warmth and acceptance they had shown Eloise when she'd returned to Five Island Cove seven years ago.

"Oh, before I forget," Robin said, reaching into her bag. "I have something for each of you." She pulled out small velvet pouches and distributed them around the table.

"What's this?" Maddy asked, opening hers to reveal a delicate silver bracelet with a small lighthouse charm.

"A little thank you," Robin said. "For being part of my crazy summer of weddings. I couldn't have done it without all of you."

Eloise examined her own bracelet, touched by the gesture. The lighthouse charm caught the light, reminding her of all the times that beacon had guided her home— literally and metaphorically.

"It's beautiful, Robin," Julia said, already fastening hers around her wrist.

"Very thoughtful," Maddy said. "Though I'm not sure what I did to help with the weddings."

"You kept me sane," Robin said simply, looking at every person for a long moment before moving to the next. "All of you did."

"Life keeps changing, doesn't it?" Alice asked. "Just when you think you have it figured out, it morphs again."

"It does," Eloise said. "But that's not always a bad thing."

"No, change isn't bad," Robin said.

"In fact," Mom said. "Sometimes change brings us exactly where we need to be."

"Mm, I agree," Maddy said softly.

She looked down at the lighthouse charm hanging from her wrist, imagining the real thing here in the cove. That lighthouse stood tall against the horizon, its white tower gleaming no matter the time of day. It had weath-ered countless storms over the decades, changed keepers, seen technologies come and go. Yet it remained, steadfast in its purpose, guiding sailors—guiding everyone—home through calm seas and tempests alike.

A sense of peace settled over her. She had found her place in the ever-shifting tides of life, so she lifted her coffee mug and said, "To change, and allowing it to change us in only the best of ways."

"Hear, hear," Tessa said.

Everyone lifted their drink of choice, and as they toasted to change, Eloise let a new sense of joy move through her, infuse into her, and she hoped she'd always embrace whatever changes life sent her way.

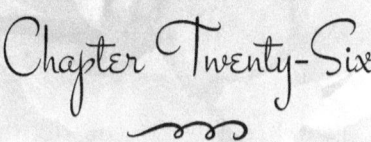

Chapter Twenty-Six

Kristen's fingers traced the simple key in her pocket as she climbed out of the car at the lighthouse. The metal had warmed to her body temperature, but she could still feel the intricate ridges of its teeth—a tangible reminder that this beacon couldn't be taken from her.

The evening air carried the first real bite of autumn, and Kristen pulled her cardigan tighter around her shoulders. October in Five Island Cove always brought this chill in the air, the promise of much colder days to come.

The sun shone for less time each day, and it would be evening before everyone got off work and joined her here at the lighthouse. She'd invited everyone to come enjoy pizza, cookies, and a nightcap. Or coffee. Whatever people wanted to eat and drink was fine with Kristen.

She just wanted them all to come.

She walked down the sidewalk, glancing down the junction toward where she and Joel had once lived. It felt strange to think that her life had transformed so much when he had died, but it had.

Her girls had all come back to the cove because of his death. Kristen had changed so much; her life looked completely different now than it had only a few short years ago.

She didn't need her key to the lighthouse, because Reuben and Jean were expecting everyone. Jean, bless her heart, had readily agreed to have everyone at the lighthouse, despite it being a very small space to live.

Kristen had arrived early, and she went down the steps into Reuben and Jean's personal living space instead of up to the lighthouse deck where she'd gather with all the ladies later.

The sound of Heidi's cries reached her as Kristen made it to the bottom level, and Kristen's heart went out to the little girl. She knocked on the door, heard, "Come in!" and pushed into the personal apartment of her son and daughter-in-law.

Jean stood in the kitchen, an apron around her waist while Heidi pulled herself up in the playpen in the living room. "Ma-ma-ma," she whimpered, a fresh wail coming out of her mouth when she laid eyes on Kristen.

"Can I get her?" Kristen asked.

"Yes," Jean said with a sigh. "She refuses to eat anything, so now she'll be cranky all night."

Kristen bent over and lifted Heidi out of her playpen. "Come on, darling," she said softly, pushing the girl's feathery, dark hair back off her forehead. "You won't eat anything?"

Heidi started to babble something, the nonsensical words punctuated with hiccupping and more tears. Kristen took her into the kitchen as Jean rounded the counter and started removing the cookies from the sheet pan. She turned on the kitchen sink and ran the water until it got warm. Then she wetted a washcloth and squeezed it out before wiping Heidi's face.

The little girl gave a shuddering breath as she finally relaxed.

"Maybe Reuben can put her to bed early," Kristen said.

Jean finished with the cookies. "Maybe. I just hate it when she goes to bed early, because then she's awake at five a.m."

"It can become a vicious cycle," Kristen said. She cuddled Heidi close and kissed the little girl. "Do you want me to try to feed her?"

"No, I've cleaned it up already," Jean said. "But thank you."

Rueben entered the part of the lighthouse where he lived, saying, "Hey, my girls."

"Your mother is here," Jean said, moving toward him. In the small space, it only took a couple of steps. "And your daughter wouldn't eat her dinner."

Reuben kissed her quickly and looked over to Kristen and Heidi. "Hey, Mom."

"Hello, son." Kristen gave him a warm smile. "Thanks for letting us use the deck tonight."

"Sure," Reuben said. "Might be one of the last clear nights for a while though."

"Yeah, it's supposed to storm tomorrow." Kristen left the kitchen and sat at the dining table with Heidi on her lap.

"I'm just going to plate these up, and we can go upstairs," Jean said.

"Okay," Kristen said. She held up her key. "I brought this back."

Reuben looked at her. "You can keep it."

"I don't need it anymore," Kristen said. She wasn't sure why she had before; Reuben and Jean had been living in and maintaining the lighthouse for years now.

"All right." Reuben took the key from her, leaned down and kissed her cheek, and went down the short hall.

Jean's doorbell cam chirped, and she said, "I bet that's Robin."

Kristen wouldn't be surprised, as Robin strongly disliked being late. Everyone had readily agreed to this Friday-night lighthouse dinner, even those Kristen hadn't mentored through the Seafaring Girls program here in Five Island Cove.

Even the transplants to their group fit perfectly, and Kristen hoped their friend group would continue to expand.

Another chirp, and Jean picked up the two plates of

cookies. "I'll go up," she said. "Reuben should be back out in a minute, or you can bring her up."

"I'm taking her," Reuben said, returning in that moment. "You guys go have fun." He took Heidi from Kristen, who then got to her feet and followed Jean out of the apartment.

She made her way up the many steps, holding onto the railing as she went round and round, the sound of her girls' voices encouraging her to continue even after her knees wanted her to stop.

Robin, Alice, and Eloise had arrived together, and they stood on the deck, the breeze tugging at various hems and locks of hair.

"Oh, there she is," Robin said as Kristen arrived.

"That's quite the climb," she said, panting. "I should've used the restroom before coming up." She grinned at her girls and gave them each a hug.

"AJ and Kelli are almost here," Alice said. "They have the pizza, and Laurel's waiting downstairs to help them if they need it."

"Okay." Kristen stood near the top of the stairs, still trying to catch her breath before she moved again to take a seat.

"Come sit," El said. "You're worrying me."

"Did your mother get fully moved in?" Kristen asked, moving toward Eloise.

"Yes, finally," El said with a weary sigh. "Since she didn't have to be out of her house by a specific date, it felt like a constant back-and-forth there for a while."

"I saw it go up for sale," Alice said.

"Yes, we got that done too." Eloise sat down, and Kristen took the chair next to her. She'd asked Reuben to make sure they had enough chairs for everyone around the circular deck, knowing that they'd be too spread out to have a whole-group conversation.

"Pizza," AJ said, and Kristen scooted back as much as she could so people could walk in front of her.

"And we have lots of cookies," Jean said from down at the table that Reuben had also set up. "Reuben will bring up the coffee in a little bit."

AJ walked past Kristen, her smile wide, and set the pizza on the table. Kelli and Laurel followed her, each of them carrying three boxes.

"Nine pizzas?" Robin asked. "There are twelve of us." She gaped at AJ as she turned from the table.

"Then some of us can take it home to our very hungry boys, who never seem to have enough to eat."

"Lena's coming," Kristen said. "So there's thirteen of us."

"We still don't need nine pizzas," Robin said, but thankfully, she dropped it after that.

"Do you want a cookie?" Alice asked, pausing in front of her.

"Yes, please, dear. Oatmeal, no raisins."

Alice smiled as she went by, and the noise level increased as Maddy, Tessa, and Julia arrived together. Kristen wasn't surprised they'd stuck close to each other.

They'd moved to the cove from Nantucket, after having some interesting and somewhat traumatic experiences.

"Are we waiting to eat?" Kelli asked. "Because I'm starving."

"We don't have to wait," Kristen said. "This is a low-key gathering." She glanced around to those crowding in around her, noting the only people missing now were Clara and Lena. She could text them and find out how close they were, but she didn't need to.

When they got here, they got here.

That was one of the things she loved most about the cove—time could sometimes be forgotten in favor of simply enjoying good company.

The night continued to stain the sky, and Kristen let Alice bring her a cookie, and then El retrieve her a piece of combination pizza.

The lighthouse had stood sentinel over Five Island Cove for generations, its beam sweeping across the water each night without fail. But tonight was different. Tonight, Kristen wanted to light it together as a celebration of everything they'd weathered together over the years.

"We finally made it," Clara said, and Kristen looked along the balcony to the steps. Clara ushered Lena onto the platform, and she followed, closing the door behind her.

A familiar ache settled in her chest at the sight of her daughter. There had been so many years when Clara wouldn't set foot near the lighthouse, when the very mention of Five Island Cove had been enough to make her voice go cold. Now, there she stood, a smile on her face, and her daughter practically vibrating with energy.

"Grandma, guess what?" Lena asked, flopping into the chair next to Kristen, where Alice had sat for a moment.

"What's going on with you?" Kristen looked over to her, and then sought Clara's gaze. She usually texted Kristen in advance, but she'd heard nothing that would put Lena in this giddy zone.

"They asked me to do a Christmas party at the grocery store!" Lena clapped her hands a few times.

"Oh, do you get to plan it?" Robin asked. "I love planning parties, especially at Christmastime."

Lena nodded. "I'm going to plan it, and it's going to be *so* amazing."

Kristen patted her hand. "I'm sure it will be, dear." She had no idea if Lena could actually pull off a company Christmas party for a staff of a few dozen people, who all worked different shifts. But she didn't have to oversee that, and she also couldn't underestimate Lena.

The girl had come so far this year, and Kristen loved her with her whole soul.

"Drinks," Reuben said as he appeared upstairs too. He brought over a couple of cases of flavored sparkling water, and Alice got up to start making mocktails for anyone who wanted one. "I'm brewing coffee right now." He glanced over to Jean and added, "Heidi is fighting sleep, so I'm keeping her awake as long as I can."

"Why don't kids ever want to sleep when we want

them to?" AJ asked. "I swear, Asher does that on purpose."

Maddy giggled and said, "My kids used to do that too. Nap at five o'clock in the afternoon type of thing."

"I'll get the lighthouse on once I get the coffee up here," Reuben said, and Kristen brushed her fingers along his forearm as he went by her.

"Thank you, dear," she said.

"Of course."

Kristen thrived on the energy of the women with her that evening, listening to their conversations, their laughter, feeding her soul in a way nothing but pure friendship could.

Reuben returned with coffee and a tray of mugs, and El raised her eyebrows at Kristen. She nodded, and El went to get her a cup of coffee. Alice finished up with the mocktails, and Robin said, "For the love, you guys, we need to eat more pizza."

Kristen smiled into the full darkness that had fallen, not bothering to hide her face. "Come sit down, dear," she said to Robin, gesturing to the chair on the other side of Lena. "In fact, everyone needs to sit down for the lighting of the beacon."

It would be bright, and she didn't want anyone to be disoriented until their eyes adjusted.

Women moved away from the railing as her phone chimed. The message from Reuben said, *I'm going to close the windows on the balcony and light the beacon. Can you warn everyone?*

I just did, Kristen said. "He's going to close the windows, then it won't be so bright." The moment she finished speaking, the huge windows that opened up and out started to sink back into place. Kristen had sat here so many times during a storm while Joel manned the controls one level up.

The view up this high never failed to move her, especially at this hour when the sky was painted in deep shades and the first stars were beginning to appear.

"I forgot how magical it is up here," Eloise murmured from beside her. "No wonder we loved it here."

"I loved it here, because it felt like nothing could go wrong," Alice said, her voice awed and quiet.

"I could see really far," AJ said. "And it taught me that life is long, and there's so much more to this world than Five Island Cove. At the time, I really needed to know both of those things."

"I just loved coming, because all of you would be here," Robin said.

Kristen smiled, because sometimes it had felt like such a fight to get her girls there. Now, they came willingly, and they sure seemed to enjoy being together.

Just then, the lighthouse's powerful beam burst to life, cutting through the darkness with its steady, rhythmic sweep from left to right, moving in a clockwise manner. It would cover the whole island, then come back around again.

As it moved around and then back toward them, Kristen watched the light illuminate their faces as it neared and found joy and wonder reflected in every pair of eyes.

Silence fell over them, as they all sat there and watched the beam circle out over the water, providing a way home for anyone who needed it.

Kristen had never felt more at home than she did in that moment, with all of her girls, a multitude of friends, and her family surrounding her.

It would go on to touch each of the five islands in turn. Diamond, where most of them now lived. Sanctuary, where Eloise had run her inn for so many years. Rocky Ridge, with its rugged coastline. Bell and Pearl, with their sandy beaches and sheltered coves.

"This is incredible," Julia breathed. "I mean, I've seen the beam before, but up here...it's magical."

"Isn't it?" Clara sighed happily. "I used to count to see how long it would take the light to go around in a full circle."

Kristen had never heard that before, and it made her heart swell. The lighthouse beam completed another rotation, momentarily bathing them all in its glow before sweeping around toward land again

"I've been thinking about what this place means," Kristen said, her voice steady despite the emotion rising in her throat. "Not just the lighthouse, but Five Island Cove itself."

She felt their attention shift to her, and she didn't usually take the spotlight. But this felt like the time to do it if she could.

"When I was a young bride, helping my husband run the lighthouse, I thought I was leaving everything behind. My family, my friends, the life I'd known. I was terrified."

Robin squeezed her hand, encouraging her to continue.

"But then I met all of you—some as little girls in my Seafaring Girls classes, some as young mothers, some much later. And I realized that home isn't a place you find. It's something you build, person by person, year by year."

Kristen looked around at their faces, illuminated briefly as the light swept past—Robin's steady strength, Alice's quiet intelligence, Eloise's thoughtful grace, Kelli's gentle resilience, AJ's fierce loyalty, Laurel's brave new beginnings, Clara's hard-won peace, Jean's nurturing spirit.

"You've all built this home with me," she continued. "Through being yourselves, and making changes when necessary. Through arguments and reconciliations. Through holiday parties, and mysteries, and YouTube channels, and weddings."

She laughed a little at the last part, and they joined her, the sound carried away by the October wind. Maddy's kindness shone through in her smile, while Julia's eyes had locked onto Kristen. Tessa, definitely the most practical of them, simply nodded, and Kristen knew that her definition of home had been changed time and time again.

"I used to worry about what would happen to this place—to *us*—when I'm gone," Kristen said. "But I don't anymore. Because I see how you take care of each other.

How you've created something that will outlast any one of us."

"Mom," Clara said softly, reaching for her hand.

"I'm not being morbid," Kristen assured her with a smile. "Just grateful. Grateful that I've lived long enough to see the seeds I planted grow into something so beautiful."

The lighthouse beam swept around again, briefly illuminating tears on more than one face.

"To the lighthouse," Robin said, raising her mocktail glass. "And to Kristen, who's always been our light."

"To Kristen," they echoed, glasses and mugs lifted in the darkness.

Kristen felt a fullness in her chest that had nothing to do with age or illness—just pure, distilled joy at being exactly where she was, with exactly the people she loved most.

The beam swept out over the water again, touching the waves with silver before disappearing into the horizon. So many nights she had stood here alone, watching that light cycle through the darkness. So many prayers she'd whispered into the wind. So many tears she'd shed, unseen by anyone but the stars, the sea animals, the very sky itself.

But she wasn't alone anymore, and she hadn't been for a very long time.

Kristen looked at the women on either side of her, the beam sweeping around them, and the sea ever-present in front of them.

"We made it," she said. "You've all made it all the way home."

READ ON FOR THE FIRST 2 CHAPTERS OF **THE HAMPTON HOUSE**, a brand new women's fiction novel that follows Mandie Grover 5 years in the future as she works with a prestigious historical preservation and reconstruction firm that restores and conserves abandoned mansions up and down the Eastern Seaboard.

Learn more about it and preorder by scanning the QR code below:

A Note from Jessie

W hat an amazing time I've had with the women in Five Island Cove! I sincerely hope you've found a place to belong among Alice, Robin, Eloise, Kelli, and AJ. I definitely identified with each of them at different times over the past eleven books.

I love Laurel and Jean too, with their quieter personalities. Kristen and Clara rounded out our Five Island Cove residents, and then I brought over my Nantucket Point ladies too. After the mysteries and events they'd been through, they all needed a fresh start, and there's no better place to do that than Five Island Cove.

I always feel like I'm visiting old friends when I come here.

So, while I have more ideas for this series, I've also been gnawing on the idea for another book. As I wrote this one, and realized so much of the focus was on Mandie Grover, that book came alive in my head.

She'll be a central figure in *The Hampton House*, the next book I'm going to release. It'll be set five or six years in the future, and you'll get to see her, Charlie, Ginny, Bobby, with some amazing cameos from the ladies in Five Island Cove.

This new series will focus on Mandie and her team of preservationists who go into abandoned mansions and restore them, clean them up, and get them ready to go back on the market. With Alice's ties to the Hamptons, and Mandie's love of history—and those YouTube videos I'm obsessed with!—I'm super excited to bring you the beginning of a planned trilogy!

You can read more about *The Hampton House* and **then read it by scanning the QR code below.**

Keep reading to get a taste for this next sweet romantic women's fiction novel.

~Jessie

PS. LOOK AT THIS BEAUTIFUL COVER! I'm in love with it! Read it now by scanning this QR code with your phone.

Sneak Peek of The Hampton House, Chapter One:

～⌒⌒〰

Mandie Grover took a sip of her coffee, now lukewarm, and told herself to go dump it out and get some water. She'd been experiencing heartburn more often than not on days when she drank the entire cup of coffee she picked up on the way in to work.

She set the to-go cup further from her and reached for the next file in the pile. Part of her job involved looking through prospective properties, and she really enjoyed browsing through the "slush pile."

At tomorrow's meeting, she'd be expected to have her top three choices for the next clean-up project, appropriately labeled CUP in her department, and literal tally marks went up on the white board as the team reviewed their personal favorites.

Mandie had two files in her favorites folder already, but she told herself to have an open mind as she looked at the picture of the mansion on the first page in the new file.

"Sixteen thousand square feet," she said. In all honesty, most mega-mansions approached ten thousand square feet, with multiple bedrooms, twice as many bathrooms, and ornate staircases.

Her heartbeat pumped out an extra beat, because she absolutely loved taking the abandoned and restoring it to full glory. That, and her phone had just sparkle-chimed with her husband's assigned ringtone.

Charlie had said, *I'm so going to pass this Pharmacology final*, with a smiley face emoji. *To celebrate, I'm stopping by Lin Chu's for dinner. You want those chickeny noodles?*

She grinned at his use of "chickeny noodles," abandoned the file, and reached for her phone to answer him. *You're finished with the final already?*

Piece of cake, he said, which was Charlie-code for *yes, I'm done and leaving campus.* He only had the one final today, and Charlie hated staying on campus when he could leave it. She'd find him in their one-bedroom apartment when she got home, and he'd most likely time dinner to arrive only a few moments before her.

She and Charlie had been married for almost five years now, and he took very, very good care of her. Mandie loved him with her whole heart, and they'd even started talking about starting a family.

Everything Mandie did required her to go through a minefield of thoughts, and she often felt like she'd made the wrong turn and gotten blown back to the beginning. She envied others who could made quick decisions with confidence, because that had never been Mandie's strong suit.

See you at home, she texted Charlie, and then she got back to the file in front of her. She had to have her choices done for tomorrow, and then she had some appointments to make with a restoration company for an apartment building here in the city that had sustained some flooding damage.

She loved her job at PastForward Restoration Company—PFRC—because they helped people who needed it while showing respect to the history of the dwellings and buildings on the East Coast. Some properties here were hundreds of years old, and Mandie felt a sense of reverence every time she got to go out on a field assignment.

The house in the file intrigued her, and Mandie leafed through the floor plan, read the story behind its abandonment, and embraced the growing excitement within her. She didn't often make her choices based on pictures, checklists, and facts. She relied on her feelings, and she reached for a green sticky note, which she attached to the front of this file.

It got placed in the yes-pile, and Mandie sat back. She loved learning about old things, and since she hadn't been on a field assignment yet this year, she muttered, "So you'll bring it up in your meeting tomorrow."

Part of her yearned to get out of this office building, though she'd once been tickled and thrilled to be riding the subway from Brooklyn, where she and Charlie lived, to the Flat Iron building every day.

She still was, but she definitely felt like some of the glitter that had first coated her job had started to flake off. She stood and stretched her back, glancing across the partition that separated her desk from the one in front of her.

The man who worked there had various camera equipment littering his space, and Flint Rogers looked up. "Hey." He leaned back in his chair. "My eyes are starting to cross."

"Editing your latest film?"

"Final edits," he said. "It's due to production by tomorrow night, and it should air next month."

"That's awesome," Mandie said. By "air," he meant the complete walk-through of one of the abandoned mansions. He led a film crew on field assignments, and they documented everything from the first step the team took onto the property to the final walk-through when a place went up for sale.

If he was lucky, he could work on one project per year, as his post-production was far more detailed than Mandie's. She was involved in field assignments from the first step to the sale, and that was it. She didn't then have hundreds of hours of film to go through and edit into a ninety-minute documentary.

"I can't believe the Maryland Mansion is almost done," she said.

"Hopefully, there will be something new at tomorrow's meeting," Flint said. He wore a neatly trimmed ginger beard, with a full head of hair to match. He was what Mandie would call a "clean hipster," as he showered regularly and didn't wear his hair long. His emerald eyes always seemed to see more than Mandie could, and he wore loafers everywhere he went, even into dangerous, abandoned mansions.

He rolled his khakis at the ankle, always wore skinny jeans and skin-tight tees—if he didn't have on a too-small polo like he did today.

"You think you'll get another assignment right away?" Mandie asked. She leaned against the chest-high divider and took in more of his mess. How he worked in those conditions, she didn't understand. He had yellow legal pads filled with notes and numbers in black pen she couldn't read. But Flint somehow knew what it all meant, and she supposed that was all that mattered.

"Jo Ann's quitting," Flint said. "Which means they'll have to promote up another film lead, and last time Candace needed to do that, it took four months for me to go through multiple interviews, present my portfolios, and get named to the position."

Mandie drew in a breath. "Jo Ann's quitting?"

Flint looked away. "I guess that isn't common knowledge." He looked at Mandie with puppy-dog eyes. "Don't say anything, okay?"

"Yeah, of course not," she said.

Flint stood and stretched his arms above his head, his tiny shirt pulling up over the waistband of his khakis. "You haven't been out in the field in a while."

"Tell me about it." Mandie rolled her eyes. "I think Candace thought I'd get pregnant, and she didn't want to assign me to anything."

"So you're not pregnant?" Flint grinned at her, and Mandie smiled and shook her head.

"Even if I was," she said. "That shouldn't exclude me from field work. It's pregnancy discrimination."

"Sometimes those old houses are full of mold."

"We have protective gear for that." Mandie folded her arms, becoming more and more determined to get an assignment tomorrow. She'd had enough of desk work, phone calls, and file browsing. She swatted at Flint's chest. "Plus, you tromp through those sites in shoes with barely any soles and no socks. It's a miracle you haven't contracted gangrene or something."

Flint bellowed out a laugh, and Mandie allowed herself to smile. As he quieted, she said, "All right, Flint. Tell me how to get assigned to something tomorrow."

"Step into my office," he said, and Mandie scrambled to go around the dividers and into his disorganization. If it would help her get a field assignment, she could sit among cameras, flash lights, and micro SD cards.

———

"So the final went well?" Mandie asked as she entered her apartment. She tapped the door with her foot to close it, then noticed the candles on the table. She froze. "What anniversary did I forget?"

Charlie turned from the back counter, a plate of orange chicken in his hand. "Final went amazing. There's no anniversary."

"There's something," Mandie said as she got moving again. She'd brought home her top three files so she could obsess over them while she and Charlie watched TV tonight. He sometimes had her quiz him, especially with anything math-related, but he'd already taken that final, so she anticipated an evening filled with some sort of action-adventure movie, and she could easily keep up with the plot while she looked through her files again.

"There's me finishing another year of school," he said. "That's it."

"Only one more," Mandie said as she dropped her bag over the back of the couch and shrugged out of her jacket. Springtime in New York could still be chilly, and Mandie hated nothing more than being cold on the subway.

She wrapped her arms around Charlie once he'd set down the plate of chicken. "You're amazing, baby. One more year of pharmacy school." She kissed him, glad she got to spend her evenings with her best friend in the whole world.

"Tomorrow, they're making assignments for the next major field assignment, and I want it so badly." She whispered the last few words, almost afraid to speak her desires.

"You'll get it," Charlie said. "You haven't been out of the office in a while."

"For six months," she said. "And I know Candace just

got a whole heap of new funding. She might even schedule two projects."

"Where are they?"

"My favorite one is in The Hamptons," Mandie said as he pulled out her chair and she sat down. "It would be a dream to work on it. It's close, so I wouldn't have to live on-site. My other two favorites are out of the city. One in South Carolina—a really old plantation that would be pretty cool—and one up in Cape Cod."

"Mm." Charlie sat down too. He dished up some of her chickeny noodles, and Mandie simply watched him.

"Did you hear about the internship?"

"Another interview next week," he said casually, but Mandie knew he hated the multiple interview process. *Honestly*, he'd said. *If they don't know by now, I don't know what else to do to win them over.*

She smiled at him. "So we'll both have amazing news by this time next week."

"You'll have yours tomorrow." He grinned at her and took orange chicken and ham fried rice for himself.

"What if I don't get it?" Mandie let her vulnerability show. Only for him, and Charlie heard her and looked right at her. "She's been passing me over for some reason, and I just—what if I've gotten my hopes up and I don't get it?"

"You're going to get it."

She sighed, because frustration frothed through her. "Thank you, baby." She did like his confidence in her, but they'd been together long enough to see that sometimes confidence didn't always equate to getting what they wanted.

He hadn't gotten into the Pharm.D. program at Rutgers, for example. He'd had to settle for his second choice of St. John's, and while he loved his program there now, Charlie had definitely been disappointed.

"And if you don't," he said. "I'll have mint chocolate chip ice cream here tomorrow night, and we'll go away for the weekend. Go see your mom and dad in the cove." He raised his eyebrows. "Okay? It won't be the end of the world."

"It'll just feel like it," she said miserably.

"Hey, let's be positive," he said. "You've got a strong case for getting assigned, and they've picked your top choice the last four times."

"Yeah." Mandie twirled up some noodles and stuck them in her mouth. Salty, savory deliciousness moved through her. "Mm."

Charlie grinned at her, and suddenly everything was okay.

"And hey," she said. "If I do get it, I know I won't have to work with The Bulldozer."

Charlie choked on his chicken as he started to laugh. Mandie smiled too, though she truly didn't like working with Suzette Paxman. She'd been nicknamed The Bulldozer by everyone in the office, because she rammed through old houses like one. She held a degree in Anthropology, and she acted like she was the only human being alive who did.

In some cases, working with her meant Mandie didn't have to get her hands and feet as dirty, as Suzie wasn't afraid of anything. She'd go into any room, any broken-down pool house, over any surface, to get the footage and information they needed.

Every team had a bulldozer, actually, but none of the other employees at PastForward carried the nickname the way Suzie did.

She giggled with Charlie, because suddenly everything felt lighter. "I'm going to get it," she said, mustering up all the optimism she could. "And I'm going to have the best team ever, and it'll be the house in The Hamptons, and when we go home to Five Island Cove this weekend, it'll be to celebrate my new field assignment."

"There you go." Her husband beamed at her, and Mandie reached over and covered his hand with hers.

"Should I really get us tickets for the Steamer?" she asked.

He nodded. "Yeah, my mom would like it too. She'll take us to lunch to celebrate another semester done."

"Free food," Mandie mused. "I see how you are."

"Hey, I never say no to free food." Charlie grinned, and Mandie did too. She suddenly had so much to look forward to in the next few days, and her stomach flipped over tomorrow morning's meeting.

She just had to get a field assignment. She simply had to.

Sneak Peek of The Hampton House, Chapter Two:

~∞~

A licia Halverson stepped onto the elevator ahead of Mandie, and when she turned, she gave the other woman a look that spoke volumes. Thankfully, Mandie could understand looks where words weren't spoken, and she edged behind a tall African American man to position herself closer to Alicia.

"What have you got?" she whispered on the third floor, when half the people in the elevator exited. "Lish, don't hold out on me. I'm here an hour early to go over files I have memorized."

"Please." Alicia half-scoffed and half-laughed. "You're here early so you can pace in the bathroom and pitch yourself to your reflection."

Mandie's shoulder shivered back and forth, her way of conceding to Alicia without words. Alicia laughed, because she knew Mandie so well. She reminded her of her younger sister, and a powerful wave of missing rolled through Alicia completely unbidden.

"My thumbs are aching from how much I texted last night," Alicia said as the elevator struggled to get moving again.

"It better have been with Michael." Mandie sighed, and Alicia felt her frustration. She hadn't been assigned a field trip in months either, and once Mandie had texted last night, Alicia had taken it upon herself to figure out how to get the two of them assigned to whatever went up on the board today at PastForward.

"Michael, I wish." Alicia rolled her neck, and the day hadn't even started yet.

"He's going to ask you out. You just need to keep stopping by for those chocolate croissants."

"Yeah, and then I have to run fifty miles on the treadmill." Alicia shook her head now, the ends of her long, dark hair brushing against her elbows. She'd braided into pigtails today in an attempt to make herself look younger. Candace seemed to discriminate on any grounds she could, and only she knew what those were.

Alicia and Mandie had brainstormed that they changed all the time too, and it could be because Alicia left her food in the microwave too long or that she'd just turned thirty-five. No one really knew, and she wished there was a system for how people got selected for field assignments.

"Rory says there's no way Suzie will get picked," Alicia

said once they'd passed the seventh floor. "She's still finishing up with the New Hampshire mansion."

"So we'll need another bulldozer," Mandie said, her eyes glued to the numbers above the doors. They were nearing ten now, and had five more to go. "Who?"

"Rory says the two of us would make a killer research and checklist team, with Flint behind the camera."

Mandie only hummed, but that said so much. Alicia knew she wanted this field assignment more than anything, and she'd known before Mandie had texted last night. She knew, because Alicia needed this assignment like she needed oxygen.

"You love Flint."

"Flint's the best," Mandie agreed. "So John as the third?"

"Could be." Alicia nodded as the elevator made another stop and then continued up. "Maybe Chevy. He hasn't been out since that Baltimore fiasco."

She and Mandie got off on the fifteenth floor and went past the ritzy real estate firm to their private historical restoration and reconstruction firm.

They both worked in the Preservation and Conservation Department, but they both also handled local clients who needed help getting natural disasters cleaned up when they weren't working on historical cases.

"I'm so bored," Alicia whispered as she opened the glass door and held it for Mandie.

"I might scream if I don't get assigned today," she

whispered back. "Just right out loud, in the middle of the meeting."

Alicia laughed lightly. "I doubt it. Assignments always come at the *end* of the meeting."

Mandie scoffed and veered off into her desk area while Alicia continued down another two rows to hers. She quickly put her purse in her bottom desk drawer, grabbed her files, and went back to Mandie's desk.

"Top three. We have to be in perfect alignment."

Mandie already had her folders out too. She loved sticky notes and color-coding, which was why she'd be perfect for any field crew. The woman literally never missed a detail, and she had three folders, one each labeled with a green note, a yellow one, and a pink one.

"Is pink above green or below?"

"Pink is the prize, my friend." Mandie smiled as she slipped the marked folder to the top.

Please let it be the Hampton House, Alicia prayed as Mandie seemed to fall into slow motion. Alicia really couldn't leave her children for an off-site field assignment, and she wondered if Candace had somehow found out about her recent divorce.

She commuted from Queens, from the tiny two-bedroom house where her son slept in the second bedroom while her daughter shared her room with her. She and her ex had been living there for a few years now, so that hadn't changed. It would simply be difficult to be on-site for any amount of time, and she'd chosen the Hampton House as her top pick simply in the hopes that it would be chosen, and she could get the field assignment.

She earned more when on assignment, as they received a per diem for food for every day worked out at the site. Plus, the house held a magic to it that leapt off the printed page and permeated the air.

"I knew you'd like the Hampton place too." Alicia grinned widely when she saw the pillared mansion on the front page inside the pink-sticky-note-marked folder.

"It's the best property," Mandie said. "Though I did like that one in the Appalachians."

"The Mountain Mansion?" Alicia fake-swooned. "Isn't it amazing? Even full of someone else's stuff and those ghastly all-terrain vehicles. I can't even imagine the views." Alicia could admit she was somewhat of a romantic, but the images of her eight-year-old's and her five-year-old's faces grounded her. Brought her back to reality, and that meant she couldn't run off to Virginia even for an amazing mountain mansion.

"I didn't put it in my top three," Mandie said. "I don't really want to travel for the field assignment." She tucked her honey-blonde hair behind her ear as she bent over the Hampton House. "I'm worried that if it comes up a lot, Candace will choose it even if it doesn't have the most votes."

"She is so unpredictable," Alicia complained. "That's what I dislike the most. If I knew how things could go, if I could predict it, I wouldn't be so nervous." She flapped her hands a couple of times, then told herself to stop it.

She got to her feet. "Look, you're the natural choice for the researcher. I'm the perfect fit for the financial advisor. All we need is a bulldozer and a film crew, and this is going to be the best summer and fall of our lives."

Mandie clapped her hands together. "Yes! This is the kind of pep talk we need."

No one else had come into the office this early, and Alicia had psyched herself up appropriately. "Okay," she said, pacing to get out some of her extra energy. "We are going to pitch ourselves today. I *want* this assignment."

"I *need* it," Mandie said. "I'm tired of assisting on research and then staying here while the team goes out."

"This is ours."

"What's yours?" someone asked, and Alicia's gaze flew past Mandie to another blonde, this one with plenty of strawberry in her hair and so not someone she wanted to talk to this early in the morning. Or ever, really.

"Hey, Suzie," she chirped in a falsely bright voice. "You're here early."

"I've got to get this last form filed for the West Hills Monster."

Mandie got to her feet, her irritation like a scent on the air. Suzie barely looked at her, as if Mandie didn't hold any importance at all. Alicia reached out and grabbed onto her forearm, and that stopped Mandie. Thankfully.

"Leave it," she hissed as Suzie went by them. "We'll play our cards in the meeting."

Several seconds passed while they both waited for the blonde bulldozer to get out of earshot, and then both she and Mandie sat down in Mandie's desk area. "She thinks she's going to get another assignment," Mandie said. "Unbelievable."

"She's not going to get it," Alicia said. "There are so many deserving people—like us."

"Like us," Mandie agreed with a nod. "Okay, more people are starting to come in. We can't be seen conspiring, or Candace will for-sure give the assignment to someone else."

"Right." Alicia squeezed her friend's hands, then stood, and made her way over to her desk. The office started to fill, and before she knew it, Candace had stepped out of the conference room, the silver bell in her hand.

"Let's go, people," she called as she started to ding the bell over and over and over. *Ding! Ding! Ding!*

Everyone got to their feet like dogs, like the bell had triggered something Pavlovian inside them. Alicia joined them, her three folders and her notebook in her hands. She deliberately didn't allow herself to migrate to Mandie's side. Candace didn't like it when friends tried to get on the same teams, and Alicia panicked that her friendship with Mandie—which was well-known around PastForward—would suddenly hinder her.

Fourteen people crowded into the room, and Candace indicated the three trays in the middle of the oblong table. "First, second, third," she said, indicating a tray with each one. "Folders in."

Someone swore, and Jackson—another accountant

with a degree in construction management—jumped to his feet. "I forgot my folders."

"Door's closing in ten seconds," Candace called after him, and though he was one of Alicia's main competitors for this field assignment, she hated seeing him humiliated. Candace had locked people out of meetings before, so her ten-second rule was not an empty threat.

Ten seconds later, Jackson sprinted into the room just as Candace said, "Doors, please."

He practically threw his folders into the trays. Candace glared at him as she pulled the first tray toward her. "Paula, please tally."

Another woman scrambled to her feet, and Alicia wondered why they all kept showing up here, day after day, to be ordered around and treated subserviently. Paula uncapped a blue white board marker, and Candace flipped open the first folder.

"Hamptons," she said, and Alicia shot a look over to Mandie. She sat very still, her gaze trained on Candace. "Cape Cod." Another folder. "Hamptons." She continued on until all the folders in the first pile had been read, and it was obvious that the majority of people in the office wanted to work on the Hampton House next.

Candace turned and looked at the tally marks. "Nine, wow." She smiled as she turned back and picked up the second stack of folders. She read through those, and the Cape Cod Complex came in second.

Their boss didn't even turn to get the remaining pile of folders. She steepled her fingers and considered the board. "I'm a bit surprised more of you didn't pick the Appalachian Jewel." She simply let the words hang there, and Alicia had learned not to justify anything.

If Candace asked her a direct question, she'd answer. Otherwise, she wouldn't. If she didn't get an assignment today, Alicia wasn't sure what she'd do. Screaming, like Mandie had suggested, sounded about right.

She looked down the table to her friend again, and this time, Mandie's eyes darted to hers too. Then Candace spun, and Alicia jerked her attention back to her. The tension in the conference room pressed against the ceiling, against all the walls and windows, straining to get out. Alicia could barely get a decent breath, and she wondered if anyone else felt that.

"We might as well go over what's third." Candace started reading through those, and Paula dutifully tallied them all up. Candace, in all her bleach-blonde-bunned glory, turned to face the board again.

She never went out in the field, except to check-in once, maybe twice, during a project. She demanded detailed reports which she religiously read, and she'd email questions or call private meetings with teams. Alicia had never seen her wear anything but skirts that fell precisely to her knees, heels, and fluttery blouses.

Today's was pale blue, with a navy skirt and navy heels, and perfectly matching robin's egg blue earrings in the shape of dragonflies.

"Ah, there's my Appalachian Jewel." She grinned at the

board, then swiveled back to the group at-large. "Thank you, Paula. Please take your seat."

Paula did just that, and Alicia looked down at her notebook, almost afraid to make eye contact with Candace. She forced herself to look up, because she couldn't show her boss any weakness.

"We have enough funding for two teams to get started," she said. "I'm going to send some of you to Virginia and this mountain mansion. I think it's the best in the bunch, and I'm honestly surprised it's not number one."

No one said anything, because it sounded like Candace had just started a lecture. Alicia gazed at her, and Candace looked her way.

"Let's start down there." Candace looked down at some notes in front of her. "Jackson." Alicia's heart started to pound through her whole body. If Jackson got the Jewel, she'd be the most logical choice for the Hampton House. "You'll manage the finances."

"Yes," he said, his smile spreading across his whole face. It only made Alicia want to squirm.

"Vanessa, I need you on point," Candace said.

"Yes, ma'am," Vanessa said.

"Chevy." Candace glanced over to him, and he was a bulldozer like Suzie.

"You got it, Candy," he said, and he was the only one who'd ever called Candace such a thing. A thread of horror moved through Alicia, but Candace only laughed.

"And on film…" She paused and sighed. "I'm going to pause on that for a minute. I want you guys to clear your afternoon on Monday. We'll meet to go over everything then."

Murmurs of assent moved through the group, and the tension in the room skyrocketed. Alicia shifted in her seat, and Candace looked at her. Her eyebrows went up, and Alicia's did too. That was about as big of a challenge as she could lay down, and she hoped the message had gotten across.

"The Hampton House," Candace said, consulting her notebook again. A few seconds went by, then a few more.

"Ma'am?"

Every eye flew to Mandie. She'd half-raised her hand, and she'd gone pale, like she might throw up. Candace looked at her, blinking rapidly a few times.

"I'm in love with this house," Mandie said. "I'd love to take point on it. I've already sketched out a few things to get started."

"You have?" Candace folded her arms and considered Mandie, her gaze sharp and hooked. Alicia's mouth had gone dry, and she had no idea how Mandie had the nerve to speak up in a meeting where people didn't do such things.

"Yes, ma'am," Mandie said. "And I'm completely available to meet with you and whoever else you appoint to the team anytime."

"Anytime." Candace nodded, though something cold definitely emanated from her. She leaned back in her chair and appraised Mandie for several long seconds. Then a couple more. Right when Alicia thought the air would snap, she said, "All right, Miss Kelton. Oops, I mean *Mrs.* Kelton. You can have point."

"Thank you, ma'am."

Alicia couldn't speak up now, but she wasn't a bulldozer, nor on film. If she didn't get named next, she wouldn't have an assignment. A voice started shrieking in her head, an internal monologue that left her feeling desperate, irritated, and hopeless all at the same time.

She had to get out of this room.

Now.

Get out. Get out. Get out!

She stayed right where she was, and Candace looked at her notes and then right at her. "Alicia, can you keep *Mrs.* Kelton within budget?"

"Yes, ma'am," she said, her voice grating like rusty nails against cement. "Absolutely, I can."

Candace nodded and looked around. Alicia's heartbeat now bobbed somewhere outside her body, but she still had enough wherewithal to pray, *Not Suzie. Please, not Suzie.*

"Brandt," she said. "You'll be on bulldozer, and Flint, I know you're just barely finishing up the Maryland Mansion, but I need you in The Hamptons."

"Sure thing," Flint said.

"Apparently, *Mrs.* Kelton has some notes already for us," Candace said dryly, and Alicia thought Mandie might blow her top. She'd turned bright red now, and since Alicia sat on the same side of the table as her, she could see her fisted hands.

"Mandie's the best," Flint said. "I'm sure she and Lish

can get started without me and Brandt. We're more of the on-site crew." Flint threw Alicia a smile, and that settled some of the acid boiling in her stomach.

"I want the Hampton House team in my office first thing Monday morning." She got to her feet. "I'll have my own notes to go over." She gave Mandie a pointed look. "All right. Back to work."

She started stacking the folders, and Alicia filed out of the conference room along with everyone else...except Mandie. Alicia met her eyes and gestured for her to *come on! Don't stay in here with the Big Bad Wolf!*

Mandie shook her head slightly, her jaw set and her eyes filled with pure determination. Alicia moved out of the way, wondering if she needed to stay and back-up whatever Mandie said.

But Mandie asked, "Miss Ewing? Can I speak to you privately for just five minutes?" and Alicia ducked out of the room. She'd hear all about this five-minute meeting soon enough, and she didn't want to step on her friend's toes.

She closed the door behind her and practically rammed into Flint.

"What's she doing?" he murmured.

"It's suicide," Alicia said, turning to face the conference room. All of the blinds were open, but Mandie stood with her back to the office.

"So we'll be going to lunch today," Flint said easily. "If she's still alive, we'll hear all about it." He nudged Alicia with his elbow. "And hey, you guys got Brandt."

Relief filled her again and then again, and she finally felt like she could breathe properly. "Yeah," she said. "We got Brandt." Her gaze went back to the conference room. "And if Mandie doesn't get fired, we pretty much have the dream team for the Hampton House."

Then she turned and walked back to her desk, praying for her friend in a constant internal stream of words.

READ THE HAMPTON HOUSE ON YOUR favorite retailer by scanning the QR code below:

Books in the Five Island Cove series

The Lighthouse, Book 1: As these 5 best friends work together to find the truth, they learn to let go of what doesn't matter and cling to what does: faith, family, and most of all, friendship.

Secrets, safety, and sisterhood...it all happens at the lighthouse on Five Island Cove.

The Summer Sand Pact, Book 2: These five best friends made a Summer Sand Pact as teens and have only kept it once or twice—until they reunite decades later and renew their agreement to meet in Five Island Cove every summer.

Books in the Five Island Cove series

The House on Seabreeze Shore, Book 5: Your next trip to Five Island Cove...this time to face a fresh future and leave all the secrets and fears in the past. Join best friends, old and new, as they learn about themselves, strengthen their bonds of friendship, and learn what it truly means to thrive.

Four Weddings and a Baby,

Book 6: When disaster strikes, whose wedding will be postponed? Whose dreams will be underwater?

And there's a baby coming too... Best friends, old and new, must learn to work together to clean up after a natural disaster that leaves bouquets and altars, bassinets and baby blankets, in a soggy heap.

Books in the Five Island Cove series

The Seafaring Girls, Book 7:
Journey to Five Island Cove for a roaring good time with friends old and new, their sons and daughters, and all their new husbands as they navigate the heartaches and celebrations of life and love.

But when someone returns to the Cove that no one ever expected to see again, old wounds open just as they'd started to heal. This group of women will be tested again, both on land and at sea, just as they once were as teens.

Rebuilding Friendship Inn, Book 8:
Clara Tanner has lost it all. Her husband is accused in one of the biggest heists on the East Coast, and she relocates her family to Five Island Cove–the hometown she hates.

Clara needs all of their help and support in order to rebuild Friendship Inn, and as all the women pitch in, there's so much more getting fixed up, put in place, and restored.

Then a single phone call changes everything.

Will these women in Five Island Cove rally around one another as they've been doing? Or will this finally be the thing that breaks them?

Books in the Five Island Cove series

The Glass Dolphin, Book 9: With new friends in Five Island Cove, has the group grown too big? Is there room for all the different personalities, their problems, and their expanding population?

The Bicycle Book Club, Book 10: Summer is upon Five Island Cove, and that means beach days with friends and family and summer reading programs! When Tessa decides to look into the past to help shape the future, what she finds in the Five Island Cove library archives could bring them closer together...or splinter them forever.

Books in the Five Island Cove series

The Holiday House, Book 11: Revisit Five Island Cove at Christmastime! Join the women in the cove as they come together for a wedding, the holidays, and new ideals to what it means to be a mother, daughter, sister, aunt, and friend.

The Summer of Weddings, Book 12: In the picturesque setting of Five Island Cove, the bonds of friendship are as enduring as the tides. **This summer, the cove is abuzz with wedding bells as Mandie and Charlie, Ginny and Bob, and Julia and Liam prepare to say their vows!**

Books in the Nantucket Point series

The Cottage on Nantucket, Book 1:
When two sisters arrive at the cottage on
Nantucket after their mother's death, they
begin down a road filled with the ghosts of
their past. And when Tessa finds a final
letter addressed only to her in a locked
desk drawer, the two sisters will uncover
secret after secret that exposes them to
danger at their Nantucket cottage.

The Lighthouse Inn, Book 2: The
Nantucket Historical Society pairs two
women together to begin running a
defunct inn, not knowing that they're
bitter enemies. When they come face-to-
face, Julia and Madelynne are horrified
and dumbstruck—and bound together by
their future commitment and their
obstacles in their pasts...

Books in the Nantucket Point series

The Seashell Promise, Book 3: When two sisters arrive at the cottage on Nantucket after their mother's death, they begin down a road filled with the ghosts of their past. And when Tessa finds a final letter addressed only to her in a locked desk drawer, the two sisters will uncover secret after secret that exposes them to danger at their Nantucket cottage.

Books in The Hamptons series

The Hampton House, Book 1: Mandie Kelton, Alicia Halverson, and Suzette Paxman are drawn together by the allure of forgotten elegance and the shadows of the past. They'll have to learn to get along if they have any hope of keeping their jobs, and as they restore an abandoned mansion in The Hamptons, they'll also discover the lost and hidden parts of themselves that make them into the women they're meant to be.

The Yacht Club, Book 2: Mandie Kelton, fresh from the triumphant restoration of the Hampton House, faces a new challenge when her boss, Candace Ewing, reveals their next project: restoring a famous historical yacht once owned by a legendary figure. Tasked with breathing new life into the venerable vessel, Mandie, along with her trusted friends and colleagues—Suzie, Alicia, and the enigmatic Candace—embarks on a journey that will test their skills and uncover long-buried secrets.

The Cove Cottage, Book 3: As the summer in Five Island Cove unfolds, Mandie Kelton, Alicia Halverson, and Suzette Paxman find themselves navigating the serene yet tumultuous waters of another massive restoration project. After the whirlwind of the wedding season, the three best friends are eager to immerse themselves in their new project: restoring the enigmatic Cove Cottage, a historic seaside home with a rich tapestry of secrets woven into its walls.

About Jessie

Jessie Newton is a saleswoman during the day and escapes into romance and women's fiction in the evening, usually with a cat and a cup of tea nearby. She is a Top 30 KU All-Star Author and a USA Today Bestselling Author. She also writes as Elana Johnson and Liz Isaacson as well, with almost 200 books to all of her names. Find out more at www.feelgoodfictionbooks.com.